Eyes of Eagles

This Large Print Book carries the
Seal of Approval of N.A.V.H.

EYES OF EAGLES

WILLIAM W. JOHNSTONE

WHEELER PUBLISHING

A part of Gale, Cengage Learning

GALE
CENGAGE Learning·

Farmington Hills, Mich • San Francisco • New York • Waterville, Maine
Meriden, Conn • Mason, Ohio • Chicago

GALE
CENGAGE Learning·

Copyright © 1993 by William W. Johnstone.
Wheeler Publishing, a part of Gale, Cengage Learning.

LIBRARY OF CONGRESS CATALOGING-IN-PUBLICATION DATA

Johnstone, William W.
    Eyes of eagles / by William W. Johnstone. — Large Print edition.
    pages cm. — (Wheeler Publishing Large Print Western)
    ISBN-13: 978-1-4104-6708-9 (softcover)
    ISBN-10: 1-4104-6708-2 (softcover)
    1. Fathers and sons—Fiction. 2. Kidnapping—Ohio—Fiction. 3. Shawnee
Indians—Ohio—Fiction. 4. Large type books. I. Title.
    PS3560.O415E94 2014
    813'.54—dc23   2014003461

Published in 2014 by arrangement with Pinnacle Books, an imprint of
Kensington Publishing Corp.

Printed in the United States of America
2 3 4 5 6   18 17 16 15 14

IT BEGAN IN 1817
IN THE WESTERN
OHIO WILDERNESS . . .

JAMIE IAN MacCALLISTER: As a boy of seven, he could only watch in horror as the Indian war party murdered his mother and father. Raised by the Shawnee chief who had taken him prisoner, he would escape four years later and find his way back to a white society unwilling to accept him.

KATE OLMSTEAD: The prettiest girl in Western Kentucky, she fell in love with Jamie at first sight. They ran away together, heading west . . . but hard on their trail were vengeful men who had vowed to kill them both.

MOSES WASHINGTON: A runaway slave who had found refuge for himself and his family in the Big Thicket country of East Texas, he risked his life for Jamie and Kate when they decided to settle down, raise a family and live out their lives . . .

... BUT SAM HOUSTON, JIM BOWIE, DAVY CROCKETT AND ALL THE OTHER DEFENDERS OF THE ALAMO WOULD DRAMATICALLY AND FOREVER CHANGE THE LIFE OF JAMIE IAN MacCALLISTER!

This book is dedicated with respect to Deana James, Dan Parkinson, and Martin Roberts, who had the patience to answer my hundreds of questions about Texas history.

PROLOGUE

No man is an island, entire of itself; every man is a piece of the continent.

— John Donne

It wasn't much, but to Jamie Ian MacCallister the cabin was a castle. Actually, and Jamie knew it well, the cabin was better than most, for it had a real puncheon floor, leveled timber slabs, where many had only a dirt floor. His friend Robert lived in a cabin with a dirt floor, just about two miles down what passed as the road; two ruts that wound through dark woods.

If it was a hard life, Ian didn't know it. He'd been born right here in this snug cabin in the Western Ohio Wilderness. Oh, Jamie worked hard for a boy of almost seven, but it was important work. He knew that was true 'cause his pa and ma told him so. And now with the new baby in the cabin, his work was more important than ever, for his ma had never really gotten well after having the baby and Jamie was now doing a lot of the chores his ma used to do. She was just so weak all the time, and had to be abed for rest several times a day. But Jamie didn't mind the extra work, for his pa said life was hard on the frontier.

Jamie was making candles while his pa and ma were in the village, seeing the doctor. He'd gotten out the spun milkweed candlewicks and had threaded the candlewicks through the base holes and tied a knot in each, then fastened the tops to a stick. Carefully, Jamie got the pot of melted fat from the fire and poured it into the tapered molds, then sat back while it hardened. He tried to remember what else he was supposed to do. Oh, yes. Give the beans in the pot a stir and put out the potatoes for baking in the ashes. Was that all? The boy pondered for a moment. He thought it was.

Then he heard the sounds of the wagon coming slowly up the rutted road and he ran to the windows and opened the inner plank shutters. Light was fading fast as the day was coming to a close. His ma and pa were home. Even though his pa called him his little man, it got kinda lonesome with everyone gone.

His ma and pa were laughing softly, so

everything must have gone well at the doctor's cabin. Jamie opened the door and caught a glimpse of something moving at the edge of the timber. Deer probably, he thought, and closed the door as his parents stepped into the cabin.

The sleeping baby was placed in the cradle and Jamie's ma turned and smiled at him and Jamie returned the smile. She sure was pretty, and his pa was a big handsome man. Both of them blond and naturally fair, although the sun had turned their skin brown from being outside so much.

"We have a birthday boy somewhere around here," his pa said, unable to hide his grin. "Where do you reckon he is, Priscilla?"

"Why, bless me, Ian," Jamie's ma said, "I just don't know. He might be hiding under the table. Let's ask this stranger to look."

"Aw, Ma!" Jamie said. He would be seven come the next day, and his parents always gave him some store-bought candy or a little foofaraw for his birthday.

"Here he is!" Jamie's pa said, grabbing Jamie and holding him out in his strong hands. "He's gotten so big I didn't know him right off." He set Jamie down on the floor and looked around the cabin. "You done real good, son," he said seriously. "Swept the place clean and made candles and something sure smells good in the pot yonder."

"Beans, Pa," Jamie said.

"And naturally you tipped over the honey pot and added a bit, too, didn't you?" his ma asked with a smile.

"Well . . ." the boy ducked his head to hide his dimpled smile.

Ian ruffled his son's hair. "That's all right, son. I like 'em sweetened a bit myself."

"I'll set the table while you see to the team, Ian," Priscilla said. "Help me, Jamie. The ride has tired me."

Ian stepped outside and closed the door. As Jamie was reaching for the bowls, he thought he heard a cry, a noise of some sort, coming from the outside. He paused, listening. But it was not repeated. He shook his head and began setting the table as his ma gave the beans a last stir. Jamie whirled around and dropped the bowls as the cabin door was slammed open. Painted Indians filled the cabin, one of them holding a bloody war club. Priscilla screamed and ran for the cradle. Before she could reach it, a warrior swung his war club and her head was split open, her skull smashed. She fell to the floor. Jamie leaped for his ma and his own head exploded in pain, sending him spinning into darkness, a single cry on his lips.

Jamie did not see his mother scalped. He did not see one Shawnee warrior pick up the baby and smash its brains out against the stone of the fireplace and then hurl the little lifeless body into the fire. Jamie lay on the floor, blood pouring from his head, staining the freshly swept and mopped floor of the cabin.

One big Shawnee, the leader of this raiding party, squatted down beside Jamie. He turned the boy over and put his hand on Jamie's chest. The heartbeat was strong and steady. The warrior slung Jamie over one shoulder and walked out through the smashed door into the night.

He ordered the cabin burned.

Jamie awakened several times during the night. He always wakened to pain. He knew he was being carried, passed from one Indian to another as they ran through the forest. He did not think they ever stopped for rest. The moon was full and gave ample light as long as it lasted but Jamie could recognize nothing familiar. Once he awakened as they crossed a river. He had no clear idea what river. Once he tried to fight the Indians. He was beaten and his wrists and ankles bound tightly. They soon became numb and Jamie wondered if he was going to be tortured before they killed him. He'd heard men talk about the terrible things Indians did to white captives. He wondered if his mother had survived. He felt she had not, for he had seen the awful blow delivered to her head. His father? No, he'd seen the blond scalp dangling from the big warrior's club. So his family was dead. Jamie began to cry. That got him another beating until he stopped sobbing.

Once they stopped, a young Indian — Jamie felt he couldn't be more than a boy — whispered to him. "You must be brave. You must be strong. If you are not, they will kill you. Be brave and be silent. We have a long way to go." The young Indian slipped away into the darkness. He smelled of sweat and woodsmoke. And blood.

Jamie nodded his head and tried to rest. His bound hands and feet hurt so bad he had to clench his teeth to keep from crying out from the pain. But he made not a sound. He was cold, but tried not to shiver. He had to be brave. He had to be. He knew his life depended on it.

The boy tried hard not to think of his parents, and his baby sister. He fought hard to put them out of his mind. Young, he was.

But he was born on the frontier, and was a realist for his age. He knew he was alone now. If he was to survive, he had to depend on his wits. The young Indian had seemed friendly enough, but his pa had always said that Indians were notional folks. They didn't think like white people. So Jamie — seven years old today — lying on the cold ground in a part of the country he had never seen before, made up his mind. Where his captors were concerned, he would be like a leaf: whichever way the wind blew, that's how he'd go.

He just couldn't see any other way. At least for the moment. But one thing he did know for a certainty. If the savages didn't kill him, he would escape. He didn't know how, he just knew he would. Someday. Or his name wasn't Jamie Ian MacCallister.

■ ■ ■ ■

Part One:
The Way West

■ ■ ■ ■

'Tis grand! 'Tis solemn!
'Tis an education of itself to look upon!
— James Fenimore Cooper

ONE

They traveled for three days and nights, first on foot, then in canoes on a big river. When they finally paddled their canoes toward shore, the boy was so lost and so tired and so sore he couldn't tell up from down.

His hands and feet were untied, but his feet were so numb he could not walk. The Shawnee who had taken him picked him up and threw him onto the bank. Then the whole band turned their backs to him and walked into the village amid shouts of greeting from the others.

The Indian boy knelt down beside Jamie. "I am called Little Wolf," he said in broken English. "You must rub your ankles and wrists to get the blood flowing. And you must not try to run away. This is a test. The first of many. If you cause trouble, Tall Bull will kill you."

"Why are you helping me?"

Little Wolf smiled. "Don't be fooled. I am

not helping you. But you are a boy and if you live, you will be a warrior. I heard Tall Bull say this from his own mouth."

Jamie thought about that for a second or two. Then fierce pain hit him hard as the feeling began returning to his feet and hands. He did not make a sound. Little Wolf watched this and was pleased. Jamie rubbed his ankles harder and more pain nearly put him out.

"You see!" the Indian said, as others gathered around. "You have pain, yet you do not cry out. You will be a warrior someday. Now get on your feet and walk to the village. Stay to one side and behind me."

"Where are we going?"

Little Wolf struck him across the face with a stick. Jamie felt the warm trickle of blood on his skin.

"Do not ask questions," Little Wolf said, a mean look in his eyes. "Not yet. Learn this now. Do as you are told when you are told to do it. You will endure many beatings before the testing is over. Now do as I told you!"

As they walked from the river, Jamie limping badly on his swollen feet, he looked at the twin lines of Indians up ahead of him, mostly women and young boys and girls. They all had sticks in their hands and were waving them, shouting at Jamie. Jamie did not have to understand the Shawnee language to know the shouts were strong insults upon him. He also knew from listening to adults talk what was about to happen to him. The Shawnees made captives run through a long and cruel gauntlet. And sometimes people did not live through the double line of tormentors. Jamie was determined that he would. He began stamping his feet on the ground and rubbing his wrists harder to hasten the flow of blood to his feet and hands.

Little Wolf turned and his smile was hard. "Now we will see how brave you are, White Hair."

"Braver than you think." Jamie met the older and taller boy's eyes. "I bet I knock some of them to the ground."

"Oh?" Little Wolf said. "And when, or if, you are able to do that, you might die."

"I'll take that chance." Jamie looked deep into the Indian's eyes, and with a start realized Little Wolf's eyes were *green*!

"What are you staring at, White Hair?"

"Your eyes."

"What about my eyes?"

"They're green. And your hair is brown. You're *white*!"

Little Wolf knocked him down with his

club. "I am Shawnee."

Jamie got up with blood running down from the gash on his forehead and mad enough to spit. He tackled the bigger boy and they rolled on the ground. The older men of the village ran to the kicking and punching boys and pointed and laughed. But they made no move to separate them. If the boy with white hair bested Little Wolf, so be it.

Jamie took a wild swing and his hard little fist landed solidly on Little Wolf's nose. The blood spurted and Little Wolf jumped back, astonishment and pain mirrored on his face. He raised his club to strike Jamie, and Tall Bull jerked it from his hand.

"No!" Tall Bull ordered. "Wrestle him. Tell him if he can best you, he is spared the gauntlet."

Little Wolf didn't like it, but he told Jamie his father's orders, adding, "I think I will kill you this day, White Hair."

"I don't think so," Jamie told him, and then hit Little Wolf as hard as he could, right on the mouth.

Jamie didn't know anything about Indian wrestling, but he did know a little something about fist-fighting, for his father had seen to that.

Little Wolf went down hard, landing on

his butt. His lips were red with blood. He became furious when some of the young girls giggled at him. He sprang to his feet and tried to grab Jamie. But the seven-year-old twisted away and kicked out with one shoe, the hard leather catching Little Wolf on the knee. The Indian boy gasped with pain and Jamie set himself and swung. The blow struck Little Wolf on the side of his neck and dropped him like a stone. Jamie had lucked out and quite by accident struck the Indian boy in just the right spot. Little Wolf was unable to get up.

"Enough!" Tall Bull said, holding up his hand. He knelt down beside his adopted son just as Little Wolf was beginning to come around from the nerve-numbing blow. Tall Bull was a brave warrior and a respected subchief of this particular band of Shawnees, but he was also very superstitious. He cut his eyes to the white-haired boy. He knew he should kill the captive immediately. There was open defiance in the boy's eyes. But still he held back. It was rare that Little Wolf ever lost in any contest. He had never lost to a person of Jamie's age and size. He was confused.

A woman stepped out from the crowd and walked to Jamie's side and put a hand on his shoulder. Tall Bull's mind was made up for him. The woman was his wife.

Jamie looked up at the woman and met her eyes. He was not expecting to see compassion or tenderness, and he was not disappointed. Jamie would find out soon enough that he had been spared because the woman needed a slave to work, and work he would, brutally hard work, with daily beatings for many weeks. But he was alive. And for now, that was all that mattered.

Tall Bull stood up, Little Wolf beside him. There was blood on the boy's face and wild, open hate in his eyes. Jamie met the Indian boy's gaze and knew he had made a bitter enemy. He knew, too, that he would have to be very careful, for he sensed, correctly so, that Little Wolf would plot to do him harm, even to kill him, if Jamie ever let down his guard.

Little Wolf spat at Jamie's feet and stalked away, his back stiff with anger.

"You are making a mistake, woman," Tall Bull said to his wife.

"I need a slave and the boy is strong. I want him."

"He is trouble. I made a mistake. I should have killed him with the others."

"But you didn't," she replied smugly.

"Don't point out the obvious to me! All

right. Take him. But he is your responsibility."

Deer Woman looked down at Jamie and pointed to the Shawnee town. When Jamie hesitated, she picked up a stick and beat him across the back and shoulders, the blows stinging and bringing blood. Jamie got the message and walked toward the town. Deer Woman stayed right behind him. Every few steps she would whack him again with the stick.

But I'm alive, Jamie thought. I'm alive. Although there would be many times in the months to come when the thought that he would be better off dead would enter his mind.

His parents had always felt that Jamie was exceptionally bright and very perceptive for his age — of course all parents feel that way — but in Jamie's case it was true. He did as he was ordered to do and did it without question or hesitation. The beatings began to slacken and finally all but stopped as Deer Woman very quickly became pleased with White Hair, as Jamie was called.

Jamie was her personal slave and instantly did her bidding. Since Deer Woman was the wife of a very important man, the others in the camp did not torment Jamie. Indeed, most began to like the boy who did his work without complaint and quickly caught on to the Shawnee way of life.

And Jamie made no effort to escape. That was noticed by all and soon Jamie was free to walk unguarded throughout the Shawnee town. The Shawnee town was a large one, and Jamie soon found three other white captives, all women. Two of them had been with the Shawnees so long they were more Indian than white, and shrank away from the boy at his approach. But the third woman, just out of her teen years, was friendly toward him and was as hungry for news from the outside as Jamie was anxious for knowledge as to where he was and what he might expect in the weeks or months that lay ahead of him.

"In the wilderness," Hannah told him. "I have never been more than two or three miles from this place."

"How long have you been a captive?"

"Five years, I think. What year is this?"

"1817."

"Four years, then. Seems like forever. Listen to me. We can only talk for a few minutes or they will become suspicious. We'll talk each day when we gather firewood, or gather berries come the spring."

"I don't plan on being here come the

spring," Jamie informed her.

Hannah smiled. "You'll be here."

Jamie began to sprout up and grow stronger. Deer Woman jokingly complained that she had to work all the time just to keep Jamie clothed. When the spring came, Jamie was still a captive and worked the Shawnee gardens, for like most Indian tribes of that part of the country, the Shawnees depended heavily on agriculture for their existence. Jamie helped the women tend the corn, beans, squash, and other vegetables. Since he was so young, he quickly mastered the Shawnee tongue, although he never let on that he knew as much as he did. He preferred to listen.

He learned his approximate location, and was heartsick for a time. He was several hundred miles, at least, from the village near his home. My home, he thought. I don't have a home. For Little Wolf had been more than eager to brag about how the cabin had been burned to the ground. He also went into great detail about how Jamie's mother and father had been scalped and then mutilated. He had taken great glee in the telling, over and over, until Tall Bull had finally ordered him to shut up.

Hannah talked with him briefly each day,

and each day he learned more and more about the Shawnees. And to Jamie, none of it was good.

The Shawnee, Jamie learned, were a much feared tribe, and were rarely defeated in battle. They were masters of guerrilla warfare, and were expert in the use of camouflage. The men were for the most part of average height, but with a very stocky build. They were quite strong, with tremendous endurance. The men shaved their heads, using sharpened shells from the rivers, and almost always were elaborately painted. And the Shawnee were very warlike.

They lived in homes, not that much different from the cabin where Jamie had been born. The lodges were long and snug, sometimes forty or fifty feet long, and were built without windows. The smoke from interior fires drifted out through holes built in the roof. When it rained, sliding panels were used to keep out the elements. The Shawnee slept on raised platforms which were covered with bearskin rugs. Since air circulation was poor, the lodges were a mixture of smells, ranging from cooking odors to tobacco.

The Shawnee towns were always built close to a river or stream, and were always built in a circle, with a huge longhouse in the middle of the walled compound that was used for important meetings; such as the declaring of war on another tribe. Jamie learned about the tribe's history and who they called friend (which could change like the wind) and who they had hated forever and ever. At the top of that list were the Cherokees, the only Indian tribe to ever give the Shawnees a thorough beating on the battlefield. The Shawnees hated the Cherokees, also feared them, and avoided them whenever possible.

The Shawnee were noted for constructing the best bows and arrows of any tribe, and they were deadly accurate with them. The horse did not play an important part in their lives — not yet. They had horses, stolen from white settlers, but for the most part the Shawnee of the early 1800s either walked, ran, or used canoes to travel; when possible, they used all three methods.

Jamie MacCallister did his assigned chores, kept his mouth shut, stayed out of trouble, and learned by listening. Their society, he learned, while vastly different from his own, was, oddly enough, similar in many ways. Nothing of any importance was ever done without first having a meeting and discussing the problem. The chief was a great and important man, but his word was not final and could be overruled by a vote. Although that was not often the case.

The language was Algonquian, but Jamie and Hannah spoke in whispered English whenever possible, so they would not forget their native tongue. The other white captives had been in the hands of the Shawnees for so long they had forgotten most of their English.

"They were brought here from far to the east," Hannah told Jamie. "So I was told. They were traded from another tribe. The Indians who took them as wives were long dead before I arrived here. They died cowardly, so no other Shawnee will take them. They are looked upon as outcasts. They could both leave if they wanted to, no one in the tribe would care. But they don't choose to do that."

"Why, Hannah?"

"Because they know they would be outcasts in a white society more so than they are here. At least here they have a place to sleep, food to eat, and some degree of protection."

"That's sad."

"Yes, it is. But in a few ways, Jamie, the Indian way of life is better than what we grew up in. Not in very many ways, but in some. They are truly savages, but in their own way, generous and giving."

"I haven't found any that are generous and giving yet," Jamie replied bitterly.

Hannah looked at the boy and smiled. "Deer Woman saved your life, Jamie. And don't think she didn't take a risk by standing up to Tall Bull. For she certainly did."

Jamie stole a furtive look around him. No one appeared to be watching them, but that was something he could not be sure of. For Little Wolf had a tight circle of friends and Jamie knew one of those friends was constantly watching, usually from hiding. Jamie spotted his watcher. A big hulking boy called Bad Leg because one leg was shorter than the other. Bad Leg disliked Jamie as much as Little Wolf did. Although Jamie had never done anything to warrant that dislike. Little Wolf and his gang tormented Jamie whenever they found him alone and outside the lodge, for they knew that no matter what they did to him, Jamie would never tattle on them to Tall Bull or Deer Woman. Consequently, they did their best to make life miserable for White Hair. Why that name remained was a mystery for Jamie, since Deer Woman regularly put plant dye on his hair to darken the blond.

"I see him, too," Hannah said, resting her back for a moment from the gathering of firewood in the fields and cutting her eyes to where Bad Leg was hiding behind a tree. "He is an evil boy, Jamie. And wicked because the other children used to taunt him when he was little — so I am told. Although I don't believe the parents would have permitted very much of that. Indians are very strict about that sort of thing."

"Hannah? Is Little Wolf white?"

"That is a question you must never ask, Jamie. Not to any Shawnee. I believe he is, yes. Or at least has some white blood in him. And no, I don't know the story as to how he came here. I know only that he is adopted. Deer Woman is barren."

"Oh, I know not to ask Tall Bull or Deer Woman. The worst beating I ever had came after I asked her about Little Wolf."

A woman screeched out for them to stop chattering and to get back to work.

It was the winter of Jamie's second year in the Shawnee town.

The thought of escaping was never far from Jamie's mind, awake or sleeping. He dreamed of seeing his own kind once more. Of having some candy, like a peppermint stick or a piece of johnnycake or a thick wedge of apple pie or some of his mother's sugar cookies. Home-baked bread all dripping with fresh-churned butter and a glass of cool milk from the well.

But he never let on that he was unhappy. By the end of his second year of captivity, Jamie was allowed to roam unescorted from the village for several miles in any direction. He made snares and caught rabbits, always bringing them back to the lodge and skinning and cleaning them before handing them to Deer Woman to add to the stew or to cook over an open fire on a wooden spit. She always told him what a good boy he was.

But she never told him that when Little Wolf was around. She knew that her adopted son hated White Hair and knew only too well that her husband still did not fully trust the white boy. But that distrust was tempering as the months went by. The turning point came one early spring, when Jamie was very late in returning from a foray into the deep woods, and Little Wolf was urging his father to let him find and kill White Hair. Tall Bull had told his son — over the protestations of Deer Woman — to go, find his friends, and wait.

"He is gone, Woman," Tall Bull told her. "I suspect he hid food in the woods in preparation for this day. I made a mistake. I should have killed him."

"The boy will return," Deer Woman insisted. "Give him time. I know he will return."

"It is nearly dark. You are a fool!"

A shout came from a sentry by the log wall of the Shawnee town and everyone came running. Tall Bull and Deer Woman watched the small figure come slowly walking out of the woods, dragging a travois. All could see the doe on the travois. And it was a good-size doe, too.

Deer Woman looked up at Tall Bull. Her husband sighed but made no other comment. He knew better.

The villagers watched as Jamie dragged the heavy load in through the open gates. All could see that the boy was nearly exhausted. But he would not ask for help.

Jamie stopped and looked at all the people gathered around. "Did something important happen while I was gone?" he asked.

"We were worried about you," Deer Woman said quickly. "That is such a fine deer. Where did you get the bow and arrows, White Hair?"

Jamie's bow and quiver of arrows lay on the travois. He had decided to test his status with the tribe. "I made them," he said. "I've been practicing in the meadow beyond the trees. There!" He pointed.

Tall Bull walked to Jamie's side, his eyes taking in the load which was far too heavy for Jamie, even though he was growing rapidly and was big and strong for his age. "It is a good deer," he said. He first picked up the bow and carefully inspected it. He grunted with satisfaction. "You *made* this, White Hair? How?"

"By watching you," Jamie said. "Everybody says you make the best bows in the town, so who better to watch?"

Deer Woman hid her smile. White Hair certainly knew how to play the right song with Tall Bull, she thought.

Tall Bull grunted, but he was obviously pleased. He took out each arrow and looked it over. "Good," he finally said. "You do good work. I told Deer Woman you would be a good hunter. I knew that all along."

Deer Woman rolled her eyes.

Little Wolf and his friends had gathered, all looking at the deer on the travois. None of them had ever killed a deer that size when they were so young.

Tall Bull's eyes saw the blood on Jamie's shirt and unlaced the front. There was a deep gouge on the boy's chest. "What is this?"

"Some wolves wanted the deer. I faced

35

them down and one accidentally scratched me."

"You . . . faced down wolves?" Tall Bull said. Then he leaned closer and sniffed Jamie's clothing. No doubt about it. The boy was telling the truth. He smelled like a wolf's den.

"Yes, sir. Well . . ." Jamie smiled. "They weren't very big wolves. There were only two of them. I think they were young."

A woman came over, uninvited, and bathed the scratch. Then she applied some ointment and smiled at him before turning and rejoining the crowd.

"He's lying!" Little Wolf said.

"No," Tall Bull said. "He is not lying. What color were these wolves?"

"One was black and the other gray," Jamie said.

"I have seen them," a man spoke. "The little one speaks truth."

"I knew all along he would be a great hunter," Tall Bull said. "I knew I was right in sparing him."

Deer Woman again rolled her eyes.

"I will skin the deer and scrape the hide," Jamie said. "Then I shall . . ."

"That is woman's work!" Tall Bull said sharply, and Deer Woman gasped and put a hand to her breast. "Not work for a man.

Tomorrow you start training to be a warrior." There were sudden tears in Deer Woman's eyes. "Little Wolf, help your brother with his load. You will want some of the meat to fill your belly, I'm sure, so work for it."

"My *what?*" Little Wolf screamed the words. "What did you say?"

That got him a clout on the side of the head from his father. "Never speak to me in that tone!" Tall Bull told his son. "Never again. Do you hear me?"

"Yes, father," Little Wolf said humbly, and sincerely, for he held his father in great respect.

"Hear me!" Tall Bull shouted. He turned in all directions and spoke the words to the north, south, east, and west. And the Shawnees crowded closer. "White Hair is no more. Never speak the name again." He put a hand on Jamie's shoulder. "From this moment forward, this boy is my son and he shall be called Man Who Is Not Afraid. He is my son. Insult him, and you insult me." He ruffled Jamie's hair. "Let us go to the lodge, son. Tomorrow will be a full day."

TWO

Jamie did not sleep on the floor that night. He had his own raised platform and his own new robes, not the hand-me-down and worn skins he had been using.

Just before he fell into a deep and heavy sleep, for they had all gorged themselves that night on meat, Jamie thought about his encounter with the wolves. They had been hungry, that was evident, and before Jamie left he did throw them some scraps and entrails. But when he faced the pair, curiously, he had not been afraid. He had faced bigger dogs before, and he had often heard his father say that wolves will leave you alone if you leave them alone. His father had said that he had never heard of a wolf just up and attacking a human being. There had to be a reason. Maybe that's why Jamie had not been afraid this day.

But he had taken an awful chance by killing the deer and exposing the fact that he now had weapons. Hannah had tried to talk him out of doing it, telling him that she had seen captives killed for doing just what Jamie planned. But Jamie could not be dissuaded. He was determined to better his status with the tribe. The more freedom he could have, the better his chances would be for escape.

Just as soon as he knew exactly where he was, that is.

Jamie had thought of hiding clothes out in the woods, but he was growing so fast that when the time came the clothes would not fit him. He gave up that idea.

As sleep took him, he thought, one step closer. One step closer.

Jamie's life changed drastically from that day on. He was permitted now to play games with the other boys and he quickly made friends with most of the boys his own age. And by listening to them talk, discovered that he was south of the Ohio River. South? If that was so, he was several hundred miles from where he'd been born.

But the faces of those in the village near his cabin had faded in his mind. He couldn't even really remember what his best friend, Robert, looked like. He wondered if the Shawnee raiding party that night had killed

Robert and his family, too? And how many others?

Jamie made up his mind. He would not attempt to return to the area where he used to live. What would be the point? He had no family left. He would listen to the older people of the tribe talk, and more importantly, warriors who had returned from recent raids, and try to find out where the nearest town was. He would listen carefully, and memorize any landmarks they might mention. He had to know for certain how to get to the Ohio River. For once there, he could make it to freedom. He just knew he could.

His days were busy ones now, for Tall Bull began his instructions on the art of being a Shawnee warrior. Jamie was very young for this harsh and uncompromising study, but Tall Bull puffed with pride when he was with the boy. How many men could say they had a son who, no more than a child, could kill a deer that weighed double the boy's weight and drag it home? How many men could boast that their son had faced down wolves, and won? And Tall Bull also kept picking away at any scab that grew over the wound on Jamie's chest so that a scar would remain forever.

"People will always want to see the scar

where you battled wolves and won," he told Jamie. "It is something to be proud of."

Jamie had stopped trying to tell Tall Bull that he had received the slight wound quite by accident. The black wolf had been afraid of him and had lost its balance and fell over on his back. Kicking out with its legs, one paw had struck Jamie, ripping his shirt and scratching his flesh.

Jamie had yelled in pain and the wolves had become frightened and ran back about fifty yards. It was no major thing to Jamie. Actually, he'd felt sorry for the hungry animals, for it had been a hard winter. But he sure wasn't going to argue with Tall Bull about it.

Jamie took to the bow as if he had been born to it. Tall Bull made him a much better bow than the one Jamie had made, and before the summer was over, he was the best shot in the Shawnee town, for his age group, and even better than some of the men, which did not set well at all with those warriors. Jamie could read the looks on their faces, but none vocalized their unhappiness. To do so would incur the wrath of Tall Bull, and none among them wanted that.

By the time Jamie was ten, he was very tall for his age and very strong. He could run and jump and wrestle with the best of the boys. As a hunter, he had no equal among his age group and even those several years older. He brought back to the lodge more than his share of game.

The hatred that Little Wolf felt for him had deepened, but only Little Wolf, his band of friends, and Jamie knew that. Inside the lodge, it was all brotherly love and good feelings. Deer Woman suspected that all was not wonderful, but she maintained her silence concerning her suspicions. Tall Bull did not have a clue. He knew only that he had two fine sons and he was proud of both of them.

By the time Jamie was eleven, he looked and behaved as a boy much older than his years. Even Little Wolf, who was about nineteen — no one knew for sure — was more than a little wary of the boy called Man Who Is Not Afraid. He and Bad Leg talked often, and secretly, of how best to get rid of Jamie, but so far it was all talk and no action.

Jamie and Hannah were doing some secret talking, too. A particularly cruel and quite ugly Shawnee had taken Hannah as his wife, and she was miserable.

"It's time, Hannah," Jamie told her as she worked one afternoon.

She paused only for a second, and then

resumed her berry picking.

"You have a plan?"

"Yes. But it's a dangerous one. We might be putting ourselves in more peril."

"I have to get away from Big Head. I think he might kill me soon."

"Meet me in the woods at noon tomorrow. By the blow-down. I have food and robes hidden there. Also a pistol I stole from the possessions of Sour Belly before they buried him. We're escaping, Hannah. We're going to be free."

She cut her eyes to this boy — really just a child. But Jamie had left his childhood far behind him. He was serious, seldom smiling. Much more man than boy. And she felt sorry about that. For Jamie, the joys of being a child had been ripped cruelly from him, leaving a deep scar that nothing would ever erase.

"Jamie, you know what will happen to us if we are found."

"We will be tortured to death. I know. I've seen it. We both have."

"I'll meet you in the blow-down at noon tomorrow. I would prefer death over my life as it is now."

The boy called Man Who Is Not Afraid met her eyes for a moment. "I will not let them take you alive, Hannah. That is why I stole the pistol. I will kill you first."

"I hope you mean that, Jamie."

"I do."

"I will bring back a buck for you, Mother," Jamie told Deer Woman the next morning. "One that you can make me a fine shirt and leggings from."

She looked at him and smiled.

"I shall go with you," Little Wolf said.

"I need you here," Deer Woman said quickly.

"Why?" Tall Bull demanded.

"To fix the panels on the smoke holes." She pointed upward toward the ceiling.

Tall Bull grunted. "You were to have repaired them last week, Little Wolf. I am becoming weary of your laziness. Stay here at the lodge and do what your mother asks you to do. I must go to a council meeting. Good hunting, son," he said to Jamie with a smile.

Little Wolf left moments after his father, grumbling and complaining.

Jamie picked up his bow, quiver of arrows, and secured his knife.

"Man Who Is Not Afraid?" Deer Woman said.

Jamie turned. He was now as tall as Deer Woman.

She put a hand to his face and touched him gently, then ruffled his dyed brown hair. "I knew this day would come. You are not Shawnee and never will be. Head south toward the tall mountains, to the Cherokees. They will see that you and Quiet Woman get back to your people. Do not reply to my words. Just go, my son. But go with this knowledge; someday Tall Bull and Little Wolf will find you. That will be the day when you must decide whether you live or die. And whether you will, or can, kill your father and brother. Goodbye, son."

She turned her back to him and Jamie knew, with that gesture, she was forever cutting the Indian ties to him.

Jamie stepped out of the lodge and did not look back.

He walked away with all the dignity an eleven-year-old can muster, and that is about on a par with the Queen of England. And it does not matter whether the eleven-year-old is a so-called uneducated savage or the son or daughter of a royal family.

Very few in the Shawnee town paid Jamie any attention as he walked out of the enclosed village and headed in the opposite direction of the blow-down in the timber. Where Hannah was waiting. Bad Leg watched him leave, however, and noted

Man Who Is Not Afraid was heading north.

"He'll probably kill a bear and there will be singing and dancing and more praising of him," Bad Leg muttered sourly. "I hate him."

Deer Woman busied herself in the lodge. She had grown to love the white-haired boy, much more so than Little Wolf, who she suspected was not quite right in the head. There was something very dark and twisted about Little Wolf.

When Jamie was in the deep timber, certain he could not be spotted from the town, he changed directions and began running. He ran at a steady, distance-eating lope and was not even winded when he reached the blow-down.

"Here!" Hannah called, standing up amid a jumble of brush and old fallen logs.

"Follow me!" Jamie said, and took off at a trot, slowing his pace so Hannah would be able to keep up.

He jogged along for another five minutes before reaching the spot where he'd been caching supplies. While Hannah rested, Jamie removed the supplies from the hiding place and then carefully concealed the spot.

Jamie said, "Follow me, Hannah. Put your feet where I put mine. Do not break off any twigs or bruise any leaves. Do not step in any mud or soft ground. I think they will first search to the north. But they will, in time, find our trail. Of that, I am certain. Probably by this time tomorrow. There is a small river that flows south about a day's run from here. Once we reach that, we will enter the river and cling to logs for a time and let the current take us . . ."

"There are great scaly creatures in the waters!" Hannah said, very much afraid. She had heard talk of the huge alligators that slid through the dark waters of the creeks. Huge beasts that preyed on humans and animals alike.

"No," Jamie assured her. "Those are to the south and east of here. Nearer the big waters. The old men say they used to be here. But no more. Let's go, Hannah. We're running for our lives."

"And freedom," Hannah said, adjusting the straps to her pack.

"Yes," the boy/man said. "And freedom."

By full dark, Tall Bull knew that one of two things had happened: Jamie had been attacked by a panther or a bear, or he had run away to seek out his own kind.

Since the boy had an uncanny ability to get along with wild animals, Tall Bull had to conclude that Man Who Is Not Afraid had run away.

"Bad Leg saw him going north," Little Wolf told his father. "That would be the logical thing for him to do."

Tall Bull grunted. "Man Who Is Not Afraid would not necessarily do the logical thing. He is uncommonly bright and filled with wisdom for one so young. We can do nothing in the night. There is no moon and we would only blunder around in the dark, destroying any sign they might have left. Which will be few," he added dryly. "We will commence the search at first light."

Jamie had first set a hard pace. He was young and his muscles strong. But when he saw that Hannah was beginning to falter, he slowed to a walk for a time, allowing her to catch her breath. For seven hours that is how they traveled, running, jogging, walking, then resting for only a few minutes every hour. At full dark, with Jamie in a part of the country he had never before seen, he found a good place to rest. Hannah sank wearily to the branch-protected grassy spot. Jamie had no way of knowing just how many miles they had traveled from the Shawnee town, but he guessed at least fifteen or so miles. Maybe twenty. They were heading into dangerous country; disputed country.

While there were ever-growing spots of civilization in this country, it was still very dangerous. And to make matters worse, Jamie really did not know where he was. For as the white people pushed further west, the Shawnee town had been moved several times during Jamie's captive years.

Jamie thought it was 1820, but he wasn't sure about that, either. He had heard talk among the elders that there were thousands of whites living in the territory that bordered the latest Shawnee town, considerably smaller and hidden much better than the first one Jamie had been taken to. Many of the Shawnees had moved much further north, but Tall Bull and those who followed him stayed to the south.

"Where are we, Jamie?" Hannah asked the next morning.

"I don't know," the boy gave her an honest answer. "But we're free."

They walked and ran all that day, and the next, heading south. Jamie never did find the river he was looking for. But he did stumble onto a creek and he and Hannah followed that for miles, sometimes on the bank, sometimes wading to hide their footprints. On the ninth day out, Jamie was forced to admit that he was as lost as a goose. He and Hannah had gotten turned around in the dark woods and he had absolutely no idea where they might be.

"What do we do?" Hannah asked.

"I climb a tree," Jamie said.

He climbed the tallest tree he could find, and when he finally settled on a limb, he was so startled he almost lost his balance and fell. He was looking at more smoke than he had seen in his life. Smoke from dozens of chimneys. This was no Indian village or town. No Indian would allow that much smoke to fill the air and give away their location. Jamie figured the town, surely a white town, was no more than three or four miles away, over the hills.

He quickly climbed down and told Hannah the news. She was deliriously happy for a few moments, then a worried look sprang into her eyes.

"What's the matter, Hannah?"

"They'll shoot us, Jamie. They'll think we're Indians. Look at us. We're more Shawnee than white."

Jamie had not given that any thought. But he did now. "Hannah, you have a petticoat in your pack. I saw it. It's white. We'll rip off some pieces and tie them on sticks. We'll walk in holding the sticks in the air. That way we'll be safe. But first we'll wash as best we can. We're both filthy. Then we'll put on our spare clothing." Buckskin clothing. But it was all they had.

It would have to do.

They scrubbed themselves clean at a spring and changed clothes, then looked at each other, the grown woman and the eleven-year-old man/boy who had thought up the escape plan, and carried it out.

They still looked like a couple of Indians.

Hannah started giggling and Jamie lost his usual serious demeanor and let the child free. Soon they were howling with laughter.

They finally sat down on a log and wiped their eyes with pieces of Hannah's torn petticoat. She looked at what was left of the undergarment. "I've been so careful with this all these years. It was my last hold on reason and order and . . . sanity, I suppose. It sounds stupid, but it was all I had left."

"No, it wasn't, Hannah," the man within the boy once more surfaced. "You had memories and you had hope. Just like I did. And we had each other. And now we're free to start over." He stood up and held out his hand. "Let's go make a new start for ourselves, Hannah."

That new start almost ended before it could begin. As they walked up the rutted road that led to more buildings than Jamie had ever seen, they both heard the call.

"Indians! Indians! To your posts. Man your posts."

Jamie and Hannah froze and held up their white pieces of petticoat and waved them.

"We're not Indians!" Jamie called. "We're white. We've been captives for years. We're not Indians."

A dozen mounted men, all heavily armed, rode out to the pair, standing still in the road.

"My name is Jamie Ian MacCallister. And this is Hannah Parker. We escaped from a Shawnee town about eight or nine days ago. Far north of here. Tall Bull's tribe."

"Good Lord!" a man breathed. "Where are you from, lad?"

"The western edge of Ohio Territory, sir. I think it was four, maybe five years ago. I'm just not sure. I know it was the day before my seventh birthday when they came out of the night. Tall Bull led a raiding party to my cabin. They killed my pa and ma and smashed my baby sister to death against the stones of the fireplace. Tall Bull and his wife, Deer Woman, adopted me. Hannah here . . ." He paused for only a second, thinking fast. He knew that if any settler knew she had been touched by an Indian, much less shared the robes with a savage, she would be shunned; an outcast. "She

52

played like she was crazy so the Indians would leave her alone. It worked."

"Smart thinking, lass," another man said. "Damn filthy savages."

The men all swung down from their saddles and looked at the pair.

"They dyed Jamie's hair with coloring from plants," Hannah told the men.

"Sure did," another man spoke. "You can see the blond roots."

"After Jamie faced down a pack of wolves . . ."

"Faced down a pack of wolves!" yet another man said, clearly startled.

"Yes," Hannah said quickly. "The boy was hunting and became separated from his guards. He was only nine years old and had killed a huge deer with the bow and arrows he'd made. The wolves were about to fight him for the meat" — Jamie struggled to keep a straight face, but it was done only with a lot of effort — "and he grabbed one by the throat and stared it down. The animal clawed him fiercely but Jamie refused to drop his eyes. Jamie and this huge wolf stayed that way for several minutes, as the other wolves became afraid." Jamie rolled his eyes. "Finally, Jamie threw the big wolf from him and all the wolves ran away. Look!" She opened Jamie's shirt, exposing the long scar.

"Would you look at that?" a young man exclaimed. "What a fearsome mark the beast left on you, boy."

"And after that," Hannah continued. "Jamie was called Man Who Is Not Afraid. The Shawnees sang songs about his bravery and danced in his honor." She put her arm around Jamie's shoulders. "He saved my life, and I shall forever be in his debt."

Jamie decided to change the subject before the manure got too deep. "Where are we, if I may ask?"

"Why, you're in Kentucky, lad. And you and the lady here are safe. Come on, the both of you. Let's get you out of them savage's clothes and into a tub of hot soapy water. How does that sound."

"As near to heaven as I might ever get," Hannah said.

And the men laughed. All but one.

THREE

Jamie and Hannah had traveled many more miles than they thought. They had come about a hundred and seventy-five miles from the Shawnee town on the river.

"You must have gone right by a dozen or more settlements," Reverend Hugh Callaway told them. "Why, the country is filling up fast, I tell you."

"Tall Bull's band is one of the last real holdouts in this area," a farmer named Mason said. He leaned forward. "Lad, what are you going to do? Will you seek to find relatives up yonder whence you came?"

Jamie shook his head, conscious of Hannah's eyes on him. "No, sir. I think not. I had no kin there. Just Pa and Ma and the baby. They're all dead. I see no reason to go back."

The men looked at one another. Callaway said, "Then what do you intend to do, lad?"

Jamie met the reverend's gaze with one of

his own. "Survive, sir. I'm really very good at it."

"But where, lad?" Mason asked.

"In the woods, if I have to."

"But you're only a child!" the reverend's wife said. "You can't live out in the woods in a cave like a sav—" She bit the words off.

"Like a savage Indian, mum?" Jamie said that with a smile. "It's all right. I don't mind. I learned a lot from the Shawnees."

"From a filthy pack of red niggers?" another man spoke up. A man that Jamie had taken an instant dislike to back on the road.

"Beggin' your pardon, sir," Jamie said. "But this band of Shawnee bathed regularly. They make their own soap, just like we do."

"Sounds to me like you're defendin' them savages," the man said angrily.

"Now, calm down, John Jackson," the reverend said. "You've no call to address the boy in such a manner."

"How do we know that both the boy and the wench ain't spies for the red devils?" Jackson demanded. "I say we banish them both from town."

"I say nay to that!" a merchant man named Abe Caney spoke up. "John, you've no right to accuse these people of any wrongdoing. They've been put through

56

enough without adding false charges from you."

The others in the meeting room were quick to agree with Caney. John Jackson stood up, jerked his hat from the peg, and stormed out into the late afternoon.

"Pay the man no heed," Mason said. "He's an ill-tempered man but a good man in his own way. We've all fought the savages and John will stand with the best of them."

"Aye," Caney said. "And he'll be the first to help with the building of a cabin." He smiled. "Although he does grouse about it the whole time."

"My child," the Reverend Callaway said, speaking to Hannah, who was anything but a child, with a well-rounded figure and full bosom. The only thing the ladies of that time would object to were her tanned cheeks and arms. But that would be the case in the cities, not on the frontier, where women usually worked alongside their men in the fields. "Have you given thought as to the rest of your life now that you are free from the hostiles?"

Hannah smiled. "My life was interrupted at age fourteen, Reverend Callaway. I'm afraid I haven't been free long enough to do much thinking about the rest of it."

"Of course, of course!" He patted her

hand. "Well, you can stay with us for a time, and Jamie, a young couple will be along shortly to fetch you to their home. They're a lovely Christian couple without children and they were delighted when I sent a boy riding to their farm with news about you."

Jamie nodded his head. "Yes, sir," he said.

"You'll not be needing that bow and quiver of arrows now, Jamie," Mason said.

"I'll keep them," Jamie replied. He smiled. "As souvenirs."

Sam and Sarah Montgomery were a nice young couple, and Jamie found himself liking them from the start. They were amazed at Jamie's size, expecting to see a small boy of eleven, not this strong and quite capable appearing young man who, despite his young age, exuded strength and quiet confidence.

After supper at the Callaway home, on the wagon ride back to their farm that evening, Sam asked, "Do you have much knowledge of the fields, Jamie?"

"I helped Pa when I was little, yes, sir. And I had a section of the garden that was mine."

"Wonderful. I'm in the process of clearing land to raise more crops."

"I haven't had much experience with an

axe, sir," Jamie said dryly.

Sam cut his eyes to the boy/man sitting between he and his wife. Jamie had a sense of humor, Sam discovered. But he doubted the boy rarely let it show. Probably wasn't much to laugh about while a slave in a Shawnee town. "I imagine that's true, Jamie," he replied.

Jamie knew why the quick glance. "Indians have a good sense of humor, Mr. Montgomery," Jamie said. "They just don't show it much around people not of their kind."

Sam started to say that the only good he'd ever found about Indians was when they were dead. But he held his tongue. There were dozens, hundreds, of questions the couple wanted to ask Jamie, but they did not know how or where to begin.

"You live a long way out of town," Jamie observed, after a few moments of silence.

"We have a little settlement out here," Sarah said. "About a dozen families live within a two- or three-mile radius of one another. There are enough children that we now have our own school. I do some of the teaching."

"I could read and write some when Tall Bull took me. I think I've forgotten how."

"It'll come back to you in jig-time," Sam said. "We won't push you, Jamie. You've got

59

a lot of adjusting ahead of you." Like learning how to wear shoes again, he thought. Jamie wore his moccasins; said the shoes he'd received hurt his feet.

"Do the Indians bother you out here?"

"Sometimes," Sam admitted. "There are a lot of areas close by that are not settled. But the savages are slowly being forced out as more and more settlers come in. Some are saying that the nations will someday be settled from coast to coast. Probably not in our lifetime," he added. "What lies beyond the Mississippi is pretty much a mystery."

"Not to my grandfather," Jamie said, suddenly remembering the stories his pa used to tell him.

"What's that?" Sarah asked.

"My grandfather. The man I'm named after. He went west to the big mountains years before I was born. Seventeen ninety, I think Pa said. He came back once, Pa said. Years before Pa and Ma got married. Said he looked like a wild man. All done up in beaded buckskins and hair long as a woman's. Then he went west again and no one's ever heard no more from him."

"Wasn't there a MacCallister with the Lewis and Clark expedition, Sarah?" Sam asked.

"I believe there was. Seems like I've read

something about that. He joined up with them in the west as a guide."

"That's my grandpa, then," Jamie said. "I wonder if he's still alive?"

Sam did not want to tell the boy that he'd heard nothing good about the white men who lived in the mountains of the west. They were, for the most part, a wild and Godless lot, more savage than civilized, heathen to the soul. Some had taken to calling them mountain men. And there sure was a MacCallister among them. A bad man, some said, who had killed other men with knife and gun. He would tell Sarah not to mention the man to Jamie. In time the boy would forget all about his wild and Godless grandpa.

There was to be a shindig, Sam told Jamie. All the people who lived in the small community were going to gather the first warm Saturday and there would be singing and eating on the grounds. Jamie would get to meet all the folks and make new friends. It would be a grand to-do, Sam promised.

The cabin of Sam and Sarah Montgomery was much finer, larger and better built than the one Jamie vaguely remembered from his childhood. Sam and Sarah came from monied families, and that was evident in the cabin's construction, for it was a two-story log house with several rooms. It had a central chimney — something that Jamie had never seen before — and it was made of stone and was fireproof. It was the grandest house that Jamie had ever seen, and he said so.

"Is it, now?" Sam said. "Well, let's take the grand tour then, lad. I'll show you your room."

The boy surfaced. "My own room?"

"All your very own, Jamie," Sarah said softly. "We want you to be happy here. We think you've had quite enough unhappiness in your life."

Jamie couldn't believe his eyes. His room, his very own room, was bigger than the whole cabin in which he had been born. And he had a whole big bed to himself, with a feather tick and two pillows.

"The corner logs of the house are not square-notched, Jamie," Sam explained. "I had a skilled worker come in and dovetail them all. Makes for a sturdier structure. The home is built on stones for support and it's stone-walled all around the base. The roof don't leak. Put together with nails. They're expensive, too. This home is solid, Jamie," he said proudly. "She'll be standing for years to come."

"You best get ready for bed, Jamie," Sarah said. "You must be exhausted and here we've been prattling on."

Long after the candles had been pinched out and the lamp wicks had cooled, Jamie lay wide awake in the soft bed. It was too soft. He couldn't get comfortable. Finally, he took his blankets and rolled up in them on the floor, on the rag rug beside the bed. That was much better. He was asleep in minutes.

Jamie was jerked out of sleep by a slight noise. While the senses of anyone living in the frontier had to be keen to stay alive, Jamie's were Indian-keen. And something had brought him wide awake. Jamie slipped from under the blankets and padded sound-lessly to the shutters. He cracked them and looked out. Two men were slipping across the clearing toward the barn where Mr. Montgomery's fine horses were kept. Mr. Montgomery worked the land himself, and had no paid hands or indentured people on the place. Sam and Sarah did not believe in indenturing people and frowned mightily on slavery. Jamie dressed quickly and silently and took up his bow and quiver of arrows. He strung the bow — it was a powerful one, made just recently by Tall Bull — and slipped his way silently down the steps. He had already tested to see which steps squeaked and which did not. He stayed close to the wall on his way down and fixed the latch-string so he could get back into the home.

Jamie slipped around to the side, where an overhang had been built, to both afford shelter from the rain and allow Sarah to wash clothes in the big pot while enjoying the shade. Mr. Montgomery hadn't missed much when he had the home built.

Jamie had overheard Mason and Caney talking about the rash of horse-stealing that had been going on in the community and about how the man appointed sheriff seemed unable to do anything to stop it. Jamie knew how to stop it. For his Shawnee town had come under attack by Indians several times since he'd been renamed and accepted by the tribe. Jamie had put arrows into several enemies. He didn't know if he'd ever killed anyone, or not. But he had sure tried.

Jamie had helped Mr. Montgomery put away the team earlier that evening, and had seen the fine horses kept in the barn. They would be a prize for anyone, and would bring a lot of money for a person who didn't particularly care where they came from.

The men were dressed all in dark clothing

and had kerchiefs tied around the lower part of their face. They carried bridles in their hands. Jamie slipped closer; close enough to hear them talk.

"We'll ride to Tennessee," one said. "Sell them down there. I got a man who'll fix up papers for us."

Jamie notched an arrow.

"Too bad we can't knock Sam in the head and have us a time with Sarah," the other one said.

Jamie drew back.

"Maybe next time we're in the country. I could have me a high ol' time with that wench."

Jamie let fly.

The arrow flew straight and true and embedded deeply in the man's rump and he let out a fearsome shriek and fell to the ground, on his knees. Jamie put his second arrow into the other man's leg, knocking him down. Within seconds, Sam Montgomery was outside, a pistol in each hand.

"Over here, Mr. Montgomery," Jamie called. "Horse thieves."

"By the Lord!" Sam said, as Sarah came outside in a dressing gown. She carried a lantern. "Ring the warning bell, Sarah," Sam told her. "Ring it loud and long."

He looked at Jamie, standing calmly,

another arrow notched and ready to fly. "Lad, you should have called me. You might have been killed."

"Not by those two," the boy said, no sign of fear in his voice. "I've stood and faced Yuchi, Miami, and Creek, and got arrows into all of them. Those two are cowards."

Sarah was ringing the large bell set at the front of the house. "We all have those bells, Jamie," Sam explained. "It's a warning system for Indian attacks or a house afire. There'll be ten men here in that many minutes."

Sam had lit a lantern from a peg under the overhang and he and Jamie walked over to the groaning men. "Masked brigands," Sam said contemptuously. "Thieves in the night coming to steal from honest men."

"I'm bleedin' to death, man!" one of the horse thieves said. "Help me."

With his next gesture and following words, Jamie knew that Sam was no man to play with. He lifted one heavy pistol, cocked it, and said, "Want me to put you out of your misery? I can. Just say the words."

The man screamed, "No. For the love of God. Are ye daft, man? And who is that little savage with ye?"

"My son," Sam said, the words proudly spoken. "And if you call him a savage again,

I'll put a ball between your eyes."

The man with the arrow in one buttock cried out. "I been grievously wounded, Mr. Montgomery. Will you see to it that I come under a doctor's care?"

The pounding of hooves stopped any further words. Armed men jumped off their mounts and rushed to the scene. They looked at the arrow-punctured bandits and then at Jamie.

"I think you done well by takin' this lad under your roof, Sam," one said. "These are the Saxon brothers from down Tennessee way. My oldest boy said he thought he seen them a-skulkin' around your place the other afternoon. I was raised up with their oldest brother over in Virginia. He's a good man, but these two is nothing but white trash."

"Where'd you stand to put the points in them, boy?" another man asked.

"Over there by the overhang," Jamie said, slipping the sinew bow string off to save both string and bow. "They were talking about knocking you in the head, Mr. Sam, and then . . . well, doing things to your wife."

"That's a filthy calumny!" one of the Saxon brothers yelled. "We done no such thing. He's just tryin' to get us hanged!"

"I do not lie," Jamie said. "There is no reason for me to lie. If I had wanted you both dead, I could have easily done so."

One of the men who had ridden to the scene said, "That's a good twenty-five/thirty yards over yonder, boy. You right sure you didn't just luck out these shots?"

Jamie looked at the man. Without changing expression, he restrung his bow and notched an arrow. The barn door was fifty yards from where he stood. "The dark spot just above the latch," he said, and lifted the bow. The arrow flew to the dark spot with a thud. "This one will go beside the first one." The arrow landed within an inch of the first arrow.

The men laughed. One said, "You got any more questions about the boy's skill, Luke?"

Luke good-naturedly joined in the laughter and replied, "Nope. My wife always said I beat all for puttin' my foot in my mouth. Looks like I done it again." When the laughter had once more subsided, he smiled down at Jamie. "You're all right, son. You're all right."

"I got me a arrey in my arse and y'all's havin' a arrey shoot!" the rump-shot brigand yelled. "How about givin' me some relief?"

Luke spat on the ground. "When the jury

hears the boy's testimony about what you wanted to do with Mrs. Montgomery, you'll get some relief, Saxon. Thirteen steps and a rope."

The men were trussed up and tossed, not too gently, into the back of a wagon and since it was only a couple of hours until dawn, they were taken into town to the jail, escorted by several of Sam's neighbors.

"Stay here and protect Sarah, Jamie," Sam told him.

The boy nodded his head, a solemn expression on his face. "I will do that, sir. You do not have to worry while I am here."

"I do believe he means it, too," a man muttered. "I shore do."

On the way into town, one of the neighbors said, "The boy don't smile much, do he, Sam?"

"I guess if you're raised as a captive by Shawnees," Sam replied, "you wouldn't have a lot to smile about."

"Raised by Shawnees!" one of the Saxon brothers hollered, lying on his stomach in the bed of the wagon. "Why, that's got to be the Wolf-boy that there Cherokee told us about a couple of months ago, brother. The one that was taken captive as a tadpole."

"Wolf-boy?" a neighbor said.

And the conversation was lively on the

ride into town, with Sam telling the story — he still wasn't sure he believed it — about Jamie facing down the pack of wolves and gaining the Shawnee name of Man Who Is Not Afraid.

"Damn!" Luke said. "You shore nuff got you a ring-tailed-tooter, Sam."

"Yes, I sure did," Sam replied. "I don't believe anyone would argue that."

"I damn sure won't," a Saxon said. "Oh, Lordy, my arse is on fire!"

FOUR

The news of Jamie's felling two horse thieves with arrows was all over the small community by breakfast time. Most of the people applauded the boy's actions and most of them lamented that Jamie did not aim higher and once and for all rid the land of the worthless Saxon Brothers.

"Vengeance is mine, sayeth the Lord," the Reverend Callaway told a gathering of men.

"The Lord also works in mysterious ways," one of Jamie's supporters countered.

But a few were on the other side.

"I told them at the meetin' hall that damn boy was nothin' but a savage," John Jackson said to Hart Olmstead, the only man in the community with a worse disposition and attitude than John. Hart was an ignorant, opinionated, overbearing, crude, hulking lout. And his four sons were just like him, one of whom was Jamie's age.

"Oncest them damn Shawnees git holt of

a person, that person ain't never fitten to live in a white society agin," Hart said. "I'll not have my boys rubbin' elbows with no damn red nigger. He ain't white no more. He's Injun, through and through."

Very few in the community agreed with that opinion, but it only takes a few.

"And I don't believe that wench's story about her bein' off in the head, neither," Hart opined. "Some stinkin' buck bedded her down first night in that Shawnee town and that's that." He shuddered at the thought. "That's almost as bad as bein' had by a nigger. Let's go see Sheriff Marwick. I know them Saxon boys. They ain't bad people. I don't believe they was tryin' to steal Montgomery's hosses."

The sheriff, a large pus-gutted man named Burl Harwick, was about as qualified to uphold and enforce the law as he was to be pope. But when elections were held, no one else wanted the job so he got it, more by default than popularity. Burl was even more ignorant than Hart Olmstead, and on top of that, he was a coward. He was also inherently lazy. Few really liked the man, so it was only natural he would be friends with John Jackson and Hart Olmstead.

"I ain't met the boy as yet," Burl said to his two friends. Just about his only friends.

"But ever'body says he's a right nice boy. Big for his age and solemnlike."

"Well, you got to talk to him, Burl," John said. "And since we're your duly sworn deputies, we'll ride along with you out to the Montgomery place. I think once you talk to him, you'll see what me and Hart already know: he's an Injun. And we don't want no damn Injuns around here."

John and Hart were sworn deputies, albeit unpaid ones. However, they both knew that few in the community took them very seriously.

Burl checked on his prisoners before he locked up the sturdy log jail. Both men were in leg irons and behind bars, and that, coupled with their wounds, insured that they were not going anywhere. The "doctor," actually a barber and bartender by profession, had to dig and cut the arrowheads out of the rump and leg of the Saxon brothers. Not a very pleasant experience. The brothers lay on their bunks and suffered with a great deal of loud complaining.

"Be a relief just to get away from those two," Sheriff Marwick said, as he locked the outer door. It was a long ride out to the Montgomery place, and Burl was not a good horseman. By the time he arrived, his "deputies" with him, the sheriff was not in a good mood.

And John had been right: Burl took an immediate dislike to Jamie. The boy was big for his age, and there was cold defiance in those pale eyes. And something else, too: the boy was not afraid of him. That was unsettling to Burl. He'd never met a boy who wasn't afraid of, if not the man, as least the badge pinned on the outside of his black coat. But not this boy. And Burl had never been comfortable in the Montgomery home. It was too fancy for his tastes.

Burl questioned the boy, and got the same story as he had earlier from Sam Montgomery.

"Let fly them arrows a bit quick, I'd say," Hart Olmstead said.

"You weren't here," Jamie said, meeting the man's gaze. "So how would you know?"

"Don't you sass me, you smart-mouthed half Injun pup!" Hart said.

"That'll do, Hart!" Sam stepped between them. "You're forgetting that you are in my home. I'll not permit you to browbeat this boy."

"I'm an officer of the law, Sam. You interfere with my questionin' of this boy and I'll put you behind bars."

"I'd like to see you try that, Hart," Sam's

words were quietly offered. But they were edged with tempered steel. "As far as you being an officer of the law, you're nothing but a joke. You and John both. Now get out of my house."

Hart Olmstead marched to the front door of the fine home near the edge of wilderness, his boots thudding heavily. At the door, he turned and pointed a blunt finger at Sam. "I'll thrash no man in front of a good woman, Sam Montgomery, and your Sarah is a good woman. But I give you warnin' now, first time I see you alone in town, I'd challenge you to fists, by God."

Sam stiffened in anger. He was not as big as Hart Olmstead, but was very strong. And Jamie suspected, from looking at Sam's big, flat-knuckled hands, the man knew how to fight.

"Sam . . ." Sarah said.

"Stay out of this, Sarah. I'll have no man throw down a challenge and expect me to stand by and do nothing. Get outside, Olmstead. I am going to teach you a lesson you will never forget." Sam had no way of knowing how prophetic his words would turn out to be.

Hart Olmstead's face turned first chalk white and then beet red. He very nearly tore the door down getting out of the home. Sam

Montgomery removed his coat and took off his shirt. His muscles fairly rippled as he flexed his arms. He winked at Jamie. "I don't hold with fighting, lad. But there comes a time when a man must fight for what he believes in. Sarah, would you be so kind as to grind some beans and have a fresh pot of coffee for me. And also have some hot water to bathe my cuts and bruises. Mr. Olmstead is a brute, and I shall not come out of this unscathed."

Sarah waited until the heavy bell stopped ringing in the front yard.

"Certainly," Sarah said, her face pale. She cut her eyes to Jamie. "The boy . . ."

"The boy has been a man for some time, I suspect. He will be outside, with me."

"Why the bell, Sam?" Sarah asked.

"Olmstead wants everyone in our community to be here to see me receive a thrashing at his hands. I am afraid he is to be sorely disappointed. Sorely, in more ways than one," he added with a small smile.

Sam and Jamie walked out of the house while the neighbors were gathering. The women hurried into the house. In the front yard, Sam said, "Get away from Sarah's flowers. I don't want them trampled on." Sam walked out of the yard and to the side of the road. "Get over here, Olmstead, and toe the mark."

Jamie looked back at the home. All the women had gathered at the windows and thrown open the shutters. He turned to look at Hart Olmstead. Sam had been right; the man was a brute, with massive shoulders and arms. And Jamie could tell he was spoiling for a fight.

Olmstead spat on the ground and lifted his fists. "Now, rich boy, you'll get your comeuppance. I intend to knock you off that ivory tower you sit on like a king."

Jamie had been right in guessing that Sam Montgomery was a man of substance. And people like John Jackson and Hart Olmstead always resented those with money.

Jamie's pa had told him that.

Unbeknownst to anyone, Jamie had taken a pistol from Sam's holster that hung from a peg in the hallway and shoved it behind his belt and pulled out his shirttail to cover the butt. He didn't trust the sheriff or John Jackson. He believed neither of them to be honorable men.

Hart walked up to Sam and Sam hit him twice in the face before Hart could blink. The blows were powerful ones that rocked Hart's head back and bloodied the bigger man's lips and nose.

Hart cursed Sam and took a wild swing

that, had it connected, would have done some damage. Sam ducked under the whistling fist and struck Hart a terrible blow to the stomach. The air wheezed out of Olmstead and before he could recover, Sam had knocked him down in the mud with a hard left.

"I'm probably making a bad mistake, but I'll not put the boots to you, Olmstead," Sam told him, backing up and giving the man room. "Although if the position were reversed, I believe you would not hesitate to kick me."

Hart Olmstead rose slowly to his feet, hate and fury in his eyes and on his bloody face. "No man does this to me," he panted the words. "No man!"

"I just did," Sam spoke calmly. "But it need not continue. Whether it does or not, depends entirely on you."

With a roar of rage and a wild obscenity on his lips, Hart charged Sam, hoping to get him in a bear hug and crush some ribs. But Sam had anticipated that and merely stepped to one side and tripped the bigger and heavier man, sending him crashing to the ground, sliding in the mud for a few feet, on his belly, chest, and face.

The men all laughed and that made Hart Olmstead even angrier. "Damn you all!" he screamed, getting to his knees and squatting there in the mud and the blood. "I'm an officer of the law in this county. I demand respect. And I command the whole damn lot of you to stop laughing."

That brought even more laughter and hoots and catcalls of derision from the crowd of men. Over it all, Jamie could faintly hear giggling coming from the house. Jamie cut his eyes to Sheriff Marwick. The man looked embarrassed.

Hart got to his feet and the man was a mess, mud and blood dripping from him. Sam stood nonchalantly, still neat as a pin. He had not even broken a sweat.

"Give this up, Hart," Sam said. "We'll call it a draw and shake hands and you can clean up over yonder at the rain barrel. What say you, Hart?"

"I'll kill you!" Hart screamed, and rushed at Sam.

Hart was swinging both fists and they both connected against Sam, knocking the man backward and bloodying his lips. Sam regained his balance and clubbed the maddened Olmstead hard on the back of the neck, knocking him down. Olmstead was up on his feet fast and rushed Sam. For a moment, the two men stood toe to toe and slugged it out, both of them landing hard punches.

But soon Sam's blows began to have an effect on Olmstead, backing the man up, blood streaming from the man's mouth and nose. Olmstead's lips were pulped and his nose was nearly flat.

Hart back-heeled Sam and sent him crashing to the ground. Hart tried to put the boots to the smaller man and Sam rolled away, jumping to his feet. Hart rushed him and Sam stopped the man cold in his tracks with a solid left and right to both sides of the man's jaw. Hart's knees wobbled and Sam bored in relentlessly, hammering hard with blows to the head and the body.

Hart covered up his face and backed away, trying to clear his head and recover his waning strength. But Sam pressed him, hitting hard with body blows. Hart lowered his fists to protect his bruised and aching belly and Sam wound up a right and blasted the big man flush in the mouth, following that with a left that when it landed sounded like someone hit a watermelon with the flat side of an axe. Hart's eyes rolled back and he went down to his knees in the churned-up mud. He stayed on his knees for a few seconds, then slowly toppled over, face first in the rutted road.

The crowd stood silent, but every man

there had a smile on his lips. And that did not go unnoticed by Sheriff Marwick and John Jackson. It was at that point when Jackson realized just how much he and Marwick and Olmstead were disliked by the members of the community.

"Is anybody gonna help me get Hart to his feet?" Marwick said, walking over to the unconscious Olmstead.

No one in the crowd made a move.

Jamie felt eyes on him and turned his head. John Jackson was staring straight at him, the hate shining bright and hard. Jamie knew then, but did not know why, that he had made a terrible enemy of the man.

Sheriff Marwick dragged Hart Olmstead off the road while Jackson fetched a bucket of water from the well. Sam was drying his face and upper body with a rag one of the neighbors had handed him. Jackson poured the bucket of well water on Olmstead's head and the man groaned and rolled over. Jamie had never before witnessed such a beating as this one — and he was not alone, neither had most of the others present.

Hart Olmstead's face was cut, battered, bruised, and bloody. One eye was completely closed and one ear swollen nearly three times its normal size. His lips were swollen and his nose was mashed all over the center of his face. On his bare torso, there were huge splotches of red and blue/ green where Sam's fists had landed.

Olmstead moaned and sat up, with a little help from Marwick. Through his one good eye, he glared balefully first at Sam Montgomery then at Jamie. He didn't have to say a word. The eye spoke silent hatred.

"This is not over, Montgomery," Hart pushed the words past swollen lips.

"It is as far as I am concerned," Sam told him, slipping into his shirt he'd hung on the split-rail fence.

"I'll kill you someday," Hart said.

"Shut up, Hart," Sheriff Marwick told him. "Don't talk like that."

"Son of a bitch!" Hart said to Sam.

Sam stiffened, for that was an insult that warranted killing.

"He didn't necessarily say that to you, Sam!" John Jackson said hurriedly. "Just take it easy, Sam. Your name wasn't connected with that oath."

"That's true, Sam," a neighbor said. He looked at Hart, now standing on his feet, leaning against the sheriff. "You best clear this up, Olmstead. Did you hurl that insult at Sam?"

Hart stood for a few seconds, then slowly shook his head. He was in no shape for a pistol affair, and he knew it. "No. Of course not."

"I'll accept that," Sam said.

Both Marwick and Jackson breathed a bit easier. Neither of them wanted to see a duel between Sam and Hart. Dueling was still very common. It had not been that many years back that Andrew Jackson and Thomas Hart Benton had gone at each other with pistol and dirk in a Nashville, Tennessee, hotel, with Jackson coming out on the short end of that fight.

It took both Marwick and John Jackson to get Olmstead into the saddle, with Olmstead muttering fearful curses, carefully directed at no one in particular. Olmstead did not once look at Sam. John passed the reins to him and then the men climbed onto their mounts and started slowly up the road.

"No good will come of this," Sam said to no one in particular. "I have just made a mortal enemy, for Hart Olmstead is a good hater."

"You whipped him fair, Sam," Luke said. "You did not use no boots on him nor bitin' or eye-gougin'."

"That's the problem, Luke. I whipped him. And he'll not forget it. Not ever."

"You men gather over yonder under the shade tree," Sarah called from the open door to the house. "We'll bring coffee and bread and molasses out. I don't want you stomping around in this house with your muddy boots."

"By the Lord!" Mason said. "That was a good fight, it was. I don't recall ever seein' none better."

While the men laughed and gathered under the huge old tree by the side of the house, Jamie slipped inside and put Sam's pistol back into the holster, then quickly rejoined the men as Sarah and the other ladies were bringing out refreshments.

Sam sidled over to Jamie and whispered, "Did you put my pistol back, Jamie?"

Without changing expression, Jamie said, "Yes, sir."

"Would you have used it, lad?"

"Yes, sir."

"Ummm," was all Sam ever said about that.

FIVE

The following morning, Jamie started doing chores before Sam or Sarah were even out of bed. He had not forgotten how to milk — but he had forgotten how a tail full of burrs felt when it came in fast and hard contact with the side of his head — and had the cow milked, the hogs slopped, the eggs gathered, and firewood stacked neatly when a still tousled-haired and sleepy-eyed Sam stuck his head out the back door and called to him.

"Yes, sir?" Jamie said, walking up to the back door of the home.

"How long have you been up, lad?"

"Since the cow started lowing."

Sam smiled. "That fight yesterday must have taken more out of me than I thought. Well . . . Sarah says to tell you that breakfast will be ready in a few minutes. Why don't you come on inside and help me grind the

85

beans and we'll have some coffee in no time."

"All right, sir."

Sam did not say anything about the way Jamie was dressed. In his buckskins. It was not that it was unusual dress for the time, for many men still wore skins, but for Jamie . . . he would have to somehow point out that it would be best if he dressed more like a schoolboy, which he would be in a short time. The sooner the townspeople forgot he had once been a Shawnee captive, the better for everybody. He lifted his gaze. Jamie was seated at the table, watching him.

The boy was so damn quick it startled Sam.

"I'll wear my skins working out here, sir. But I had to save the other clothes. I've only got the one set."

Sarah gasped as she worked at the stove and Sam closed his eyes and shook his head. "Jamie . . . I'm sorry. Sarah, how's about us going into town today? We'll get Jamie all decked out in store-bought shirts and britches."

"What a grand idea!" She whirled around from the stove. "And I have to get some things for the to-do this Saturday night. Yes. We'll all go into town to Abe Caney's store. But first the cow has to be milked, the hogs slopped, the eggs . . ." Her eyes fell on the basket of eggs on a chopping block.

"Jamie did all that while we were still abed, Sarah," Sam said softly. "I think we have us a godsend here."

"You did it all, Jamie?" Sarah asked.

"It wasn't that much. If I didn't do at least that much before the others got out of their robes back at the Shawnee town, I got a beating. I learned to do things fast and right the first time."

Tears sprang into Sarah's eyes. Sam ducked his head for a few seconds. "You'll get no beatings here, Jamie," she said.

Sam lifted his head and there was a twinkle in his eyes. "Besides, I'm not so sure I could whip Jamie."

Abe Caney pulled Sam off to one side while Sarah was busy shopping. "That must have been some fight out at your place yesterday, Sam. The whole town's talking about it."

"It's over, Abe. I hope I never have to have another one."

But Abe was eager for details. "Where'd you learn to fight, Sam? You're known as a peaceable man."

"My father insisted I learn all forms of self-defense, Abe. From fencing to bare-knuckle boxing. His father knew James

Figg, really the first bare-knuckle champion."

While Sarah shopped and Sam and Abe chatted, Jamie stood on the porch of the store and watched as several boys walked up the street. He had a hunch they would angle over to him, and they did.

Jamie did not see the Reverend Hugh Callaway walk up the short street and stop a dozen yards from where Jamie stood, leaning up against a post and sucking on a piece of peppermint candy. Nor did he know that two of the boys were sons of John Jackson and Hart Olmstead. He would learn that very soon.

"Hey, there's the Injun boy," Jubal Olmstead said.

"Yeah," Abel Jackson said. "Let's go over and see if he wants to fight."

"You better leave him alone," the third boy said. "My pa said if I called him names or caused him any trouble, he'd take a piss-elm branch to my butt. And he will, too."

"Then you just stand aside and stay out of this," Abel said. He was built like his father, and had just about as much sense. The three boys were all thirteen years old and as boys were prone to be during that hard and brutal time, they were strong from long hours of chopping wood, clearing timber, moving huge rocks, and putting in back-breaking hours in the fields.

Jamie sucked on his peppermint stick and watched the trio move toward him. One of the boys left the group and walked over to sit on the edge of a watering trough.

"Hey, you!" Abel called to Jamie. "Red nigger. Why don't you leave town. Nobody wants you here."

Jamie's eyes narrowed slightly but other than that his expression did not change. He said nothing.

"Maybe he's forgot how to talk English," Jubal said. "I bet that's it."

"Let's learn him," Abel suggested. "Hey, Injun-boy, can you say, 'I'm 'bout to get a heap big butt-kickin'?"

The two boys thought that was hysterically funny. The third boy sat on the edge of the trough and did not laugh. He watched Jamie. He thought that maybe Abel and Jubal were about to make a big mistake. His pa had been among those who'd met Jamie, and his pa had been plenty impressed by the boy. More man than boy, his pa had said. And added that his son had best walk light around the Shawnee-raised young fellow. There was a mean glint to the lad's eyes.

I will witness this, Reverend Callaway thought. And when the dust settles, I will

89

testify that the two young scalawags egged this on.

"Get off that porch, Injun-nigger," Abel said. "And take your whopping, 'cause you're sure gonna get one." He added a most disgusting phrase concerning Jamie's mother.

Jamie left the porch like a mainspring that had been wound too tight. His moccasins hit Abel flush in the face and Reverend Callaway winced as the sound of Abel's nose breaking crunched its way to him. Jamie whirled and kicked out, his foot striking Jubal behind one knee and bringing the boy down in the dirt. Then Jamie was all over him and had drawn first blood before Sam and Abe could rush out of the store and separate the boys. From the look on Jubal's face, the older and bigger boy was mightily relieved that somebody had broken up the fight.

Reverend Callaway stepped out. "Jamie didn't start this, Sam, Abe. And the Jefferson boy didn't have anything to do with it." He told the merchant and the farmer what had happened just about the time Sheriff Marwick came puffing up.

"You again!" he shouted to Jamie. "Damn little half Injun troublemaker." He started toward Jamie and Sam stepped in front of him.

"I'd suggest you hear what Reverend Callaway has to say about it, Sheriff. And don't you ever call Jamie that again. Or I'll call you out and we'll settle this with pistols or blade. Your choice."

Marwick sputtered for a few seconds, but he really wanted no trouble with Sam Montgomery. Sam was rich — to Marwick's mind — and wielded considerable power in the community. Besides that, after he'd witnessed the beating Sam had administered to Hart Olmstead, he was more than a little afraid of him.

The sheriff listened to the preacher and shook his head. "Them boy's daddies ain't gonna like this none, Reverend. They's gonna be trouble and it's gonna be bad. One boy's nose is busted and the other got kicked in the privates and can't even get up. Lord God, where'd that kid learn to fight?"

Sam looked at Jamie. The boy stood expressionless, his arms folded across his chest. There did not appear to be a mark on him. Sam looked at Reverend Callaway, who was also staring at Jamie. The preacher lifted one eyebrow in silent questioning.

Marwick helped Jubal to his feet. The boy stood half bent over, both hands holding his aching groin and tears of pain and rage streaming down his face. "I'll kill you!" he shouted to Jamie.

Jamie shrugged his shoulders in reply.

"You boys get on home," Marwick told the two agitators. "Move!" He looked at Robert Jefferson, still sitting on the edge of the trough. "What's your part in all this, boy?"

"Nothing, Sheriff. I didn't do nothin'."

"He's telling the truth," Jamie spoke. He walked over to the boy and stuck out his hand.

Robert looked at the hand for a few seconds, then stood up with a grin and shook the hand.

Sheriff Marwick snorted in disgust and stalked off. Sam and Abe walked back into the store, Reverend Callaway with them. Jamie sat down on the edge of the watering trough with his new friend. He hesitated for a second, then gave Robert his last piece of peppermint candy.

"Hey, thanks! Where'd you learn to fight like that?"

"At the Shawnee town — warrior training."

"You really took Injun warrior training?"

"Since I was nine. I think," he added. "I'm not really sure how old I am."

"You look like you're about fifteen."

Jamie shook his head. "Eleven or twelve. One or the other. I'm sure of that. You going to be at the to-do this Saturday?"

"Plan to be. Pa says it's gonna be a whingding of an affair. Ma's got her party dress from the trunk and letting the wrinkles fall out. Pa's gonna cut my hair this week." He looked at Jamie's long blond, shoulder-length hair, with all the berry dye washed out. "I wish I could grow my hair that way. You gonna cut it off?"

"I see no reason to."

"Jamie? You made some bad enemies today. Them two won't forget it. They'll be lookin' to waylay you. You best walk careful from now on."

"I always do," Jamie said softly. And probably always will, he added silently.

The ladies began bringing food over Saturday morning. Jamie had never seen so much food — pies, cakes, cookies, roasts, and the like.

Jamie wondered if the families of Olmstead and Jackson would come to the party?

"Doubtful," Sam told him. "We both made bad enemies, Jamie. Those two are spiteful, revengeful men. And their children are just like them." He smiled. "All except Kate."

"Kate who?"

"Kate Olmstead. Prettiest girl in this part of the state. Just about your age. And she's as sweet as honey. She spends a lot of time with Reverend Callaway's daughter, Judith. More time with them than she does at home. I don't think she likes her home life very much. She might be here for the party. She's a very sweet girl, Jamie. You'll like her."

Sarah looked up from her kitchen work and smiled. "I'm glad you made a friend with Robert Jefferson, Jamie. He comes from a good Christian family."

"We get along fine," Jamie said.

Jamie scrubbed himself until he shone, bathing in the creek that ran not far from the house. During the summer months, Sam, too, bathed in the creek — it was a common practice on the frontier. When the first folks began arriving at the house, Sam and Jamie were all decked out in clean clothes, and in Jamie's case, new store-bought clothes. Hannah came out with Reverend and Mrs. Callaway . . . and Kate Olmstead. Hannah was escorted by a huge young man everybody called Swede. But even though Hannah was beautiful, Jamie only had eyes for Kate. He thought she was just about the prettiest thing he had ever seen. She had hair the color of wheat and dark blue eyes. All the young boys followed her around. But Kate had eyes only for Jamie. Jamie got so discombobulated looking at her he walked right into a tree and put a knot on his forehead.

Sam and Sarah were amused at the boy's antics.

"I think he's in love," Sarah said.

"Oh, honey, they're just kids," Sam replied.

"So were we, remember?" she reminded him.

"You're right. As usual."

Hannah and Swede joined the young couple. They too had noticed Jamie and Kate.

"It's about time Jamie had some fun," Hannah said. "God knows he's lost most of his childhood."

The four of them stood apart from the laughing and gossiping crowd that spilled from the front to both sides of the yard. The Jackons and the Olmsteads were not in attendance, and the general consensus among everybody there was relief.

"Is Jamie really just eleven years old?" Sarah asked.

"Twelve, I believe. But he could easily pass for someone much older. He hadn't been at the Shawnee town five minutes before he whipped Tall Bull's son, Little Wolf. Jamie's a fighter."

"Yes," Sam said dryly. "I can attest to that."

"And so can them rowdy boys who picked on him in town," Swede said, his eyes sparkling. He chuckled. "I would have very much liked to have seen that."

"It was brutal," Sam said. "And frightening in a way. The boy fights with a coldness that is scary. And he is very skillful."

"I'll tell you what he is now," Hannah said, and they looked at her. "In love!"

Six

Four people taught at the local school: Reverend Callaway, his wife, Elizabeth, Abe Caney's wife, Mary, and Sarah Montgomery. The community had tried to hire a full-time teacher, but so far had no luck in doing so. That summer Sarah tutored Jamie at home, in preparation for the next term. She found him to be exceptionally bright and to be a voracious reader. Whenever he had a spare moment, he had his nose stuck in a book.

News from town was not good. The Saxon brothers had broken out of jail . . . with some outside help, and nearly everyone thought they knew who had helped them: Hart Olmstead and John Jackson. But nobody could prove it.

Hart Olmstead had forbidden his daughter, Kate, from ever again going out to the Montgomery's. He had given the child a terrible beating when she mentioned Jamie's name one evening at the supper table.

Robert Jefferson told Jamie about Kate's beating one day in town and the boy's thoughts turned dark and savage, but no one knew it except Jamie. Like the Indians who had taken him, Jamie had mastered well the art of facial stoicism.

"Did he hurt her bad?" Jamie asked.

"He marked her some," Robert told him, as the boys sat on the ground and played mumbly-peg with their knives.

Jamie still carried his Shawnee skinning knife, but he carried it out of sight, tucked into his high-topped moccasins. He did so without Sam having to ask. He wanted to do everything he possibly could to make life easier for the couple who were so kind to take him in. But there was one thing he refused to do: wear shoes. And Sam and Sarah had stopped asking him to. During his formative years, from seven to nearly twelve years of age, he had not had a shoe on either foot, so his feet just weren't comfortable in anything except moccasins.

"How bad?"

"Not too bad, 'way I heared it. Heard it." Since school was about to start, he had begun to watch his grammar. Getting rapped on the knuckles or a twisted ear hurt. "He was careful not to mark her on the face. He beat her back and backside with a belt. She had to stay abed for several days."

The boys were silent for a time. Robert looked at Jamie. "You got a funny look in your eyes, Jamie."

The look vanished instantly. Jamie smiled. "Just thinking, that's all."

"You anxious for school to start?"

"Yeah. I really am."

School on the frontier was primitive at best. The buildings were ill-heated in the winter and insufferably hot in the summer. If a child got four full months of schooling a year, that was considered good. And those four months almost always were in the dead of winter, when his or her parents did not need them to work in the fields, plowing, planting, harvesting, mending fences, chasing down strayed cattle or hogs, or hunting for food or gathering berries.

But Jamie cherished every moment in school, for he was fully aware that he was far behind the others his age. However, there was also another reason why Jamie loved school: he got to sit next to Kate Olmstead.

During his first year of his stay at the home of Sam and Sarah Montgomery, Jubal

Olmstead, Abel Jackson, and the few others who called them friends pretty much left Jamie alone. But Jamie knew it wouldn't last and he was careful not to get caught out alone. It wasn't that he was afraid, for he was not. He just didn't want to cause trouble for Sam and Sarah.

Jamie was growing fast and filling out. Already big for his age, he was going to be a tall man, wide shouldered, lean hipped, and heavily muscled. Already he could more than hold his own with Sam in the fields, but he always held back, so as not to embarrass Sam.

Sam had presented Jamie with a fine Kentucky horse, a midnight-black stallion named Lightning that he'd bought for no more than a song because no one could ride the animal.

"If you can ride him, you can have him, Jamie."

"I'll ride him, sir."

"Just keep him away from the other horses. This one's a bad one."

"He's just misunderstood, sir. That's all. Believe me, I know the feeling."

Jamie gently broke the horse, constantly talking to him and not even attempting to ride the stallion for weeks, until the animal became used to Jamie's touch and voice.

Sam and Sarah watched him work and both knew the boy had an almost unnatural ability to handle animals.

"Eerie," Sarah called it.

Sam agreed.

The big black had tried numerous times to bite and kick Sam, but never with Jamie.

Jamie turned out to be a fine horseman, taking to the saddle as if born to it. He could be seen often on the road into town, riding in to fetch something for Sarah. He carried a short-barreled rifle in a saddle boot — a cut-down version of a Kentucky rifle — and kept his pistol in a saddlebag. The carrying of weapons caused no head to turn, for brigands prowled the roads and dark paths of the timber, and Indian attacks were still occurring, although the latter were slowly tapering off as the various tribes were killed off, pushed westward, or breaking apart and attempting to assimilate into white society.

Jamie had heard that Tall Bull's band had left the country and gone west. Where in the west no one seemed to know. But Jamie had not forgotten Deer Woman's dire prediction: "Someday Tall Bull and Little Wolf will find you. That will be the day when you must decide whether you live or die. And whether you will, or can, kill your father and brother."

Deer Woman might have had some doubts as to whether Jamie could kill in defense of his life or loved one. Jamie had no doubts at all.

Since the day of that terrible fight in the road that passed in front of Sam and Sarah's land, Hart Olmstead had spoken not one word to Sam, Sarah, or Jamie. John Jackson spoke, but it was forced, and never more than a very terse greeting or farewell. Hart and his boys had stopped attending Reverend Callaway's church. Kate and her mother still came to Sunday services, and to the occasional singin' and eatin' on the grounds, and Kate was rapidly turning into quite the young woman, beginning to fill out in all the right places and turning heads whenever she entered a building. But she had eyes only for Jamie.

Hart Olmstead had once again stated his objection to Jamie and forbidden his only daughter to see the boy. But Kate paid no attention to the warning and managed to see Jamie whenever he came to town, if only at a distance or to exchange a few words in Abe's General Store.

Jamie's life took on a darker and more dangerous note as the small town in Kentucky began to grow, not always with the right people. Hart Olmstead's brothers moved into the area, as did kin of John Jackson, and with them they brought several friends, mostly white trash with criminal tendencies. And as is so often the case with trash, they had an army of children, most of whom were, tragically, just as ignorant as their parents.

"Apples do not fall far from the tree," Reverend Callaway remarked over coffee after supper at the Montgomery home. "I fear that our community is rapidly being populated with individuals of less than honorable intent."

Jamie said nothing; just listened. Several times in the past few weeks he had been forced to gallop Lightning in order to get away from the growing gang that hung around Jubal Olmstead and Abel Jackson. Those two had dropped out of school and were very nearly men grown. And they were dangerous. Thefts had increased a dozen times over since the new additions to the community had arrived and there had been several men badly beaten and left by the side of the road after being robbed. Two women had been assaulted and raped in their cabins.

Several men had gone to Sheriff Marwick and warned him that if something wasn't done to curb the crime, the citizens just might have to take to night-riding.

Sam Montgomery's holdings had grow dramatically as farmers whose lands bordered his gave up and moved away, selling out to Sam. Sam now had two men working for him; good Christian men, with families. The community several miles from town had grown, and the citizens met and voted to start their own town, complete with church, school, general store, and marshal.

They named it New Town, which in a few years would be changed to Montgomery, and before the turn of the century would be gone, with not even a building standing. Abe Caney built a general store in New Town, Reverend Callaway moved into New Town and a church was built. Gradually, over the months, New Town became a safe haven for decent, hard-working people, while trash took over the old town. They built saloons, gambling parlors, and houses of ill repute, elected John Jackson as mayor and Hart Olmstead as tax assessor of the county.

Jamie was fourteen years old, looked twenty, and was tree-tall and strong as a bull. He still wore his thick blond hair shoulder length and wore his high-top moccasins. Several times, young men who followed the dictates of Abel Jackson and Jubal

Olmstead had made the mistake of challenging Jamie, confronting him on the dark, twisted roads that wound amid a sea of trees. Twice Jamie had been able to outdistance them on Lightning. The last time he had been forced to fight.

Jamie galloped into the yard and leaped from the saddle, running to the house, startling Sam and Sarah, who had just sat down for the noon meal.

"What's wrong, Jamie?" Sam asked, rising from his chair.

"I didn't make it to the north field, Sam." As Jamie grew older, the couple had insisted that Jamie call them by their first names. "The gang that Hart's nephew, Edgar, heads waylaid me. There was a shooting, Sam."

Sam asked no questions. He knew in his heart that Jamie had not provoked it; knew that for almost three years Jamie had carefully avoided trouble, ignoring taunts that he, personally, would have killed over. "Ring the bell, Sarah," he said. "The sheriff and a posse will be along soon, and they'll be wanting to take Jamie. That will not happen as long as there is breath left in me."

"What do you want me to do, Sam?" Jamie asked.

"Charge your rifle and pistol, lad."

Jamie shook his head. "No, Sam. Wait, Sarah. Don't ring that bell. We have a few minutes; probably more than an hour. Listen to me. There will be a dozen or more men and boys ready to swear that I provoked this trouble. You know that. I don't know if I killed that fellow or not, but I think I did. It was close range, and my ball was true. The jury will be rigged, and I'll hang." Sarah started crying and Sam was trembling with rage. "It's over here for me."

"No!" Sam shouted, his big fists clenched.

"Yes," Jamie said softly. "I've been expecting this. And I'm ready for it. Even if I should beat this false charge, those who hate me will never let me live in peace. Not here. I have a place chosen in the dark timber two day's ride west of here. I've food and blankets ready to go in the barn. It's better this way. You both know it in your hearts. I love you both dearly, but I can't stay. I don't want blood spilled over me. The wilderness is my home. I'm as comfortable there as a wolf, a panther, or an eagle. I'll see you both from time to time. Tell Kate that I love her and to wait for my return. I will be back for her." He hesitated. "Sam, I will soon have the name of an outlaw. The sheriff, Hart Olmstead, and John Jackson and their kind will have me known as a highwayman.

Don't you believe it." A twinkle came into his eyes. "Oh, I might take something from them every now and then, to help those they've taxed into poverty and the like . . ."

"Jamie," Sam said. "I . . ."

The young man waved him silent. "I must go. Be sure to tell Kate I will be back." He kissed Sarah, shook Sam's hand, and walked out of the house. He did not look back.

WANTED FOR MURDER
JAMIE IAN MacCALLISTER

Jamie unfolded and looked at the badly faded wanted notice he'd found tacked to a tree and smiled. There was a fairly accurate description of his likeness on the page.

"So I did kill the man," Jamie muttered. "But what else could I do? He was trying to kill me!"

He was sitting in his camp, deep in the woods of unsettled Kentucky, and in 1826, there were a lot of those places. It had been months since he'd left the comfortable home of Sam and Sarah Montgomery, and just as many months since he'd seen Kate. But he'd been back to their secret place several times for the messages she would leave in a hollow tree. It was on the way back west to his camp that he'd found the wanted notice. Now, sitting by his lonely fire in the cave in Western Kentucky, Jamie allowed himself the luxury of a few moments of feeling sorry for himself. Would he ever find peace? The summer was nearly gone, and soon he would have another birthday. His fifteenth. These were supposed to be the fun years of life . . . so he'd read. If these were the fun years, he sure wasn't looking forward to the bad years.

He shook those thoughts away and once more reread the letter from Kate. Even under these dangerous and dire circumstances, it was difficult for Jamie to get very low for very long. It just wasn't his nature. He was a survivor.

My darling Jamie,

First of all, let me tell you how much I love and miss you. I have bad news. I told you last time that Hannah was to marry the Swede. The date was all set and everybody was rejoicing. Then, just last week she was set upon by brigands and raped. She claimed John Jackson's oldest boy, John Jr., and his father. I believe her. Of course, they alibied for each other and the sheriff laughed it off. I positively *loathe* that stupid oaf! The Swede says he doesn't care if the entire

Shawnee nation assaulted her, he loves her and wants her to be his wife. But Hannah feels that given time, he would grow to hate her. I don't believe that.

Jamie folded the letter carefully. He had read the letter several times and had memorized it all.

Sitting by his fire, he cooked his supper and then rolled up in his blanket. His mind was made up. He was going back and speaking to Hannah. She had been his friend and deserved some happiness. And maybe he'd just settle some old scores with the Jackson family while he was at it.

SEVEN

Jamie just about scared the Swede out of his boots when the door was opened and there stood Jamie. There was a confused look on his face, for Jamie had cut his long hair. Then the big man recognized him, hollered one, grabbed him in a bear hug, and hauled him inside the snug cabin.

"Swede, you're crushing me! Put me down, you ox!"

"Jamie!" Swede said. "It's so good to see you. But you are taking a terrible chance, lad!"

"Sit down, Swede. I want to talk to you," Jamie said, sitting down at the rough kitchen table. The Swede first poured them coffee and then sat down, his face serious. "Pack it up, Swede. Sam will buy your land at a fair price. You get Hannah and head for Illinois. I've talked to people and they said the land there was fine. The soil so rich and black it'll grow nearly anything. I —"

"But Hannah won't even talk to me, Jamie!" the big man said with nearly a sob. "Not since the . . . trouble."

"I'm going to her cabin as soon as I leave here, Swede. I can talk some sense into her. She'll listen to me. Swede, you have to know this: she was the wife of a Shawnee."

The man smiled. "I guessed that, Jamie. It makes no difference to me. None of that matters. What matters is here and now, lad." He sobered for a few seconds. "You're heavily armed, Jamie."

"I'm an outlaw, Swede. A young desperado who is wanted for murder. I have a price on my head."

Swede nodded his head. "And Sam's place is watched all the time, Jamie. Don't go there."

"I must. I have to say goodbye when all that I have returned to do is done."

"You're going to kill John Jackson and his son." It was not a question.

Jamie nodded. "And then I am taking Kate and we are heading west. We probably will never see you and Hannah again, Swede."

"Damn! but it's a sorry time. Lad, if you run off with Kate, her father and brothers will pursue you both to the ends of the earth."

"Let them. I'm taking Kate and leaving."

"Jamie, think about this. You've killed one man . . . let it alone, lad. Just take your loved one and leave."

Jamie smiled. "Swede, you are the biggest, strongest, yet the gentlest of men. You couldn't harm anything. It even upsets you to have to kill game for food. Yet, I can understand that. And I know this too: Hannah must be avenged. And I can do that." He stood up. "After I am gone, you and Hannah leave. Make a fresh start. Will you promise me that?"

"If you can bring my Hannah back to me, Jamie, I will promise to move Heaven and Earth for you . . . and do it."

After Jamie had left the cabin, Swede sat for a time. "That's a *boy*?" he questioned the silence. "No. He left his boyhood back at that damnable Shawnee town. He became a man at age seven."

Kate almost fainted when she opened the shutters to her bedroom and saw Jamie. "No time for anything but this, Kate," he said. "Start packing a few things, including blankets. But just enough to get by. I've left a packet of food by the hollow tree. When the house is quiet, you go there this night and wait for me. I have things to do that are dark and suited for the night. It might be noon tomorrow before I can meet you there. But the place is safe and no one will find you there. When I do come, I will have a mount for you with a proper saddle for a lady." He leaned in and kissed her lips. "I'll see you at the tree, Kate. And then we'll be rid of this damnable place forever."

Jamie was gone in the night. Kate closed the shutters and smiled. Then she set about packing a few things.

The guard who was assigned to guard the Montgomery house never knew what hit him and laid him out cold on the ground. But what hit him was the butt of one of Jamie's pistols. Jamie hog-tied the man — he knew him as a thug and ne'er-do-well who would do anything for money — and left him trussed up tight. Jamie had circled the house twice, and knew there was only this one guard. He boldly walked in the back door and called out his presence.

Sarah threw her arms around him and Sam shook his head. "You've grown some in the months, Jamie. And you've a hard look in your eyes. Sit down, lad, and have some food and drink."

"I would like that, for I've eaten little this day." Over food, Jamie said, "I want the gelding for Kate. The bay."

"Take him. He's yours. And take the saddle, too. Jamie, I've a poke of money for you. It's enough to last you several years if you're careful. What else is on your mind?"

Jamie lifted eyes that were a cold and bright hard blue. "You don't want to know, Sam. Leave it at that."

"All right, Jamie. Jamie! The guard outside . . . ?"

"Will not be moving for several hours. I didn't kill him because I want no harm to come to either of you."

Sam waved that aside. "No harm will come to us, Jamie. We've formed our own militia here in New Town and are left strictly alone. We outnumber those in old town. And they are mightily afraid of us. But that will do you no good, for the warrant against you came after a true bill."

"I'm not worried about that, Sam. For when I leave here this night, I will not be heard from or seen again in this area." Jamie explained what he wanted Sam to do, and the man instantly agreed.

"You've seen Hannah? We have not been able to convince her that the Swede doesn't care what happened. He just loves her."

"I just left her cabin. I managed to get through to her. She'll be leaving with the

114

Swede."

Sarah put her hand over his. "Oh, Jamie. Where did your childhood go? You're shouldering a terrible burden to be so young."

"I guess I'm like the eagle, Sarah. I am what I am and can no more change than the eagle."

"I'll fix you enough food to last several days, and we've had your buckskins and other clothes packed ever since you left." She rose from the table and busied herself so Jamie would not see the tears in her eyes.

Sam left the room and returned with a small leather sack. He placed it on the table. "With care this should last you for quite some time, Jamie. Take it with our love and blessing. Why don't you go up to your room for one last time and change into your buckskins."

Viewing his old room was hard, for Jamie knew he would never see it, or Sam and Sarah, again. He was not yet out of his teen years and was starting over — again. For the first time in years, he fought back tears. He stepped out of the bedroom and closed the door behind him, forever sealing off another part of his life. When Jamie came back to the kitchen, Sarah had composed herself and a packet of food was on the table.

"I've saddled the horse for Kate," Sam said. "Both of you go with our blessings, Jamie. And Godspeed."

Sarah kissed him and then fled from the room, her apron to her face, no longer able to control her tears. Sam stuck out his hand and Jamie took it.

"Goodbye, Jamie Ian MacCallister. Man Who Is Not Afraid."

"Goodbye, sir. And . . . thank you and Sarah for everything."

Jamie picked up the food packet and turned away, walking from the warm home, out into the cool and dangerous night. He rode straight to the Jackson farm. During the months of his fleeing the false charges, he had learned that John Jackson's wife had left him, unable to endure the abuse any longer. So there would be John, John Jr., and Abel at home.

Jamie left the horses a few hundred yards from the darkened cabin. He knew that John Jackson hated dogs, so he did not have to worry about any barking to announce his presence. He slipped up to the cabin and looked through the slightly cracked shutters into Abel's sleeping quarters. The pallet was empty. Abel was probably staying with his friend, Jubal. Good. One less to worry about.

Jamie opened the shutters and climbed into the cabin, making his way carefully through the home. John Jackson was snoring in his bed, and his son John Jr. was snorting and blubbering in his bed. Jamie, a pistol in each hand, walked up to the elder Jackson's bed and stuck the muzzle against the man's temple. Jackson jerked awake, his eyes wide with fear.

"John Jackson," Jamie said softly, just loud enough for the man to hear. "I'm judge and jury and I find you guilty of rape and sentence you to die."

The cocking of the heavy pistol was enormous in the quiet house.

"Get up, John Jackson, and go awaken that scum you call a son."

The man rose from the tick, dressed in a long nightshirt. He padded barefoot to his son's room and called out, his voice quaking with fear.

The son stood up, also dressed in a long nightshirt.

"In the big room," Jamie said. "Build up the fire so you can see the man who kills you."

John Jr. started squalling out his fear as he stoked the coals into flames.

"Now tell me the story about how you two brave men raped Hannah. And you'd better

117

speak the truth."

John Jr. broke apart, babbling out the rape, telling the awfulness of it.

Jamie cocked the second pistol, both of them double-shotted. Jackson started crying, the tears running down his face, begging for his life. Not his son's life, just his. Jamie leveled a pistol and both father and son began weeping and begging, the snot running from their noses and slobber dripping from their lips.

Jamie couldn't do it. He just could not kill the men, although both of them surely deserved it. He slowly lowered the pistol.

"God knows I should kill you both," he said, his voice hard. "But I cannot. I see you now for what you are. Cowards, the both of you. Live in your own private hell, for you created it."

Jamie turned to leave. John Jr. leaped for the shotgun over the fireplace and started to bring it down just as Jamie turned. Jamie fired, one ball striking the man in the chest and the second ball tearing into his throat, drenching the father with the son's blood. John Jr. fell into the fire, his nightshirt catching on fire and his greasy hair exploding. The shotgun discharged, the blast blowing a hole into the roof, and sending dust showering down into the cabin.

"No!" the father screamed. "My boy. Oh, you've killed my fine boy." He pulled his son from the fire, spreading flames across the floor. "My God, MacCallister, help me."

"Not damn likely," Jamie said.

"Goddamn you!"

Jamie turned and walked out into the night. He wasn't worried about pursuit, for the father would be too busy trying, in vain, Jamie hoped, to save his cabin from the flames.

Jamie charged his pistol as he walked and holstered it before stepping into the saddle and taking up the reins of the horse for Kate. The flames from the burning cabin were beginning to dance in the night sky.

"I'll kill you!" John Jackson's wild screaming reached him. "As God is my witness I'll track you to the gates of hell, you Injun bastard."

"Wrong, I'm not an Indian, you ignorant oaf." Jamie turned Lightning's head.

"Do you hear me, you sorry son? I swear on my boy's dead body you'll pay."

Jamie ignored the man's howling.

"You're a dead man, MacCallister! Do you hear me?"

"Not by your hand, Jackson," Jamie muttered, and put his horse into a gallop. He rode westward, toward Kate and a new life.

EIGHT

By dawn, the young couple had put miles behind them. Jamie had traveled no roads, staying with game trails that he knew well. By dawn, both he and Kate and their mounts were exhausted. He had chosen their first stop earlier, on the way east, and the closest settlers were miles away. Jamie made a bed of fresh cut boughs for Kate and she was asleep in seconds.

He rubbed down the horses and picketed them on good grass, then made a walk-through of the area surrounding the camp. He ate a biscuit and sat with his back to a tree and dozed. Lightning would wake him if anyone drew near. He was better than any watchdog Jamie had ever seen.

They both awakened at noon and were ravenous. Jamie built a small fire, using dry wood and placing the fire directly under a low overhang of branches to break up the smoke.

"We'll start cutting slightly south tonight, Kate. I've not been much in that country. But I'm thinking John and your father will feel that we plan on joining Hannah and Swede in Illinois. I hope."

"I don't care where we go, Jamie. Just as long as we're together."

"We will be together, Kate. Forever. When we get down into the southern part of Tennessee, we'll find a parson and get married." Kate smiled and nodded her head.

"I want no union between us until that time. I want us blessed by God."

She again nodded her head solemnly. "Jamie? What happened last night at the Jacksons'?"

"I went there to kill them both, but I found I could not. I tried to give them their lives even after John Jr. confessed to Hannah's debasement. It was disgusting. I turned to leave and John Jr. grabbed a shotgun. I fired in self-defense. He fell into the fire and the cabin was destroyed, I think. It was an ugly scene. I do not think I shall ever forget it. Kate? Do you understand that if your father or brothers ever catch us, they will kill both of us?"

"More than you do, Jamie. My father swore that many times over, making sure I heard it each time."

Jamie sat silent for a time. "We must put many miles behind us before we stop, Kate. I think your father will never stop searching for me. And I believe John Jackson will be just as determined."

She scooted over and sat next to him. He put an arm around her and held her close.

"What are you thinking, Jamie?"

"That I wish for us a long and uneventful life together, Kate."

"Uneventful it may not be, Jamie. But we will be together."

"Liar!" Hart Olmstead shouted at Sam, pointing a trembling finger at the man. "You do know where that young killer took my daughter."

"You're crowding me awfully hard, Olmstead," Sam told the man, barely holding his own temper in check. "Back off, man. Now back off, I say! I do *not* know where they went. Deliberately so. I don't even know in which direction they went. Now curb your tongue, Hart Olmstead. Curb it before this becomes a matter of honor and I call you out with pistol or blade."

That got Hart's attention. He shuddered once and then took several deep breaths. He looked around him. All of Sam's friends had gathered in the road, and all of them were heavily armed.

"You've all conspired against me," Hart said. "Me and John Jackson both. You've all took sides with that damn savage MacCallister boy . . ."

"That's a lie, Hart," Abe Caney spoke up. "You brought all this on yourself by siding with Jackson, even after he and his boy did those terrible things to Hannah . . . a good woman if ever I saw one."

"She was nothing but a damn Injun's whore!" Hart flared.

"You better be glad the Swede ain't here, Olmstead," a farmer called out. "For he'd sure break your back for that."

"Time's a-wastin,' Pa," Hart's oldest boy, Carl said. "If we're going to pick up a trail, we'd best do it now."

"Yeah, Pa," Ernest Olmstead said. "These folks ain't gonna tell us nothin'."

"I got people out looking, boy," Hart said. "We got to wait 'til this afternoon, 'til after John buries his own. It wouldn't be proper to go off and leave a friend alone with his grief." he turned to once more face Sam Montgomery. "I'll find them, Sam. And when I kill that MacCallister bastard, I'll scalp him and bring his yeller hair back to wave under your nose."

"I hope you don't find him, Hart," Sam

replied. "For if you do, you will find nothing but grief. The boy is highly intelligent and brave."

Hart snorted and spat on the ground.

Sam said, "He didn't force your daughter to accompany him, Hart. They've been in love since the first evening they laid eyes on one another, right over there in that yard. Let them be, Hart. Let them build a life together."

"When it rains in Hell, Sam!" Hart screamed. "I'll see them both dead. And that's a promise."

"Are you daft, man!" Farmer Mason shouted. "That's your own flesh and blood you're talkin' about killin'."

"It's none of your affair!" Hart returned the shout. He whirled and mounted, galloping off, his sons and friends right behind him.

"Ride, Jamie and Kate. Ride like the wind, kids. And be happy."

Jamie changed his mind about heading south and he and Kate rode straight west. After nights of hard riding, they stopped at a crossroads store named Pekin.

In a few more years, William Clark, brother to George Rogers Clark, of Lewis and Clark fame, would establish a town here and name it after a Chickasaw Indian chief, Paduke. It would later be called Paducah.

"Where are we, Jamie?" Kate asked.

"I don't know, Kate. But I smell the river."

"What river?"

"The Mississippi."

"I'm told that's a fearsome river, Jamie. People say there are monsters in its muddy waters. Great scaly beasts called alligators."

Jamie laughed at her serious expression. "We're not going to swim it, Kate. I think there is a ferry that crosses over to a town called New Madrid. That's in Missouri."

"Sometimes the ferry runs," a man called from the porch of the store. "If the ferry ain't runnin', they's usually a boat to be hired that'll take you 'crost."

"Thank you, sir," Kate said sweetly, as Jamie helped her down from her horse. "My brother and I have far to travel."

Since they both had blue eyes and hair pretty much the same color, they had agreed to pose as brother and sister until they could find a minister and be married.

"Oh? Travelin' far, are you?"

"Central Missouri," Jamie lied. "Our parents live there."

"These are perilous times for anyone, especially for young folks travelin' alone," the man said. "But I see you be armed right well, young feller, so's I allow to how you'll be all right. Come on inside, young lady. My old woman will see to your needs. You're gonna have to see to your own hoss, son. I ain't gettin' clost to that big black. He's got a wicked eye to him."

"Yes, sir. And he will live up to his looks."

"Thought so. Biter and a kicker, is he?"

"Yes, sir."

"See to your own damn horse, then." The man walked into the store.

Jamie laughed and saw to the horse's needs, then joined Kate inside the dim store. She was buying supplies. Several men lounged at a rough table, a jug of whiskey before them. They all looked longingly and lustfully at Kate, and hard at Jamie when he walked in.

As Jamie walked to the counter, one of the men laughed, and it was not a pleasant laugh.

"The Newby brothers," the lady behind the counter whispered. "Percy, Howard, and Dick. They's eight of them, all told. They're all bad. Ride on, lad, and watch behind you for a time."

"What're you whisperin' about over there, you old hag?" one of the men yelled.

The man who had greeted Jamie and Kate looked nervously around him. "They're liquored up and snake-mean, young feller," he whispered. "I cain't be held good for what they'll do."

"Old man," one of the Newby brothers hollered. "I done tole you 'bout that damn whisperin.' We don't like it."

"Sorry, Percy," the man called.

"You there," another brother called. "Gal with the gold hair. I ain't seen you afore. What's your name?"

Kate and Jamie had decided on trail names to help throw off Olmstead and Jackson. Jamie turned to face the loudmouth. "Tess," he said.

"I ain't talkin' to you, boy."

"You are now," Jamie replied, a cold calmness to his voice.

One of the brothers laughed at the expression on his brother's face. "I do believe, Dick, that there young feller tole you square, didn't he?"

"Run!" the woman behind the counter hissed.

Dick Newby stood up. He was dirty, unshaven, and smelled bad. "You need to be larned some manners, boy."

"Choose your purchases, Tess," Jamie said, placing money on the counter.

"Boy's got gold, Percy," Dick said.

"Has he now?" the brother replied.

127

"Where'd you get that there gold, boy?" he tossed the question to Jamie.

"That is none of your affair," Jamie said, feeling the old wildness well up strong within him.

Percy stood up, standing beside his brother. "Mayhaps I think it is. Mayhaps I think a young couple like y'all might need bodyguards on the trail, seein' as how you're totin' all that money. Travel ain't safe these days."

"So we've been told," Jamie fought the wildness down. "Thank you for your concern. We'll do nicely as we are."

"My, but don't he talk proper?" Howard Newby said. "He's a regular little prince, ain't he?"

A calmness took Jamie. He was familiar with it. But with the calmness came cold, a freezing wind that blew across the highlands of his ancestry. Hooded Druids, their faces hidden, began chanting, their voices all combined with the ancient and strong warrior sounds of Celts, Anglos, and Normans. It was a volatile and dangerous mixture, and Jamie would fight with it and for it all his life.

"I'm no prince, sir," Jamie said, a tightness to his voice. "But what I am is a person who minds his own business and goes his own way in peace, if others will let me. Will you be so kind as to allow that courtesy?"

The Newby brother smiled, exposing a mouth full of yellow, rotting teeth. "No," he said softly.

"Then state your intentions, sir."

The brigand looked at Kate and licked his lips. He cut his eyes back to Jamie and smiled. "Lay your poke on the counter and walk out that door. Leave the girl."

Kate hissed in fright and Jamie said, "Do you not be afraid, Tess. No harm will come to you."

The third Newby brother stood up. "Old man, take your hag and go to the back. Close the door."

The man and woman scurried to their living quarters and closed the door. The sound of the door being barred chilled Kate. Her eyes were wide and frightened. Jamie seemed not to have noticed, his eyes never leaving the Newby brothers.

"Last chance, lad," Percy said.

"The same might be said for you," Jamie replied.

"He's a game one, Percy," Howard said with an ugly laugh. "Give him that."

"Pick up your purchases, Tess," Jamie said. "And step to the door."

"You stay where you is, wench," Percy said.

"Do what I say, Tess," Jamie told her. "You do not take orders from this wretched hulk."

Holding her purchases, Kate started for the door. Percy stepped around the table and started for her. Jamie shot him.

The double-shotted, heavy caliber balls struck the outlaw in chest and face, making a dreadful mess of the man's head. Dick Newby grabbed for his pistol and Jamie jerked out his second pistol, cocked, and fired. One ball went wide and the other ball struck the brigand in the throat. He went down, making horrible gurgling sounds. Jamie leaped at the third Newby brother, clubbing him to the floor before he could free his pistol. Again and again, Jamie smashed the man's face and head with the butt of his pistol, working with the rage of an ancient Viking berserker.

"Enough!" Kate screamed from the door. "He's done, love."

Jamie let the thug fall to the floor, his face and head streaming blood. The old couple threw open the door and ran from the rear and looked with a curious mixture of horror and satisfaction at the scene.

"Finish him, lad!" the old man shouted. "Kill him for sure or he and his kind will forever be on your trail."

The old man grabbed up an axe and ran to the Newby brother. Before Jamie could stop him, he had brought the axe down on the unconscious man's head.

"Now it's done and good riddance," the old man said, leaning the bloody axe against a table leg. "Run, lad. Take your sister and run. I'll tell their brothers you was headin' south for New Orleans. Go, boy. Now! Them other brothers could show up anytime."

Several miles from the store, Jamie halted and dismounted. He knelt by the trail and retched up the contents of his stomach. He wiped his mouth and said, "I swear before the Almighty God, Kate, I just want some peace for us."

Kate came to him and put her arms around him and held him close. "You did what you had to do, Jamie. They would have killed you and then passed me around like a common whore and then murdered me . . . or worse. You did the only thing you could do."

He nodded his head. "There is terrible, furious wildness in me, Kate. I've had it all my life. When I'm angered, it's like . . . like a freezing rain that blots out all else. I'm afraid of it, Kate. When it takes control it's all-consuming in me. I have no fear of those who challenge me. And that's not a normal thing. Now I know why my father rarely spoke of his father. I'm like him, Kate. I'm like that man who rode west and lived in the mountains . . . maybe he still lives there. Maybe he's more savage than white. I don't know. But I have my grandfather's hot blood within me."

"Perhaps that isn't a bad thing, Jamie. We're heading into a savage land where it will take that wildness to survive. You have to look at it that way."

"Did you see me back there, Kate? The pistols actually seemed to be a part of my arm and hand. I don't even remember jerking and firing. It was . . . it was . . . a natural thing to do. Three men are dead, Kate. Two at my hand. And if you had not screamed, I would have surely killed that third man."

She did not know how to respond to that, so she said nothing.

After a moment, Jamie said, "If the remaining brothers are as bad as those we saw back there, they'll torture the truth out of that old man and woman."

"They wouldn't!"

"Oh, yes, they would. And they will. And I've seen brave warriors break under pain. We've got to ride, Kate. And ride far." He shook his head. "I've got you in an awful mess, Kate."

She smiled and kissed him. "*We* got ourselves in the mess, Jamie. Us. Together. Just like we planned for months. Together. Forever."

I just hope forever isn't as short as the future looks right now, Jamie thought, helping Kate to her feet and giving her a hand up into the sidesaddle. 'Cause right now, it looks bleak.

NINE

Jamie and Kate had no choice but to head for the river crossing at New Madrid, for this was all new country to Jamie, and he didn't know where else to cross. The river curved just north of the store, effectively trapping them in its upside-down U. He kept them as close to the river as possible, and they saw a few boats on the mighty river. Once they came upon a band of Chickasaw Indians, but they were friendly, and friendlier still when one of them recognized Jamie as Man Who Is Not Afraid.

"Tall Bull and Little Wolf hunt you, Man Who Is Not Afraid," the Indian said. "They have sworn that you will die."

"They don't worry me as much as those white men behind us," Jamie said, in tongue and in sign. "If you see them, stay away, for they are bad."

"As are most white men," the leader of the band said. "Even though you were taken by the hated Shawnee, you are a good white man. You learned the true ways and follow them." He shrugged his shoulders. "You are good even though you are a white man," he added. "Go in peace."

A few more days and they found a boatman who would cross them, for a fee that Jamie felt was a bit high, and then they were in New Madrid. The town had been destroyed during the earthquakes of 1811 and 1812, when the upheavals had been so tremendous the Mississippi River had actually run backward and the town they were seeing now had been forced to relocate several times.

Jamie found a boarding house and got a room for Kate, so she could bathe and change clothes, while the lady who ran the place kept an eagle eye on him. Then they found a minister who agreed to marry them and Jamie slipped the ring that Sarah had given him onto Kate's finger and kissed her. They decided to ride on that day, rather than risk a night in the town, for Jamie was sure that the Newby Brothers were hard on their trail. They cut straight across Missouri, heading for the hills. That night they were truly joined and it was magic for both of them, as they made the sweetest of love under God's canopy of diamonds set in velvet. They promised their undying love for each other.

They were both fourteen years old.

When the young couple reached a series of foothills, Jamie cut south, into Arkansas, still a few years away from being admitted into the Union. Behind them and still on the east side of the Mississippi River, Hart Olmstead and John Jackson and their sons were trying to pick up their trail. The country store where Jamie had encountered the Newby Brothers was nothing but charred ash. The surviving Newby Brothers had tortured the old man and woman until they told them that the young couple had planned to cross the river at New Madrid. The Newby Brothers then killed the man and woman and burned down the store.

On the banks of the east side of the river, the brothers cleaned up as best they could and then paid to cross the Mississippi. In New Madrid, they made a few polite inquiries and found that a young couple had been there a few days earlier and had been married. The last anyone saw of them they were heading west, toward Crowley's Ridge.

The Newby brothers were riding westward five minutes later.

Jamie and Kate were near adults for their

time, but really they were still kids, and this trip was a grand adventure for both of them. They were in a wilderness, where few white people lived and Indians still roamed. Here they would find a few Osage, but mostly Quapaw and Caddo. Jamie did not know if the Indians here were warlike or peaceful, and he wasn't about to take any chances.

Jamie led them on game trails, staying away from what few roads there were, and being very careful to stop every so often and check for smoke. Jamie used his bow to hunt game, choosing the silent kill over the more accurate and long-range rifle, which might have attracted unwanted attention.

For days they rode south and slightly west, through heavily forested hills and valleys. They saw the smoke from cabins and a few settlements, but stayed clear of them. Their supplies ran out when they were a few miles north and west of the territorial capital, a place called Little Rock, which was once a Quapaw Indian settlement, then a trading post, founded by a French trapper named Bernard de la Harpe back in 1722.

Now the young couple had a hard decision to make.

"If we go into Little Rock," Jamie said, "for sure we'll attract attention, even though I'm told it's a huge place, with maybe a thousand people there."

"All together?" Kate asked.

"That's what I was told. And I feel that those tracking us will go there to make inquiries. There are sure to be trading posts along the river, but going to one of them would be worse than the city."

"I've never seen a thousand people all together," Kate said wistfully. "The city must be filled with all sorts of grand shops."

"Do you want to go there, Kate?"

"That's up to you, Jamie. But we've got to have supplies; we're out of everything."

"And we've got to pick up a pack horse and a new tent," Jamie said with a sigh. At times he felt like the weight of the world was on his strong young shoulders. "Well . . . it can't be helped. We've got to go there, and we've got to outfit. We've got to stock up with powder and lead. Kate, when we leave the city, we'll head straight west, into the Ouachitas. That Quapaw I talked to said we could lose our pursuers in there." The friendly Quapaw had also told Jamie it was a dandy place for him to set up an ambush, and kill those tracking them, but Jamie didn't tell Kate that. Although he certainly kept that thought in the back of his mind.

"Whatever you say, Jamie."

Kate was tired and her face showed the

strain of traveling through the wilderness. Having known nothing but brutally hard work since childhood, this venture was no more than a lark to Jamie. But he knew it was tough on Kate. Riding sidesaddle through the wilderness was awkward and uncomfortable.

"Ah, Kate," Jamie said, not quite sure how she would receive this suggestion. "There is one other thing we can buy when we get to the city."

"Oh?"

"A regular saddle and some men's britches for you to wear."

She smiled mischievously. "Why, Jamie, you know that a proper young lady does not sit a horse astride."

"It was just a suggestion, Kate."

She laughed at the crestfallen look on his face. "Oh, Jamie! I think it's a wonderful suggestion. With me not having to sit perched on that stupid saddle like a queen, we can make much better time. And if I get a big floppy hat and loose clothing, I can cut my hair short and pass for a boy."

Jamie looked at her. He had his doubts about that last bit. Nobody but a babbling idiot would ever take Kate for a boy. But he was learning fast about being married. "Uh . . . right, Kate. You're right."

"We got a big group of men followin' us," Trent Newby said, flopping down on the ground and pouring a cup of coffee from the battered pot.

"The law?" Waymore Newby asked.

"What law?" Ford Newby asked. "There ain't no damn law in this territory — at least none that could, or would, tackle us. Mayhaps them folks is trailin' the same two we is?"

"Possibility," John Newby said. "You mighty quiet, Bart. What you got rumblin' 'round in your noggin?"

"Where are we goin' with this, John? We done left hearth and home way back behind us. Are we west of the river for good?"

"For as long as it takes us to find them two kids and avenge our brothers."

"That might take years, John."

"Then it'll take years. What the hell have we got to go back to?"

"Good point," Waymore said. "Best thing for us is never to go east of the Mississippi. By now, the law has done put together who kilt them old people and torched their store. We cain't never go back."

The five brothers sat around the fire,

morosely staring at the flames, letting that information slowly sink in.

Waymore broke the silence. "I'm gonna kill that kid and use that gold-haired girl hard."

"And then pass her around," Bart said.

"Yeah. That too."

Jamie paid a farmer on the outskirts of town a dollar to look after their horses, and two dollars to let them use his wagon to go into the city. The farmer hadn't seen three dollars in hard money in months, so he jumped at the offer. He was happier still when Jamie said he would bring the man back a sack of sugar and flour and some coffee.

"Bless your hearts," his wife said.

Jamie had been astonished when he'd opened the bag of money Sam had given him. He knew it had been awfully heavy, but since he had a little money of his own — Sam had insisted on paying him for the work around the farm, and Jamie had saved most of it — he had not opened the bag until a few days before reaching Little Rock.

"Sam is very wealthy, Jamie," Kate told him. "He comes from a very rich family back east. So does Sarah. Both families see to it that they want for naught." She smiled and her eyes sparkled. "Did you ever hear why two educated and sophisticated people like them left the lights of the city and came to be in the wilds of Kentucky?"

"No. But I often wondered."

"Well, I don't know all the story, but Sarah has told me a little bit about it. Sam and Sarah were quite young when they fell in love. Even younger than us. But another family wanted their son to marry Sarah. There was a fight, and Sam killed the boy's father and had to flee just ahead of the law. The warrants have long since been cleared, but they like it on the frontier and just don't want to go back."

"That's why he was so eager to help us," Jamie said slowly, as the two of them bumped and lurched along in the wagon.

"I'm sure that's part of the reason. The main reason is they both love you."

Jamie didn't know how he felt about that. He did know that it made him feel bad, sort of.

Kate picked up on his mood and put a hand on his arm. "Don't feel badly about it, Jamie. Sarah told me they could never expect to hold you back there. She said you were like an eagle, you had to fly and see through the eyes of eagles. Sam was there and he agreed. He said you were born for the wild country, for the mountains and desert and the wilderness. They questioned me at length about my love for you and the type of life I would probably lead if I left with you. It isn't going to be easy, Jamie. I know that. We're going into country that few white people have ever seen. But it's what I want. That, and to be with you."

"I don't really know where we're going, Kate. Not yet. But no man could ask a woman for more than you just said. And there's the city, Kate."

Neither one of them knew if there really were a thousand people in the city, but it was more people than either one of them had ever seen all gathered in one place.

"I'd love to shop some," Kate said. "But I know that we cannot risk lingering long. We'll shop together as quickly as we can, and then leave. All right?"

Jamie nodded his head and pulled the wagon around to the side of a huge general store. He let the horses drink and then he and Kate walked into the store. Place had more stuff in it than either of them had ever seen. It would make Abe Caney's store back in Kentucky pale in comparison.

Jamie had spread his money around to various pockets of his homespuns that he had changed into at the farmer's cabin. Kate had also sewn pockets at the top of his high-top moccasins for most of the money. He knew better than to flash a lot of gold around. While Kate did her woman's shopping, Jamie bought lead and powder and a mold. Then, after signaling Kate he was stepping outside for a moment, he went next door to a gun and leather shop and bought four used pistols, another rifle, more powder, and a saddle. He could make powder if he had to, for he'd watched the Shawnees do it, combining saltpeter, found in certain types of caves, sulfur, and charcoal . . . but the homemade stuff was not dependable and tended to be very volatile, igniting when one least expected it, often with disastrous results to the party not expecting harm. He loaded that in the wagon and returned to Kate's side. The store was very busy, and that was good, for it gave no one a chance to really stare long at them or to ask any questions. Jamie bought several sheets of canvas and a small container of tar, which he would use to thinly coat the material to make it waterproof. He bought lengths of rope, two good knives, two hatchets and two axes and a small sharpening stone. Then they loaded up and drove on down the street to another store and bought the rest of their supplies, including eating utensils and britches and shirts for Kate. At the livery, Jamie dickered some with a man and left leading two strong pack horses and rigs to carry all their supplies.

"It's so much, Jamie!" Kate said.

"It'll seem like nothing when we're on the trail, Kate. And I've still got most of the money Sam gave me . . . us."

Kate smiled. "You're catching on real quick, Jamie." She laughed and hugged him, and Jamie had him a thought that maybe the horses needed a rest and while they were resting, he and Kate could find some bushes to get behind and . . .

He shook his head. Best to not think about that. Kate had told him there was a time and a place for everything.

He gave the farmer and his wife their promised sacks of sugar and flour and salt and a few other articles that Kate had picked out for the woman and her two young children, a boy and a girl. The man and his wife were embarrassed by the generosity of the young couple.

Jamie leveled with the man and the wife while the kids ran off to play with their new geegaws. "We're running, folks. We've committed no crimes and we're not living in sin. We were married back up the trail. But there are some killers after us. They're bad people. If they should stop here, and they might, you never saw us."

"You go with God, young feller," the settler said. "And don't you worry none about us sayin' a thing. We can be right tight-lipped when we taken a mind to it."

Jamie and Kate packed up and pulled out within the hour, the farmer's wife shaking her head at Kate's wearing men's britches, and horrified at her riding astride.

"That girl will come to no good end," she said to her husband.

"Maybe that's the way they do it back east now," he replied. "This younger generation is sure goin' to hell in a handbasket. No tellin' what they'll be doin' next."

"It's the devil's work, for sure."

Jamie and Kate pushed westward, riding deeper into the wilderness, behind them came the Newby Brothers and behind them rode John Jackson and Hart Olmstead and their followers. Jamie and Kate both felt that John and Hart would eventually give up and return to Kentucky, for they had businesses to run and farms to tend back there, and neither was a wealthy man. The Newby Brothers were a different story however. Jamie and Kate had learned from talking to people along the way that the Newbys were highwaymen, wanted in several states and territories, and they were also friends with the Saxon gang. Since the Saxon Brothers escaped from jail, several years back, they had become the leaders of one of the most infamous and feared gangs in the country, robbing and raping and killing and plundering wherever they rode, which was wherever and whenever they chose.

Although both Jamie and Kate would have liked to visit the hot springs, which they had read and heard about, and which had been used by Indians for centuries, believing the hot water had magical healing powers, the springs lay south of where the young couple rode, and they felt sure their pursuers would go there in search of them. The two pressed on westward. They encountered Indians, but the Caddos gave them no trouble and most were friendly.

On the fourth day out of Little Rock, camped at the edge of a little lake in the Ouachita Mountains, a voice halloed their camp. Jamie put his hand on the butt of a pistol and waited.

"I be friendly, young folks," the man said, walking his horse closer. "And I be alone. Smelled your food a-cookin' and the coffee boilin'. I'll ride on if you say to."

"Come on in," Jamie told him. "We're as

friendly as you are."

The man dismounted and saw to his horse's needs. He squatted by the fire and took the cup of coffee Kate handed him. "Obliged, missy."

Jamie noted that the man was not that much older than he was. He figured him maybe twenty or so at the most. The full beard made him appear much older.

"I been to St. Louis to see the sights and sell my pelts," the man said. "Thought I'd just take me a look-see down this way 'fore I headed back to the mountains. I been to Fort Pickering; some folks has taken to callin' it Memphis. Silliest name I ever did hear. What's it mean, anyways?"

"I think it has something to do with Egypt," Kate said.

"Do tell."

"My name's Sonny and this is Tess," Jamie said.

"It ain't done it, neither," the buckskin-clad man said with a smile. "But you'll find the further west you head, names don't account for much. It's more what a man does now than what he's got behind him. And right now, you got a mess of trouble comin' hard on your heels . . . Jamie and Kate Mac-Callister."

The stranger's eyes hardened, his smile

vanished, and he reached for a pistol stuck in his sash.

TEN

The young couple tensed as the stranger's hand closed on the butt of the pistol.

"Relax, kids," he said. "I'm just tired of this thing pokin' me in the ribs." He laid the pistol on the ground, beside him.

Jamie eyed his rifle and pistol, out of his reach.

"Don't never get away from your guns, boy," the stranger said. "Not out here. It was smart of you, buying them extree guns back at Little Rock. Man can't never have too many."

"Are you spying on us, sir?" Kate asked, her eyes flashing with anger.

"Nope. You might say I'm sort of your guardian for part of this trip you're on."

"Why?" Jamie asked.

"I know your grandpa, boy. That's why."

"Will you stop calling me *boy*? You're not more than five or six years older than I am."

The man smiled. "In man's years, son,

that's right. But in experience, you'll never catch up with me. I went west when I was a lot younger than you." He smiled that strange smile. "Man Who Is Not Afraid."

"You said you know my grandfather?"

"Yep. And he's alive and well and damn spry for his age, too." He looked at Kate. "Kindly pardon my language, ma'am." He looked back at Jamie. "When I heard a young feller name of MacCallister was being tracked — I was told that over at a tradin' post on the White — I done me a little investigatin' and decided to drift on over this way. I picked up your trail north of the city and been watchin' you. You do tolerable well in the wilderness, boy. Tolerable. Them Shawnees taught you good. Now I'm fixin' to teach you a bit more whilst we head west. I'll leave you a ways after we cross the Red, 'cause I've got me a yearnin' for the mountains and the plains. I been missin' 'em something fierce, I have."

"I'll see them someday," Jamie said. "Me and Kate."

"Probably," the man agreed. "And once you do, you'll never leave 'em for long. They pull at you. The plains is something a body's got to see to believe. And the mountains? Well, words can't describe 'em."

The stranger sighed and shook his head.

"The mountains get to a man. I've been ramblin' on some. You mind if I have me a taste of that stew you got cookin' in the pot, Missy?"

"Of course not. I'll get you a plate."

"Then you're a mountain man?" Jamie asked.

"I reckon," the stranger replied, taking the plate filled with stew. He ate several spoonfuls. "Good grub, Missy. Man gets tired of his own cookin'." He smiled. "And I 'spect a woman does too, now, ain't that right?"

Kate laughed at him. "Oh, yes."

Jamie and Kate took a liking to the friendly and easygoing stranger. As he ate, he told them about Jamie's grandfather, and about the way of life of the mountain men. Then he had Jamie tell him what type of supplies they'd purchased back in the "city".

The stranger grunted his approval. "You'll do, Jamie MacCallister. You'll do. You brought just what you'll need and no more. You didn't waste good cash money on gee-gaws and foofaws. And you got a good eye for horseflesh. That big black of yours is better than a watchdog — ain't I right?"

Jamie allowed as how he was.

"Thought so. But seeing Kate in men's britches is gonna take some getting used to, I reckon."

■ ■ ■ ■

The stranger made his camp about fifty yards away from Jamie and Kate, to give them some privacy and also, Jamie felt, not to offer any attacker a bunched-up camp.

"We don't even know his name," Kate whispered that night, snuggled close together in their blankets.

"I guess if he wants us to know it, he'll tell us. Kate? Tomorrow I start teaching you about guns. You've got to be able to fire both rifle and pistol and know how to reload."

"I know how to reload. But I'm not much of a shot."

"You will be. You've got to learn. I'm told that the danger of Indians is not much where I've got in mind for us to live. But we must never forget those who are trailing us. And you've got to be able not just to shoot, but to kill."

Kate was silent, mentally recalling the ugly, savage viciousness of her father and of John Jackson and those awful Newby Brothers. "I'll stand when the time comes, Jamie. Of that, you may be sure."

The next afternoon, by the banks of the Fourche River, Jamie and the stranger began Kate's introduction to weapons. They practiced with her for an hour, until she began to complain that her shoulder and hands were aching.

"Best to stop now," the stranger said. "We don't want to push this. Accidents happen when a body does that."

"You go take your bath, Kate," Jamie told her. "We'll stand guard and start fixing supper. We'll fry up those big fish we caught."

"She's a good girl," the stranger said, kneeling by the fire and pouring a cup of coffee. "You're a lucky man. She'll stand beside you."

"Are you married?" Jamie asked.

The stranger smiled. "Married to the mountains, I reckon. The wind is my woman. You two gonna settle in Texas, huh?"

"Planning on it."

"Gonna be a war there, Jamie. The Mexicans is not takin' kindly to the talk of independence."

"Then I'll fight."

The stranger looked at this boy/man. Big feller. Arms and wrists on him held more power than the boy probably realized. The years with the Shawnees shaped him, body and mind. He'll be a rough one to tangle with, for a fact. Carried a hide-out knife in one leggin, too. And the stranger had no doubts about Jamie's ability and will to use it.

"You want to tell me why you got all these people after you, Jamie?"

Jamie looked across the fire. He could hear Kate singing softly from the river. "One group is led by two men, Olmstead and Jackson. Kate is Olmstead's daughter. We ran off. I killed Jackson's son, John Jr., after the two of them raped a good lady back in Kentucky. The other bunch will be the Newby Brothers. I killed two of their brothers at a trading post just off the Mississippi River. The old man at the store killed the third one with an axe."

That brought a grunt from the mountain man. He'd pegged Jamie MacCallister right: the boy wouldn't back up and take water from nobody. "What about the third bunch?"

Jamie stared at him for a moment. "*What* third bunch?"

"You got three groups of men trailin' you, Jamie. What do you know about the Saxon Brothers?"

Jamie shook his head and cursed, something he rarely did. He told the stranger about his encounter, several years back, with the Saxon Brothers.

The mountain man laughed. "Twelve

155

years old and shoot a man in the ass with an arrow. I reckon that would get his attention, all right. That might be enough to make him carry a grudge." He chuckled.

Jamie grinned boyishly. "He didn't see the humor in it, that's for sure."

"I reckon not."

Kate walked up, smelling of soap and cleanliness, her blond hair dark with water. "What's so funny?" she asked.

"We also have the Saxon Brothers after us," Jamie said.

"And you think that's funny?"

"Not really. But shooting one in the butt that night was."

Kate laughed and turned around. She had cut short her bath when she felt eyes on her. But she could detect no one. Now she mentioned it to Jamie and the stranger. The mountain man was on his feet in an instant, rifle in hand.

"Get the horses behind them rocks over yonder," he said, jerking his head. "Missy, you get all them spare guns and start loadin' 'em up. Double-shot the pistols for close work."

"Indians?" Jamie asked, working quickly.

"I don't think so. I can't give you no good reason why I think that, I just do."

"I'm not familiar with any of the tribes in

this area," Jamie said.

"No one is no more. Whites keep pushin' the tribes out of the east and shovin' 'em west. Some tribes has joined with other tribes, some packed up and went west, and others just disappeared. I don't know where the hell they went. Last year I seen a bunch of Yuchis and Shawnee out on the plains. Heading west to get shut of the white man. Can't blame 'em none."

Jamie cut his eyes. "I think I just spotted a blue shirt across the river. Not that that means a whole lot. Could be an Indian wearing it."

"Could be but I'll bet it ain't. I think we're about to get fell on by a bunch of white trash."

"I doubt it's Olmstead and Jackson. We're at least a week ahead of them."

"No more than that," the stranger said. "Come the mornin,' we start hidin' our tracks."

"Hallo the camp!" the shout came from across the river. "We're friendly folks and wouldn't harm nary a butterfly. Can we come over and share our meager food with y'all, kind gents and beautiful lady?"

"Goddamn ridge-runners," the mountain man said. "Worthless, shiftless trash. From this distance, they wouldn't have known your lady was a woman . . . unless they spied on her bathing. And that makes 'em lower than a snake's belly far as I'm concerned." He looked at Jamie. "If I wasn't here, what would you do?"

"First I'd find out how many of them are over there. Then I'd tell them to keep on traveling and make sure they did. Then I'd break camp and move on for several miles."

The mountain man smiled, and with that smile, Jamie knew he was maybe twenty, at the most. "You'll do, Jamie MacCallister. You'll do." He raised his voice. "Keep on travelin'. We ain't in the mood for no company."

"That's a terrible unchristian thing, friend," the shout was returned. "We are all poor pilgrims wandering in a vast and hostile land, ain't we?"

The mountain man's language coarsened considerably and he told the as yet unseen man where he could go and the shortest way to get there . . . in a manner of speaking.

Kate covered her mouth to smother her giggle.

"I don't think you're a very friendly person," the shout came from across the river.

"I don't much give a damn what you

think!" the mountain man hollered. "But I know you best keep on travelin'."

"Whatever you say, friend. We'll pray for you over our supper."

"Say a prayer or go to hell. Just get gone from here," the mountain man replied. He turned to Jamie. "They're sure to have people all around us. Damnit, I thought I heard something in the woods about twenty or so minutes ago."

"Who are they?"

"Movers. Shiftless rawhiders who squat in some homesteader's abandoned cabin and live until it falls down around them. Then they move on. And they steal anything that ain't pegged down good. They're too lazy to work; think the world owes them something. And they've always got a hard-luck story to tell. I was crossin' Missouri some months ago and run into a bunch of them. I never heard such whinin' and complainin' in all my life. Give me a headache. I hadn't gone ten miles up the road 'fore I run into the sheriff and a posse chasin' 'em. And their women is the worse. Whoors and trash and the like. Don't never turn your back to them. Them women'll have a dirk in you faster than you can spit."

"What do we do?" Kate called from the rocks.

"Get ready to kill some white trash," the mountain man said shortly.

"Just like that?" Jamie questioned.

"Just like that. Believe me, they'd kill you and leave you for the ants without never blinkin' a eye."

"I must have missed something those years living in the Shawnee town," Jamie said.

"You missed puttin' up with white trash. Next time you see a Shawnee, thank him for that."

Even though Jamie knew they were surrounded by danger, he had to chuckle at that. "Why do you hate them so?"

"Oh, I don't hate them, Jamie. I don't hate very much. Takes a lot to make me hate somebody. I just don't have no use for them. They're takers. Anytime a person takes more from his community or his fellow man than he gives back, that feller is what I call a taker. A lot of bankers is takers. A lot of lawyers is takers. You don't have to be trash to be a taker."

"I never thought about that."

"You never had to. Until you left that Shawnee town and come back to live with the whites. Injuns won't put up with takers. They'll run them off or kill them. Well, most Injuns, that is. They's a couple of tribes up

160

in the northwest that's pretty damn shiftless, but as a rule your Injuns have a fairly
strict code they live by."

"Everything is loaded up full and I've
patches and balls ready," Kate said.

"That's a good girl, Jamie," the mountain
man said. "Don't never treat her bad."

"You don't have to worry about that.
Say . . . what is your name? I can't go on
calling you 'hey.' "

The young mountain man laughed.
" 'Bout three years ago, folks started callin'
me Preacher. I'll tell you why later. Right
now, cock that rifle. 'Cause here they
come!"

ELEVEN

Jamie did not hesitate once the first shot was fired from across the river. A second after the ball whizzed past his head, Jamie pulled his rifle to his shoulder and fired. Across the river, the shooter dropped his rifle, threw his arms into the air, and pitched face-forward onto the bank.

The young mountain man fired and the ball struck a man in the stomach, doubling him over, screaming. He dropped to his knees and wailed in pain.

Kate fired from the rocks and her shot struck a man in the hip, spinning him around. Like the others, he dropped his rifle and went down.

"Three shots, three down," Preacher said. "Can't ask for no better than that."

"Damn your black hearts!" the same unseen voice called from across the river. "Now you've done it. We come into this land as poor homeless pilgrims and all we asked was for compassion. Now you heathens has kilt kin. You'll pay. You'll all pay for this unjust mistreatment."

"Unjust mistreatment?" Jamie muttered, reloaded and ready. "They started it, not us."

"That's the way them sort of people think, Jamie," Preacher said. "They blame others for their misfortune. They don't never put the blame where it belongs — on themselves."

"That's stupid!"

"Yep. Sure is. But they'll never change. It'll be the same a hundred and fifty years from now. Probably worser as government seems to be gettin' bigger."

"What do you mean?"

"The government'll be payin' folks not to work. That's what I heard somebody say in St. Louis a few weeks back."

"That day will never come," Jamie argued.

"Don't bet on it," the mountain man replied. "See 'em movin' over yonder?"

"Yes. They are very clumsy . . . and stupid if they think we haven't spotted them."

Preacher sighted in and let a ball fly. From the other side came a fearful shriek and a man thrashed around in the brush and then fell out into the clear and rolled down the bank, coming to a stop at the water's edge.

"I 'spect that'll just about do it," Preacher said, reloading quickly. "They lost a goodly number to us and by now they know we ain't a bunch of pilgrims." He held up a hand. "Listen."

Jamie and Kate could hear the faint sounds of wagons bouncing and creaking away.

"Stay here with your woman," the mountain man said. He picked up his rifle and was gone.

Kate left the rocks at a run and came to Jamie's side. Her face was pale and her eyes were startlingly wide. "I shot a man, Jamie. I killed him!"

"No, you didn't, Kate. He was hip-shot and crawled into the brush. I saw him. Don't worry about it, Kate. We did what we had to do. I'm proud of you."

The young couple stood silent for a few moments. "They're gone," Preacher called. "Come on across and help me gather up this gear and such. You'll need it."

Kate went across with Jamie and stopped by a dead man, staring down at him. "Why . . . this wretch has *fleas*!" she said, looking at the tiny parasites hopping about, not yet realizing that their host was dead.

"That probably ain't all he's got," Preacher called out, his tone very dry.

"Jamie, strip him of his shot and powder and pistols."

"I don't rob from the dead, Preacher."

Preacher stepped out of the brush. "Learn something valuable now, Jamie." He was carrying several rifles and pistols. "This ain't no church picnic. Where you and Kate are goin' there ain't no white people, much less stores and the like. Whatever y'all gonna have, you got to tote it in with you and make it do. You got that through your head, now, boy?"

It still irritated Jamie for the young mountain man to call him *boy,* but he realized that Preacher, while only a few years older, was vastly more knowledgeable in such matters than he and Kate. "I understand," he said softly.

"Fine," Preacher said. "Kate, you get on back 'crost the stream and get some lye soap and hot water ready. We got to wash these britches and shirts and coats."

"You're going to *strip* the bodies?" she asked. "All three of them?"

"Five of them," Preacher corrected. "They was two waitin' for us over here. I used my good knife on them. Now go on acrost. It ain't fitten for you to witness what me and Jamie got to do."

"Are we going to bury them?" Jamie asked.

"Cave that bank yonder on them," the mountain man said. "That'll do for this bunch."

Kate beat it back across the river and Jamie and Preacher fell to their grisly task.

"They left a wagon and a team," Preacher said. "That might be what you and Kate had better use to get to where you're going. They also left four saddle horses. Pretty good stock. That will help y'all get started when you reach your stoppin' point. We'll hide all signs of a fight and then I'll take the spare horses and lay a false trail west. That will throw off them comin' in behind you. By the time they realize they're mistooken, y'all's real trail will be gone. I'll hook up with y'all in a few days."

"You're a real friend, Preacher," Jamie said, his eyes serious.

"You're a MacCallister. Your grandpa took me under his wing soon as I got to the high lonesome. If he hadn't a-done that, I'd have died, probably. 'Sides, I like you and Kate. Now close your mouth and get to work, 'fore you start blubberin' on me."

The next morning, Preacher was gone before the dawning, leading the spare mounts and laying down a false trail. Jamie and Kate pulled out in the wagon. Both

166

knew, in all probability, the wagon had been stolen, for it was filled with provisions and other gear. They didn't even know for sure what all was in the wagon for they did not want to take the time to inspect the load. But they did have four fine mules that would prove invaluable when they began homesteading.

The going was much slower now, for there were no roads and Jamie had to scout ahead for the best route through the western Arkansas wilderness. Kate drove the wagon and it did not take her long to master the reins.

Jamie chose their campsites with care, always picking a spot that the two of them could easily defend. But they encountered no trouble during the days that Preacher was gone. And they were glad to see the young mountain man, days later, when he finally caught up with them, riding up from the south and joining them just as they were making camp for the evening.

He swung down from the saddle and saw to his horse while Jamie took the spare mounts over to the picket line. "Got news," Preacher said. "But first I'll have me a taste of that coffee. I run out day 'fore yesterday." He squatted down and took the cup that Kate handed him. He blew to cool and then swallowed. "Good. I'm a coffee-drinkin' man. Talked with some Injuns. Seems like Kate's pa and them ridin' with him have done give it up and headed back to Kaintuck. Now all y'all got to worry with is the Newby Brothers and the Saxon gang. But they'll play hell findin' your trail. I rode south for a time, then cut east and went over to the hot springs. Damndest sight I ever did see . . . almost." He took a gulp of coffee. "Y'all ever heard of the Big Thicket country?"

Kate and Jamie shook their heads.

Preacher brushed a space clean on the ground and drew a rough map. "It's right here. And I'm told it's wild. I like wild things, so I'll drift on down that way with you two. When you first see it, so I was told by them Caddos, you'll think it ain't nothin' but a dark swamp. Tain't so. They's areas within it that's good farm land. Rich and never seen a plow. I think that's y'all's best bet." He looked at them. "What say you both?"

Jamie glanced at Kate and she smiled and nodded her head. "Let's go look at it," Jamie said.

With Preacher back to help, Jamie could now relieve Kate at the reins, spelling her when she got tired, or when Jamie thought she was tiring. But Kate was a lot tougher than Jamie realized, and although she was tired at day's end, she enjoyed driving the team. Not that handling four big mules was any pleasure, mind you, she just liked the feeling of contributing to this journey. But she let Jamie think he was doing her a big favor.

And with the young mountain man along, Jamie was slowly being eased and teased out of his usual somber and serious mood. For with Preacher, life was a grand joke — unless it came to a shooting or a cutting and then he could get real serious.

They saw no one. They did spot distant smoke from time to time, but they did not wish to call attention to themselves so the smoke went uninvestigated.

They moved slowly through a series of rolling hills and came to a long valley. Preacher rode back to the wagon, where Jamie had been riding along, talking with Kate as she handled the reins.

"We'll make another two/three miles and then bed down for the night. This time tomorrow, we'll have cut straight south. Arkansas River's to the north of us 'bout forty or fifty miles, I reckon."

"How far down to this Big Thicket country?" Kate asked.

"Pretty good ways, missy. Hundreds of miles. I'd say. Weeks of travel. Tell the truth, I ain't real sure where it is."

"Let's go," Jamie said.

The days stretched endlessly behind them and loomed the same way ahead of them. During their stops for the night, Kate went through the contents of the big wagon and discovered a treasure trove of goods. Kegs of powder and sheets of lead. Flour and sugar and bolts of material. A case of rifles and pistols. Cooking pots and pans and other utensils. Needles and thread. Medical supplies and potions and bandages. Hatchets and axes.

"Had to have belonged to a traveling salesman," Jamie said. "I wonder if those movers killed him for this?"

"Probably," the mountain man said. "But this'll help y'all get set up and settled in. Oncest we get down south and I have me a look around, I'm gone back to the mountains. Y'all might not never see me again. I warn you now that when I go, I ain't much on goodbyes. You'll just get up one mornin' and I'll be gone. But I want the both of you to know this has been a right pleasurable time for me. Just wanted y'all to know that."

They rolled on and saw no one. Jamie

began to suspect that Preacher, always ranging out from the wagon, was deliberately taking them around any settlers' cabins so they'd remain unseen. Several times both he and Kate had smelled the odor of food cooking. Preacher had dismissed it as their imagination. But Jamie knew it had not been only in his mind. He knew what salt meat and biscuits smelled like.

Jamie had once more allowed his blond hair to grow long, and sometimes Kate would braid it for him to keep it from tangling. He was well into his fifteenth year and had reached his height. He was three inches over six feet and muscular. Anyone who tried guessing his weight would usually be twenty-five pounds short. He had taken to riding with his short-barreled rifle over the saddle horn, like the mountain man did. None of them had any idea what month it was, and they weren't real sure of the year. They believed it was 1823.

After months on the trail, Preacher rode back to the wagon one afternoon and pointed. "There she be, people. That's the start of it. It'll run, off and on, for several hundred miles, so I was told. Whether that's true or not, I don't know. How far down you want to go, Jamie?"

"Two or three more days, at least."

171

"All right. Then I'll be back in about a week or so. I heard tell there was a tradin' post down here around a place the Frenchies call Beau Mont and other folks is callin' the Bluff. I don't know whether it's there or not. I'll check it out. Don't get lost. See you."

Kate and Jamie traveled southward for several more days, until Jamie found a place where he could pull the wagon off into an area where it was very nearly invisible from ten feet away. He spent a day building a brush corral for the livestock and getting Kate used to the idea that he would be gone all day, for the next several days. She didn't like it, but knew it had to be.

"Jamie," she asked over supper. "Who owns this land?"

"I . . . ah, don't know. Mexico or France or somebody. But in two or three days, we're going to own a chunk of it."

"How?"

That brought him up short again. "Well, we'll settle on it. That's how. We'll build us a cabin and that'll show that we're here to stay."

"That's how it's done?"

He smiled. "That's how we're going to do it."

■ ■ ■ ■

Jamie fell in love with the country. Five hundred yards from where he'd left Kate by the wagon, the land turned soggy and soon he was surrounded by a tangle of brush and woods so thick he had to hack his way through. In the dark still waters — bayous, Preacher had called them — he saw huge alligators, twelve-to fourteen-feet long, and rattlesnakes and water moccasins as thick as his wrists. He found signs of bear and wolves.

He loved it, but it wasn't what he was seeking. He wasn't sure in his mind what he was looking for, only that he'd know it when he came to it.

Then, on his fourth day of exploring, he found what he was looking for. The area was set back in the thickets, but there was firm ground leading to it and clearings dotted the location. He knelt down and tore up a handful of earth. Rich soil that would grow good crops and produce fine gardens. When he got back to the wagon, Preacher had returned.

"She's there, all right," the mountain man said, drawing a crude map in the dirt. "You got tradin' posts set south, west, to the north, right up here, and one right acrost the Sabine River over in Frenchy land. The settled Injuns here won't bother you if you leave them alone. They's Alabama and Coushatta. Been here about twenty or so years. They's Kiowa and Comanche all over the damn place, but mostly to the west of here. Ain't many white folks around here, but I heard talk that some feller name of Austin has done settled three or four hundred families in various spots in Texas and he riled up the Mexicans by doin' so. But they'll get over it, I reckon. They's a bunch of Frenchies down here just north of pirate city — some call it Galveston. Them Frenchies has settled in the valley of the Trinity River. So now y'all know as much as I do about this area of the country. I seen what I want to see of this country. It's all right. But I got a hankerin' to get back to the High Lonesome."

"You're not going to wait until the morning, are you?" Kate asked him.

The mountain man shook his head. "Nope. I'm takin' out right now. My feets is gettin' itchy." He stood up and stuck out his hand to Jamie. "But I wanted to come back and see y'all one more time. See you."

The young mountain man walked to his horses and rode away to the northwest without looking back.

"Do you suppose we'll ever see him again?" Kate asked.

"I don't know, love." Jamie stood behind her. He put his arms around her, under her breasts, and pulled her close. "But I do know this: except for each other, we are alone."

Kate smiled. "We won't be for long."

"What do you mean?"

"Jamie Ian MacCallister, you'd better get a cabin built pretty quick. We're going to have a baby."

TWELVE

It didn't take Jamie long to recover from his shock and within minutes Kate was laughing so hard at the way her young husband was acting toward her, she had to sit down on the tailgate of their wagon.

"Jamie! I'm not some delicate flower or piece of fine china. I'm pregnant, that's all. It'll be several more months before I better not do any really hard work." She took his hands in hers. "Now listen to me. We can still get a garden in. It's late, but we'll salvage something out of it. We can't plant potatoes, but we can plant other vegetables. And we're going to need a milk cow."

"A *milk cow*? Where am I going to get a milk cow out here?"

"I don't know. That's your job. Just get us a milk cow. Right now, let's move back to where you've picked the spot for us to live and get busy."

"I'll get some sort of shelter up for you,

Kate, and then I'll have to leave to find some cows . . . or a nanny goat."

"Either one will do."

Jamie sighed as a little bit more weight settled on his strong young shoulders. "Let's just hope it isn't twins," he said.

Kate smiled. "Triplets run on my mother's side of the family."

"Oh, *Lord*!"

Kate was still laughing as Jamie hitched up a mule and started plowing up a garden for Kate — with a mule who wasn't real happy about pulling a plow. But he got the job done and then Jamie got busy working on cabin and corral. He wasn't going to hurry on the cabin and regret it later. He took his time shaping the logs. The wagon had contained mauls and froes, several drawknives, and a broadax and adz. Jamie had the tools, and he knew how to use them. He was also determined that the cabin would have a wood floor.

"It isn't necessary, Jamie," Kate said softly.

"Yes, it is," he said, and went back to work with the foot adz, which was normally used for squaring logs.

Hands on her hips as she watched the sweat streak the dusty skin of his bare upper torso, she said, "I suppose you're going to want windows, too?"

"Certainly," Jamie said. "But at first we'll use doeskin membranes."

"What?"

"Yes. But I'll have to kill several bears for you to use the grease to coat the membranes. That lets the light come through."

"That's *disgusting!*"

Jamie paused in his work and cut loose with one of his rare laughs. After taking a swig from the water jug Kate handed him, he said. "You're a pioneer lady now, Kate. Now get thee back to work, wench!"

She tossed the remaining contents of the water jug on him and then ran off to her garden, leaving Jamie dripping wet and laughing. She looked at the mess Jamie had made of the earth and shook her head. She didn't have the heart to tell him he'd used the wrong kind of plow . . . Jamie had broken the earth for field crops, not a garden.

She stood at the edge of the plowed-up mess and did some thinking. They had plenty of flour, so wheat could wait until next spring. Corn, too, with pole beans among them so the vines could grow up the tall stalks. And they had pumpkin seed, and gourds would also grow among the corn. Jamie would have to get some potatoes at one of the trading posts, for they would have to have potatoes. And beans, peas, cabbage, turnips, and sweet potatoes. But that was next year. Kate wasn't sure what month it was, but she knew it was pushing the seasons to try to plant very much right now. But she'd give it her best and say a little prayer. That never hurt.

Kate was showing when Jamie finished the cabin. She thought it was funny-looking at first, but she never cracked a smile. Now, looking at it, it made sense. Jamie had built a double cabin, with a dogtrot between them and two stone fireplaces with stone chimneys to prevent fire. On one side was the kitchen and sort of a living room, the other side a bedroom. It made sense in this warm climate, for they could sit in the dogtrot on warm evenings and enjoy a breeze.

"If you like, I'll put some sort of floor down later," he said.

They had seen no white men, but lots of Indians. Jamie quickly made friends with them and there was no trouble . . . not yet. But Jamie knew that in even the friendliest of tribes, there were those who harbored terrible blind hatred for all whites.

"Black man lives other side of this swamp," a elder in the tribe told him one

179

day. He pointed. "That way. Woman and three children. Came here four winters ago. Good man. Work hard. Friendly to all. He ask about you. I tell him that I believe you good. Then I tell him about your Shawnee name: Man Who Is Not Afraid. I tell him that I don't think you like slavery."

"I don't. I hate it. No man has the right to hold another as a slave. It's wrong."

The Indian smiled. "Tomorrow, I bring my woman and daughters to stay with your woman during her time. We go see Moses. Is good for you?"

"Good for me," Jamie replied.

The Alabama gripped Jamie's strong arm. "You good man, Jamie . . ."

Jamie had to burst out laughing, for the elder could no more pronounce MacCallister than he could fly to the moon. It came out sounding like MacCabaister-bucket. But the elder was a man of high humor and he joined in the laughter, taking no offense at Jamie's mirth, as Jamie knew he wouldn't.

The Alabama showed Jamie passageways through the country called the Big Thicket, and Jamie committed them to memory. On some of them, the water was knee deep and one had to carefully count the steps to gain safe passageway. Miss a count, and you found yourself sinking into the black water, or worse yet, mired in deadly quicksand. And one had to constantly watch for deadly snakes and alligators.

"I'd hate to be on horseback coming through here," Jamie remarked.

"That is your next lesson," the Alabama told him. "It can be done. I will show you. It is also very interesting when you meet a bear or a panther on these narrow paths," the Alabama said, with more than a hint of a twinkle in his dark eyes.

"You ever do that?"

"Yes. That is how I got my second name."

"Your *second* name?"

"Yes." The elder chuckled. "Man Who Walks On Water." Then he burst out laughing as did the others with them.

Most people had the mistaken belief that all Indians would rather die than turn tail and flee for their lives when faced with a hopeless situation. Jamie mentioned this to the elder.

"Only the very stupid ones," the elder replied. "And they're all dead."

Jamie had discovered that the Alabama and Coushatta tribes were very pragmatic realists. And that is one of the reasons why they would survive when the Texans made their purge of the red man in the late 1830s. The other was Sam Houston, who rewarded the tribes for their neutrality during the Texas fight for independence.

Moses Washington was a man Jamie guessed to be in his late thirties. He had a son, Robert, who looked to be a few years older than Jamie. And another son, Jed, and daughter, Sally. His wife was named Liza and both their parents had been brought over on a slave ship from Africa.

Jamie stuck out his hand and smiled. "If you ran for your freedom, I sure don't blame you. And don't worry about me. I'm running, too."

Moses shook the hand and returned the smile. "But they'll hang me if they ever find me."

"Well, they'll just shoot me," Jamie replied.

Both men laughed and an instant friendship was formed. Only death would break the bond.

Sitting under the shade of a huge old tree, as they talked, Jamie could easily tell that Moses and his family were having a tough time of it. They were getting by, but just barely. Their clothing was very nearly in rags. But how to offer them help without offending the man's pride?

"You know," Jamie said slowly, thinking as fast and hard as he could. "Come this spring

I sure could use some help in getting in a crop."

"I'm a pretty good farmer," Moses said. "Back in Virginia I could make almost anything grow."

"That's good. I'm not much of a farmer. This might solve another problem for me. You see, me and Kate brought so many supplies with us, I'm afraid one of the barrels of flour is going to be filled with bugs before we could use it. Could you use it?"

"I suppose we could," Moses said slowly. "But I would take it only as part payment for next spring's work."

"That would be fine with me. And we have so many clothes and bolts of cloth, perhaps you could use them."

"Oh, I reckon Liza could put them to use. They sure wouldn't go to waste."

"Well, that's settled then. And when Kate's time comes, she'd sure appreciate it if another woman was present. I sure don't know anything about childbirth."

"Womenfolk like another of their kind with them when they birth," Moses said solemnly. "Liza and Sally will come only a day or two before and stay."

"That's a relief. You have a weapon, Moses?"

"Got a piece of a shotgun."

183

"When you find time, come over. I've got more rifles and pistols than I'll ever need. Horses, too. Some movers tried to kill us over in Arkansas. I didn't figure the dead they left behind would be needing their weapons."

Moses cut his eyes at this young white man. He concluded right then and there that Jamie Ian MacCallister would be a bad enemy to have . . . and a fine friend. "I can shore understand that," he said dryly.

"You'll come over then and let me share with you?"

"Would tomorrow be too soon?"

Kate and Liza and Sally hit it off from the first moment and Moses and Robert and Jed marveled at the newly built cabin in the thicket. Robert inspected every aspect of the work and Jamie could practically hear the wheels turning in the young man's head. He suspected that soon another cabin would replace the one Moses and his sons had hurriedly thrown together.

"Anytime you want to borrow tools, help yourself," Jamie offered.

"Kind of you," Moses said, clearly embarrassed.

"That's what friends and neighbors are for," Jamie replied.

Kate and Liza and Sally were busy sitting in the shade of the dogtrot sewing and taking up clothing for the boys. Jamie put a side of venison on the outside spit and then accompanied Moses as the man showed him the best places in the clearing to plant, and what to plant where.

"I got milk cows," Moses said. "Bring one over for you and some chickens, too. Don't know where the cows come from. We sort of found them on the way out here."

Jamie cut his eyes to the man and smiled. "That was very fortunate."

"We thought so," Moses said, a very slight smile playing on his lips. "Man over in Arkansas had a whole bunch of cows. I reckon them that followed us just figured their boss man, why he had too many and we didn't have naught."

"I'm sure that was it. And the chickens, did they follow along, too?"

"No. How the chickens got here is a strange story. Big wind come up last year. Sort of a cyclone, I guess. Right out of the east. Them chickens just sort of sailed into our yard. Why, you never seen such confused hens. And the roosters was even more confused. Took them chickens two/three days to start layin'. But I reckon they like where they are. Didn't none of them try to go back to where they come from."

"Stranger things have happened, I suppose."

"The Lord does work in mysterious ways."

"Sure does."

Up until the time he had met Jamie, Moses had been relying on traps to snare meat for his family. With the gift of guns from Jamie, he and Robert could now not only have adequate means to hunt the deer and wild pigs that abounded in the thicket, but they had the means to protect themselves against any enemy that might come along.

Jamie and Moses found a place in the thicket where their land very nearly joined. That winter they worked clearing out trees and stumps so their land could join and they could jointly work the fields come that spring, and also make the journey to and from each other's home much easier.

Liza brought the men their nooning one day and smiled at Jamie.

"That smile worries me," Jamie said.

"Me, too," Moses said, staring hard at his wife. "Female type people get sort of mysterious at times. Speak your mind, woman."

"Kate's time is near," Liza said. "And it will be twins."

"*Twins!*" Jamie's mouth dropped open.

186

"Twins," Liza repeated. "I put her to bed and left Sally with her. Tomorrow you will have two more mouths to feed."

"How do you know this?" Jamie questioned.

"Two heartbeats," Lisa replied. "Two childs. One is bigger than the other. A boy and a girl, I am sure." She turned and began the walk back to Jamie's cabin.

"Sometimes women spook me," Jamie said.

"And they always will," Moses added.

The next day, Jamie and Moses were working close to the cabin when Jamie noticed Jed coming at them at a flat run across the cleared field. Jamie and Moses dropped their axes and took off running.

"It's time!" the boy hollered. "Mamma done said the babies is a-comin'."

The three of them raced toward the cabin. They met a very determined Sally standing outside the cabin, a stick in her hand. "You stay out!" she warned the men, menace in her voice. "This ain't no affair of menfolks."

"Damned if that's so, girl," her father said. "How do you think babies is made — by wishin' and hopin'? Stand aside."

Sally raised the stick. "You'd hit me?" Moses asked.

"Mamma tole me to if you tried to come inside. I does what mamma tells me."

"I'll get me a limb and wear your fanny out, girl," the father warned.

"Shut up!" Lisa called from the cabin. "And go away!"

"Do *what,* woman?" Moses yelled.

"Go work on the barn. Go huntin'. Do somethin'. Just go away."

"What do we do, Papa?" Jed asked. Robert was working in a far field and unaware of what was taking place.

"Go away," the father replied. He cast a hard look at his daughter. She raised the stick.

"No respect for elders," Moses said, turning away and he walked toward the half-finished barn "No tellin' what it'll be like a hundred years from now."

THIRTEEN

When Kate screamed, Jamie jumped up and started for the cabin, Sally and stick forgotten. Moses grabbed him by the seat of his britches and hauled him back down to the log bench. "All women holler when they give birth, Jamie. Don't git upset."

"Something must be wrong, Moses!" He jumped up again and Moses grabbed him again. "Turn me loose."

"If something was wrong, Jamie, my woman would have yelled for us. Just settle down. This could take some time."

"But Kate is suffering!"

"We's all born into pain with love, boy. That's the way life begins. Kate probably ain't doin' no more sufferin' than any other birthin' woman. Maybe less than a lot of 'em. Just settle back down."

"I feel like I should be doing something."

"Kate's doin' it for the both of you, boy."

It seemed like hours, but Kate actually

had a quick and relatively easy birth. When Jamie and Moses were finally allowed into the cabin to see Kate and the twins, the babies had been cleaned up and wrapped in soft warm cloth, and Kate was lying on the bed in a clean gown. Liza had washed her face and helped with her hair. But Kate looked tired.

"We have a son and a daughter, Jamie." Jamie was amazed at how strong her voice sounded. "Get the Bible."

Jamie fetched the Bible and quill and well. He entered the date of birth and looked up when it came to names. "Just like we discussed, Jamie," Kate said.

Jamie wrote: *Jamie Ian and Ellen Kathleen. Born in the wilderness of Big Thicket, Texas.* He looked up as Liza placed the babies beside Kate and shooed Moses outside before Kate began nursing them. "You still want eight kids, Kate?"

"More than ever. I want this name of MacCallister to ring clear all over the land." She smiled. "But we'll wait awhile before we start working on that again."

Jamie looked at the twins. "Amazing," he said.

Jamie, Kate, and the twins sat snug in their cabin during the winter. It was amazingly mild, when compared to the winters the young couple had known in their past. Jamie was over at Moses's every day, weather permitting, helping him build a new cabin. He was putting off going to the trading post down south, and Kate was beginning to give him looks that told him he would have to go, and do it quickly.

The weather began turning warmer and Jamie knew he'd have to make the trip for seed — it would be planting time soon — and the trip was necessary for the many things that Kate had listed. He saddled up one of the fine horses left behind by the movers over by the river in Arkansas, and cinched the pack frames on two pack horses. The big black, Lightning, was too recognizable, and Hart Olmstead might have signed arrest warrants against Jamie, describing the horse he rode.

"I still think I should go with you, Jamie," Moses said for the umpteenth time.

"No. It's too risky."

"Young man," Moses said. "I could go as your *slave*. Think about it."

"No." Jamie put cool eyes on him. "Moses? Have you ever killed a man?"

"No."

"I have. Several of them. I wouldn't

hesitate to kill again. Can you truthfully say that?"

"I would kill if my life were threatened," the runaway slave said. "Or the lives of my family."

"Of course, you would. But that's not what I mean and you know it."

Moses sighed and nodded his head. "All right, young Jamie. All right. Which post do you travel?"

"I don't know. I haven't made up my mind. But I think I'm going south. To that trading post north of Pirate City . . . or whatever it's called now."

"When are you leaving?"

"Now."

Jamie kissed Kate and the babies, shook hands with Moses, and pulled out, once more riding into the unknown — alone. He carried two pistols in his waistband, two more in holsters on his saddle, his rifle was at hand, the short-barreled carbine saddle-booted. The trip down was, for the most part, uneventful. Twice he took to cover to avoid groups of mounted men. One of the groups was all dressed up in fancy uniforms, with banners on long poles flapping as they rode. Jamie did not know who they were, and was not that interested in finding out. The other group was a rough-dressed bunch that looked like trouble. Jamie kept to his cover until they were well out of sight.

As he drew nearer to the settlement, he began to see more signs of people, and there was no way he could avoid being seen. But his caution was needless. The people he encountered were all friendly, many of them speaking in a strange language . . . a beautiful language that seemed to flow from their mouths. Jamie had discovered while a Shawnee prisoner that he had a gift for languages. But he knew he had no time for lessons on this trip.

The settlement was a few buildings, and that was all. But the post was large, and Jamie swung down from the saddle by the side of the building. He saw to his horses and then entered the trading post. A familiar smell struck him, the mixture of odors taking him back to Caney's General Store, hundreds of miles away to the north and east. Leather and tobacco and foodstuffs assailed his nostrils as he stepped into the post. One end served as the bar, and half a dozen men lounged there. All turned to look at the tall young man who walked like a big cat.

"Set your rifle over here, son," a man behind the counter said. "You won't need it in here."

"I'll carry it," Jamie told him.

"Suit yourself."

"Boy must be a-skirred," a man at the bar said. "Maybe his mamma just cut him a-loose from her dress-tail."

His companions thought that was very funny. The man behind the counter did not. There was something about this tall young man that spelled trouble with a capital *T*.

Jamie contained the flare of wildness that leaped up strong within him and turned to the counterman, handing him a list. "Would you please fill this?"

"Be glad to. Say! This is quite a list."

"I live a long way off. Don't figure on getting here more than once a year."

"Ain't he polite, now?" one of the rough dressed men at the bar said. He put one hand on his hip and mimicked, *"Please!"*

The counterman watched Jamie's eyes narrow and his features grow taut. And he watched the young man's inner struggle to maintain control. At first he had guessed Jamie's age to be twenty-four or five. Now he revised that, figuring the lad to be no more than twenty-one.

Jamie was in his sixteenth year.

"Which direction you come from, Slim?" the same loudmouth asked.

"South," Jamie replied shortly.

"*South?* Hell, I just heared you say you come a-far. You didn't come far from the south."

"Me and my horses swam over from China."

The counterman and several others in the large store, none of them associated with the thugs at the bar, had a good laugh at that. One of those who saw the humor in it was a well-dressed man of middle age. He had been quietly giving the tall young frontiersman a careful inspection and liked what he saw.

The loudmouth flushed under his tanned and dirty face. "Yeah? Well, I don't think that's a damn bit funny."

Jamie turned slowly and the counterman and the well-dressed man both watched him. There was something in the way that he moved that made both of them think of a big panther, or a huge, stalking timber wolf.

Both men watched the young man once more control his temper. But both knew it was being done with an effort.

"I don't really care what you think," Jamie said evenly. "And where I came from is none of your business, now, is it?"

The lout stiffened in anger. "I just might decide to make it my business."

195

"That is your choice," Jamie replied.

"Bradford," the counterman warned. "I've told you before, I'll not have trouble in my place. Now, by the Lord, back off, man."

"I don't take orders from you, Smith," Bradford said, his back stiff with anger. "This kid is makin' light of me, and I'll have my due respects from him 'fore I'm through."

"I have a thought that you might get more than you bargained for here, Bradford," the well-dressed man said, his words soft.

Bradford turned to him. "Nor do I need advice from the likes of you, Fontaine. When I want advice from a damn Injun lover, I'll ask for it."

The well-dressed man did not take offense. Instead, he merely smiled. "Bradford, I think before this moment passes, you will never need advice from anyone again."

Bradford blinked, the message in those words going right by him. He shook his head and turned back to Jamie, who had turned his back to him and was shopping for something for Kate.

"Boy!" Bradford's tone was sharp. "You do not turn your ass to me."

Bradford did not see the tight smile briefly pass Jamie's lips. The lout had no way of seeing into Jamie's soul; of being a witness to the cold savage wildness welling up within him. The ruffian had no way of knowing how close he stood to death. Jamie turned, ever so slowly and faced the man. His blue eyes blazed with fury.

Jamie said, "Sir, I do not know who you are, nor do I care. But you are pushing me. And I do not like to be pushed. I beg you to leave me alone. I will say no more on the matter."

He once more turned to look at a glass case containing women's brooches and other foofaraws that women liked so much. Jamie heard boots thud against the floor and watched in the reflection from the glass as the angry man rushed toward him. Just as he could smell the whiskey on the man's breath and the smell of his unwashed body, just as he watched the man reach for him, Jamie drove the butt of his rifle into the man's stomach. The air whooshed out of the man and he doubled over, dropping to his knees on the floor. Jamie returned his gaze to the assortment of jewelry.

Fontaine smiled. He had been right in his assessment of the lad. This young man was one calm and collected person to be so young.

Bradford struggled to his feet, one hand holding his bruised belly. The hand hovered near the butt of a pistol jammed behind his wide belt.

"Don't," Jamie warned him, his tone icy cold. "I wish no further trouble with you. Just leave me alone."

Bradford looked about him. The others in the store, except for his few equally dirty and untidy friends at the plank bar, were frowning at him. Several of the men had their hands ready to jerk pistols in defense of the tall young man. The women in the store had taken cover behind counters.

"You put that rifle down and step outside," Bradford threw down the challenge. "We'll settle this man to man."

"Fists or knives?" Jamie asked coolly.

Fontaine smiled and cut his eyes to Smith, standing behind the counter. Smith minutely nodded his head in silent agreement.

Bradford was taken aback by the coldness of the question.

"Watch him, young man," a man called from the depths of the store. "He's a bad one."

"No," Jamie said. "He just smells bad, that's all."

Bradford cried out and jumped at Jamie, one big fist swinging at Jamie's head. Jamie caught the arm, one strong hand gripping the wrist and the other hand gripping the forearm, turned, and threw the angry thug over his hip and shoulder. Bradford landed near the doors with a thud that shook the contents of the shelves.

Several men customers drew their pistols and faced Bradford's friends. One of them held out his hands. "It's his fight. We'll not interfere. But Bradford was only funnin' with the lad. There was no need for it to go this far."

Jamie laid his rifle on the counter. "Keep an eye on that for me, please, sir. I shall be back in a moment." Jamie stepped around the still addled Bradford and walked outside. He stood in the road, waiting.

"Bradford," one of the men at the bar called, as the fallen thug was getting slowly to his boots. "Return to the bar and have a drink. Don't pursue that lad. There's something almighty queer about this."

"Sound advice, Bradford," Fontaine said. "Take it."

"You go to hell!" Bradford said, and stormed out the open doors. He hit the covered porch on the run and threw himself at Jamie.

Jamie sidestepped and Bradford kissed the dirt of the road, landing on his belly and face and knocking the wind from himself. He crawled to his knees, spitting out dirt and fouling the air with his wild cursing.

The customers in the store all gathered on the porch, well-dressed gentlemen, buckskin-clad men, and ladies with parasols. Entertainment was where one found it in the young settlement.

"You'll die for this!" Bradford said.

Jamie said nothing. He stood in the road and waited. Bradford rushed him, making the same mistake as before. Jamie tripped the man and sent him stumbling along like a drunkard. Bradford recovered only when a hitchrail stopped him. He caught his breath and turned around, finally learning his lesson. He raised his fists and advanced slowly toward Jamie.

When Bradford drew close, Jamie suddenly leaped at the man, both his moccasins striking the older man in the chest and knocking him to the ground. Jamie landed gracefully on his feet and waited.

No one noticed the lone dusty rider who had come in from the north and dismounted. He now stood watching the fight with undisguised interest.

Angry to his core, for he was known throughout as a rough and tumble fighter who rarely was bested, Bradford lost all sense of reason and charged Jamie, wanting to crush the life from the tall young man.

Jamie stopped the man cold with a crashing right fist that pulped the man's lips and sprayed blood. Jamie followed that with a left to the stomach and another right to Bradford's jaw that rocked the man back. Jamie hammered at the lout with lefts and rights that smashed his nose, split the skin under his eyes, and knocked out several teeth. As Bradford stood nearly helpless, swaying in the road, Jamie struck him over the heart and Bradford's face paled with the sometimes deadly blow. Jamie back-heeled the man and sent him tumbling to the ground.

"No more, lad!" Fontaine called from the porch. "You'll kill the man."

Jamie turned, his blue eyes cold. "And that would be a loss to this community?"

"Nay, lad," Smith called. "But the man is down now. He can't get up."

Jamie looked at the battered and bloody man lying in the dust of the street. Bradford was near unconsciousness. Jamie turned his back to him and walked to the porch and then into the store.

Smith turned to Bradford's shocked friends. "Get him out of the street and see to him. And don't return here until you can conduct yourselves with some degree of civility." He followed Jamie into the store and set about filling the young man's shopping list.

"The lad is a cool one," Fontaine remarked, as he watched Bradford's friends drag the man off to the shade of a tree.

"Aye," a man agreed. "The kind we need in this country . . . when the time comes."

"Curb your tongue," Fontaine said, cutting his eyes all about him. "Words of Texas independence falling on the wrong ears means death in the night. I shall befriend this young man and sound him out."

A few buildings away, the lone rider had slapped the dust from his clothing and was walking toward the huge general store. He carried two pistols behind his waistband. That in itself was not unusual, for most men carried at least one pistol and oftentimes several of them. It was the way this man carried them: the butt of each pistol facing forward and slanted toward the other, enabling the man to draw with either hand.

And the placement of the pistols did not escape the attention of Jamie as the man walked into the store. He had learned long ago to miss nothing. Jamie put some tobacco on the counter for Moses — the ex-slave made his own pipes — and watched as the pile of articles began to grow.

"You must really live a long way off, lad?"

Smith said with a smile.

Jamie returned the smile. If he was a bit ruffled by the savage fight he'd just been in — savage for Bradford, not for him — he did not show it. Fact is, he wasn't. "A very long way," he said.

And Smith knew he was not about to get more out of the lad. But he did know by what Jamie was purchasing that he was buying for several women and babies. And for several men, judging by the clothing sizes.

Smith noticed the stranger edging closer to Jamie, pretending to be looking at goods. And he knew that Jamie was very aware of the man. The lad's eyes had lost their friendliness and had taken on that cold frosty look once more.

"Quite a fight out there," the stranger spoke from just behind Jamie. "Where'd you learn to fight like that?"

"From my father and his friends," Jamie replied. Not exactly a lie, for Tall Bull had adopted him.

"Queer way of fightin'. Don't see many white men fight like that."

"Whatever it takes to win."

"You know a mite of Injun wrestlin', I'd say."

"Could be." Jamie tensed as the man moved closer.

The ladies had not reentered the store after the fight, choosing to be escorted back to their homes, and the place was empty except for Smith, who owned it, and Fontaine, who was one of Austin's men and who, back when he was working openly for the U.S. government, had been one of those instrumental in persuading the pirate, Lafitte, to leave Galveztown, as it was then called, only a few years back.

Smith said, "Can I help you, Mister?"

"No. But Jamie here can."

Jamie smiled. This did not come as a surprise; he knew he'd be found eventually, for Kate's father was a vengeful man, and hate ran strong in him. And Caddo Indians had told Jamie that while visiting over across the river in Louisiana they'd heard that Jamie had a price on his head.

He lifted his eyes to Smith. "I'm no highwayman, sir. And I killed in self-defense. Killed one of the men who beat and raped a dear friend of mine. I suspect that my wife's father has placed a bounty on my head for running off with his daughter. Is that not true, Mr. Whoever-You-Are?"

"You're comin' back to Kaintuck with me, Jamie Ian MacCallister," the man said.

"I doubt it," Jamie said calmly. Jamie's right hand was hidden from the bounty hunter by his body and from Smith by the rough counter. Only Fontaine saw him slip the razor-sharp knife from the sheath. "How much is Olmstead paying you for this travesty of justice?"

"That ain't none of your concern."

"How about Kate, my wife?"

"Mr. Olmstead don't want no more to do with that slut. She's on her own."

Smith and Fontaine both shook their heads at the callousness of the father.

"But you're goin' back, one way or 'tother, MacCallister. Alive, or with your stinkin' head in a sack for proof."

The man's hand flew to the butt of a pistol and Jamie whirled, his knife flashing, cutting the man from side to side, the blade sinking deep.

The bounty hunter screamed hideously and fell to the floor, the blood gushing from him. He put both hands to his stomach in a futile attempt to stop the blood. He looked up at Jamie. "Damn your eyes! You've killed me!"

Jamie wiped his blade clean and sheathed his knife. "I didn't start this. You did."

"You . . . You won't get away. There are others with me. They'll . . ." The man fell back, stretching out on the floor. Jamie's knife had cut deep, ripping vital organs.

"I'd have done the same, lad," Fontaine was the first to speak. "You had no choice."

"None at all," Smith agreed. "He's fair done for. We don't have a doctor anyway."

"No doctor would do this one any good," Fontaine said.

"Goddamn you, MacCallister!" the dying man cursed.

"Here now!" Smith admonished. "That's no way to depart this life to stand before your Maker."

The bounty hunter mouthed a terrible oath.

"I didn't want this," Jamie said. "I'll stand before the court of law and plead my case."

Fontaine gave a short humorless bark and Smith chuckled grimly. "*What* courts of law, Jamie?" the store owner said. "We have no law here. Not to speak of. I'll have my people carry the body out and bury it. No one need ever know of this. I'll fetch my manservants. Close and bar the front door, Louis. Then Jamie can tell us his story." Smith walked to the rear of the store and called out, then returned to the counter.

Jamie looked down at the now dead man. "I just wanted to be left alone with Kate and the babies."

"And you shall be, Jamie," Fontaine said, walking back from barring the door. "We need men like you in this country. Your secret is safe with us. I promise you that."

"Why?" Jamie asked.

Smith threw a ragged blanket over the dead man. "Because men like you are going to have to settle this land. Strong men, brave men, men who will stand and fight for what they believe in. Not human vultures like this wretch on the floor, who feed off the misery and misfortune of others. No bad man buys candy and foofaraws and geegaws for kids and women. No bad person lays in supplies for others first and buys nothing for himself. That's why."

Two Indians came silently in from the back and Jamie signed with them. Their eyes shone their approval and they spoke silently with their hands for a moment.

"Man Who Is Not Afraid," one finally said in English. "Man Who Tames Wolves and Panthers. We heard you were here."

"What?" Fontaine said, his eyes holding a puzzled look. "What's this?"

"It's a long story," Jamie said, as the Indians picked up the body and walked out the rear of the store.

"They'll bury him deep in the woods," Smith said, working at the blood stains with a wet mop. "His horse has already been taken outside of town."

How many more dead men lie before me? Jamie questioned his mind. How many more before I can live in peace?

"Do you be careful on the ride back to hearth and home, Jamie," Smith said. "For he said he had others with him."

"I'll be careful," Jamie said. "Kate's waiting for me."

FOURTEEN

Jamie packed up his supplies and left that afternoon, first heading west, then cutting north when he was a few miles out of the settlement. He still wasn't sure why Smith and Fontaine had been so quick to help him, only that he was glad they did. But he trusted the men. He had told them his story, and neither man had pressed him as to where he lived. They had simply accepted him for what he was.

One thing Jamie was sure of: he could not return to the Big Thicket until he dealt with the dead bounty hunter's friends. He could not lead his enemies back to home territory and risk Kate and the babies getting hurt.

He knew what he had to do, and just the thought of it was disturbing to him, leaving a bitter, coppery taste in his mouth.

He was going to have to find and kill those other bounty hunters. Or let them find him.

In the 1820s East Texas was virtually an

unbroken sea of forests, dotted only by a few meadows where the soil wasn't quite right for trees. The Caddoan Indians had cleared small patches of land for farming, and the few white settlers living there had done the same. But in the mid-1820s, East Texas was a magnificent forested sight, with game abounding, from deer to wolf. Jamie knew the woods, and could survive in them even should he be faced with no supplies nor weapons. Here, one could eat one's fill of persimmons and pawpaws, make tea of the sassafras root, lotions of witch hazel, and fragrant candles of the bayberries.

Jamie, not yet wishing for a campfire, breakfasted on a handful of chinquapin nuts, those tasty morsels enclosed in prickly burrs, then followed that treat with berries and a drink of cold spring water. He checked his guns, then climbed a tall hardwood tree and carefully looked in all directions. One lone finger of smoke drifted upward, from a few miles to the east, the direction he must travel. He had no doubts as to what the smoke represented: the bounty hunters.

Jamie climbed down and saddled up. He booted his long-barreled rifle and chose the shorter-barreled Army carbine. It was of a heavier caliber and carried a fearsome recoil, but the big ball was a man-stopper, capable of inflicting grievous wounds.

Fontaine had told him of a little settlement north of his present location, where whites were settling around an old Spanish mission, and where a sawmill had been operating since 1819. The settlement was called Nacogdoches, after a local Indian tribe. Fontaine had said that for his next supply run, Jamie should go there and make contact with a man; Fontaine said he would send word for the man to be expecting Jamie in a few months.

But for now, Jamie had a more pressing matter to deal with. The bounty hunter had not said how many friends he had with him; but in this day and time, no one but the most foolhardy, adventurous, or skilled traveled the frontier alone, and Jamie did not think the bounty hunter was very skilled. Three or four more, he guessed.

He traveled a couple of miles, following a game path, until coming to a place his eyes had been seeking: a tiny glen where his horses and supplies would be safe. It was a natural corral. There was a small creek and graze enough for what he had to do. Should he fail, the horses would eventually break free and wander.

From a hardened leather case, he removed

his bow and strung it. He did not have to inspect his arrows. He had made them and knew they would fly true. He spoke softly to his horses and comforted them, petting each one and allowing them to nuzzle him. Then the boy/man slipped into the lush and quiet forest, his moccasins making no sound as he set about his deadly business.

He did not like what he was about to do, but felt he had no choice in the matter. He would have preferred to live and let live. But Olmstead and Jackson had now made that impossible by sending armed men after him, with orders to bring him back alive, or kill him and bring back his head in a sack.

So be it.

The Shawnees had trained Jamie brutally hard, but well. He was the consummate guerrilla fighter. It had been said of the Shawnees, that when it came to camouflage, the only way you could tell a Shawnee from a tree or bush was to look closely to see if the tree or bush had eyes. Jamie had muddied his face and leafed and vined his person with green. He was death, making his way slowly through the lushness of forest.

He could now smell the woodsmoke and taste the odor of food cooking. With each step, he moved no more than a few inches, stopping, the only movement his eyes. He was surprised at the number of men. He counted six. Then he smiled. Olmstead must be very afraid of him to send so many. If these men were really after him. Of that, he must be sure. He moved closer, taking twenty minutes to cover a hundred feet and another half hour to come within easy hearing distance of the dirty and loutish-looking lot.

"Hankins should have been back by now," the voice drifted to him. "Somethin's gone awry."

"Aye," another said. "Or else he's killed the boy and taken the head back alone, to claim the bounty for himself."

The men were silent for a moment. "Yeah, Clarence," one finally spoke. "He might just do that."

"I think the kid got him," another one said.

"I say nay to that, Cabot. This kid don't have the sand to take Hankins."

Jamie was sure now that he would not be ambushing pioneers on their way west to settle a new land. These men had come to take him back or kill him and cut off his head. Jamie moved closer, the sounds of their talking and arguing covering any slight noise he might make.

When he was in easy pistol range, he cocked the pistols, one at a time, covering the sound with a hand, and then leveled them. He had recharged his guns before leaving the glen, double shotting each pistol.

"Me and Kate just wanted to be left alone," he muttered, then pulled the triggers.

The double report was enormous and when the smoke had cleared, three of the brigands were down by the fire. One had been shot in the center of the face and he was dead. The other two had taken a ball or two in the chest and stomach and were thrashing around, making fearsome noises.

Jamie shifted positions quickly, not taking the time to reload just yet. He still had his short-barreled rifle fully charged, but Jamie figured from this point on, it would be arrow or blade. But he planned on discharging his rifle against one of the bounty hunters before settling down with bow and arrow. Jamie knew it would be useless to even think about wounding those hunting him. That would accomplish nothing. He had to finish this, here and now.

One of those back at the campsite had ceased his moaning, but the other one was shrieking hideously. Jamie ignored the sound and concentrated on the woods all

214

around him. He silently cocked his rifle and waited motionless in the tangle of brush and tall virgin trees.

"Do you think it's Injuns, Clarence?" the call sprang out of the forest to Jamie's right.

"No, Cabot, I don't. I think it's that damn MacCallister kid."

"Then . . ." The third voice trailed off.

"That's right, Dick. He got Hankins."

The one called Dick cursed Jamie, very loud, long, and violently. He had some terrible things to say about Jamie. Dick was on the other side of the small clearing. Jamie shifted ever so slowly, until he was facing where the sound of Dick's voice had come. He slowly pulled the rifle to his shoulder and waited. One of them would move first; he was sure of that. He knew he wouldn't.

"Kid?" the call came from the position where the one called Clarence had last spoken. "Kid, I know you ain't goin' to answer, but listen to me. What's done is done. There don't have to be no more killin'. Let us go and you'll not see us again."

Jamie wanted to believe the man meant it, but he knew in his heart that could not be. He could not let them go back to Olmstead and Jackson and tell of them finding him. Olmstead's hate ran deep as any dark river,

215

and just about as unstoppable.

"What say you, MacCallister?" Clarence called.

Jamie remained silent.

When Clarence called again, Jamie knew the man had been lying. For his position had changed; he was working closer to where he'd seen the smoke from Jamie's pistols.

But Jamie was far away from that spot. Jamie sighed silently and waited. The third man in the clearing had fallen silent, either dead or unconscious.

Then the man called Dick got careless. He shifted slightly and exposed part of one dirty pant leg. He was behind a thick flowering bush that Jamie had seen before but did not know what it was called. Jamie studied the bush for a long moment, finally being able to make out Dick's shape. The fool was squatting instead of lying belly down. Jamie sighted him in, slowly took up slack on the trigger, and his rifle boomed.

Jamie instantly changed position, having already worked that move out in his mind. Two rifles roared, the balls slamming into the area where Jamie had just vacated. Jamie quickly reloaded his rifle and pistols, again double-shotting the pistols. He thought about his bow, and then rejected that idea.

The brush was just too thick. This would be settled with guns.

There was no sound from Dick. The man was either unconscious or dead, probably the latter.

"Pretty good, kid," Clarence called softly, the whisper deceptive as to his location. "Olmstead and Jackson said you'd be easy. But I kinda doubted that right off. I figure you got Hankins, so that makes you a dangerous one. Hankins was a manhunter, and a good one."

He kept talking, and Jamie sensed that the other one, Cabot, was circling while Clarence rattled on. Jamie slithered away on his belly, crawling under bushes and low foliage, hoping he would not come nose to nose with a big rattlesnake. Once his quiver of arrows caught on a vine and the leaves shook softly. Jamie lay still for a thirty count, but no shots came his way. He moved on, working in a half circle. Then he saw Cabot just ahead of him, squatting at the edge of a tiny clearing. Jamie slowly drew himself up on one knee, his bow in his hands, arrow notched. He pulled back and let fly, the arrow driving deep into the man's chest. Cabot's mouth opened, but no sound came out. He toppled over, dead, the arrow through his heart.

Jamie whirled as the bushes rattled behind him. Clarence was rushing at him, both hands filled with pistols, but the bushes prevented a clear shot. Jamie rolled to one side and jammed out with his bow. The brigand's legs got all tangled up in the bow and down he came, landing heavily on his belly. One pistol discharged, the ball digging up dirt inches from Jamie's face. Jamie thrust his bow again with all his considerable strength and a horrible, gurgling sound filled the soft forest air. The second pistol discharged harmlessly into the air. He pulled his bow back and looked at it. One end, about six inches up the wood, was slick with blood.

He jerked out a pistol and cocked it, but it was not needed. Clarence lay on his back, both hands holding onto his neck, trying to stop the gushing blood. The tip of Jamie's bow had entered the man's throat at the soft hollow and rammed all the way through the back of his neck.

The bounty hunter tried to speak, but could not. Jamie looked down at him, no pity in his eyes. "You should have left me alone," he said.

Clarence gurgled at him.

"I'll bury you all," Jamie said. "I shouldn't, but I will. But I won't ask the Lord for any favors on your behalf."

Clarence pulled out a knife and tried to throw it at Jamie. Jamie kicked it out of the man's hand before he could hurl it.

Jamie shook his head and walked away, after picking up the man's weapons and removing his powder horn and shot pouch. From the amount of blood the man was losing, he would be dead in a little while.

Jamie inspected all the dead, remembering what Preacher had told him. "Don't leave nothin' behind that's valuable, Jamie. They're dead and you ain't. You and yours can use it, and they cain't. So take it."

Jamie didn't like doing it, but he saw the practicality in it. He took all the money on the men, and it was a surprising tidy sum after all was counted. He found their horses and was delighted, for they were fine mounts, and one of them had not been cut and the lone mare among them was a beautiful animal. And, to his surprise, he found several pack horses with their loads already racked and ready to toss on and cinch up. They must have just resupplied at the trading post to the north. Added to what he'd bought, they now had supplies to last for months.

Jamie took the brand new shovel he'd just purchased at the trading post and dug a large common grave, dragging the bodies over and toppling them in; there was no respectful way to do it. He covered the dead, jammed a crude cross he'd made into the earth, and turned to walk away. Then, with a sigh, he returned to the mound of earth and took off his battered hat. "Lord, I give them to You. I don't know what else to say."

Then he set about packing up all the guns and supplies and getting the horses ready for the trail. He had a long way to go, and was anxious to get there. He would tell Kate everything that happened, for they had vowed never to hide anything from the other.

In the saddle, he looked back at the mound of earth for a moment. "I just wanted to be left alone. That's all."

Kate and Liza and Sally oohhed and aahhed and carried on so much about the stuff Jamie had bought it got embarrassing for him. He finally went out to sit in the dogtrot with Moses.

"Gonna tell Miss Kate about your troubles on the trail, Jamie?"

"What do you mean?"

"You got blood on your shirt and britches, Jamie. How many set upon you?"

"Seven, all told."

Moses stiffened in the wood-and-hide chair. *"Seven!"*

"They're dead. I doubt anyone will ever find the bodies. But I did bury them and speak words over the grave."

"Seven!"

Moses was astonished and could not hide that emotion. While the runaway slave liked and trusted the young man, no more than a boy, really, he found his calmness in discussing his killing of seven men disquieting and disturbing.

Jamie's eyes were cool and calm on Moses. "They came after me, Moses. They were to bring me back alive, if possible, or kill me and cut off my head and bring it back in a sack as proof. I could not wound them and let them return to Olmstead and Jackson. They would have sent more men after me. They probably will anyway, but this way they don't know where I am. So what choice did I have, Moses?"

The ex-slave thought about that for a moment or two. He slowly nodded his head in agreement. "None, young Jamie. But. . . let me ask you this: do you feel anything about the deaths of those men?"

"No," Jamie was quick to reply. "They came after me, Moses. I'm not going to drape myself in sackcloth and ashes and flay myself over the deaths of hired killers. You've got to overcome your natural, and understandable, fear of the white man, Moses. If not your distrust; for which I certainly can't fault you. We both have a chance to start over here. I think we can have a fresh start and live out our lives here, and prosper, to some degree. I have no desire for great wealth, and I know you don't, either. We both want basically the same things: a roof over our heads that doesn't leak, a warm snug cabin, clothing for our backs, food for our families, and peace. You can probably attain the latter. I think that will never come for me."

Moses was silent. He cut his eyes to Jamie, waiting for an explanation.

"Texas will fight for independence someday, and I think I shall be a part of that fight. I believe that is why Smith and Fontaine befriended me at the trading post. At least part of the reason."

Moses said nothing. His own life as a slave had been brutal and sometimes savage, but he could clearly remember having a childhood, even though he had to work. He still had time to play, go fishing, swimming, attend worship services, and listen to the old people tell stories in the cool of the evening after the work in the fields was over. Jamie had missed all that. One day he was a boy, the next day he was thrown into adulthood, forced to use all his wits to survive. Moses had never been savagely beaten; he'd seen very little of that on the Virginia plantation where he'd been worked and played. Only a very foolish white man would pay hundreds of dollars for a strong slave and then mistreat him to the point where the slave could not work. Moses Washington, ex-slave who would be hanged or horsewhipped to death if ever found, suddenly realized that he felt sorry for Jamie Ian MacCallister. Moses realized that, in an odd way, he was more free than Jamie.

Kate and Liza and Sally came out to join the men. They brought coffee and cups and little cakes just baked. Robert and Jed were over at Moses's place, seeing to chores. Before Jamie could tell them what had happened on his journey, Kate unexpectedly said, "Someday, Jamie, you might have to kill my father and probably my brothers, as well. It does not matter. For they are all long dead in my mind. My own brothers tried to rape me during your absence, Jamie," she finally admitted something that Jamie had suspected all along. "Several times I had to run away from them and stay gone for days.

Twice I slept in the woods with the beasts. I assure you, I much preferred their company to the company of my family. Now I'm sure my father has disowned me. They are all vile, evil people. We won't talk of this again."

Jamie had brought back some real sugar, and they all savored the sweetness in their coffee, sitting quietly together, enjoying each other's company, amid the beauty and silent grandeur of the Big Thicket.

All around them, events were slowly taking place that would lead to, in less than ten years time, thirteen days of a standoff in an old mission that would become a part of world history. But the fugitives in the dark reaches of the Big Thicket knew nothing of that now. They were cognizant only of the day-to-day survival that faced them. Of them all, only Jamie really knew in his heart that Olmstead and Jackson would never give up. Kate thought that he might, someday, have to kill her father and brothers. Jamie knew that just as surely as the sun rose in the east that day faced him. There was no "might" or "perhaps" about it.

One of the twins began to cry for attention and Kate and Sally rose to see to the child. Moses looked at Jamie. "Another slave family come into the area while you were gone, Master Jamie," he said.

"Stop calling me master, Moses. I'm not your master. Have you met them?"

"Yes. They're of high color. They ran away because neither world would accept them."

"That's stupid. People are people. We all bleed the same color. You're telling me they have white blood in them."

"A lot of white blood."

"Is that supposed to make a difference to me?"

"I didn't know how you felt on the subject."

Jamie really didn't either. He knew only that if two people of different color wanted to marry, that was their business. But he knew that both those people had better understand what kind of price their children would have to pay in a world that frowned on such things. He said as much.

"Then we think alike," Liza said. "It ain't fair to saddle the children with such a burden. Not now and probably won't never be."

"Woman . . ." Moses said.

"Don't woman me," his wife warned him. "Eagles don't mate with sparrows and bears don't mate with bobcats. God made it that way. White man takes up with an Indian woman, given time, most whites will accept it. Won't never accept black and white. Not now, not never. Only a foolish or uppity nigger thinks otherwise. Them poor children over yonder has got a terrible burden to bear."

"What am I missing here?" Jamie asked.

"Two of the kids is more white than black," Moses said. "They gonna have to try to pass later on."

Jamie looked more confused than ever.

"They'll try to enter the white world as white," Liza cleared it up.

Jamie could surely understand why they would want to try. Blacks received terrible treatment at the hands of many whites. Jamie suddenly looked up, as the faint sounds of hooves reached his ears. One horse. Since he always took different trails to his cabin, and he knew he had never been followed, he had no idea who the person might be.

He looked at Moses. The man nodded his head, but did not seem at all alarmed. "Egg comes," he said.

"Egg?"

"Head of the Cherokee police. He is Chief Diwali's right-hand man. He is also called the Enforcer."

"Is he coming to try to arrest me?"

Moses smiled. "The Egg, or The Hawk, as he is sometimes called, does not *try* to do anything, Young Jamie. But no, I do not think he comes to arrest you. For killing seven bad white men he probably might try to give you some award."

"I gather he knew all along that Kate and me were here?"

"The Cherokee police miss very little, Jamie."

"The Mexican government allows this?"

"The Mexican government made Chief Diwali a colonel in their army. That answer your question?"

"Yes." Jamie watched the lone rider exit the timber and ride slowly toward the cabin. "That's the biggest damn horse I think I've ever seen!"

"Wait until you see the man riding it," Liza spoke.

He was the biggest Indian Jamie had ever seen. Egg, or Hawk, must have weighed two hundred and seventy-five pounds if he weighed an ounce. The horse he rode was a dray animal, and Jamie wondered where he got it. Kate and Sally came out, both with a baby in their arms.

Jamie stood up and made the sign for peace. The huge Indian gave no indication that he understood or gave a damn if he did understand . . . and since the sign was almost universal, Jamie was certain he did.

Egg carried a rifle in his left hand, and pistols stuck behind a wide belt. He sat his horse and stared at Jamie. His eyes were unreadable.

"Would you like to dismount and have something to eat and drink with us?" Jamie asked in English.

Egg cocked his rifle and raised it, the muzzle pointed straight at Jamie's chest.

FIFTEEN

Jamie tensed, but forced himself to continue to stare into the eyes of the Cherokee policeman. Then, to everyone's surprise, Egg began to chuckle. He carefully lowered the hammer on his rifle as the chuckle turned into a deep laugh. He dismounted with that peculiar grace that some big men have and leaned his rifle against the house.

"Man Who Is Not Afraid," he said, in nearly perfect English. "Is truly not afraid. That is good." He looked around him and grunted in approval. "You have done well. I thought you would and told Diwali so when I first visited here after you came." He smiled. "I have been here several times since then. Now, as to the matter which brought me here. I would stay away from those who would try to wrest this land from Mexico." He shrugged as only a Cherokee can. "But . . . that is your decision to make. I am here to tell you that you fought bravely and well in the woods north of the trading post owned by Smith and frequented often by Fontaine. Those were bad men who sought you out. They came to do you harm and you did what any warrior would do. That is all I have to say. You might see me again. You might not see me again. I cannot foretell the future. Hello, Moses Washington. Hello, Liza and Sally. Hello, Kate and the babies. Goodbye."

He picked up his rifle, mounted the huge horse, and without another word, rode out of the clearing and into the timber at the edge of the swamp.

"My word!" was all Kate could say. Then she frowned and looked at Jamie. "*What* fight in the woods, Jamie?"

"Well . . . Kate . . . ah . . . I was going to tell you. I really was."

Moses stood up quickly. "Time to go, Liza, Sally. We've got to be gettin' back to our cabin."

"*What* fight, Jamie Ian?" Kate demanded, sitting down in the chair just vacated by Moses.

Sally put Ellen Kathleen in Jamie's lap and quickly exited the area with her parents.

"Good luck," Moses called over his shoulder, as he and family headed for the path that would take them to their cabin. "You're gonna need it," he muttered.

"Thanks," Jamie said.

"Well?" Kate demanded.

Jamie took a deep breath. Sixteen or sixty, he thought, sometimes marriage is tough.

The summer passed uneventfully, the crops were up and looking good, no one was hurt or fell sick to any terrible illness, other than the babies coming down with the croup, which Jamie treated and eventually healed by the use of plants found in and around the Big Thicket, including coltsfoot and licorice root.

Shortly after his return from the coast, Jamie met the newest family to settle in the Big Thicket area, the runaway slave family from Alabama, Titus and Ophelia Jefferson. And Moses had certainly been correct: two of their three children — the twins, Roscoe and Anne — were white. They had absolutely no negroid features. The twins were four. Wells was about Jamie's age.

That Titus did not trust Jamie was plain. He hated whites and did not attempt to hide that. He had been a rebellious slave, and had suffered mightily because of it. Jamie shrugged off Titus's dislike and went his own way. Titus could either accept the help that Jamie freely offered, or he could go to hell. They were all starting over here, and as far as Jamie was concerned, what was past was over and done with.

"He has a right to be bitter," Robert Washington told Jamie one day, during a break in the hoeing of crops.

"I think I'm going to get very weary of hearing that," Jamie replied, conscious of the hot look Robert gave him. "My parents were killed by the Shawnee and I was taken prisoner and held as a slave, worked and beaten as much or more as Titus. But I don't hate all Indians. People who hate will always find some excuse to do that."

"You're white. You don't understand," Robert said. "Your people weren't torn from their homeland and brought over here in chains."

"No," Jamie replied, remembering some of what his father had told him as a child. "That's right. My people were just run out of their country because of their religious beliefs. It's over, Robert. Behind us."

Robert threw down the hoe and stalked off, his back stiff with anger. They all were working in Moses's fields that day, and Sally brought out a gourd of water for Jamie. "What's wrong with Robert?" she asked.

"Oh, he's angry with me because I won't beg Titus to take my help."

"That whole family is trouble," the young woman said. "All except for Wells."

Jamie hid his smile, knowing that Sally was sweet on Titus's oldest son. He drank the cool water and offered no comment. Titus had thrown together a shack a few miles away and had bitterly and with open hostility refused Jamie's repeated offers of help. Jamie had made up his mind that he would offer no more. He thanked Sally and watched her walk away. She was a good-looking young woman and he expected that she would marry Wells. Wells had quarreled with his father and stormed out of the shack, building — with the help of Moses and Jamie — his own snug and small cabin in the Thicket. Wells was eager to work for Jamie and Moses, and was a fine hand, easygoing, quick to smile and joke, and hardworking.

Jamie finished his row and walked over to Wells, working on the far side of the field with Moses. Moses leaned on his hoe and said, "We might have some trouble comin' our way, Jamie."

"How so?"

"Wells told me that his pa's gone back east. He didn't know it until this mornin' when he went over to see his ma. He's gonna bring back some slave families that's hidin' out over 'crost the Sabine."

"That's all right with me, Moses," Jamie said, puzzled at the ex-slave's attitude.

"You don't understand, Mr. Jamie," Wells said. Jamie had tried to get him to stop calling him "Mr. Jamie," but so far had not succeeded.

"I guess I don't," Jamie admitted. "You know I don't hold with slavery."

"I know you don't, Jamie. But the ones Titus has gone to fetch are bad ones, Jamie," Moses explained. "They're followers of Nat Turner."

"Who is Nat Turner?"

"Well," Moses took off what passed for a hat and scratched his graying head. "I guess I could say he's just a Virginia slave who wants to be free, but that wouldn't tell it all. He hates all whites. Maybe with good reason; I don't know. But if Titus brings those people in here, you and Kate and the babies will be in danger. But that ain't all. If them runaways come in, the whites will be sure to come after them . . . then we'll all be in trouble."

Jamie leaned on his hoe and thought about that for a moment. "There's more, right?"

Moses nodded his head. "Some slave owners in Mississippi and Alabama has commissioned a group of men to bring back their slaves. For each runaway slave they bring back alive, they're payin' twenty-five cents a pound. You know a good slave sells for five hundred dollars and up."

"No, I didn't know that. That's disgusting. And where are you getting all this information?"

Moses smiled. "You know the Indians travel and bring back stories. Some are true and some aren't. This one is. Those men who hunt down runaway slaves is under the command of a man named Jackson. And Olmstead has moved down into Southern Louisiana. He's a slave dealer now, and makin' a fortune. Jackson's right-hand men are two sets of brothers, named Saxon and Newby."

"Oh, *shit!*" Jamie shouted, throwing down his hoe.

"Yassur, master," Moses mush-mouthed and rolled his eyes and hung his head and shuffled his feet, a twinkle in his eyes, knowing how Jamie hated it when he joked like that.

"Stop that, Moses," Jamie said. "That isn't funny."

But both Wells and Moses laughed, knowing that Jamie did not understand black slave humor. The mush-mouthing, eye-rolling, head-hanging, and foot-shuffling was one way the slaves could ridicule their white owners and the slave owners couldn't do a damn thing about it because they didn't know what was going on.

Jamie shook his head and waited for the men to settle down. When they had sobered, he asked, "And what do you propose doing about this situation?"

It was obvious to Jamie that the men had discussed this more than once, for they exchanged glances several times before Moses finally spoke. "We have to stop them from flooding into this area, Jamie. Not the good, decent slaves who are running for their freedom; but the ones who want to start some sort of black-and-white war."

"That is a war that the negro will never win, Moses. Not now, not a hundred and fifty years from now. Hear me well, both of you. For I know better than you about such matters. There are, or were, far more Indians than whites east of the Mississippi. Look at them now. You either conform to the white man's ways, or eventually, the white man will destroy you." He turned to Wells. "Are you telling me that you would take up arms against your own father?"

"I don't know that, Jamie. That's an honest answer. But I do know that he has to be stopped from floodin' this place with angry, runaway slaves who want only to kill whites."

"I see. Yes. In other words, you both want me to do your killing for you?"

"Jamie," Moses said.

"No!" Jamie's reply was hard. "We're either in this together, or not at all. I'm not some Hessian mercenary with my gun and sword for hire. Now what say you both?"

Wells looked sick and Moses's eyes held a haunted look. Jamie knew the turmoil within them must be terrible; Wells because he was faced with taking up arms against flesh and blood, Moses because he was a man of color being forced to decide whether to fight against his own people . . . and he might have to fight his own son, Robert.

Wells was the first to speak. "All right, Mr. Jamie. We ride together."

Jamie looked at Moses. The older man slowly nodded his head. "I'll get my guns. We'll have to ride out now if we're to catch Titus in time."

Jamie rode to an Alabama encampment and told Putting His Foot Down — second name: Man Who Walks On Water — what was happening. "Fear not for your wife and children, Man Who Is Not Afraid," the elder told him. "I will dispatch men to go there immediately as guards."

The Indians all around the Big Thicket country liked Jamie, for he knew their ways, had already learned their language, respected the land, and did not interfere with them in any way. The occasional Comanche and Kiowa war parties were quite another matter. So far, they had not yet discovered Jamie's home, but he knew it was only a matter of time. And Tall Bull and his hold-out band of warring Shawnee were just north and west of the Big Thicket country.

But for now, the three men rode to intercept Titus Jefferson. Since Moses and Jamie knew the shortcuts, they were at the Sabine crossing several hours before Titus arrived. Titus did not know this country, and he had, a few days before, innocently asked Moses where the best place to cross was. At the time, Moses thought nothing of it. Now, everything fit.

"On the other side," Jamie said, lowering a spy glass and handing it to Moses. "About a dozen families are waiting. And they have boats."

The men had left their horses in the brush and crawled up to the bank. Moses peered through the telescoping spy glass and grunted.

"They seem relaxed enough," he said. "Surely if they made it this far, they have guards out to watch for the slave-hunters. But this is a known crossing."

Jamie grew thoughtful for a time and Moses sensed it and watched the young man's face. "Maybe they don't want to catch them just yet. No, I don't think they do. I just learned a few weeks ago, from a trapper, that under Mexican law, no slaves are allowed in this territory. But as the whites settle, many want slaves. So in this territory, any negro that got across would have to be called a free negro. Right?"

"I've heard that, yes. So?"

"So once across this river, they'd more or less be safe?"

Moses smiled ruefully. "I wouldn't exactly say safe, but I still don't see what you're drivin' at."

"Why go to all the trouble of chasing down a few runaway slaves? Why not let them cross the river, get settled, and then fall in on them all in one bunch. If I've got my facts straight, the slavers will pay someone a dollar to a dollar and a half a pound for slaves, and then turn right around and resell them for as much as a thousand dollars — right?"

"Well, yes. But the slavers would have to

have someone on this side of the river workin' for them. They . . ." He closed his eyes and shook his head, silently mouthing the word No!

"Yes," Jamie said.

Wells put his forehead on the ground and openly wept. "It all fits now," he sobbed. "The damn escape was too easy. Daddy knew just where to go all the time. We never oncest was even in no danger. Mama said it was the Lord's will. But I knowed better. I knowed better. I had me a real bad feelin' all the while." He put his face in his hands and sobbed.

"Boy," Moses put a heavy and work-hardened hand on the young man's shoulders. "Me and Jamie is just talkin'. We ain't got no proof a-tall that your daddy is up to no good."

"But he is. I can remember times when he would openly sass the foreman and nothin' was ever done to him. And times when he was called up to the big house in the middle of the night when he didn't think none of us was awake. And ever' time he got whupped, it was done inside the barn and we wouldn't see him for weeks, sometimes. He was recuperatin', the boss man, he say. But he wasn't neither 'cuperatin'. Them whuppin' was a sham. They never happened. He was workin' for the man all them times. My own pa is a damn slaver!"

"Wells," Jamie said. "Your pa never goes without a shirt much, does he?"

"I ain't seen him without a shirt in years. He say it's to hide the scars from all the whuppin's he got. But you see, my daddy, for some years now, was the yard nigger. He kept the grass scythed and lookin' good and done little odd jobs around the big house. He never worked in the fields or loggin' or nothin' real heavy."

"Would he take trips with the boss man?" Jamie asked.

"You bet he did!" Wells wiped his eyes with a ragged shirt sleeve. "And he never objected when the master wanted to bed down mama. The twins belong to the master. They look just like him. Mama is real pretty and bright yeller, but she's not very smart. Ever' time the master would call for her to come to the barn, or down to the crick, she'd just say it was God's will."

Jamie shook his head and balled his big hands into fists, as a feeling of disgust and loathing filled him. He despised everything about slavery, and most especially the people who dealt in it. And that included some fairly prominent people of the time. Being one of the few whites who had been

241

on the wrong side of slavery, forced servitude was something that Jamie would never view as acceptable.

"I'll go sit by the trail," Moses said. "Titus has got to come this way . . . it's the only way he can come. He should be along at any time."

When Moses was gone, Wells asked, "What about them people over there on the other bank, Mr. Jamie?"

"I don't know. But now that we think we know the truth about this, I can't believe those people are followers of some rebellious person who wants to start a war. I think they're just people who want out of slavery. No one can blame them for that."

"If that's so, are we going to help them?"

"I'm not going to try to stop them," was Jamie's reply. "But I am going to tell them the truth . . . as we think it is."

"And my daddy?"

Jamie hesitated. "We'll deal with that as we come to it."

That time was now, for Moses called out, "Here he comes. He'll be here in a couple of minutes."

"Come on," Jamie said. "Let's see if we can't handle this without killing." The two of them began slipping back away from the bank of the river and into the thick brush.

Jamie, Moses, and Wells were waiting as Titus reined up, total surprise on his face. Then surprise turned to raw hatred mixed with fear. He said nothing as he dismounted from his mule; just stood facing them. He carried a rifle and had a pistol in his waistband, but he made no move to raise the rifle or grab for the pistol.

"The game's over, Titus," Jamie said. "And a dirty game it was."

Titus said nothing in his defense. He did not ask how the three had learned of his plans; did not protest his innocence. He just stood silently beside his mule.

"Say it ain't the truth, daddy," Wells begged. "Tell me we're wrong. Tell us you ain't workin' for the man as a slaver. Tell me, goddamn you!"

But Titus would only shake his head.

"Why, Titus?" Moses asked. "You a *slave*, man. Why for you help bury your own kind back into that kind of life? Why for you help them escape and then resell them? Tell me!"

"Freedom," Titus finally spoke. "The man tell me that I can be free if I do this thing. He say he give me my freedom papers if I can get together a couple hundred niggers in one spot for sellin' in this territory." He looked at his son. "You stupid just like your mama. Both of you ignorant. She ain't good but for one thing and I ain't never figured out what you good for. You ain't nothing but an ignorant swamp nigger and that's all you ever be."

"Take off your shirt," Jamie ordered.

"What?" Titus looked startled.

Jamie lifted and cocked his pistol. "Take off your shirt or I'll cripple you right here and now. I'll blow your knee apart and leave you to die. Take off your shirt and turn around. I want to see something."

Hatred and fear mingling on his face, Titus laid his rifle on the ground and then slowly pulled off his shirt and turned around. There was not one whip scar on his broad back.

Jamie grunted.

Wells took a ragged breath and cursed his father until he could not think of another thing to call him.

Moses was trembling with rage.

Titus took it all stoically, standing with his shirt in one hand. Jamie walked to him and took his pistol, picking up his rifle and then backing away.

"What you gonna do wit' me?" Titus asked.

"I don't know yet. Put your shirt back on," Jamie said wearily. "And tell us the whole story."

It was as they had guessed. Olmstead and Jackson were involved, as were the Saxon and Newby brothers, along with some prominent people in and around the New Orleans area. "They know you in here somewheres, you smart-ass white boy," Titus sneered at Jamie, after telling his dirty story of betrayal and deceit against his own people.

"Because you told them," Jamie said.

"Yeah. I did that."

"And they promised you what?"

"Your wife."

Jamie felt a coldness take him. He fought it away. "Tie him up, Moses. Good and tight."

Wells looked at Jamie. "What are you going to do, Mr. Jamie?"

"Get those people on the other side across to safety. After that, I don't know what in the hell I'm going to do."

Sixteen

The large group of runaway slaves, men, women, and children from babies to teenagers, made the crossing without incident, even though this area was infested with huge alligators. Perhaps the 'gators weren't hungry this day. Perhaps God took a hand in reshaping the so-far shattered lives of the slaves. To a person, they were scared, hungry, and ragged. Safely across, Jamie moved them back into the thicket about half a mile and then lined them up, telling them of Titus's treachery.

"I can't tell you what to do," he told them. "But if you try to settle in or around the Big Thicket, most of you will eventually be rounded up and sold back into slavery. If you go west, you're going to hit Kiowa and Comanche and Apache. I don't know what to tell you to do."

"You just a boy," an older woman said. "You that MacCallister boy, ain't you?"

"Yes."

"You got quite a reputation," a man said. "They's big reward monies on your head. White folks say you kilt a hundred men."

"They lie. But I have killed in defense of my life. And I will again if I have to. But I'm not your problem."

"I heard about a black settlement up north," Moses said. "Along the Sulphur. It may just be talk. I don't know. Maybe you folks could try for there."

"Are you goin' to try to keep us from settlin' in the Thicket?" a man asked Jamie.

Jamie shook his head. "No. I don't have the right to do that. But if you do, you'd be wise to break up into tiny groups and spread out over several hundred miles."

"No," an older man said. "We come this far together, and we're stayin' together. But you been good to us, so I'll promise that we won't settle nowheres near you."

"He's gettin' away!" a woman screamed. "And they's someone with him."

Moses lifted his rifle, then lowered it. He could not bring himself to shoot his own son, Robert. Robert and Titus leaped their horse and mule toward the river.

Jamie stood and watched them vanish in the brush and trees. He could not outrun a horse and a mule on foot, and his own horse was grazing several hundred yards away, unsaddled, unbridled, and picketed. He turned to Moses. "It would have done no good to just shoot one of them, Moses. And Robert was an uncertain target at best."

"No, Jamie. I could have shot him. And probably will some day. But not this day. And my not shootin' him will cause us grief."

"Maybe. But I have another question. Do you think your son was in on this with Titus?"

Moses slowly nodded his head. Jamie felt the man had aged ten years in as many minutes. "Yes, Jamie. I do. And it breaks my heart to have to say that." He turned to the band of runaway slaves and gave one man Titus's rifle and another his pistol and belt knife. "Split up the powder and shot. They's game a-boundin' all around you. Now you're on your own. But I say this to you: Don't settle within fifty miles of us. Go north, or go south, but stay away from the center of the Thicket."

"How will we know?" a man asked.

"The Indians will tell you," Jamie spoke. He squatted down. "Look here." With a stick, he drew a map of the Big Thicket. "There is plenty of room up here, or down there. It runs several hundred miles. All through it, there are clearings where gardens can be planted. You have axes and shovels," He stood up. "You're free now. I hope you stay free. Good luck."

He stood with Moses and Wells and watched the weary and ragged band of runaway slaves vanish into the timber. And it almost broke his heart to see them go. For he knew they were heading into a vast and hostile unknown where at best probably half of them would survive the year. Swamp fever would claim some. Others would die of snakebite or a slow suffocation in quicksand. A few would fill the bellies of 'gators. Several would drown in the black waters. They would be hunted relentlessly by the Saxon and Newby brothers and their gangs. Some would be caught and resold back into the degradation of slavery.

"But the best and the strongest and the smartest will survive," Jamie said aloud. "May God have mercy on the others. And may God forgive me for not helping them more than I did."

"You had no choice in the matter, Mr. Jamie," Wells said. "It's our survival we're talkin' 'bout, too."

"I wonder why that doesn't make me feel any better," Jamie replied.

■ ■ ■ ■

The second winter in the Big Thicket brought change. Wells and Sally were married in the fall and took in the twins, Roscoe and Anne, to raise. That was after Wells went back to his mother's shack to see about her and the twins and found them playing alone in the dirt of the front yard. They were filthy and hungry. Angry, he stormed into the shack and found his mother hanging by a rope from a beam. She left no note, because she could not read or write. She had been dead several hours. Wells grabbed up the kids and rode immediately to Jamie and Kate.

While Kate and Sally and Liza stayed in the cabin with Jed, too — he was still a little young to witness this — the men rode to the Wells's cabin and Jamie cut Ophelia down, slowly lowering the body to the carefully swept dirt floor.

"We should have brought one of the women," he said. "We'll have one of them find her best dress to be buried in."

"That was her best dress," Wells said, his voice husky. "Liza gave it to her when we first some here. Cover up her face, Mr. Jamie, would you please? I can't abide lookin' at her all swole up like that." He walked outside to stand under a tree and weep.

Moses found a tattered blanket that he recognized as having been one of his own, and carefully and as gently as he could, wrapped the woman in it while Jamie fetched a shovel and walked over to Wells.

"Where do you want her buried, Wells?"

"I ain't give that no thought, Mr. Jamie."

"Well, me and Moses picked out a nice place over between our cabins to use when the time came, and it always does. How about over there?"

"That'd be mighty fine."

"Look, you go on back to my place and stay there. Me and Moses will get things ready. In about an hour, send Jed over and we'll run him back to tell you when we're ready."

Wells nodded and mounted up. He looked back once. "Tomorrow, I'm comin' over here with a mule and tearin' this shack down. I don't want nothin' left."

"Whatever you say, Wells." Personally, Jamie thought that to be a good idea. Let it return to weeds and vines. He knew that Titus had about as much sense of direction as a lost calf. He'd gotten lost a dozen times just traveling over to Jamie's or Moses's place. If this place was not standing as a landmark, and the paths would grow over quickly, odds were good that Titus would not be able to find his. At least that was a small hope, for both Jamie and Moses knew the evil man would return . . . someday.

Moses held the woman in his arms on the ride over to the spot that would be the last resting place for the dead. Jamie rode ahead and was already digging when the older man arrived. Jed soon came over and stared at the blanket-covered body.

"Go pick some berries, boy," his daddy told him.

"Ain't got nothin' to put 'em in."

"You got a hat on your nappy head, ain't you?"

"Yes, Papa."

"Move!"

"I'd rather him gather up rocks for the grave, Moses," Jamie said.

Moses struck his forehead with the heel of his hand. "Why didn't I think of that? The boy was makin' me nervous just standin' there. Jed?"

"Yes, Papa?"

"Start lookin' for rocks you can tote over here."

"In my hat?"

Moses straightened up and started unbuckling his belt. Jed took off like his feet were on fire.

Resting on his shovel for a moment, Jamie asked, "I wonder why she did it?"

"Liza told me one time that she thought Ophelia was just about the most ignorant woman she had ever met. She was a pure pleasure to look at — not that I'd ever say that to Liza — but she didn't have nothin' between her ears. Her main business was all located elsewhere, if you know what I mean."

Jamie chuckled grimly; gallows humor to keep the men going through a terrible time. "What am I goin' to say, Moses? I don't know anything about the woman."

"I'll say something, Jamie. I don't read so good, but I remember some passages from the Bible. Liza and Sally can sing some old spirituals we used to sing back in Virginia and we'll let it go at that."

"I still don't know why she did it."

"She was alone, Jamie. Her man done took off and left her with nothin'. And she was a woman that had to have a man. She approached me 'bout a week after Titus left. Wanted to work somethin' out between us. I told her nothin' doin'. She didn't care for plantin' no garden or tendin' flowers. All her life men has done for her. Bein' a house

253

nigger like she was, some of that uppity stuff done rubbed off on her. Southern gentry white women, Jamie, they raised to wiggle and giggle, not grunt and tote."

"Then what good are they?" Jamie asked, remembering that his mother worked terribly hard and even Sarah Montgomery, with all her money, worked from can to can't.

"Oh, they mighty pretty decorations, Jamie. They get all dressed up for parties and the like. Pinch their cheeks to get 'em all rosy and such. They play the piano and dance and act the grand lady."

Jamie tossed a shovelful of dirt out of the deepening hole. "Oh, yeah? What happens when the candles are snuffed out for the night?"

Moses grinned. "The same damn thing that happens in your cabin and mine!"

Ophelia Jefferson was laid to rest and the mound covered with rocks to keep the wolves and coyotes and other animals from feasting on the body. Moses recited some passages from the Bible, some Christian songs were sung, and Ophelia was alone in the small cemetery. She was the first. She would not be the last.

At the beginning of the third year in the Big Thicket, both Kate and Sally announced that they were expecting. Wells was so proud he walked into trees and stumbled around for a while. Jamie nearly went through the roof. For twins and triplets were common in Kate's family.

Moses and Liza came over and while Liza talked with Kate in the kitchen, Moses led the young man outside, a hand on his shoulder. "Boy, me and Liza, we been over talkin' to Wells and Sally and 'bout embarrassed them down to their toes. Now it's you young folks' turn. Jamie, you do know what causes this, don't you?"

Jamie stared at him. "Well, of course I know, Moses. I'm not an idiot!"

"Uh-huh. Howsomever, that might be up to some discussion when it comes to womenfolk. You and Kate had to grow up in a hurry. And you done a dandy job of it. I reckon you really never had no childhood to amount to much. But, Jamie, do either of you know about the moon and a woman's cycles and the like?"

"Huh?"

"I thought so. You come over here and sit with me. We got to talk." And Moses and Jamie talked, and talked. Jamie was purely astonished.

Didn't do a bit of good. For the very next year after delivering her second set of twins,

Kate was pregnant again, and Sally wasn't long in announcing the same. Now there were five small mouths to feed in the Mac-Callister home. But only for a short time.

The new baby, a golden-haired, blue-eyed girl named Karen, was five months old when the bounty hunters came.

SEVENTEEN

Jamie was working alone in the fields about a mile from their cabin, breaking new ground that he and Wells and Moses had spent all winter clearing of timber. Moses was several miles away, as was Wells, each working on their own land.

Jamie was a grown man, and he had matured into the height and heft to match his adulthood. He stood well over six feet and his arms and shoulders were packed with muscle. His hands were huge and his wrists thick. Moses had opined to his son-in-law that Jamie was a man he would not like to see angered. Truthfully, Jamie did not know his own strength, but like so many big, powerful men, he was surprisingly gentle.

Jamie had heard from the Indians that white slave hunters were working up north, and that some escaped slaves and families had been recaptured and sent back across the Sabine River to go on the auction block. But there had been no reports of any slavers working in this area.

Jamie had just righted the plow and picked up the reins when he heard the shot coming from the direction of his cabin. No one in their right mind was far from pistol and rifle in East Texas during the settlement period just a few years prior to Texas officially declaring their independence and formally breaking away from Mexican rule. Jamie jerked the carbine from the boot on the plow — he carried pistol, powder horn, and shot pouch on him — and went racing on foot toward the cabin.

At the cabin, Kate had downed one slaver with her rifle and was desperately fighting with another as other men were ransacking the cabin and others were attempting to free the horses from the corral in back of the cabin. The burly man Kate was struggling with ripped her dress from throat to waist and stood for a moment, licking his lips at the sight of her full, bared breasts. He reached out with a dirty hand to caress her breasts and Kate gave him a knee in the groin and the man went down, howling in pain. Kate kicked him in the face and grabbed up a pistol just as another slaver leaped into the open doorway. Kate shot him in the chest, the heavy ball knocking the man outside, where he died amid the flowers Kate had just replanted from swamp to home.

One of the slavers in the home grabbed up Baby Karen from the cradle and grinned at Kate. "Shuck outta that there dress," he told her. "Or the baby gits its brains bashed out."

Another man grabbed her from behind and pulled up her dress, shoving his hand between her legs and fondling her. Kate screamed in rage just as Jamie dropped to one knee and leveled his rifle, knocking a man off a horse.

"Kill that kid and take the bitch with us," a bearded man said, coming out of the bedroom where he'd been unsuccessful in his attempts to find jewelry or gold.

The man holding Karen threw the child on the floor and stomped on her head. Kate became hysterical and broke free, whirling around and dragging her fingernails across the eyes and down the face of the man who had fondled her privates. He shrieked in pain and threw both hands to his suddenly bloody face.

Moses and Wells had galloped to within rifle range and two more of the bounty hunting slavers were down in the dirt, both of them belly-shot.

The leader of the band, the man who had ordered the death of Karen became frightened and bolted out the door, leaving the momentarily blinded slaver standing in the cabin, unable to see. Jamie and Moses fired as one, the heavy caliber balls striking the man in belly and chest. He fell backward, his boots on the ground and his upper body inside the cabin.

The others panicked and took off at full gallop. Jamie made no effort at immediate pursuit. He jumped into the cabin, over the body of the dead slaver, and stood in numb shock for a moment. Kate was on her knees, weeping hysterically over the still body of Baby Karen, blood and brains under the child's head.

"That bitch tried to blind me!" the slaver hollered.

Jamie drove the butt of his rifle into the man's belly, knocking him gagging and puking to the floor. Moses and Wells dragged him out and hog-tied him.

"Don't kill him," Jamie said, his word cold as ice. "I'll need to talk to him. Wells, ride for Liza and Sally." Jamie knew there was nothing he could do for Baby Karen. He quickly checked on the other children and found them safe. He had to fight Kate away from the dead baby. She hammered at him with her fists and screamed in wild rage. He finally had to pin her to the floor and hold her until Liza and Sally arrived, just moments after the raid.

Jamie wrapped up the baby in a blanket and laid her on a floor pallet. Kate had fainted.

Moses turned to Jed. "Fetch a shovel, boy, and go to the cemetery and start diggin'."

"How many got away?" Jamie asked, his voice a choked sob.

" 'Bout ten or so, I reckon," Wells said.

Jamie looked in on Kate. She was unconscious on the bed, Liza and Sally placing cool, damp cloths on her face. Jamie went outside to the hog-tied man and stood for a moment, looking down at him.

"I ain't tellin' you nothin', *bastard!*" The man spat the words at him.

"Oh, you'll tell me everything I want to know," Jamie replied. He reached down and grabbed the man's shirt front and dragged him bodily to the barn. He closed and barred the door behind him. Jamie slowly turned, pulling his skinning knife from leather and walking toward the man.

"Say, now," the man said, shrinking from the sight. "I'm a white man. You cain't do this to me."

A moment and an unanswered question later, the man began howling in pain. The painful shrieking did not last long.

Jamie dragged the bloody body into the swamps and threw the carcass into the black water. The 'gators would find the body and stuff it up under cypress roots, to ripen before they feasted.

From a canoe, two Indians watched the tall and muscular young man walk back toward his cabin. The Indians swiftly and silently paddled away. Man Who Is Not Afraid had a terrible expression on his face.

Jamie cleaned the gore off of him and walked into the cabin. Kate was awake and sitting in a chair, looking at the blanket-wrapped body of Karen. She had lost the wild look from her eyes. She looked up at Jamie.

"Who were they?" she asked.

"Part of the Newby Brothers' gang. Waymore is leading this bunch, but he wasn't along. They're camped just north of Nacogdoches."

"You'll be going after them?"

"Just as soon as we bury Baby Karen."

Kate put her hands to her face for a moment. Then she lowered her hands and nodded her head and rose from the chair. "Let me get the Bible."

And another soul was committed tearfully to the ground in the small cemetery.

An hour later, as the noonday sun beat down upon them, Jamie kissed Kate and held her for a moment. Just before he rode off to further the legend of Jamie Ian Mac-Callister, Jamie said, "They have to know that they cannot be allowed free license to torment us. They must learn that for every raid against us, I'll kill ten or more of them. Do you understand why I have to go, Kate?"

"I understand."

"I shall return, Kate. When, is something I cannot tell you. I'll be back when you see me ride up to the cabin."

"I put your supper in the saddlebags," she said, touching his face with gentle fingers. "And I put your coat behind the saddle. The nights are still cool. I love you, Jamie Ian MacCallister."

"I love you, Kate." He kissed her again, then stepped away and into the saddle.

"It's going to be a bloody time," Moses muttered. "Bloody, bloody days of retribution."

Kate turned and stared at the cemetery for a moment, just visible from the cabin. Then she looked at Moses, her eyes flashing blue fire. "I hope so, Moses."

Jamie rode for the settlement of Nacogdoches, which at this time boasted about eight hundred residents. Throughout the territory, there were some sixteen thousand Americans living, nearly four times that of the Mexican population. And that was making the president of Mexico very nervous.

Nacogdoches was where the Fredonia Rebellion had staggered into life back in December of '27, dreamed up by a cocky and crooked land dealer named Haden Edwards and his equally shady and hotheaded brother, Benjamin. The Rebellion pitted the older settlers against the fifty or so families that Edwards had sold land to, land he took from the older settlers under the claim that Edwards had the authorization to do so from the president of Mexico. What he had was the authorization to sell land the Mexican government had given him through a grant. The only problem was the land had already been settled on by Mexicans and Americans, most of whom had clear title to the land, given to them by Spanish grants, which the Mexican government honored. For a few weeks, the area around Nacogdoches had Americans fighting Americans, and Mexicans fighting Mexicans. Finally they all turned on Haden Edwards and his brother Ben, who with a few colonists with more guts than sense, on December 30, 1826, seized an old Spanish fort and loudly proclaimed the settlement and the land around it the New Republic of Fredonia.

What Haden and Ben did not realize was that their deal with the Cherokee Indians, which they thought was their ace up the sleeve, had been thrown out by the tribal council. That harebrained scheme had been to sign a treaty with a few Cherokees dividing up Texas among all members of the tribe . . . because Mexico would not grant or even sell the Cherokees any land.

The New Republic of Fredonia lasted six weeks. When the Edwards brothers learned that the Mexican army along with several hundred of Austin's men were advancing on the old fort, they fled back to the safety of the States.

Jamie rode into the settlement and left his horse at a livery, walking toward the general store which was owned by a German emigrant named Adolphus Sterne, who would be elected mayor of Nacogdoches in 1833. He carried his short-barreled carbine and two pistols stuck behind his wide belt. He was dressed in buckskins. With his long flowing yellow hair, his tall stature, and his magnificent build, Jamie caused many a female heart to flutter that day. The man that Jamie had "convinced" to tell him all he knew back at his farm had told him all the names of those in the gang. They were as firmly in place in his mind as if they had been carved in stone.

Sterne himself was behind the counter, and he looked up instantly as Jamie walked in the open door. Every customer in the huge store paused to stare at the tall and striking-looking young man.

"You have an undertaker and a preacher in this town?" Jamie asked Sterne.

"Why, ah, yes, we do. Would you like me to direct you to them?"

"No," Jamie's words were as cold as his pale eyes. "But if you've law in this settlement, warn them to stay out of my affairs. You've got ten men camped just outside of town. They were part of the gang who attacked my farm over east of here, tried to rape my wife, and they killed my five-month-old baby daughter. I intend to kill them all. And I intend to start with that man right over there!"

The man had been inching toward the door as soon as Jamie had walked in. But

Jamie had recognized him. The man grabbed for a pistol but the hammer got all hung up in his shirt. Jamie was on him faster than a weasel could attack a chicken in a henhouse. The man cleared his pistol just as Jamie reached him. Jamie broke the man's arm at the elbow as easily as snapping a dry twig, and the brigand fainted from the pain.

Jamie slapped him awake. No one in the store had moved to aid the man, all believing the young man's story and all had commented on the gang of ruffians camped outside the town. They stood rooted, eyes on the deadly scene being played out before them.

Jamie drew a pistol and cocked it, placing the muzzle against the man's forehead. He screamed in fear and soiled himself, the stench strong in the general store. "I didn't touch your wife and I wasn't in the cabin when the baby was kilt, mister," he squalled, sweat running down his face and slobber leaking from his mouth.

"But you were there," Jamie said.

"Yes, yes! I was. We was lookin' for runaway slaves."

Jamie's eyes touched a Cherokee standing impassively between a cracker barrel and a pickle barrel. "You know Egg?"

The Cherokee nodded his head.

"Will you take this man to him for punishment?"

"I will take."

Jamie tossed him the slaver's pistol and let the man fall to the floor; he let him deliberately land on his shattered arm and the man howled in pain. The Cherokee smiled.

"I was raised by Indians," Jamie said to the tall Cherokee. "I do not think this man will die well."

"Nor do I," the Cherokee said. "If you wish to wait, I will tell our men to assist you in this venture."

"I don't need nor want help."

"I do understand," the Indian said. "A warrior must do what a warrior must do. May your medicine be strong, Man Who Is Not Afraid."

Jamie nodded his head and walked out of the store.

"You know that man, Paul?" Sterne asked the Cherokee, finally finding his heavily accented voice.

"All Indians know of him. Man Who Is Not Afraid. Man Who Plays with Panthers and Wolves. Jamie Ian MacCallister."

"Oh, my God! The highwayman and murderer?" a woman screeched, horrified.

"He is neither of those," the Cherokee policeman said calmly. "He is a good decent man who wishes only to farm the land, raise his family, and be left alone. Chief Diwali received a full report on Jamie years ago. But he is a good man to leave alone," the Cherokee added most dryly.

So that's the man Smith and Fontaine wrote me about, Sterne thought. I can see now why they were so impressed by him. I must make his acquaintance and convince him to join in our battle for independence. When the time comes.

After a quiet moment, the customers in the store all began talking at once about the tall handsome young man with the cold blue eyes. Only Sterne noticed the Cherokee policeman jerk the broken-armed man to his feet and shove him out the door. The man would never be seen again. Cherokee justice was oftentimes very final.

But no one saw Jamie leave town on foot, jogging his way north. He had left his horse at the livery with orders to care and feed it. He'd be back. The liveryman told Sterne the young man had taken, in addition to his rifle and pistols, a bow and a quiver of arrows and a bedroll.

"And he left on foot?" the merchant questioned.

"Yes, sir."

"What a strange young man," Sterne

remarked. "I don't recall ever meeting anyone quite like him."

"He ain't a young feller I'd want to slight," the liveryman replied.

"Oh? You had a conversation with him?"

"No, sir. But out here you learn plenty quick who the bad ones are."

"And this MacCallister is a *bad* person?"

"Not 'bad' the way you're thinkin'. No. Out here, bad means he's a man you best leave alone. It don't necessarily mean his character is tainted."

"I see," the newly arrived German-Jewish immigrant said. "The lad said he was going to kill ten men."

"He probably will, too. I wouldn't want to get in his way."

"What will happen to men like that when the law finally arrives and courts and lawyers reign over the land?"

The liveryman looked at him for a moment. "The country will probably go to hell!"

Eighteen

The slavers, bounty-hunters, and all around riffraff were camped only a few miles outside of the settlement, along the banks of a small creek. Jamie had hardly broken a sweat when he spotted the smoke from the cook-fires drifting lazily up into the air.

He cut off the road and into the timber, finding and following a probably centuries-old Indian trail. His moccasins made no sound as he drew closer to the gang of brigands. He slowed to a walk and began flitting from cover to cover. Once, caught between cover, in only a low brush-covered clearing, he saw a man turn his head in his direction and Jamie froze. The man looked for only a few seconds and then returned to his card playing on a blanket spread on the ground.

Idiot! Jamie thought.

He moved into the timber and worked his way closer. He was no longer thinking like a white man. He was a warrior of the Shawnee nation with but one thought on his mind: revenge. And it was going to be his.

Jamie worked his way around to the picket line and mingled among the horses, petting them and talking soothingly to them in a low voice that carried only a few feet. They were fine mounts, too. He'd take them when this mission was concluded, and all their supplies, as well.

A gang member, whose body odor Jamie could smell long before the man reached the picket line walked toward the horses. A heartbeat later, he was dead, his throat cut from one side of his neck to the other. Jamie scalped him, his face expressionless, his eyes blue ice.

Another gang member left the clearing to relieve himself. Jamie notched an arrow and then relieved the man of his life, the arrow from the powerful bow driving deep into his chest, piercing the heart. The man dropped soundlessly. Jamie would take his scalp later.

Two down, eight to go.

"Where the hell did Will go?" a man asked, looking up from the card game. "Will? Will!" he hollered.

Will was in no condition to reply now or ever. Jamie waited, an arrow notched and ready to fly.

Another man stood up. Jamie studied him closely. He vividly recalled the events in that trading post not far from the Mississippi River . . . hard to believe it was only a few quick years past; it seemed like ages. This one was a Newby. Hatred filled Jamie as he pulled back the bow string and let the arrow fly. Waymore Newby turned just in time to save his life. The arrow pinned his wrist to his hip, sinking deep, and Waymore screamed in pain. Jamie dropped his bow and jerked out his pistols, letting the double-shotted balls fly. He dropped his pistols and grabbed up his rifle, shooting a slaver in the belly. Through the gunsmoke, he could see the ground littered and bloodied with four bodies, two were still, the two others were jerking and twitching in pain.

But Waymore Newby was not among them.

"Damn!" Jamie whispered, as he shifted locations and quickly reloaded rifle and pistols.

"Waymore!" came the hoarse and scared call from north of the clearing. "Where you is, man?"

"Hurt!" Waymore's pain-filled voice came from Jamie's right, some distance away. "Goddamn arrey pinned my hand to my hip. Head's in deep, too. Grindin' agin my hipbone."

"If it's Injuns," came another voice, "how come they don't come on and finish it?"

"It ain't the red niggers," Waymore moaned. "It's that goddamn Jamie MacCallister!"

Jamie waited, as silent as the death he brought.

"MacCallister!" another voice called. "That cain't be!"

"Yeah, it is," Waymore said. "Soon as y'all told me 'bout that yeller-haired gal I knowed it had to be. He's out there, waitin'. Git him, boys. You can't afford to let him live. He'll track us all to the edges of hellfire."

Jamie did not move. Had they just used their vision as their Creator gave them the power to do, they could have spotted Jamie, for his cover was scant. But as long as he did not move, they seemed unable to spot him.

"Damnit, man, he's a ghost in them woods!"

"Settle down, Barton," Waymore said, and then could not stifle his moan of pain. "Just settle down. He ain't nothing but a snot-nosed kid who got lucky, that's all."

Jamie allowed himself a small smile when a shriek came from over by the picket line. Someone had found the scalped bounty hunter. The hair was hanging from Jamie's belt.

"It's Wilson! He's been scalped!"

"MacCallister was raised up by them damn Shawnees, remember?" Waymore said. "He's a savage like them. Goddamn Jesus! I hurt somethin' fierce."

Jamie had moved as the man shrieked, knowing that cry of alarm would cause all eyes to shift for a second.

Now Jamie began working his way around the edge of the clearing, slipping along the creek bank, knowing the bank would conceal him. He paused, smelling the man's unwashed body and filthy clothing to his left, not more than a few feet away. Don't these people ever bathe? he thought. He slipped on a few yards and crawled up over the lip of the bank, coming up silently behind the crouching man. Jamie cut the man's throat and took his hair.

"Osgood?" a slaver called. "You all right, Os?"

Jamie patted the dead man's shoulder, thinking: He's a better man now than he's ever been in his life.

"Anybody see where Osgood jumped to when the shootin' started?"

"Over by the edge of the crick, I think."

Jamie threw back his head and howled like

a wolf, and then jumped behind several cottonwoods that had been blown down in a storm.

Those left alive filled the air with lead balls as the call wavered silent. While the guns were roaring, Jamie had crawled the length of the cottonwoods and slipped into the brush, working up behind Waymore. But Waymore was gone, leaving a bloody trail where he had crawled away, toward the horses. A man suddenly reared up in front of him, his face pale and his eyes wide. His mouth was open, exposing stubs of blackened and yellowed teeth.

Jamie ripped him open from crotch to the V of his rib cage with his big knife, splattering Jamie with his blood. The dying man wailed once and then fell back, his innards exposed. Jamie threw himself to one side as two rifles roared, one slug knocking bark off a tree, stinging and bloodying the side of Jamie's face.

How was Waymore working a rifle with one hand? Jamie thought.

"Oh, damn, that hurt!" Waymore moaned. "I broke the arrey off and freed my hand. But the point's still layin' agin my hipbone and scrapin' when I move. How many's left, Barton?"

"Just you and me, Waymore, I think. Ain't

been airy sign of Osgood or Alfred."

"Work your way toward me, Barton. We'll have a better chance of stayin' alive if we're together."

"Comin' over."

He didn't make it. Jamie drilled him clean on his first jump and Barton went down bonelessly. Jamie knew he'd made a righteous shot.

"Just you and me now, Newby," Jamie called.

"Damn you, MacCallister! You kilt my brothers!"

"They started it, Newby. You should have left it alone and stayed away from men like Olmstead and Jackson."

"Let's deal, MacCallister."

"You have no bargaining position, Newby."

"I got gold!"

"I don't want gold."

Waymore Newby cursed him, the vile oaths ringing out over the small and bloody clearing. The clearing! Jamie studied it. Where there had been four men lying around the fire, now there were only three.

"Waymore!" a weak voice called. "I'm done for. But I got four loaded pistols and two rifles. Make for the horses and get gone from here. I'll hold MacCallister for a time."

"You're a better man than all the rest put together, Smathers," Waymore called. "I'll tell your kin how you died and on the next run, they'll be along."

"Get gone, Waymore. I can't last much longer."

To get to the picket line, Jamie would have to cross several barren spots. He wasn't going to risk it. He heard Waymore stumbling along and then heard the horse gallop away. Waymore crossed the creek and headed east.

"You can relax, Smathers," Jamie called. "I'll stay here and talk to you while you got breath."

"You show yourself and I'll shoot you, MacCallister," Smathers warned in a weak voice.

"I know it. Why'd you get tied up with a bastard like Newby?"

"Money. Hard cash is tough to come by now. I wanted enough to buy me a piece of ground. I done had it cultivated. It's goin' for a dollar an acre. Good bottom land, too. Had me a good gal an' we was betrothed."

"You'd have been better off settling for less land."

"Don't I know it now. You gonna take my hair, MacCallister?"

"No. And I'll give you a decent burial."

"Kind of you. I want you to know that I

didn't have no idee the men was gonna try to mo-lest no good woman. I never would have took no part in nothin' like that. I never even come onto your land. I was the lookout 'bout a mile up the trail."

"All right, Smathers. Will your brothers come after me?"

"Yeah, they'll come. They're fools if they do, but I reckon they will."

Jamie had nothing to say about that.

"MacCallister? How come you let me bluff you? I wanted you to shoot that damn Waymore. I ain't even got no gun."

Jamie chuckled. "You sure had me fooled, Smathers."

"My dear sainted mother always said I could charm birds out of the trees. MacCallister? I'm holdin' a flower in my hand so's you'll know who I am and won't scalp me. Look, them horses we're ridin' . . . they ain't stole. The bay . . ." He coughed violently for a moment. ". . . with the stockin' feet is mine. He's a good'un. They's all good. You can have . . ."

Jamie waited for a time, then worked his way around the camp, taking hair as he went. He found a shovel and buried Smathers deep, piling rocks on the mound to keep the varmits away. The other bodies he stacked up and caved a portion of the

279

creek bank over on them — after he took all their money, which was a nice sum of coin. He packed up all their supplies and guns and powder and lead and put out the campfire. Then he roped the horses together and swung into the saddle of the bay with the stocking feet. He headed back toward Nacogdoches, the bloody scalps dangling from his belt.

Adolphus Sterne paled at the sight of the scalps, but said nothing about it. Jamie handed him a list he'd prepared and then prowled the store, with the other customers getting quickly out of the way of the young man with the bloody buckskins and the scalps dangling from his wide belt.

Jamie suddenly realized he had not tied the scalps to his horse's mane. "Oh," he said. "Please excuse me. I'm sorry to have offended you." He went back outside and tied the scalps to the bay's mane and then cleaned off the gore from his buckskins and reentered the store.

"You get them all, MacCallister?" a swarthy skinned man wearing two pistols under his dress coat asked.

Jamie turned. "Let's just say justice was served."

"By the authority vested upon me by President Guerrero of Mexico, I now place you under arrest for murder."

Jamie laughed at him and the man's face darkened with rage. "Try it," Jamie told him.

The man reached for a pistol and Jamie's hand fell upon his wrist, seizing it in a grip as tight as any vise. "Don't be a fool," Jamie warned him. "And think like a man. Those men callously and brutally stomped the life out of a helpless five-month-old baby girl, and tried to rape my wife. Now what would you have done?"

The man's eyes lost some of their anger. A curious expression passed over his dark and handsome features. He nodded his head. "I, too, have a family. You did say your name was Curtis, did you not?"

Jamie released the man's wrist and stepped back. "That I did, señor."

"And you are from the country west of the Trinity, are you not?"

"That I am."

"For a man only five feet, four inches tall, you have quite a grip, Curtis. Now I regret that I have pressing matters outside of town that I must see to. *Buenas días,* Señor Curtis." He smiled. "And . . . *adiós.*"

Kate was working in the garden when she heard the sound of many hooves pounding the ground. She ran for her rifle, only a few feet away, and grabbed it up. She lowered the rifle as she saw the lone rider's golden hair hanging to his shoulders. He was leading a half dozen heavily laden pack horses and driving a herd of magnificent-looking riding horses. She walked out of the garden and over to the cabin, enlarged by another room the past year. Her husband was riding a fancy-stepping bay with stocking feet. She looked at the dried scalps tied to the bay's mane. The scalps did not surprise her; she knew Jamie could be as savage as any human when pushed past a certain point.

He jumped from the saddle and grabbed her up in his arms, lifting her off her feet and kissing her lips. They held each other for a long time.

When he finally released her and her feet were once more on the ground, she asked, "It's over?"

"For a time. Waymore Newby got away, swearing he'd return with more men. I won't josh you about that."

Jamie looked out at the fields he could see. They had been worked and planted. "Moses?"

"All of us worked, Jamie. Moses and the others would work the mornings in their fields, then work the afternoons in our fields."

"Titus and Robert?"

"No sign of them. But Moses said someone has been slipping about our places at night, spying."

"Just one person?"

"Several. They wear boots, Wells said."

"They play a dangerous game." He swept up Jamie Ian and Ellen Kathleen in his arms and spun around, kissing them. Andrew and Rosanna were taking their naps in cradles in the covered dogtrot, where they could catch the afternoon's breeze and still be protected from the sun. He put the older set of twins down and they ran off, shouting and playing. They would not venture far from the cabin. Several spankings had convinced them that their parents meant what they said about staying away from the edge of the swamp.

"The scalps?" Kate questioned.

"I'll keep them," Jamie said. "And if I have to hunt men again, I'll tie them to my horse's mane or my long rifle as a warning to others who try to hurt us or take from us."

Kate knew that topic of conversation was concluded. She looked at the pack horses. "Jamie, you brought back the whole store!"

Jamie smiled. "Some of those supplies were gifts from the Newby Brothers' gang."

"How very nice of them."

"Yes," Jamie's reply was dry. "Toward the end, they had nothing to say about it."

Kate let that slide. They both turned at the sounds of an approaching horse. Moses and Jed.

"Jed's grown," Jamie remarked. "And I sure haven't been gone that long."

She looked at him and smiled impishly. "That's what you think. But yes, Jed's shooting up like a stalk of corn."

Liza and the twins and Sally and Wells and their kids soon joined the group and they began unloading the supplies, with Jamie dividing them equally. It was quite a pile. When everything was unloaded, and the foodstuffs belonging to Kate were stored, the women went off to oohh and aahh over the several bolts of cloth that Jamie had returned with, and after the horses had been seen to and corralled, the men relaxed for a time, Jed among them, over cups of coffee.

"The men skulking about at night?" Jamie asked. "Tell me about them."

"Half a dozen of them," Wells said. "At least. But they don't all come at once. Two this night, two others the next night, and so on. It's got me jumpy."

"Anything been stolen?"

"Not a thing that I can see."

Jamie looked at Moses. The older man, his hair now almost totally gray, shook his head. "I don't know who they is. It's got me baffled. It's like they're playin' a game with us. But only they know the rules."

"Have any of you spoken with the Indians?"

"They haven't been around. This time of year, they're plantin', too."

"Stay close to your cabins this night," Jamie said. "The rules of this game are about to change."

NINETEEN

Hart Olmstead and John Jackson sat in Olmstead's fancy office in New Orleans and stared in silence at one another. The two teams of men they'd sent into the Big Thicket country were long overdue. And both men knew that meant only one thing: they were not coming back. They knew another thing, too: Jamie Ian MacCallister had struck again.

Hart cursed and looked at a very rough drawing, a not very precise map of the Big Thicket country. It stretched for several hundred miles and was about as accurate as trying to count the fleas on a dog.

Both men were dressed elegantly, but anyone with a knowing eye could tell they were nothing more than dressed-up white trash. Both men had been rebuked by everyone of quality in the city. Jim Bowie, a man who had made a fortune working with the pirate, Jean Lafitte, in the selling of slaves, would have nothing to do with Olm-stead or Jackson. Despite his wild reputation — Bowie had done it all, from capturing and breaking wild horses to riding on the backs of alligators for fun — Bowie was a gentleman, and knew trash when he saw it.

But Olmstead and Jackson were now reasonably well-off men, and their gangs of brigands were large, roaming all over several states and territories slaving — among other things, most of them borderline illegal or just plain outlawing.

Bowie was out of the city now, and not expected to return anytime soon. He was in Mexico, down in Saltillo, capital of the state of Coahuila, a guest of Veramendi, the vice-governor of San Antonio of de Bexar. Both of them were involved in some sort of land deal. Bowie was, according to rumors, also actively courting Veramendi's daughter, Ursula.

Hart Olmstead hated Bowie, but concealed it rather well, for he was scared to death of the man . . . most people with any sense were. Hart looked up from the crude map. "Titus could not find the cabins this trip?"

John shook his head. "No. He got everybody lost as a goose in those swamps. I tell you, Hart, you've got to see that place to believe it. It's the spookiest damn place I ever seen in all my life."

"I'll see it," Hart said. "I'm putting together an outfit now. We're going into the Big Thicket country to settle this once and for all."

The door to his office burst open, startling both men. Hart's aide said, "Waymore Newby's back. He's been hurt. His gang was wiped out by that MacCallister person."

"Goddamnit!" Hart said, slamming both hands onto his expensive desk. "Where is Waymore?"

"Bein' attended to by the doctor. His left hand is crippled and the doctor's diggin around now for the arrow in his hip."

Waymore's face was shiny with the sweat of pain, but he was conscious and able to talk, the bloody arrowhead lying in a pan on a table by his bed.

"Can you tell me what happened?" Hart asked.

"He ambushed us," Waymore said, his voice weak. He elected not to tell the man about the attempted rape of his daughter or the callous killing of his grandbaby. "MacCallister killed all the men and scalped them."

Both Hart and Jackson paled at that last

288

bit of news.

"There ain't nobody over yonder goin' to arrest him, Hart. The area is po-liced by Chief Diwali's Cherokees and Jamie's done made friends with all of them. A man can't git through the Big Thicket from the east. There just ain't no way 'cept that known to but a few, and they ain't talkin'."

Hart looked at the man's heavily bandaged hand. Waymore caught the direction of his eyes and said, "It's ruint. I ain't got but scant use of a couple of fingers. I want to go back, Hart. I got me a score to settle with Jamie MacCallister."

"We're all going," Hart promised. "I'm putting together supplies now. It'll be a couple of months before I'm ready. I've got me a man down in the south of Texas who says he knows where Jamie and that whore daughter of mine live. Says he's got a personal score to settle with MacCallister. Seems they had some trouble down in Galveztown a few years back. His name is Bradford."

"Wagons comin', Mr. Jamie," Wells said, after galloping his horse into the yard and jumping from the saddle. He caught his breath. "Three wagons."

"White men?"

289

"Yes, sir. Prosperous lookin,' too. How'd they get through?"

"I don't know. They sure took a chance." Mexico had recently forbidden any further colonization of Texas by Americans and was strictly enforcing the importation of slaves into the territory.

"They're about three miles out now," Wells said. "I ain't never seen nothin' but men of quality ride a hoss the way the man in front does. And the women drivin' the first two wagons is beautiful."

"Interesting," Jamie muttered. He had been sleeping outside for more than a week now, but no sign of those who were skulking about. Whoever they were had obviously stopped slipping about.

Jamie threw a saddle on a horse and rode out to meet the newcomers in the wagons. But they were not newcomers to Jamie, only to the territory.

It was Sam and Sarah Montgomery and Hannah and the Swede.

■ ■ ■ ■

PART TWO:
WINDS OF CHANGE

■ ■ ■ ■

Who has seen the wind?
Neither you nor I:
But when the trees bow down their heads,
The wind is passing by.
— Christina Georgina Rossetti

Twenty

"If we start to work in the morning," Sam said. "I believe we can get a crop in."

"Oh, easy," Jamie said. "Winters are very mild down here." He looked at Sam and Sarah, then at Swede and Hannah. "But why did you pull out of Kentucky?"

"Long story, Jamie," Hannah said. She and the Swede had two children, a boy three and a girl about fifteen months old. "But I'll make it short. Olmstead and Jackson somehow found out that I had been a Shawnee slave and wife for years. They rode all the way to Illinois to spread the story. Most people accepted it, but many shunned me. If we had stayed, Swede would have eventually killed someone."

"I understand. Sam, how about you and Sarah?"

"Well, Caney died during a robbery, the Reverend Callaway and family moved away, and to tell the truth, both Sarah and me were getting restless. I hired a western man to find you and report back to me. When he told us of this land, we both agreed that we just had to see it. I sold out and made a very tidy profit, indeed. And . . . here we are, Jamie."

"And there are no other people in this world that I would rather see," Kate said. "But the Cherokees will surely report you to the Mexican government."

Sam smiled. "No, they won't. I used some of the profits to insure that. The Cherokees are very intelligent people. They know the value of money."

Jamie laughed. "Then I take it you have made Egg's acquaintance?"

Sarah said, "That man is anything but a fragile egg. That's the biggest Indian I have ever seen. Does he ever come around here?"

"Egg is everywhere at all times," Jamie said.

"Now, Jamie . . ." Sarah cautioned.

"He has spies everywhere," Kate straightened that out. "They report to him. Nothing goes on that Egg doesn't know about."

"So tell us about yourself, Jamie," Swede urged.

Jamie shrugged his heavy shoulders. "Not much to tell, really."

Sam caught the quick look that passed

between Moses and Wells. Sarah noticed that Kate and Liza and Sally suddenly got very busy sewing on the patchwork quilt they were making.

"What's been happening, Jamie, my friend?" Swede asked, leaning closer.

Jamie finished his cup of coffee and sat for a few seconds staring into the cup. Then he began speaking, chronicling the years from the time they left Kentucky up to the present. He left nothing out.

The four newcomers sat in silence after Jamie had finished. Three of them were shocked at the open admission of violence and their faces showed that. Hannah smiled and winked at Jamie. She knew the warrior's way, and could understand from her years with the Shawnees why Jamie scalped all of the men but one, and why he gave that man a decent burial and did not mutilate him.

"Shocked, are you?" Jamie asked, a faint smile playing around his lips. "The last man had courage."

"I certainly understand your rage, lad," Sam said. "It was horrible what happened to your child. But it was hardly civilized behavior on your part, as well."

"It isn't a civilized time," Jamie retorted. "And I believe that one must meet uncivilized behavior with uncivilized behavior.

That is the only way the robbers and rapists and brigands of the world will cease their evil deeds."

"History proves you wrong, my friend," Swede said. "By putting a man in debtor's prison because he is unable to pay his debts is not justice."

"I agree. But as long as he's in there, he won't run up anymore bad debts, now, will he?"

The summer passed amid a flurry of work and fun. A peddler came along in a big wagon and thought a trading post would do just fine located along the El Camino Real — The Royal Road. There were already a dozen or more cabins there, along the Ayish Bayou, with others in various stages of construction. A Spanish mission had been there for more than a hundred years, but had been abandoned back in the late 1770s when Spain evacuated all East Texas missions. The old walls were still there. It was settled by Anglos in about 1818 and called San Augustine. But now the town was growing.

Jamie viewed it with mixed emotions. When questioned about it, he replied, "Even if Mexico lets them stay, which is in some doubt, a town brings people. And for us,

Kate, people mean trouble."

Even as he spoke, Hart Olmstead, John Jackson, Titus Jefferson, and Robert Washington, and a force some fifty-odd men of extremely ill repute and breeding were leaving New Orleans, heading into the territory of Texas to find and kill Jamie Ian MacCallister. Olmstead had found a man who said he could lead them through the southernmost part of the Big Thicket. They would resupply at the trading post of Beau Mont, and then head north toward the tiny village of San Augustine. He had heard that some whites had settled not too far from there in the swamps called the Big Thicket. The guide was a French trapper called LaBeau. LaBeau was not his real name. Louisiana had had warrants for his arrest for years, but he knew the bayous of South Louisiana and had family there. But even his family had finally wearied of his evil outlaw ways and told him to hit the trail, or the bayou, as it were. And don't come back unless he wanted to fill the belly of some 'gator. LaBeau got the message and told his entire family, mama, papa, brothers, sisters, aunts, uncles, and cousins what they could all do with and to themselves . . . rather vulgarly. LaBeau really started poling his pirogue when he saw his father come out of the cabin with a shotgun. LaBeau made the mistake of standing up to get better leverage with the pole and his father pulled the trigger and shot him in the ass.

But it would be weeks before the mounted column ever got close to Jamie, and in the Big Thicket life went on.

The cabins of Sam and Sarah and Swede and Hannah were built. It didn't take long with everybody working. The cabins were not nearly so grand as the one Sam and Sarah had left behind, but that didn't matter. They were once more close to Jamie and Kate.

Since he didn't really own the land, Jamie gave part of his cleared land to Sam and Swede; during the rather mild winter, they would start clearing more. Moses and Liza and Jeb, Wells and Sally, their own children and the twins were accepted as part of the unit without question. Sam and Sarah and Swede and Hannah all despised slavery.

"And Titus has never come back?" Swede asked. It was late afternoon and the day's work was done. Now it was time for rest and food and conversation. It was a Saturday, and every Saturday evening, weather permitting, the families all gathered for a communal feasting at someone's cabin. This late afternoon they were all gathered at

Jamie and Kate's.

"I'm not sure," Jamie said.

Moses said, "He'll be back." He checked to see if the twins were out of earshot. "He'll come back to get Anne to sell her to some plantation owner."

"Why?" Sarah asked. "She's just a child."

"She's a beautiful girl of eleven or so, Miss Sarah," Liza said. "Just the right age for some . . . type of slave-owner."

"Surely you jest?" Sam asked, his mug of cider forgotten.

"Goes on all the time," Moses said. " 'Sides, she could pass and that makes it even better. He'd get a good thousand dollars for Anne."

"His own child?" Swede asked, horrified.

"There are bad men of all colors," Moses said. "Yes. He would sell his child to be a white man's bed-partner."

"Disgusting!" Sarah said.

"Not civilized behavior at all," Jamie said dryly. "Wouldn't you agree, Sam?"

Sam smiled — thinly. "I would agree. But you think he has been back, Jamie?"

"I think he's tried, and gotten lost. But somebody was sure skulking about here a few weeks ago." The who and why of those night visitors was as yet unknown to Jamie. But it worried him. Whoever the visitors might be, they were not coming in from the east, through the swamps, for Jamie had picked up their trail and followed it. They were coming in from the west. He lost the trail on the now more heavily traveled road a few miles from his cabin in the thicket.

The friends and neighbors feasted and talked until after night fell, then they began the short journey back to their cabins. Kate had told the women, privately, that she was once more pregnant, but Jamie had not yet told Moses. He did not want another lecture about how babies are made.

The death of Baby Karen had hit Kate much harder than the others realized, for she was as adept as Jamie at hiding her true feelings. They had agreed that having another child would be the best thing.

It had surprised Sam and Sarah when Jamie had informed them of Hart Olmstead and John Jackson's whereabouts. Sam had said that when the men left Kentucky, they had left with much bitterness and rancor. Shortly after Jamie and Kate had left, the original town had been burned and razed by vigilantes and the gamblers and whores and outlaws either ran out or killed. Jamie did not ask if Sam had been among the night riders. But he thought not; Sam did not hold with that kind of action.

And Jamie wondered if Sam could make it out here on the frontier? Sam was a good and decent man, but he still held to the more civilized Eastern code of ethics and law, and Jamie did not know how to tell him that many of those codes simply did not apply out here. And he also wondered if Swede would last out here. Both men were honorable and brave to the soul, but neither man could shoot first and ask questions later. And out here in the raw and oftentimes lawless edge of civilization, many times that had to be the case.

"You're worried about them, aren't you?" Kate asked. The children were asleep and the husband and wife were snuggled close together in their own bed. "Sam and Swede, I mean?"

"Yes. I am. Sam can fight, and will fight. I've been a witness to that. But he's a very honorable man, and his methods of fighting are fair. Swede doesn't know his own strength and he's so slow to anger it's very likely to get him hurt or killed out here."

"Have you talked to them about that?"

"No. Not yet. But I have to, and soon."

"Don't you think they knew what they were getting into, Jamie?"

"Not really. It was a grand adventure for them. Oh, I'm glad they're here. But they've got to toughen up. And I don't think that my words alone will do that."

"Then . . . what will?"

"Savagery. It's almost as if their lives were being looked over by some guardian angel. They came all the way out here, hundreds of miles, and never encountered one hostile person or act against them." He put a big hand gently on her stomach. "You think it's twins again, Kate?"

"I don't know. But I sure am getting big awfully fast. I told you, Jamie, triplets run on my mother's side of the family."

"Good God!" Jamie muttered, and laid his head on the pillow. "Triplets! I'll have to add another room."

Kate laughed softly. As big as she was getting, she felt sure it was triplets — at least.

LaBeau was true to his word. He led the men over to the post at Beau Mont and there they resupplied for the trek north. But Hart was careful not to send but a few men in, and they went in one at a time over a period of several days. The Mexican government was really cracking down on Anglos attempting to settle in Texas, and there had been more than a few armed conflicts between the Mexican Army and Americans trying to settle. But Austin was helping to bring them in anyway, sometimes by very devious routes. And come they did.

In about eighteen months, Sam Houston, who had been living with the Cherokees up in what would someday become Oklahoma, will cross the Red River and enter Texas for the very first time. Another man who brings with him more winds of change.

Fontaine had returned from a business trip — actually, he was reporting back to Washington, to President Jackson on the freedom movement by the Americans in Texas — and had noticed the men drifting in to buy supplies. Far too many supplies for one man. Fontaine commissioned one of his own men to lounge around the post and keep tabs on how many men bought how much supplies. It did not take Fontaine long to put it all together, and he sent one of his men to follow a rough-looking fellow who had purchased far too many supplies.

"Fifty or so men camped about five miles to the east, Captain," his man reported back, using Fontaine's old Army rank. "And they're a rough-lookin' lot. I got in close and heard the names of Jackson and Olmstead."

Fontaine frowned. Where had he heard that name before? Then it came to him. Jamie MacCallister's words, several years back, at the post when that bounty hunter tried to take him back to Kentucky. "How much is Olmstead paying you for this travesty of justice?"

Fontaine turned to his man. "Get you some food and rest. Then take the best mount in my remuda and ride like the wind. You know where Jamie MacCallister has settled?"

"Aye, Captain. Just east of San Augustine. In the Big Thicket. Them thugs, they're here to do harm to the lad and his wife?"

"Yes."

"I don't need no rest and it won't take me but a moment to change saddles. That's a good boy and them are good folks who settled in there with him. Negra and white alike. I'll eat on the ride if you'll have someone fix me a poke of food."

"It'll be waiting."

But Jamie had long anticipated the day when Hart Olmstead and John Jackson would find them and launch an attack against them. Deep in the swamps, miles from where he and Kate lived and farmed the land, he had built a snug cabin and stocked it with blankets and firewood. He had built a false bottom in the floor and kept it stocked with guns and powder and balls. And he had taken the women there many, many times, until they had the route committed to memory — they could paddle there day or night.

Fontaine's man rode hard, changing horses several times along the way. He galloped into Jamie's yard and jumped from the saddle. "MacCallister!" he called, just as Jamie rounded the corner, a rifle in his hand, and Kate, heavy with child (children would be more accurate) stepped into the doorway, a rifle in her hand. "Fontaine sent me. Olmstead and Jackson have pulled out of Beau Mont by now. They've got about fifty men with them, and to a man, they're a vile, evil lot."

"You come into the cabin, sir," Kate called. "I have hot food and a bed. You're exhausted."

"Beggin' your pardon, ma'am. But I'm too nasty to soil your home."

"Then there's water right there to wash with and I'm washing clothes now," she told him. "You get out of your clothes, wash up, wrap up in a blanket, and I'll fetch you some food."

Moses had ridden up. "If you don't have no objections to wearin' clothes a black man's wore, I can have clothes here for you in ten minutes. We're about the same size."

Fontaine's man smiled. "I don't hold with

slavery, although many of my friends do. Does that make a difference to you?"

"Not nary a bit. I'll be back in a moment."

Ellen Kathleen, blond and blue-eyed, came walking out, carefully holding a big bowl of stew. Jamie Ian came along behind her, with corn bread and a wooden mug for milk from the coolness of the well.

"Sit down yonder under the dogtrot where there's shade and eat," Jamie told him. "I remember you now. I've met you. But I can't recall the name."

"Bonham. I seen you whup that trash Bradford that day at Smith's post. Bradford has linked up with Olmstead and is leadin' 'em here."

"Eat," Jamie urged the man, pointing to a chair. "Then we'll talk."

Bonham fell to his food, and from the expression on his face he was a happy man. Kate had turned into an excellent cook. Although the stew was a simple affair, it was thick with potatoes and chunks of venison and seasoned with onions and peppers. The corn bread was generously lathered with butter and the milk was cool. Bonham ate two big bowls of stew, polished off a bait of corn bread, and drank two mugs of milk before he settled back and lit up a cigar.

"Best food I've et in many a moon, ma'am," he complimented Kate. "Them Mexican peppers do give it just the right bite, don't they?" He looked at the kids, all blond-haired and blue-eyed, and at the shape of Kate. He smiled. "Jamie, you and your missus figurin' on populatin' Texas all by yourselves?"

Kate laughed and Jamie smiled. "It does look that way, doesn't it?" Jamie had brought out two mugs of coffee and set one down by Bonham.

"You got you a hidin' place, Jamie?"

"I don't figure on running."

Bonham cocked his head to one side and narrowed his eyes. "You cain't fight fifty men all by yourself, Jamie."

Jamie only smiled at that. "How much time do you think I have, Bonham?"

"Oh, ample time. Ample. It's nigh a hundred miles to here. Then when they get here, they got to find you." He stared at Jamie for a moment. "Find us," he corrected.

"It's not your fight," Jamie told him.

Moses had returned with the clean clothes. Wells and Sally and Liza had come over. And now Sam and Sarah and Swede and Hannah made their appearance.

Bonham looked at the men. "Can y'all fight?"

"When angered," Swede said.

"Well, you better get angry," Bonham told him. " 'Cause if you don't, in a few days you're all goin' to be *dead*!"

Twenty-One

The women were sent to the cabin in the swamps with enough food to last them for the duration. They did not argue when Jamie told them to go, they just packed up, kissed their men, and went.

The men, with Bonham staying despite the objections from Jamie, packed up what they could of the contents of the cabins, hid the precious articles in the woods, and made ready to defend their land and lives.

Jamie tied his scalps onto the mane of his favorite horse, a stallion he called Buck, and packed up a few supplies. Bonham was amused when he noticed the scalps. When Jamie MacCallister went huntin', the man thought, he meant business! Bonham did not have to ask what Jamie was going to do, he knew. Jamie was headin' out to cut down the odds some.

Sam Montgomery's eyes widened when he saw the dried scalps and Swede could but shake his head.

"They ought to be about a day away," Jamie said, as he swung into the saddle, his rifle in his hand. He had two pistols in holsters around his waist, and four more in leather on the saddle. His short-barreled carbine was saddle-booted and his bow and quivers of arrows was slung around him. "I'll be back." He looked at Bonham and the man nodded his head in understanding.

"I'll see to things," Fontaine's scout said.

Jamie rode out.

"He's going out to cold-bloodedly kill, isn't he?" Sam asked.

"He's goin' out to do what he has to do," Bonham said. "Come on. We got work to do."

Jamie stayed on game trails just inside the swampy edge of the thicket. He had explored the thicket and knew it as well as any living man, except, perhaps, for the Indians who lived in it. He knew it better than any white man. By late afternoon, he knew he was close to the camp for he smelled the smoke from fires and with the smoke came the odor of food being cooked. He picketed Buck on good graze and near water and began working his way to the edge of the enemy camp. Jamie's eyes were cold and his expression set. His mind was clear. He was a warrior on a warrior's path. There was no pity in him. These men had come to kill him and do harm to his family and friends. They came for blood, they would have it.

Their own.

Jamie worked in close on his belly. He was one with the land, the grass, the timber, the animals, the elements. Once, a sentry making his rounds came within a few yards of Jamie and did not see him. Jamie let him live. For now. He worked in closer until he could plainly hear the voices. One voice stood out. Hart Olmstead.

"Bradford says by noon tomorrow we'll be in MacCallister's home territory," Hart was speaking. "Dillman, you and Barnett ride out with Bradford before dawn and scout ahead. I'll give five hundred dollars in gold to the man who brings me Jamie Ian MacCallister's head."

"What about your daughter?" a man asked.

"I have no daughter," Olmstead's words were cold. "That slut made her choice years ago. Kill her."

"They got kids," Bradford said.

"Wipe them all out," Olmstead's voice reached Jamie. "They're nothing but nits and lice and fleas."

311

"That's right," Jackson said. "They're all mixed up with niggers and Injuns. God only knows who has been breeding with what. It's disgusting. We'll be doing the territory a favor when we destroy them."

Jamie could see Titus and Robert. He wondered what was going through their minds at Olmstead's words. Nothing, probably, he correctly guessed.

Jamie slowly worked away from the encampment and made his way back into the edge of the thicket. He would eat a bite or two and then rest. It was firm in his mind that he had found the right bunch, and what their intentions were — and they were anything but honorable. Tonight, then, he was going to be very busy.

Bradford lit his pipe with a burning twig from the dying fire and leaned back against the log, content in his mind. Tomorrow, he intended to be the first into the clearing where that damn MacCallister lived, and the first to reach the bastard. He was going to kill him and cut off his head for Olmstead to see. He owed MacCallister that for making a fool out of him down at Smith's Tradin' Post that time. And he'd use MacCallister's own damn axe to do the deed. And he knew that the axe was sharp. By prowlin' around the place, Bradford knew that MacCallister kept things neat and clean and ready to use at all times.

He sure did. And Jamie used his big blade now to cut Bradford's throat. The man gurgled softly and Jamie, behind the fallen log, eased him down onto his blankets with one strong hand. Bradford looked asleep. He was. Forever.

Bradford was a man who liked his privacy. He had bedded down away from the others. He would never make that mistake again.

Jamie moved to the picket line and stood silent for a few moments, letting the horses smell him and see that he meant no harm. He had already been there several times that evening; when the sentry was at one end, Jamie would be at the other, or in the middle. The horses were used to him now.

Jamie began working quickly and soundlessly. He cut partway through several dozen cinch straps; just enough so after a few miles of riding, they would break. He had picked up several dozen cockleburrs and he worked several deep into as many saddle blankets as he could find. He silently apologized to the horses for the discomfort he was about to cause them come the morning.

The Shawnee had taught him a deep respect for the land and the animals who lived on that land. They had taught him to never kill any animal for fun, for animals were as much a part of Man Above's plan as were the human people. He was taught to never kill more than was needed to feed the mouths waiting back at the lodge. They taught him to apologize to the animal after the killing, and to choose his animals with care. Kill a doe with a sucking calf, and the calf will die — that would be a wrong thing to do. The Shawnee taught Jamie Ian Mac-Callister many things during his years with them.

They also taught him how to kill silently.

When the sentry shift changed a few minutes after Jamie finished with the saddles, Jamie ruined the new guard's evening and stretched him out on the ground. He silently followed another man into the timber and watched him drop his pants, squat down, and start to grunt. Jamie's arrow drove all the way through the man's head, the point exiting out the other side. Olmstead's man would never have to worry about constipation again.

"What the hell was that sound?" a man asked, rising up from his blankets at the very slight sound of Arrow-Through-His-Head's body hitting the soft earth.

"Les," another said. "He makes more

noise takin' a crap than anybody I know."

The camp quieted down and Jamie took the man's hair and then flitted as silently as a shadow through the timber on the edge of the encampment. He had already chosen his next kill. Then sudden movement caught his eyes. He froze and watched as John Jackson stood up and walked to the fire, adding more wood, for the night was cool. It was too good an opportunity to pass up. Jamie notched an arrow, took careful aim, and let it fly. It was true, taking Jackson in the center of his chest. Jackson grunted once, and then fell forward, first on his knees, and then facedown into the fire, his hair catching on fire. Jamie stood for a moment, recalling a similar scene years back. Then he turned and ran toward the safety of the thicket as the camp exploded in sudden activity and shouts. He would return about an hour before dawn to watch the fun.

"Injuns!" a man yelled. "They's all about us, boys."

Several miles from the camp, Jamie rolled up in his blanket and went to sleep. Tomorrow was really going to be an interesting day.

Jamie did not underestimate the ability of the men Olmstead had hired on to accompany him on this dastardly mission.

Some of them, he knew, would be skilled woodsmen. But many of them, he also knew, had spent too many years in New Orleans and St. Louis, drinking and whoring and gathering flab and fat, therefore losing much of their skill in the wilderness.

He got into position long before the sky began to gray. The bodies of the four men had been wrapped in blankets and laid to one side, for burial come first light. The camp began to stir and as soon as men had swilled coffee, a few took shovels and began to dig. Jamie sat amid thick foliage, only his eyes moving. And as he had anticipated, the men were wary and Olmstead had posted many guards. To try anything now would be foolish. So Jamie sat through a short sermon and prayer — from Hart Olmstead, of all people — and waited.

Before leaving his hidden camp, Jamie had fixed up two arrows, attaching small bags of gunpowder just behind the arrowheads. Just as the men mounted up, he planned on dropping the arrows into the dying coals of the fire. With the already weakened cinch straps, the explosions would produce some very interesting results.

The scalped bodies committed to the earth and the services over — sacrilegious, to Jamie's mind, coming from such a man as Hart Olmstead — the crowd broke up and began packing up, then moving to their horses. Jamie notched an arrow and stood up, concealed behind a tree. Two men made a halfhearted attempt at putting out the fires and then moved toward their saddled horses and climbed aboard.

Jamie let his arrows fly, one to each fire pit. The explosions were enormous in the early morning air and the horses started snorting in fright and pitching and bucking. Riders went flying in all directions and a few saddle cinches broke, adding to the confusion. Abel Jackson was tossed to the ground and when he attempted to get up, he presented his big butt to Jamie and Jamie put an arrow into one cheek. Abel shrieked like a woman and started grabbing at himself. Jamie put another arrow into a man, straight into his chest, the next arrow went into Carl Olmstead's leg. Jamie jerked out his pistols and let the lead sing their death songs. Then Jamie raced back into the thicket and kept on running until he reached his saddled horse. He knew none of the men would pursue him very deep into the dark and dangerous mysteries of the thicket.

He rode hard for several minutes, then slowed to a walk, then put the big stallion into a trot, eating up the distance. He had his next ambush point already chosen.

Several miles behind him, Olmstead and his men had just managed to get things under control. By this time, Olmstead and his men had figured out that they were being harassed not by Indians, but by Jamie. Hart Olmstead was angry to the core, his face mottled by rage.

Olmstead's 'field surgeon' for this expedition, a barber from New Orleans who usually stayed about half drunk most of the time, was busy with the wounded. A cursing and shrieking Abel Jackson was forcibly held down while his buttock was sliced open and the arrowhead removed. Waymore Newby had retreated to cover and was keeping a good eye out for Jamie. He knew from experience just how dangerous the young man was.

Hart Olmstead surveyed the damage done. To his mind it was unbelievable that one young man could wreak such havoc.

"They's a doctor at Nacogdoches," La-Beau said. "Some of the wounded will make it. A couple won't."

Hart assigned men to take the wounded into the town with orders to say they were wounded during an Indian attack. His force of fifty-odd men had been cut to less than forty. And they still had a long way to go.

Titus and Robert were scared and they made no effort to hide that fear. Robert had known all along just how dangerous Jamie Ian MacCallister was and had tried his best to tell the others. But none of the men showed any interest in anything a nigger had to say. Up 'til now. Now they approached him with questions.

Shaking with fear, Robert said, "He can walk among wolves and panthers without being harmed." Not quite true, "He can stand next to a tree and you can't see him." Pretty close to truth. "He knows every inch of the swamps." Jamie knew the thicket well, but not that well. "He can move like a ghost." True. "He's as strong as any man alive." Probably. "And he don't know fear." True.

Hart Olmstead dismissed the talk as a scared nigger's babbling. But the man realized he had major problems. With Bradford gone, so went the location of Jamie's cabin and how to get to it. He had seen paths and trails and even wagon ruts leading off to the east, into the darkness of the thicket, but to follow each and every one of them would take weeks or months, and his men were not at all anxious to enter that foreboding-looking swamp. Tell the truth, neither was he.

"We know he lives just east of that settlement called San Augustine," Olmstead told his sons, Ernest, Patrick, and Jubal. Carl had gone with the wounded to Nacogdoches. "We'll concentrate our search there." He looked over at the mound of earth covering John Jackson, the best friend he'd ever had, and shook his head. Abel Jackson had been placed on a padded and horse-drawn travois and taken to Nacogdoches. "Mount up. We're pulling out."

If Hart Olmstead had possessed any sense from the outset, he would have left Jamie alone. Further evidence of how arrogant and short-sighted he was came when he did not pull the column away from the edge of the thicket and move them over to the west a mile or so. He doggedly maintained the northerly route at the edge of the dark swamps. Just as Jamie suspected he would.

A few miles up the trail, Jamie waited.

At the small settlement of cabins in the clearings, Sam and Swede noticed how calm Moses and Wells were, and commented on it.

"I doubt they'll be more than a dozen men left time they get here," Moses said. "If they even get here."

"Jamie's that good?" Bonham asked.

"He's the best," Wells said. "There ain't nobody better at this kind of warfare. He's been doin' it since he was seven years old."

Bonham shook his head. All the stories he'd heard over the past few years about Jamie MacCallister were true. The young man was scarcely twenty-one years old and already a legend. And miles to the south, that legend was growing.

Just about the only smart thing that Hart Olmstead did was not to lead the column of men. He stayed in the middle of the column, surrounded and therefore protected by his own men from shot or arrow that might come from the swamps that lay silent and deadly to his right.

After several miles had passed uneventfully, the men began to relax. Not a one of them had taken the time to inspect the belly cinches on the horses, even after a few had broken back at their encampment. Cinch straps broke every now and then, and none of them had any reason to suspect that Jamie MacCallister had anything to do with it.

When Jamie struck again, it was not a silent attack. He had brought two rifles, and he used them. Two more of Olmstead's force toppled from their saddles, dead upon impact with the ground. Before the sounds of the shots had ceased echoing, Jamie was off and running to the north, toward where he had left his horse some distance away. He paused once, to charge his rifles, and then continued running, staying in the thicket, weaving along the game trails. His long hair was braided and his head covered with a brown bandanna. His face was deliberately streaked with mud and the natural green from leaves. His buckskins blended in with his surroundings. Jamie and the swamps were as one. He reached his next chosen ambush spot and waited, catching his breath. Then he mounted up and rode out of the thicket and into a clearing. He looked south. The column of men had not stopped to bury their dead. They were riding straight toward him. Jamie lifted his rifle and screamed like a panther, taunting those to the south. Then he turned the stallion's head to the north, and staying in the open, rode away slowly.

Hart Olmstead did exactly what Jamie hoped he would do. He screamed to his men and they spurred their horses into a gallop. Jamie smiled and stopped, turning around to face the galloping charge. Cinch straps began breaking and men were tossed to the ground, many of them caught beneath the hooves of the horses galloping behind them. Olmstead hit the ground hard, as did his sons. LaBeau, realized what was happening, felt his saddle began to slide and threw himself to one side, landing hard, losing his rifle, but avoiding the deadly hooves of those horses behind him. LaBeau knew one thing: he was through with this hunt. Jamie Ian MacCallister would see no more of him. Hart Olmstead could take his money and go to hell with it.

It was bone-breaking and bloody pandemonium in East Texas. Jamie laughed at the sight and touched his heels to his horse and once more disappeared into the thicket. He rode south for a few hundred yards until he was opposite the scene of confusion. Leaping from the saddle, he fired into the tangled knot of addled men, emptying rifles and pistols. Then he was once more into the saddle, riding hard to the north. Two miles from the costly ambush, Jamie left the edge of the swamps and rode straight west for a couple of miles. Squatting in the timber, this time on the west side of the trail, he charged his empty weapons and waited.

Jamie ate a biscuit and took a drink from his water jug. He was a long way from being through with Hart Olmstead and his rapidly dwindling army of thugs and brigands.

To the south, Olmstead sat on the ground, blood streaming from a cut on his head suffered when he fell out of the saddle, and soundly cursed Jamie Ian MacCallister.

TWENTY-TWO

While Jamie munched on a biscuit and fried salt pork from his rucksack, a few miles south, Hart Olmstead surveyed his situation. It was not good. He had about twenty men left able to ride and fight, and a half a dozen of those were hurt. LaBeau had repaired his cinch strap and ridden off without saying a word. A moment later, a half dozen others exchanged silent glances and followed him. Hart did not curse them or yell out commands for them to stop. If the men did not have the backbone for the fight, he did not want them along. Besides, they were riding off without their pay, which was to be paid at Jamie MacCallister's death.

Hart walked over to Waymore Newby. "Are you with me, man?"

"I'm stayin'," Waymore assured him. "I want MacCallister nearabouts as bad as you do."

Hart nodded and walked to his sons. All of them were cut and bruised from their impacting with the ground at great speeds. Jubal had a wild and unstable look in his eyes. His hatred for Jamie, instead of diminishing over the years, had grown to a fever intensity. Jubal was a whore-master and slaver in New Orleans, making a great deal of money. But he would never be content until he stood over Jamie's body and spat on the corpse.

"We'll move west a few miles, away from that accursed swamp," Hart said. "Allen says they's another trail over yonder. Saddle up. We're riding."

Jamie waited in the deep timber. He had chosen well. His place was thick with underbrush, so thick and tangled if any tried to come in after him, they would have to do so on foot. And this tangle of trees and vines and thorny brush ran for several miles deep and a dozen miles north to south. Jamie's horse was picketed far back in the timber, on graze and ample water. Jamie waited. And it was not a long wait. He smiled when he heard the riders coming. He had guessed correctly what Hart would do.

The column was, as before, formed to protect Hart Olmstead and his sons. The men were riding in sort of a loosely formed

W, with the Olmstead family in the protected middle.

Jamie loosed an arrow and took a man down, the arrow driving in just above his belt, ripping through vital organs. The man screamed and toppled from the saddle.

Jamie instantly changed positions, notching another arrow as he moved. Guns crashed and sent balls into the brush he had just vacated. Jamie let fly another arrow and the arrow pinned a man's arm to his side. He yelled in pain and fought his horse. Jamie moved swiftly, this time on his belly, working his way through the choking underbrush, moving like a huge deadly serpent.

"Get in there and kill the bastard!" he faintly heard the words from Hart.

Yes, Jamie thought. Do come in here after me.

A half dozen men charged their horses into the timber and were stopped cold by the impenetrable growth. Jamie put an arrow into one's chest and the others, fear clouding their faces, raced back into the clearing. Hart and the others had disappeared behind a rise, for this country was gently rolling hills.

Again, Jamie changed position, on his way picking up the fallen man's rifle and powder horn and ball and patch pouch. The rifle was a good one, nearly new, and a heavy caliber. Jamie recharged the musket and slipped to the edge of the timber. He did not have to worry about anyone coming up behind him, or really, anyone coming up on either side of his position. If Hart tried anything, it would have to be a frontal assault.

The crest of the ridge was about a hundred yards away, an easy shot for Jamie if ever a target presented itself. But Hart's men were being very wary.

And Jamie saw the dark humor in that and allowed himself a cold, thin smile. He waited.

Behind the ridge, Hart was in a hard bind and knew it. That damn MacCallister had killed two more men and wounded another. He looked around at what was left of his men and grew discouraged. But the thought of calling a truce with Jamie never entered his mind. His hatred was that great.

"If we ride in any direction," Waymore said, "MacCallister will just pick us off one at a time. If we stay here until dark . . ." His voice trailed off as he received a very dirty look from Olmstead.

"He can't be alone," Patrick Olmstead said. "One man just can't do all that's been done this day."

"He's alone," one of the hired thugs from New Orleans said, as he wrapped a very dirty rag tightly around a sprained wrist, "My woman is French, deep into voodoo, and she says that Jamie MacCallister has spirits around him all the time. Good spirits and bad spirits. She warned me this mission would fail."

Waymore, just about as ignorant as they come, was fascinated. "What else did she say about him?"

"That MacCallister is what the Indians call a shape-shifter."

"What the hell is that?" Jubal asked.

"He can take the form of different animals," the New Orleans man said. "Wolves, panthers, and the like."

"Nonsense!" Hart scoffed.

Just about that time, Jamie started coughing like a panther, and then let loose with a blood-chilling panther scream from the timber.

Several of the men exchanged fearful glances. Most were ignorant to the soul, and it was a highly superstitious time. Four men made up their minds right there and then.

"We're leavin'," one said, after receiving nods from the others. "There ain't no amount of money worth dyin' for. And it wouldn't be wise to try and stop us." They walked to their horses and booted their rifles. Then they found sticks and tied rags to the ends of the sticks and mounted up.

"MacCallister!" one shouted. "They's four of us a-leavin'. We ain't joshin' none. We're a-pullin' out and you ain't never gonna see us agin. These here is sticks in our hands with rags a-tied to the end. Our rifles is booted. We're headin' south. Please let us go."

"Go and be damned!" Hart said. "I hope he shoots you all."

"He won't," the New Orleans man said. " 'Cause he's got something that don't none of us have."

"And what might that be?" Ernest Olmstead asked.

"Honor."

The four men rode out slowly and headed south, each of them expecting a bullet in the back. Jamie let them go.

"Honor!" Jubal yelled at the New Orleans man. "Jamie MacCallister ain't got no honor. He's a goddamned killer is all he is."

The New Orleans man turned his back to the angry young man without replying. MacCallister is damn sure killin' the hell out of us, he thought.

Jamie watched the four men ride out, then did some arithmetic. From the moment he rode away from his cabin, he knew he would be able to cut down the odds some; but he never dreamt he could accomplish what he had done these past twenty-four hours. Olmstead had started out with a fresh and well-equipped army. Now, if Jamie figured correctly, he was down to sixteen men, including Hart. Jamie didn't know it, but Olmstead had less than that.

Hart looked around him. He could not spot Titus or Robert. "Where the hell did those damn niggers go?" he threw out the question.

"Slipped off into the timber, I reckon," a man with a bloody bandage around his head said. "It's not likely we'll ever see them again."

Titus and Robert had stolen some supplies and during the confusion had slipped away. They headed northwest. They wanted no more of Jamie MacCallister or of Hart Olmstead. Mountain men visiting New Orleans had told them of the towering mountains, where a man could live free — if he didn't get killed by Injuns. Titus and Robert had good mounts, weapons, and food. They would ride until their pasts were far behind them, and then try to start anew. Both of them knew one thing for certain: they would never return to the Big Thicket country.

Jamie had taken a packet of food and a canteen of water from the dead man's horse. He ate the food and quenched his thirst and waited in the timber. The next move was up to Hart Olmstead.

Silently, in his mind, Hart Olmstead cursed Jamie MacCallister until he could think of nothing else to call him. He watched as his boy, Ernest, slipped to his side, being careful to stay well behind the ridge.

"Pa, it's over. We got to stay alive for the sake of our wounded kin west of here. Mac-Callister's done cut our force down to nothin'. Half of them that stayed is hurt. MacCallister's got us. It's his deck, his table, and his game."

Hart gave his son a cold look. "Boy, are you suggestin' that we . . . ?"

Ernest cut him off. "I'm suggestin' that we *live,* Pa. I'm sayin' that we call a truce with MacCallister and ride on out of here, over to Nacogdoches. When Carl and the others is able to ride, we head back to New Orleans and get on with livin.' Look, Pa, I hate Jamie MacCallister, but I love life more. We got a good thing goin' in New Orleans. Are we goin' to throw all that away for one man?"

Patrick had slipped up and was listening. He nodded his head in agreement. "Ernest is right, Pa," he said. "More'un half of the men we got left is talkin' 'bout pullin' out. If it was put to a vote, this fight would end right here and now."

Olmstead's shoulders suddenly sagged and he looked and felt his middle age. Hell, he thought, I'm past middle age. He looked down at his hands. They were filthy. He stank of sweat. His clothing was permeated with the stale smell. Slowly, he nodded his head. "Fix a stick with a white rag. Tell MacCallister it's over as far as I'm concerned."

"You ain't talkin' for me, Pa!" Jubal said. "Not now, not never. Not for me, and not for Abel Jackson. Me and him swore a blood oath a long time ago." Jubal paled at the sounds of a dozen hammers being cocked. Slowly he turned. Rifles and pistols were pointed at him.

Ernest took Jubal's pistols and rifle. "Just stand easy, brother. This here is done."

Hart took the stick with the torn shirt on it and waved it above the ridgeline. "Mac-Callister!" he shouted. "Listen to me. I know you ain't goin' to answer me, so just listen. This is Hart Olmstead talkin'. It's over, boy. You hear me? It's over. But I can't talk for my youngest, Jubal. Nor for Abel Jackson. But for me and the rest of mine, you and Kate live your lives. You'll not see me again. Ernest has got Jubal at gunpoint. And he'll be thataway 'til we're long gone. The men is headin' south, and me and mine is headin' over to the settlement to fetch the wounded back. You'll not see me again, MacCallister. Not never."

Something in his voice caused Jamie to believe the man. "All right," he called. "Ride on."

Jubal tried to wrest a rifle from Ernest and his brother gave him a good pop on the side of the head with the butt of the rifle. Jubal went down, addled.

"Jamie? This here's Waymore Newby. I'll be ridin' with Olmstead. You've seen the last of me, MacCallister."

Jamie most definitely did not believe that. But he called, "Ride on, Newby."

Jamie watched the men leave. Hart and his sons, with Waymore tagging along, rode toward Nacogdoches, the rest of the men headed south. He waited until they were out of sight, and then fetched his horse. He buried the dead man with the arrow in his chest, although he wondered why he was taking the time.

Jamie was tired. Wearily, he climbed into

the saddle and rode east. At the edge of the thicket, he turned his horse's head to the north. He had not gone a mile when he heard the sounds of hooves drumming the ground. He slipped into the thicket and waited. It was Bonham and fifteen men from in and around San Augustine. They were all heavily armed and riding with set jaws and fire in their eyes.

Jamie slowly walked his horse out of the thicket and the men reined up. They stared at the fresh scalps tied to the horse's mane and at Jamie's bloody buckskins. They looked at the camouflage on his face and hands.

Bonham was the first to speak. "I gathered up some men and we rode down to help. Looks like you didn't need any help."

Jamie nodded his head.

"How many were there, lad?" a settler asked.

"Fifty-two," Jamie replied.

"Fifty-two!" another man blurted. "Where are they, lad? Let's go finish this."

"If they's enough of us," another man added.

"It's already finished," Jamie told him. "I let the last sixteen or so ride on."

The mounted men sat their saddles and stared at him. A farmer that Jamie knew slightly — he thought his name was Stoddlemire — said, "You killed the rest?"

"Most of them. Although some chose to quit the fight and ride out on their own. I let them go. The wounded was taken over to Nacogdoches. Hart Olmstead and his sons have ridden over there to see about them. They called off the fight now and forever, and I agreed to that."

"You believe that, lad?" Bonham asked.

"For the most part. I think that one day Jubal Olmstead and Abel Jackson will return to pick up the feud. As will the Newby Brothers and the Saxon boys. But John Jackson is dead, and Hart Olmstead has had enough. And so have I."

"You look beat," another citizen from San Augustine remarked.

"I am," Jamie admitted. He'd been pumped up with adrenaline for hours, and now the letdown was visible. "But I have to get back to Kate and the others."

"Do you relax, lad," Bonham said. "They're just fine. Some of your Indian friends showed up and would've like to have scared me slap out of my boots. One second I was enjoyin' a cup of coffee, all alone by your cabin, the next second I was surrounded by Redskins. An army couldn't get to Kate and the others, even if they was to home."

"You and your family have got to start socializing, Jamie," another man said. "After all, we're all well within riding distance of your cabins."

"Yes," said a man Jamie knew only as Howard. "It's time we had a long talk with you. We've grand plans for Texas."

"I know," Jamie said. "Egg told me."

"He *told* you?" another blurted.

"What did he say?" yet another man asked.

"Later, Ralph," Stoddlemire said, dismounting. "Come on, Jamie. Let's get some hot food in you and some coffee. Then we'll ride back with you." He looked over at Jamie, a twinkle in his eyes. "I was going to say that the next time you're in trouble, all you have to do is holler, and we'll come runnin'. But you're a regular one-man army."

"Yes," Bonham said. "You can bet that the story of this fight will spread all over the land."

He was right. When Jim Bowie heard the story of how one man, Jamie Ian MacCallister, successfully fought more than fifty men, and killed more than half of them, he startled the diners in the elegant restaurant by shouting, "By God, boys. That's a man. I want to meet this young fellow."

When the news reached Davy Crockett, way up in Tennessee, he whooped, "Thar's a man's man, boys. I hope I get to meet this grizzly bar someday."

Bowie and Crockett would get their wish, in just about four years. During a cold winter in early 1836 at a crumbling old church built by Franciscan friars and named the Mission of San Antonio de Valero, where some one hundred and eighty-two men would withstand nearly two weeks of siege and ninety blood-drenched minutes on the final day . . . at The Alamo.

TWENTY-THREE

Jamie put the fight behind him and concentrated on living. He told Sam and Sarah, Swede and Hannah, Moses and Liza, Wells and Sally, and of course, Kate, what had happened, once, and then he would speak no more of it. He learned that three of those taken to the doctor at Nacogdoches had died, one before reaching there, and that Hart Olmstead and sons were gone back to Louisiana, Waymore Newby with them.

Jamie put all that out of his mind and settled down to the chores of everyday living on a rapidly growing farm. Young as he was, Jamie had to sit down to stop the dizziness in his head when Liza and Hannah and Sarah and Sally came out onto the newly built porch one day with the news. Jamie was the father of triplets. Matthew, Megan, and Morgan.

"Boy," Moses said, putting an arm around Jamie's shoulders. "This has got to stop!"

Jamie numbly nodded his head.

"What are you, twenty-one or twenty-two years old and already the father of *seven*?"

"Seven," Jamie said, his voice weak. *"Seven?"*

"Son," Sam said. "When Kate allows you close to her again, which I hope won't be for a couple of years, and you feel amorous, go jump in the creek, will you?"

"Bayou," Jamie automatically corrected.

"Whatever!" Sam said.

"Maybe separate bedrooms?" Wells mused aloud.

Jamie gave him a dirty look.

"Or a bundlin' board," Moses suggested.

Jamie sighed and took the good-natured ribbing.

"Hell, he'd just climb over it," Swede said.

"He won't for a long time," Sarah said, joining the men. "These were hard birthings for her, Jamie. She'll be all right. But she's got to rest and rest plenty."

"But she'll be all right?" Jamie asked, anxiety in the question.

"Yes. I'm as sure of that as I can be."

"I had a dog once," Swede said. "She gave birth to nine puppies. All of them lived. And her with only eight teats. You should have seen her moving those pups around from teat to teat. I guess Kate will have to . . ."

340

He caught himself and fell silent, glancing up at Sarah. The look she gave him would have withered a cactus.

Swede covered his mouth with a big hand and blushed from his nose to his toes.

Jamie stood up. "Can I see Kate and the babies?"

"Oh, yes," Sarah said. "But only for a brief time." As Jamie walked toward the house, Sarah sat down beside her husband and he put an arm around her shoulders.

"Was it bad, love?" he asked.

"Very bad. I don't think she should have any more children. And Hannah and Liza agree."

"What does Kate say?"

Sarah shook her head. "She says that's nonsense. She says she wants nine children, and nine children she will have. Sam, Jamie and Kate are not much more than children themselves! What are they going to do?"

Sam looked at all the little MacCallisters running around, in the front yard. They all looked alike: fair-skinned, blond hair, and blue eyes. "Kate is as hardheaded as Jamie. And in her own way, just as strong."

"That doesn't answer my question."

Sam smiled. "Oh, they'll probably have nine kids."

"You're not much help," Sarah said dryly.

"What do you want me to do, sleep between them?"

After the laughter had faded and the conversation shifted to other, less important matters, Sam looked at Roscoe and Anne, playing with the other children in the yard. Although their mother had been half white — he'd been told the whole sordid story — the twins were as lily white as the MacCallister kids.

Heartbreak and grief plays yonder, Sam thought. In here, in this cocoon, they are isolated and protected from the cruel and cold outside world. But as they grow older, they are going to be slapped hard by reality. If they are truthful about their heritage, they will not be totally admitted into either world. I feel sorry for them.

The twins, now either eight or nine, no one knew for sure, not even Wells, were lovely children. Roscoe would surely turn into a handsome man, and Anne into a beautiful woman. But both twins had developed a sneaky and sly streak. They weren't always truthful and sometimes they "borrowed" things without telling the owner. When confronted about it, they both would become tearful and claim complete innocence.

Sam felt eyes on him and he looked up

into the eyes of Moses. Moses arched one eyebrow, as if knowing what Sam had been thinking. Then he slowly and minutely nodded his head, as if silently confirming Sam's suspicions. Then Moses stood up and walked away.

Sam watched as Anne looked quickly around her to see if any of the other children were watching, and then picked up a ribbon that had fallen from the hair of Ellen Kathleen and slipped it into the side pocket of her dress. She went right back to playing hopscotch as if nothing had happened.

After dozens of meetings, over the next eighteen months, with some of the men from the village of San Augustine, Jamie elected to ride south, down to Smith's Trading Post. Both Smith and Fontaine had sent word that they wanted to see him. Almost two years before, Mexico's Centralist government, under the cruel and dictatorial Anastacio Bustamante, had moved to crush any rebellion the free-spirited Texans might be dreaming up. Bustamante passed a law that ordered the military occupation of Texas with convict soldiers, who were to remain on the land when their 'enlistment' was up, and the law also stopped any further immigration of Americans into Texas.

It was June 25, 1832, when Jamie stepped down from his horse in front of Smith's General Store, as it was now called. Jamie was twenty-two years old, and a man grown. He was almost six feet, four inches tall, and weighed two hundred and thirty pounds, with shoulders packed with muscle and arms so huge that it was a good thing Kate made his homespuns — when he elected to get out of buckskins — for no store-bought shirt would fit him. He walked through the store, and every eye turned to look at the tall young man with the long blond hair, tanned face, and cold blue eyes. He picked out a few things he would buy, for Kate and the children, and then adjourned to the bar for a drink. Jamie rarely tasted whiskey, but he did enjoy a drink now and then. He preferred wine — a glass or two before sup-per — and made gallons of it from wild ber-ries every year, as did the others in the small community in the thicket.

Smith and Fontaine joined Jamie at the bar. "Revolution is in the air, Jamie," Fontaine said, speaking in low tones. "Both here and down in Mexico. Santa Anna is preparing to oust Bustamante, and some think the man is less a monster than Busta-mante, and will listen to our grievances. I'm not so sure. But we have problems closer to

home. Have you ever heard of John Bradburn?"

Jamie shook his head and sipped his whiskey.

"Well, he's an American mercenary colonel in the Mexican Army. He took over the
garrison in Anahuac, not far from here.
Now he's about to abolish the town of
Liberty and seize the American settlers'
land. When he does, all hell is going to break
loose."

"What is he, a fool?" Jamie asked.

"Yes. And an arrogant one, at that. We are
well known to him, but you are not. We
would like for you to ride to Liberty and assess the situation. Will you do that?"

Jamie nodded his head. His crops were all
in and looking good. He had just worked
his fields and could take time off. "Yes. Tell
me what you want me to do."

"We'll talk about it over supper this
evening, and come the morning, you can
ride out fresh. Don't worry; I'm not being
watched. I'm certain of that."

But Fontaine and Smith had been a few
days late in calling on Jamie to ride in and
assess the situation. Before Jamie could even
get started on his trip to Liberty, Fontaine
received word that about a hundred and
fifty Texas colonists were on the march

toward Liberty to rescue the settlers that Colonel Bradburn had jailed. A battle ensued between Texas colonists and Mexican troops near the mouth of the Brazos River. Both sides took casualties but the colonists emerged the clear victors when the Mexicans threw away their weapons and ran for their lives.

"It's started," Smith said. "There is no stopping us now, lad."

"That depends on whether Wharton or Austin prevails at the self-government convention we've called for in October." Fontaine's words dashed cold water on Smith's hopes.

Jamie fixed the man with a blank look.

"Austin is the cooler head," Fontaine explained. "He prefers to take it one step at a time. President Jackson agrees with that. Wharton is somewhat of a hothead, albeit a good and loyal man. Wharton is demanding total independence from Mexico. It's too soon for that." He patted Jamie on the shoulder. "Well, let us older heads continue to fight the war of words, lad. As for you, keep your powder dry."

Jamie rode back to his cabin in the thicket. He was not a politician; he had absolutely no interest in great flowery speeches — either in making them or listening to them.

He was a farmer. Nothing more. So he thought. Jamie got along well with the Mexicans who lived close by — ten miles away meant a close neighbor — and he had learned Spanish and spoke it well. But as far as he was concerned, Texas belonged to America, not Mexico, and so did most of the Mexicans who lived nearby. And if ever Mexican soldiers tried to seize his land, or put Jamie Ian MacCallister in jail, they'd have a fight on their hands.

Kate was delighted to see him return so quickly. "I thought you'd be gone for weeks," she said.

"So did I." He explained to her, and to the rest of his immediate neighbors, what he had been told by Smith and Fontaine.

"So this means war?" Sam asked, a worried look on his face.

Jamie shrugged. "Maybe. Fontaine and Smith seem to think that this Santa Anna person will be easier to get along with than Bustamante. I guess only time will tell about that."

Jamie and his neighbors worked their fields and lived in peace for two years, gathering their crops and enjoying life. Kate had a child early in '34. A girl they named Joleen. Jamie and Sam and Swede occasionally rode into San Augustine for news — Moses and Wells never left the thicket — and sometimes Kate and Sarah and Hannah piled into wagons and accompanied the men into the village, just for a break in the routine and to talk to other people.

Back in October of 1832, a group of Texans held a convention in San Felipe on the Brazos. It was to be the first of many on the march for independence. The firebrand, William Wharton, delivered a stormy speech, demanding absolute independence from Mexico. He tried to get elected president of the convention, but Austin, a cooler head, defeated him. The delegates wrote a petition and approved its delivery to Mexico. The petition's main points demanded separation from the state of Coahuila and full Mexican statehood for Texas.

But the petition, for whatever reasons, never reached Mexico City, probably due to the bitter civil war raging in that country.

Those living in the thicket knew nothing of this, for the winters were bitter those years and most stayed close to hearth and home. They did not know until several months after it happened that in January of 1833, General Antonio Lopez de Santa Anna succeeded in driving Anastacio Bustamante from the office of president of Mexico. The Texans were excited at the news and immediately called for a new convention to be held in San Felipe in April of '33.

Neither did those in the Big Thicket country know that it was during this time of struggle that Sam Houston crossed the Red River and rode some one hundred and seventy-odd miles south to Nacogdoches, then the most populated and largest American town in Texas. Houston met with two old friends of earlier days, Adolphus Sterne and Henry Raguet, and they told him of the young warrior called Man Who Is Not Afraid, Jamie Ian MacCallister. Later, after Houston had left Nacogdoches and ridden down to San Felipe and rejoined an old drinking pal of his, Jim Bowie, Houston told Bowie of MacCallister.

Bowie, who had settled in Texas a few years earlier, after marrying Maria Ursula de Veramendi, the daughter of the most prominent family in Coahuila y Texas, nodded his head.

"I keep hearing the name. I want to meet this man. He is my kind of man, and we'll need men like him when we make our move for independence, and that is surely coming."

Houston explained to Bowie his real reason for coming to Texas: to meet, at President Jackson's request, with the Comanches in an effort to bring peace between them and the white settlers.

It would turn out to be only a token gesture that would accomplish nothing. And when Mexico learned of the meeting, they drafted a formal letter of protest to Washington, stating they resented the interference from the American president. The president never received it.

After Houston met with several chiefs of the Comanches, he returned to San Felipe and spent a day, in private, with Stephen Austin. While the two men were not best of friends, neither were they enemies — they were just different. Austin was a quiet sort, much given to introspection, quite the diplomat, and very idealistic. Houston, on the other hand, was quite vocal, extremely aggressive, dashing and lively in dress, and somewhat of an adventurer.

But they both put any differences aside and placed their minds together to map out the future of Texas.

When Houston returned to Nacogdoches, he found that the citizens there had placed his name in nomination to be their delegate at the upcoming convention in April, in San

Felipe. He accepted and helped draft the first constitution for the state, and the delegates asked Stephen Austin to take the petition and the new constitution to Mexico and meet with Santa Anna. Austin, although still a relatively young man of thirty-nine, was not in good health, but he agreed to go. That trip got him arrested in Mexico and cost him eight months in a Mexican calaboose. After three months in solitary confinement, he was moved to better quarters and could write letters, telling his friends and family where he was and pleading for the Texans to remain calm, and take no violent action. The Texans agreed to that. Austin would not return home for nearly two years; no longer under arrest after eight months, but not allowed to leave Mexico.

Like Austin, Houston asked for calm and restraint. During this time, Sam Houston, a lifelong atheist, joined the Catholic church — as was required of all landowners — and took the name of Don Samuel Pablo Houston. Before doing all this, he divorced his wife, Eliza.

Also during this period of time, Jim Bowie lost his wife and two children to cholera. For months, he all but slept in a barrel of whiskey and his health deteriorated badly.

■ ■ ■ ■

Over in the swamps and cleared fields of the Big Thicket, life went on, with Jamie and Kate and family snug in their cabin — although it would be inaccurate to call the now six-room structure a cabin.

In March of 1834, just as Jamie and the others were sharpening their axes and getting ready their plows and teams for the spring planting, Bonham sent him word: some rascally-looking men had been making inquiries about Jamie down at Beau Mont, in the saloons that catered to the less desirable clientele. One of them was named Saxon.

TWENTY-FOUR

"When will it end, Jamie?" Kate asked, as she watched him carefully clean his guns and stroke the blade of his big knife over the sharpening stone.

"When they're all dead, I reckon, Kate." He smiled at her. "Texas is on the move and I need to be in the fields."

"The Nunez boys can plow and plant, Jamie. You know they idolize you."

The Juan Nunez family lived right on the edge of the thicket and Jamie and Kate had become friends with them. During the winter, Juan and his wife, Maria, became seriously ill and Jamie and Kate nursed them back to health and saw to the needs of their children during their illness. Jamie and Kate had made friends for life.

"I thought those horrible Saxon brothers and their kin were working for my father." Kate said.

"I guess they branched out on their own."

He stood up, treetop tall and with shoulders so broad he had to turn sideways to go through many doorways, and leaned down and kissed his wife. "I've already arranged for the Nunez boys to get the land ready and to plant if I'm not back."

She handed him a packet of food and waited until he had looked in on all the children, standing for a time looking down at the sleeping Joleen, and then walked with him outside, where young Jamie, now eight years old, stood holding the reins to Jamie's horse.

"Boy," Jamie told his son, whose head was so far back looking up at his father he was in danger of falling over, "you take care of your ma, now, you hear?"

"Yes, Pa. I will."

"And you mind her, too, you hear?"

"Yes, Pa." Then he quite unintentionally toppled over backward, landing on his butt. He grinned up at his parents, and made a face at his twin sister, who was by the corner of the house, sticking her tongue out at him.

Laughing at young Jamie's antics, Jamie and Kate walked out to where Sam and Sarah, Swede and Hannah, Moses and Liza, and Wells and Sally had gathered. All the men were a little miffed at Jamie's refusal to let them accompany him.

"I'll be back," Jamie told them. "Two weeks, a month, two months. I don't know. But I am going to resolve this matter. One way or the other."

Sam looked at the horse's mane, now holding more than two dozen dried scalps. He just never would understand the lad, he thought. And Lord knows he had tried.

Swede tried not to look at the scalps. One side of him thought they were disgusting and certainly not something any civilized man would so proudly place on exhibit. However, the other side of him was proud of Jamie for doing what most people did not have the courage to do: defending his family and himself and openly defying tradition by silently telling others: this is what happens when you commit lawless acts against me or mine. So beware. Same principle as a Keep Off sign, albeit just a tad more graphic. Hannah had quietly changed Swede since their marriage. And Swede was not nearly as reluctant to fight as Jamie thought he was.

At the same moment Jamie was speaking to his friends, Jim Bowie was leaving San Felipe for a visit with a friend, Fontaine, who would meet with him and a few others caught up in the Texas independence movement, in the back of Smith's store.

Bowie rode with only a few friends accompanying him, not at all concerned about Indian attack . . . he rather looked forward to any fracas that might occur. Bowie had since stopped his wild drinking as the grief over the death of his wife and children abated. But he was still a good hand with the jug from time to time.

During one of their meetings, Louis Fontaine had admitted to Jamie that he was a government agent, acting on orders from President Jackson. Only Smith, Austin, and Adolphus Sterne knew that, and now Jamie knew it.

On his ride south, Jamie was amazed at the number of new cabins up and going up. Americans were ignoring Mexico's ban on immigration and coming across the borders and settling. Jamie reckoned there must now be hundreds of American families living in Texas. He was right. By 1837, there would be fourteen thousand American families living in Texas.

Jamie encountered no trouble on his ride south. He did receive some rather curious looks from the new people settling in; and the scalps tied to his horse's mane did, too. But nobody had any comments to make about them. When the man sitting the saddle looked as though he had been hewn out of oak, only the most unwise or foolhardy would be prompted to have anything derogatory to say.

Jamie took his time getting to his destination, stopping often to talk with people, so Bowie and friends were there before he arrived. Jim Bowie, a big strapping man of over six feet and weighing nearly a hundred and ninety pounds, was standing on the porch of Smith's General Store when Jamie rode in. Bowie took one look and made up his mind. Jamie Ian MacCallister was a man to ride the river with. That they were opposites held no doubt in Jim's mind, for Jamie's manner suggested that he was a quiet man, while Jim could be and usually was, loud and boisterous. Bowie was also a drinking and hard partying man. Looking at Jamie, Bowie had the thought that the young mountain of a man had never been drunk in his life and probably never would be. He was correct. Bowie had been told by Fontaine that Jamie was antislavery. Bowie smiled at that. In one year's time, the Kentucky born Jim and his brothers, John and Rezin, had made thousands of dollars working with the pirate, Jean Lafitte, smuggling slaves. Jim had done it all and was ashamed of none of it. But he also held that each man had the right to his personal opinion on issues and was not to be faulted if that opinion ran across the grain of his own.

And Bowie was amused when he saw the scalps tied to the mane of Jamie's horse. Here, he thought, was a man clearly warning all he met that he would tolerate no excess liberties to be taken upon him. Bowie had heard of the men camped outside of the town, and Fontaine and Smith had brought him up to date on the bounty hunters and their relentless pursuit of Jamie MacCallister. This was shaping up to be a very interesting day, Jim thought, for two of the men who were hunting Jamie were in the grog shop just across the rutted street. Yes, Jim thought, lighting a cheroot, it was shaping up to be a very interesting day.

Jim watched as Fontaine's scout, Bonham, a good, steady men, Jim thought, hailed Jamie and then walked into the street to speak with him.

"They's a passel of them in town, Jamie," the scout told him. "And they're spread all over, but most of them is down to that Mex joint. They's two of them over yonder acrost the street. One says his name is Andy Saxon. Come on," Bonham said. "There is someone I want you to meet."

Jim Bowie was not a man easily impressed. But Jamie Ian MacCallister impressed the hell out of him. The young man — Jim guessed him to be in his early twenties — was huge, with wrists that Bowie guessed would be an easy ten or twelve inches around. The lad does not know his own strength, Bowie guessed again, and knew he was right.

Bowie smiled at Jamie's easy handshake. A lot of men liked to show off their strength by grinding the other fellow's knuckles together. That was done to Bowie once. Jim told the oaf that if he ever did it again, he'd spread him wide open and let him look at his own guts.

But not Jamie. Jamie was no show-off. He was a man who knew his own capabilities and limits and that was something that most men never realized. Jim Bowie liked the tall, long-haired young man immediately. Jim started to offer his help in dealing with the Saxon gang, then decided against it. He wanted to see Jamie in action.

Smith and Fontaine were indisposed for a time, Jim told Jamie.

"Well, how about a drink then?" Jamie said. Then he smiled and added, "Across the street."

Bowie returned the smile. "I have been

known to tipple from time to time."

"Well, let's go tipple then," Jamie said, handing the reins to one of Smith's manservants. The Indian smiled secretly at Jamie.

Bonhan chuckled as the three of them walked across the road. This was going to be fun!

Bowie had noticed — not much escaped the adventurer's eyes — that Jamie had booted his rifle and carried only his two pistols behind his sash. But the knife Jamie carried in a beaded sheath looked familiar and he asked him about it.

"Made by Noah Smithwick," Jamie said. "I believe you have made his acquaintance."

Bowie smiled and then laughed. For it was Noah who had made the knife he now carried in a sheath at his side. "I've met the gentleman a time or two," Bowie responded, as the men stepped to the door of the shady saloon.

The saloon stank of stale sweat, unwashed bodies, and clothing worn too long. The noses of Jamie, Bonham, and Bowie wrinkled against the unnecessary foulness as they stepped into the semigloom of the grog shop and walked to the plank bar.

The saloon was full for this time of day, and as Bonham had whispered to Jamie upon his arrival, he knew none of the men.

"What a foul lot," Bowie said, in a voice that was deliberately loud and intended to reach the ears of everyone present. It did.

Some of the men stirred in anger, but none among them had any desire whatsoever to match blades with Jim Bowie. For if they challenged him, it would be Bowie's choice of weapons, and they all knew what that would be.

"Whiskey," Jamie said. "And wash out the cups," he added. "Carefully."

Bowie and Bonham laughed at that.

The barkeep gave Jamie a hot look, but was wise enough to add nothing vocally. He dunked three cups in a bucket of water and set them and a jug on the planks. Then the man behind the bar moved to the far end, just as far as he could go, putting himself well out of the line of fire he felt was inevitable.

Bowie splashed whiskey in his cup and downed it. "Awful stuff," he said, then smiled. "Don't know why anyone would want to drink it." Then he picked up the jug and refilled his cup.

Why anyone would want to tangle with a person of Jamie's size and near legend reputation was a mystery to both Bonham and Bowie. Even quietly standing at the rough bar, slowly sipping his cup of whiskey, even a fool could see that MacCallister had the power in those massive arms to snap a grown man's back like a twig. But the Good Lord, in all His wisdom, for whatever reason, placed a large number of fools on this earth. And on this day, in the spring of 1834, the dark, smelly saloon held no small number of them.

One of them stood up and walked to the bar, stopping directly behind Jamie. "Mac-Callister! You're wanted back in the States on a number of charges."

"All those warrants have long been dismissed," Jamie said, without turning around. "Do you be a wise man, now, and return to your seat. I wish no trouble."

"Jamie Ian MacCallister," the man persisted in a loud voice. "Surrender or die, you back-shootin', murderin' son of a bitch!"

Jamie turned around and hit the man. His big fist struck the man just above the left ear and it sounded like a melon hit with the flat side of a shovel. The man's boots flew out from under him and he was sent crashing to the floor, about ten feet from where he had stood. He did not move.

Jamie's swing had not seemed rushed, but Bowie knew he had just witnessed one of the most powerful blows he had ever seen.

Blood was leaking from the prostrate man's nose and mouth and left ear. Bowie had seen many a dead man in his wild and oftentimes violent life, and he knew he was looking at another.

An unshaven and loutish-looking man knelt down beside the man on the dirty floor. "You've killed him!" he said.

Jamie shrugged his heavy shoulders in complete indifference. "He threatened me," was all he had to say.

"Do you know who this is?" the kneeling man asked.

"No, and I don't care," Jamie replied, taking another small sip of whiskey.

"This here's Andy Saxon."

"Am I supposed to be impressed?"

The man rose to his boots and slowly made his way to the door. "You're a dead man, Jamie MacCallister," he said. "Andy's kin will track you to hell for this."

Jamie turned to face the man. "That's been tried by better men than that scum on the floor. They're dead and I'm still here."

The man turned and ran from the saloon. He jumped into the saddle of a horse tied at the hitchrail and galloped off.

Bowie tossed some coins on the planks. "The service was lousy, the whiskey raw, and the clientele surly. But the show was excellent. Let's go, boys. We have a meeting to attend."

"What about that there feller on the floor?" the counterman cried.

"The way I see it," Bowie said, "you have two options. You can leave him there until he petrifies, and then prop him in a corner as a conversation piece. Or you can bury him. My suggestion is the latter. In this climate he's going to get very rank, very quickly."

Bowie, Bonham, and Jamie walked out.

Twenty-Five

Bowie studied Jamie as they walked. He could detect no change in the man's demeanor. Jamie had just stretched a man out dead on the floor, either with a broken neck or a broken skull, and he had not changed expression yet. Fontaine had told Bowie that Jamie was very bright, and Bowie had realized almost instantly that he certainly was not dealing with some sort of dullard. Then he had to suppress a chuckle. When had *he* ever been terribly overcome with grief after a killing?

Now he knew why he had taken such an immediate cotton to the lad — they were both as much alike as two peas in a pod.

At the meeting, Fontaine and Smith were uncommonly blunt. "War is looming on the horizon, Jamie. I would guess no more than a year away. We need to know exactly where you stand."

"I stand for Texas independence," Jamie

said without hesitation. "I thought I had made that clear."

Fontaine nodded his head, as did Smith. "This is something we're asking of all our people, Jamie. You have not been singled out for questioning."

"You have your answer," Bowie said shortly. "Now, what about Santa Anna?"

"Santa Anna is no friend of ours," Fontaine said. "We were all wrong about him."

They certainly were. By now it was clear that Santa Anna was a tyrant. He was rapidly becoming a dictator, with the Mexican congress snugly in his pocket. Santa Anna had made it abundantly clear that under no circumstances was Texas to be free of Mexico's control.

But Santa Anna had made a few other mistakes along the way. One was allowing land to be more easily acquired, and two was modification of the laws allowing new settlers to come in, and come in they did, by the thousands.

Austin had smuggled a letter out of Mexico, the contents of which, had they been seen by Santa Anna, would have put Austin up in front of a firing squad. Austin had some pretty strong things to say about Santa Anna, and called for war.

"Our army?" Jamie questioned.

Smith smiled. "Loose and highly disorganized. It's far too soon to call openly for volunteers. But they will be there when the time comes."

"And I am to do what?" Jamie asked.

"Wait," Bowie told him. "That's all any of us can do."

After Jamie had excused himself, saying he had some business to attend to, Fontaine looked at Bowie. "What do you think?"

"He's solid as an oak."

"Tell us what happened across the street," Smith urged.

"He killed a man with one blow from his fist," Bowie said simply. "Dispatching him without a change of expression."

"Do you think he's a killer without conscience?" Fontaine asked.

Bowie smiled. "No more than I am."

Jamie rode toward the encampment of the Saxon gang with every intention of ending this years-long pursuit once and for all. But when he reached the camp, it was deserted. The coals were still hot and scraps of food and bits of ragged and discarded clothing were scattered about, but the Saxons and their followers were gone.

Jamie picked up their trail and found they had gone south for a few miles, then cut east toward the Sabine River. He followed the obvious trail for a few miles, then gave it up when it became clear the gang was quitting the hunt. For what reasons, Jamie did not have a clue.

"Good," he muttered, and turned his horse's head north, toward Kate and home.

Everyone was both surprised and pleased to see him return so soon. Kate had feared that he might be gone for weeks, or even months. And, secretly, she feared for her husband's life, for she knew him better than anyone, and knew the chances he took. Hannah had explained the warrior's way to her. And even though Jamie had spent only a few years with the Shawnees, the lessons he had learned there were burned deep within him, and they would remain there all his life.

So for nearly a year, the political struggling and rumors of war were forgotten by those in the Big Thicket as they concentrated on their own struggling to stay alive, work their fields, and raise their families. Jamie did not know why the Saxon Brothers had given up their hunt for him, but he felt sure that one day he would meet them and it would have to be settled.

In the world outside the Big Thicket, events were rushing toward war. Santa Anna had sent his brother-in-law, General Martin Perfecto do Cos, to Saltillo, with orders to get rid of the Federalist governor and his staff, who were openly opposed to Santa Anna's dictatorial ways. War between the Texans and the forces of Santa Anna moved closer.

Sam Houston continued to tell his followers to stay calm. War was coming, but not just yet.

Over in San Felipe, a flamboyant young attorney, William Barret Travis had put together a small force of some twenty-five men. Hardly an army, but it was the beginning of one. Some say it was Travis and his little force, a few months later, who really fired the first shot of the revolution — but Texas was huge, and there were shots being fired all over the place, so no one is really sure.

Fontaine sent Bonham to fetch Jamie. Travis wanted to meet him. Jamie agreed, but could not understand why the special interest in him. There were hundreds of men who knew Texas better, so why him?

Bonham shrugged his shoulders. A few days later, at the rear of Smith's store, Fontaine cleared it up. "Because you represent what Texas is all about, Jamie. It doesn't make any difference whether you were born here, or not. At this point in time, most Texans have come in here from somewhere else. But you're free, and you're willing to die for that freedom. You're a little bit wild, and you don't give a tinker's damn whether others approve of that, or not. You're true to yourself and to your family. That's Texas. You stand up for what you believe in, and if the law, or lack of it, can't handle it, you will and to hell with those who don't have the backbone to fight for what they believe in. That's Texas, Jamie." The government man smiled and called, "All right, Mr. Travis, please come in."

Jamie Ian MacCallister and William Barret Travis shook hands and sized each other up. Jamie had heard that Jim Bowie and Travis did not really like one another, and Jamie could see why.

As they drank coffee and talked, Jamie could see that the two men were opposites. Bowie was wild and unruly and oftentimes quite unpredictable, while Travis was outwardly cold and calculating. But Travis was also hotheaded and did not like his orders questioned, and he was the sort who felt that his way was the only way. Regardless of that, Jamie and Travis, in only a few short hours that day, grew to like and respect each other. And Jamie could sense that Travis, like Bowie, was fearless. When everybody involved finally made their declaration and committed, it was going to be a matter of wills as to who would actually lead the Texas Army of Independence, Travis or Bowie.

Travis left Jamie with these words: "Stand ready for the call, Jamie MacCallister."

"Blowhard," Bowie muttered.

Jamie was back home in time to help with the spring planting.

On a warm and not unpleasant Saturday evening, when all were gathered at Jamie and Kate's for an evening of conversation and food and some hard cider for the men (the men didn't know it, but the ladies had a jug hid out behind the woodpile for themselves), Jamie broke the news to them all.

"I might get the call to go and fight at any time. So I've arranged for help to come over. Juan has brothers just recently moved into this area, and they're good people and need to work. I . . ." He shook his head and smiled. "We don't even have an army yet. But Bowie, Travis, Smith, and Fontaine want me to leave the land and become a scout for them. I'm torn, I tell you."

"Do you want to go, Jamie?" Kate asked.

"Yes. I do."

"Then it's settled. You'll go."

"Texas obviously needs you, Jamie," Sam said. "I believe it's your duty."

"Jamie," Swede said, leaning closer. "We all live within shouting distance of each other. We've quite a little settlement here and we can put together a fighting force in a matter of seconds."

That was true. Jamie had insisted upon all the women mastering rifle and pistol.

Jamie nodded his head. "All right. But I'll be gone for months, surely."

Kate looked at him, her blue eyes twinkling. "But won't it be fun when you do return?"

Jamie reached San Felipe in time to speak briefly with a very excited Travis. "They've done it, lad!" Travis said. "General Cos has reopened the garrison and the customs house at Anahuac and is sending troops in to reinforce those stationed there. We grabbed a Mexican courier and took these dispatches from him." He waved several papers under Jamie's nose. "But wait! There is more. Much more. In here," he thumped the papers, "is a signed statement from a ranking Mexican general, clearly stating that when the conquest of Zacatecas is complete, Santa Anna himself will lead the Mexican

Army to us and crush us!"

Actually, Travis's Spanish was not that good. Nowhere in the dispatches did it mention the word "crush," which is *aplastar.* The word *castigar* was used, which meant punish or chastise.

"We ride for the garrison?" Jamie asked.

"We ride, lad!"

"How many in your army?"

"Twenty-five brave Texans and one cannon!" Travis said proudly.

Jamie blinked at that. "Against how many?"

"That's what you are to find out, Jamie. Ride like the wind and report back to me immediately."

"Yes, sir, ah . . . ?"

"Colonel, Jamie. In the Texas Army of Independence."

"Yes, sir, Colonel Travis."

When Jim Bowie heard of that he, too, became a colonel and started putting together his own command. It was sort of an odd way to fight a war.

"We'll meet you on your way back!" Travis shouted.

Jamie lifted a hand and was gone.

What Jamie found in the garrison at the tiny settlement of Anahuac was one officer and about fifty enlisted men. He learned this by sitting in a cantina and watching the post.

That the Mexican officer in charge was hated by most of the Mexican locals was summed up when a man engaged Jamie in conversation and called the Mexican officer a rotten son of a bitch.

But the man was watching Jamie closely, too closely. And Jamie sensed he was an informer and merely smiled and shrugged his shoulders. "I never get involved in local politics," he told the man. "I'm from Louisiana over here visiting friends." He jerked a thumb. "Up north."

The man smiled and Jamie could see him relax. "You are wise, señor. If you are hungry, they serve excellent food here. I know. My sister is the cook!"

Jamie ate the hot spicy food and drank about a gallon of water to cool the flames. Then he began the long ride back east. About halfway there, he met Travis and his command.

"About fifty men, Colonel," Jamie reported. "I only saw one officer. But that officer has spies all over the settlement. One approached me."

"You obviously convinced him you were not involved in any skullduggery."

"I believe so."

"Good. Ride with me at the head of the column. We're on the march."

On June the 29th, 1835, Colonel William Barret Travis and his small army, rode up to within shelling distance of the garrison in Anahuac and sent Jamie, under a white flag of truce, to relay a message.

"And that message is?" the officer in charge said with a sneer.

"Surrender, señor," Jamie told him.

The Mexican commander spat on the ground by Jamie's feet. "There is your reply. Come the dawning, I will see you all dead!"

"I doubt it. But *gracias* anyway." Jamie walked back to his horse and returned to Colonel Travis with the message.

"Make ready the cannon!" Travis ordered.

The cannonball crashed into the compound without killing anyone but scaring the hell out of everyone. The Mexican officer was certain that this tiny force was the vanguard of a much larger force and immediately ran up the white flag of surrender.

Travis rode up to the gate. "Stack your arms and deliver them to us. Tomorrow, at first light, you and your command will leave Texas."

"Sí, señor!" the officer said.

As he watched them leave just after dawn, Jamie wondered if all wars were as easily won as this one?

When Travis and his victorious force returned to San Felipe, they found, much to their surprise, that the majority of people there had suddenly had a change of heart and were soundly condemning Travis's actions at the Mexican garrison.

"You acted in haste!" one clearly frightened citizen told the startled Travis. "We could all be wiped out because of your brashness."

Travis was furious, but managed to contain his anger when a committee from the town wrote a letter of apology to the commander of the small garrison at Anahuac. He even kept his temper in check when that same committee demanded that he do the same. He finally wrote the note of apology, but those that knew him could clearly see that beneath the words, it was definitely tongue in cheek. Jamie knew then that the seemingly straight-laced Travis had a wicked sense of humor.

Jamie kept in touch with Kate and his friends back in the thicket by posting letters to the village of San Augustine whenever he could, which was not often, for Travis had him riding all over the south part of Texas, gathering little tidbits of information. For the first time since leaving the Big Thicket, Jamie felt he was finally doing something worthwhile, both for the independence movement and for himself.

Jamie was learning the country and the people who lived there. Since he had mastered Spanish, he moved easily among the Spanish and the Anglos. Several times he encountered bands of Kiowa and Comanche on his lonely rides. But he was not attacked by them. Like Houston, the Indians knew Jamie was a friend if they would let him be, and they did, reluctantly, even though the Comanches were probably the most hated of all Indians in Texas . . . much of that hatred richly deserved, for the Comanche and their allies, the Kiowa, certainly earned the name savage in their wars against the white settlers. They butchered their way through Texas history, until the Texans finally had enough of it and very nearly wiped them out; those that were left were placed on reservations up in Indian Territory, an area that would later become Oklahoma.

"Man Who Is Not Afraid just might be a fool!" one Comanche chief told Jamie one hot afternoon.

"And Big Bear just might not live out this day if he does not watch his words," Jamie retorted. Jamie knew only too well that the Indian admired and respected courage, if nothing else. If he showed one second of fear, they would kill him on the spot. Jamie also knew that the chief — actually a sub-chief — was watching the muzzle of Jamie's carbine, which was pointed directly at the Indian's chest.

The Comanche grunted. "I think you would die well, but not on this day." He led his band away in a swirling cloud of dust.

Jamie rode on, toward San Antonio.

After bathing and shaving, Jamie walked through the streets of the town. San Antonio was the largest town in Texas at the time, boasted more than two thousand citizens. Jamie enjoyed his first meal cooked by someone other than himself in days, and watched the passing parade of colorfully dressed men and women. But his eyes kept drifting to an old mission some distance away. He felt somehow drawn to the church. Finishing his drink, he walked over to the mission and stood for a moment by the entrance of the south gate.

"It's the Mission of San Antonio de Valero, señor," a man told him. "People around here call it The Alamo."

Twenty-Six

As Jamie rode, he stopped often and listened. If the talk was favorable, he quietly told the men to keep their weapons handy and lay in a stock of powder and shot. And Jamie was amazed that nearly everyone he talked with knew of him and his exploits.

General Cos was loudly demanding that Colonel Travis be arrested and handed over to him for the raid at Anahuac. Wrong thing to demand as far as the Texans were concerned. If they wanted to chastise Travis for acting impudently, that was all right. He was one of them. But to hand Travis over for a Mexican firing squad was out of the question.

General Cos retaliated by starting a steady flow of troops into Texas. This, Jamie saw personally and he beat it back to San Felipe to tell Travis.

"How many did you see, Jamie?"

"Several companies, at least."

Travis nodded his head. "Bonham has just returned from near the border. This only reinforces what he heard. That General Cos is preparing to enter Texas with several battalions of Mexican regulars. War is very close, Jamie. Take some time off and return to your family. Stay a few days, a few days only, Jamie, and then report back here."

Jamie took two spare mounts and hardly stopped until he reached Kate's side.

His friends left them alone for the first day, but on the second day, everybody came over, hungry for news.

"I'll tell you what I know," Jamie said, after everyone had their drinks and was settled down in the yard. The only movement was the occasional batting and swatting at a mosquito. "There will be another convention — at least one is called for. But I doubt there will be time for it. According to both Travis and Bowie, war is on our heels. This will probably be the last time I'll be back for several months, at least. Perhaps longer. Probably longer."

It was August 1835.

"Tell us about the army, Jamie," Hannah urged. "It must be a grand sight."

Jamie smiled. How to tell them Texas was about to enter into a war and so far, he'd seen no sign of any organized army? He'd been told that Houston and Fannin did have men. But they were poorly organized. "And, Houston and Fannin have quarreled on more than one occasion," Jamie told them. "Bowie told me that Fannin wanted to be a general. Houston made him settle for a colonelcy. It isn't that people aren't really getting along — the quarrels are minor — it's just that everything is so disorganized. That's got a lot of people worried."

The friends talked well into the night, and then departed. Kate said, "I have clean clothes all ready for you, Jamie. Puts His Foot Down brought you new moccasins and leggin's that his wife made for you. Hannah made you a new pair of gloves. And Juan sent over a nice serape for you. It will be warm this winter." She broke down then, and came into his arms.

Jamie held her, letting her weep and get it out of her system. Kate was a strong woman, but she had kept her emotions all bottled up for too long, so the children would not see her shed tears and get them upset.

After a time, she pulled away from him and dabbed at her eyes with a piece of cloth. "There now!" she said, patting her hair. "That's over and done with. It will not happen again."

Jamie smiled in the darkness. "Cry if you want to, Kate. When I saw what we're going to be up against, I felt like shedding a few tears myself."

She waited.

"So far, we've fought soldiers that were pressed into serving. Prisoners, for the most part, who agreed to serve in the army in return for their sentences being lifted. Those troops I saw down along the border were professionals. And there are thousands more just like them not far behind."

"Juan says he will take up arms and fight alongside you, Jamie."

"Yes. There are a lot of Mexicans who will be doing that. I just hope in the years to come, after Texas gets her freedom, and she will, that those people are not forgotten. I've met once with a fine gentlemen named Juan Sequin. He's political chief of the San Antonio district. He's solidly on our side and has pledged to fight with us."

He put his arm around her shoulders. "Enough talk of war and politics, Kate. Can't we think of anything better to do?"

She smiled and they rose from the bench together and walked into the cabin. Moments later, the candle in their bedroom was snuffed out.

■ ■ ■ ■

"Jamie Ian MacCallister," Travis said proudly. "I want you to meet Mr. Stephen Austin."

The Mexicans had finally released Austin under a grant of general amnesty. But the time in prison had nearly done him in. He was only forty-two years old, but looked twenty years older when Jamie met him in September of 1835. His health was broken and he coughed persistently. He was Secretary of the State of Texas when he would die two days after Christmas 1836.

"I've heard much good about you, Jamie," Austin said. "I want to thank you for volunteering to serve with us."

"My pleasure, sir."

"I've been told by Bowie that you are a natural leader of men. Would you take a commission and lead a company of Texas volunteers?"

"Sir, I know nothing of leading great groups of men in battle. As you no doubt have been told, I was taught warfare by the Shawnees. That is the way I prefer to wage war."

Austin smiled, as did Travis and Bowie, who had managed to be together in the same room for twenty minutes without one giving the other an acid piece of his mind.

"Very well, Jamie," Austin said. "At any rate, I'm glad to have you with us."

Jamie knew a dismissal when he heard one, and he was glad to leave that stuffy room. Austin had the smell of death about him and he said as much to Bonham, just as the voices of Travis and Bowie in loud argument drifted out of the closed door.

"Prison broke him, Jamie. He isn't a well man. But he's a good man."

"That I could see plainly."

"He needs rest and lots of it, but I fear he'll not get it."

That would prove to be true. In just over a month, Austin would be chosen as a field commander, even though he was not a soldier and did not want the job. Being the man he was, Austin did not turn away from the job.

Travis's spies reported to him that the Mexican commander at San Antonio, Colonel Domingo de Ugartecha, was about to mount an expedition against the people of Gonzales, a small community to the east of San Antonio.

"Why?" Travis asked. "They've done nothing."

"To take back a cannon given to them

some years ago," the spy replied.

The small brass cannon had been given the people of Gonzales some years back to help protect them against Indian attack. The cannon itself was very nearly useless. But the very idea of a large Mexican force of soldiers attacking civilians over a cannon that was practically worthless rankled the Texans. Jamie was ordered to ride to Gonzales, to warn the settlers there. When he arrived, he found the citizens already knew of the impending attack and had strung up two huge banners. One said, GO TO HELL, SANTA ANNA. The other banner was hung over the tiny cannon, now mounted on a cart. It read, COME AND TAKE IT.

Jamie, as ordered, let the settlers handle their own affairs, and handle it they did. One hundred fancy-dressed and helmet-plumed mounted Mexican dragoons came face to face with some one hundred and fifty Texans armed with long rifles on the Guadalupe River on October 2, 1835.

The commander of the dragoons laughed at the sight and made a very loud and very derogatory remark concerning the Texans. Bad mistake. One sharpshooter knocked the plumed helmet from his head and the commander fell off his horse as the Texans opened fire.

The Texas war for independence from Mexico had officially begun.

"Don't get too cocky," Bowie warned his men. "So far, we've not come up against professional and seasoned troops."

"Bowie's right," Travis said, in one of their rare agreements. "Most of the soldiers we've faced had little or no training. Believe me, the worst is yet to come."

Then they started arguing about who was really in command.

Jamie had waited in Gonzales for a message from a scout in Goliad, about seventy miles southeast of San Antonio. Jamie had already received word that General Cos was in San Antonio with a force of about fifteen hundred men and he was anxious to get that news to Travis. As soon as the scout from Goliad handed him the pouch, Jamie was in the saddle and riding.

The message read: *General Cos left a small force in Goliad. Attacking.*

Just before midnight on October the 9th, a force of Texas volunteers overpowered the Mexican garrison at Goliad and seized arms and powder and shot.

General Cos was furious and swore dire revenge on the heads of any Texan who dared oppose him.

Over in Gonzales, Austin now found himself commanding a force of over five hundred men. Further east, in Nacogdoches, Sam Houston was calling for volunteers, having accepted the call for him to be commander. Bowie was commander of about a hundred men, all tough and spirited and loyal to Jim. But Bowie elected to stay loyal to Travis, who was forced to stay in San Felipe awaiting the convention, and take his orders, at least for a time.

The whole situation was chaos and turmoil. Hundreds of Texas men had taken up arms, but nobody knew whose orders to obey. They were all volunteers and if they decided to go home for whatever reason, they went. They had no uniforms and looked terribly ragtag, albeit very spirited, as some three hundred to four hundred Texans — no accurate record was kept — marched toward San Antonio in the middle of October, hell-bent to attack General Cos. They dragged along the brass cannon from Gonzales, but unfortunately, the wheels fell off the cart, and the cannon — which was useless anyway — had to be discarded alongside the road.

Jim Bowie and his hundred or so men were scouting far ahead of the main column, Jim, as usual, wanting to be in the vanguard of any good scrap. Jamie had been assigned to Bowie's company. And was scouting ahead when he saw a large force of Mexican cavalry approaching. He raced back to Bowie with the news and the company barely had time to take cover before the Mexicans attacked.

Outnumbered more than four to one, the Texans beat back charge after charge.

"Stay calm, boys," Bowie called to his men. "And keep your heads down. We can't afford to lose a man."

Jamie was deadly accurate with his long rifle and that did not go unnoticed by Bowie and the other men.

"They're bringing up artillery!" Bowie shouted, lowering a spy glass. "Give them everything we've got, boys!"

Within minutes, the Mexicans had re-treated under the withering fire from the Texans, leaving their artillery behind.

"Charge!" Bowie yelled, and the Texans surged forward, capturing the artillery pieces of the Mexicans. "Load 'em up and turn 'em around!" Bowie shouted. "Give them a taste of their own cannon."

The Texans began pounding the retreating Mexican army with their own cannon. The Mexicans lost some sixty men, with about that many wounded. The Texans had one man killed and only a few wounded.

Bowie and his men were jubilant, but cautious. Bowie was under no illusions. He argued against attacking San Antonio, which was defended by General Cos's force of more than fifteen hundred troops.

"Surround the town as best we can and settle in," one of the commanders of the Texans, Ben Milam, said. "We'll wait them out."

It was October 28th.

"If we wait long," Jamie said, after walking through the camp and listening to the men talk, "the spirit will wane."

"You'd attack a much larger force, lad?" he was asked.

"I would, Indian style."

Edward Burleson, an old Indian fighter from way back, agreed with Jamie. He was overruled and the volunteers settled in to wait.

"We're making a mistake," Jamie warned.

Bowie nodded his head in agreement but did not argue the command. He had other things on his mind.

"A bad mistake," Ben Milam said sourly.

Bowie left camp to attend the convention in San Felipe, where he promptly got drunk and insulted one of the attendees, Anson Jones, who would later be governor of the

Republic of Texas. One thing about Bowie: he didn't give a tinker's damn who he insulted.

The convention ended with Austin ordered to go to the United States to ask for money to pay for the war and to round up volunteers. Houston was appointed supreme commander of all the troops except those now garrisoned around San Antonio, the command of those men now given to Edward Burleson.

Back at San Antonio, conditions among the volunteers were terrible and getting worse. The men were running out of food and most did not have adequate clothing for the winter, which was hard upon them. Many of the men were thinking about the upcoming spring and the planting of their crops. Some left to return to hearth and home.

Burleson wanted to attack General Cos but his field officers overruled him and voted to withdraw the men.

"Hell, no!" Ben Milam said hotly. "I'll not back up a damn inch!"

Jamie had spoken with several Americans who had just broken out of jail in San Antonio and they had told him that the morale among the Mexican defenders in the town was not good. He went to Ben Milam with the news.

"You'll follow me, lad?" Ben asked.

"I will," Jamie told him. "And many of the men still here will, too."

"You're a game one, Jamie." Ben Milam then drew his sword and cut a line in the Texas dust. "Who will follow Ben Milam into San Antonio?" he threw out the challenge. "Those who will, step across this line."

Several hundred men shouted back that they would and surged over the line to stand by Ben and Jamie. Then Francis Johnson and his men agreed to go with Ben.

Ben now had about three hundred volunteers ready to follow him into San Antonio and, as Ben put it, "Kick the pants off of General Cos."

It was December 5th, 1835. Jamie had climbed up on a rooftop for a better view before entering the town. The first thing to catch his eye was the Mission of San Antonio de Valero.

What was it that local fellow said it was called? Yes, he remembered.

The Alamo.

TWENTY-SEVEN

Jamie, Bonham, and three other men did not enter the town with the two regular columns of about a hundred and fifty men each, commanded by Tom Milam and Francis Johnson. They were not keen on fighting all bunched up with others. Instead, when they got into the town, they smiled at each other and with a nod, parted company to fight the way they liked best: alone.

Jamie crouched just off the mouth of an alley, his bow ready, an arrow notched. He saw a fancy-dressed Mexican officer, a plume on his helmet, come prancing his horse up the alley. Jamie made a silent kill, the arrow driving deep into the man's chest.

"Teniente?" a man called for his lieutenant.

Jamie waited, another arrow notched, ready to fly. The soldier stepped into view and his eyes widened in shock and horror when he spotted Jamie. The horror did not last long as the arrow from Jamie's bow took the man in the chest. He fell, his rifle clattering on the stones.

Jamie ran to the mouth of the alley and almost ran into a huge Mexican sergeant. The *sargento* lifted his rifle, a smile on his lips. Jamie laid the hard bow across the man's face, the blow knocking him to the ground, blood streaming from a broken nose. Jamie was on him, knife in hand. When the blade rose again, it was dripping crimson.

Jamie dragged the body out of the mouth of the alley and squatted down, assessing his situation. There were sounds of fierce fighting all around him, and the booming of cannon as the Mexicans fought the assault. But the Mexican gunners, for whatever reason, weren't too proficient with the cannon; the cannonballs tore up more local homes than hurt any attackers.

Jamie made a dozen more kills that day, with arrow, knife, and musket ball. He was catching his breath late that afternoon when he heard his name called.

"Jamie!" Bonham called from behind him. Jamie turned. "Ben Milam wants you, right now."

"Jamie," Ben said, handing him a paper. "This is a report on the first day's fighting.

Take this to the provisional government. By the time you reach there, this scrap will be over. You go on home and visit for a time." He winked at him. "I'll see you later on, lad."

Those were the last words he ever spoke to Jamie. Early on the third day of fighting, "Ol' Ben," as his volunteers called him, was shot in the head and died instantly. Francis Johnson took over total command. The Texans, enraged at the death of Ben Milam, fought like wild men. Over a hundred and fifty miles away, Jamie was handing the report to a member of the provisional government.

General Cos found many of his troops frightened and demoralized. Almost two hundred men, including some officers, had already deserted him. General Cos, fighting down his own growing panic, retreated to the Alamo mission, but the Texans used the captured cannon and hammered at the trapped troops. Late on the fifth day, Cos had had enough. He surrendered himself and over a thousand men to Burleson.

It was a glorious time for the Texas volunteers. Outnumbered, they had beaten a much larger force.

Burleson accepted General Cos's surrender and then let the man go after Cos promised he would never again fight Texans. It was a promise he was to break, very soon.

Back in the Big Thicket country, with Kate and his family, Jamie could not believe it when he heard that General Cos and over a thousand of his men had been set free and even provided with guns and powder and shot to protect them against possible Indian attacks.

"We tweaked their noses, Kate," he said to his wife. "Santa Anna will never forgive or forget that."

But few agreed with that assessment. Only a handful of people felt the Mexican government would retaliate for the humiliation of General Cos at San Antonio. The provisional government issued a call for a new convention to be held at Washington-on-the-Brazos on March 1, 1836.

Houston pleaded with the Texas provisional government to send out a call for troops. He was ignored.

He was told the war was over. Texas had won. Mexico will give in to our demands for statehood within the Republic. Everybody go home.

But not everybody went home. A few felt sure that Mexico would send troops into Texas. A small force of Texas volunteers was left behind at the Alamo, with Green Jameson in charge of making the old mission more fortlike. Austin was in Louisiana, seeking loans and volunteers. Houston was trying to rally Texans to make ready for a fight few believed was coming; Houston also wanted to abandon the Alamo and blow it up, believing the place could not be defended. He sent Bowie and a small force to San Antonio to do just that. But Bowie found the men at the Alamo in good spirits and ready for a fight, so the Alamo remained intact, under the command of Colonel James Neil.

Meanwhile, the provisional government's legislative council in San Felipe came up with a strange idea to invade the Mexican city of Matamoros. Their reasoning behind this was that most of the city's population despised Santa Anna and would certainly embrace and support a Texas expeditionary force. Houston thought the scheme a nutty one and refused to have anything to do with it. So the council picked James Fannin to command the force and was named a colonel. Fannin pulled out over two hundred men from the San Antonio area. That left Neil with only about a hundred men to defend the Alamo. Fannin had also stripped the place of most of its supplies, leaving Neil with little food and no medicines.

Governor Henry Smith was furious and a big row now developed between the council and the governor's office, with cuss words flying back and forth. The governor claimed that he was in charge and the council claimed they were in charge. Chaos reigned when calm should have been the order of the day.

Back east, Jamie Ian MacCallister packed up a few things, kissed Kate and the children, and rode west, soon linking up with a few volunteers who felt as Houston did.

Houston was in charge of the Texas army, but Fannin took his orders from the council and Houston had no authority over him. Colonel Fannin blissfully went about the business of getting his troops ready to invade Matamoros. But Houston was a charmer, and he rode to Goliad and spoke to the men encamped there.

"They'll be plenty of fighting for all, boys," he told them. "We don't need to go off half-cocked and split our forces."

He convinced enough of the men so that for the moment, the plan to invade Matamoros was tabled.

Fannin was furious but there was nothing he could do about the situation except fume and pout. Which he did, quite well and often.

Jamie had paused in Nacogdoches and had linked up with Davy Crockett and his Tennessee Mounted Volunteers.

A few weeks earlier, Travis had been commissioned by Governor Smith to put together a force and quickly march to the Alamo. Upon arrival, Colonel James Neil left because of illness in his family and Travis and Bowie immediately started arguing about who was in command. When they weren't arguing, they were in agreement on one point: they had to have reinforcements and they sent out messages to that effect. But Colonel Fannin, still smarting over Houston's interference with his men and his grand plan, and still dreaming of capturing Matamoros, refused to allow any of the men in his command to go to the Alamo.

But Crockett was on the way, as were the First Company of Volunteers from New Orleans. And from all over Texas, in small groups and alone, men were riding toward the Alamo, to defend the dream of liberty.

When they camped each night, Jamie was amused by the antics and the stories from Davy Crockett and his Tennessee boys. To Jamie, Crockett seemed an unlikely choice to be elected to the United States Congress, but he certainly had been elected, in 1827, '29, and '33. And he came close to being nominated for the vice president's slot on the Whig ticket.

"Last year," Crockett told Jamie, "Ol' Andy Jackson conspired agin me and refused to support me. So I told 'em all to go to hell . . . among other places. I was goin' to Texas. And by God, here I am."

"Why?" Jamie asked.

Davy chuckled. "To fight, boy. To fight for freedom. Why are you here?"

Jamie smiled, the light from the dancing flames of the campfire highlighting his strong face. "To fight, Mr. Crockett."

Crockett's men laughed at that and Jamie looked around at the circled group.

"Just Davy, Jamie," Crockett said. "My daddy were Mr. Crockett. Tell me about Bowie and Travis."

"They don't much like each other, but they'll fight side by side."

"I 'spect we'll all fight side by side, Jamie," Davy said, becoming serious. "And mightily outnumbered we'll be, too, I'm thinkin'."

That was understating it somewhat. The defenders of the Alamo would be outnumbered by over forty to one.

The camp fell silent as the men rolled up

in their blankets against the cold of the night. Most of them stared at the stars above for a time, thinking of what they had left behind them, and wondering what lay ahead of them. Finally the fire burned down to dying coals and the men slept.

Far to the south, General Santa Anna was massing some six thousand men, all highly professional and solidly trained combat soldiers. He had spent millions building his army. Another advance force of more than fifteen hundred men, under the command of General Joaquin Ramirez y Sesma was already in place, bivouacked near Laredo. Santa Anna's troops were gathering near Saltillo, some two hundred miles south of the Rio Grande.

Santa Anna's plan was a simple one. He was going to march his troops all the way to the Sabine River, using the old *El Camino Real* — the Spanish Road — and teach these damn Texans a hard lesson along the way. The route he had chosen would take him through San Antonio, but he did not expect any trouble there, or anywhere else along the way, for that matter. He was that confident.

With Bowie now at the Alamo, the mood of

those defenders in place soared. Bowie had many friends in San Antonio and soon they were bringing welcome food and much needed warm clothing to the men behind the walls. One of Bowie's men, James Bonham — no relation to Jamie's friend who had returned south upon receiving orders from his boss, Louis Fontaine — suggested that a resolution be drawn up, in which the defenders of the Alamo would demand the Texas provisional government to send supplies. Everyone present signed it . . . for all the good it would do them, which, when it came, was damn little and too late.

Crockett sent Jamie on ahead with the news that help was coming and Bowie and Travis put their daily differences aside and warmly greeted the young man.

"How many men, lad?" Travis asked.

"About fifteen, sir."

Both Travis and Bowie blinked. Bowie spoke first. "Fifteen, Jamie?"

"Yes, sir. All sharpshooters and spoiling for a fight."

Travis turned, a numb expression on his face. He walked off, muttering, "Fifteen?"

Jamie looked at Bowie. "Are you well, sir?"

"I'm fine, Jamie!" Bowie clasped Jamie's strong arms. "Just fine."

But he was not. Bowie was, in reality, a very sick man and probably dying. He coughed often and sometimes brought up blood with the phlegm. He more than likely had tuberculosis and adding to that, might have been in the grips of typhoid and pneumonia, for the winter had been brutally cold and none of the men were adequately dressed. Ever since he'd arrived at the Alamo, he had annoyed Travis by leading drunken and oftentimes rowdy parades up and down the streets and into the cantinas of San Antonio. Travis wrote lengthy reports about Jim Bowie's drunken behavior. Bowie knew of the reports and laughed them off. But he did agree, much to the surprise of Travis, to share command of the Alamo. Bowie would command the volunteers, and Travis would be in charge of the regulars . . . who had yet to receive a penny's worth of pay. They would never be paid, but they would pay, in blood. Their own.

"When will Crockett arrive, Jamie?" Bowie asked.

Jamie smiled. "Before the fight starts, Jim. You may be sure of that."

Jim laughed, then broke into a fit of violent coughing. He hawked up phlegm and spat on the ground. Jamie noticed there was blood in the phlegm.

"Damn whiskey's going to kill me yet," Jim joked, then walked off, shouting and laughing to his men.

Jamie walked the nearly three-acre compound, noting the walls, which were twelve feet high and three feet thick. Makeshift platforms had been hurriedly erected for riflemen to stand on, but there were not enough of them. The Mexicans had left behind plenty of cannon, but even though the defenders had been working hard, many of the cannon would never be used effectively because there would not be enough cannon slits cut in the thick walls to use them. The mission church was very nearly a ruin, only the stone walls and part of the roof still intact. Log and plank cannon mounts had been built around the high walls.

On the hurriedly reinforced roof of the mission church, three twelve-pounder cannons faced due east. On the south side, mounted on a log platform, were four four-pounders. Eighteen-pounders were at each end of the west wall, and one in the center. Two eight-pounders were mounted on the north wall, just to the west of the earthen barricade that had been thrown up across a seventy-five-foot gap in the wall. There were light cannon set up on several roofs, and in the courtyard a small battery of eight-pounders pointing due south.

Once those gates are closed for good, Jamie thought, there will be no escape, for the horses were pastured, incredibly, Jamie felt, nearly *five miles* away along Saldo Creek. Jamie had stabled his horses in the cattle pen, just west of the irrigation ditch, easily accessible to him. After taking a look at Jamie, no one questioned him about it.

Courage was one thing. Foolishness was quite another matter.

A thousand men would be hard-pressed to defend this place, Jamie felt, strolling along, speaking politely to men he scarcely knew, and tallying the number of defenders as he walked. When he finished, he was depressed, and leaned against the outer wall of the long barracks, near what would soon be the hospital entrance.

"Grim, isn't it, lad?" Travis asked.

Travis sometimes irritated Jamie if for no other reason than to have a man several years away from being thirty years old call him "lad." But he concealed his slight irritation. "Yes, sir. It is."

"We'll soon have reinforcements," Travis said confidently. "Our supporters won't let us down. You'll see."

Jamie nodded his head and Travis said, "I

want you to ride south, Jamie. After you've rested a bit," he quickly added. He showed Jamie a map. "Down here," he pointed. "Toward the Rio Grande. Bowie seems to think Santa Anna will march his men across the barren area. I tend to doubt it. But I want you to check it out and report back to me."

"Only if he wishes to do that," Bowie said, walking up. "Jamie is a volunteer, not one of your regulars, William. What say you, Jamie?"

"I'm here to help in any way I can," Jamie replied quickly, noticing the flush that reddened Travis's face upon Bowie's interference.

"There is little water for miles in some stretches," Bowie told him. "And damn little forage for your horse. Ride with care, Jamie."

But before Jamie could give any reply, a shout came from a sentry in the bell tower. "Riders coming in!" he called.

Davy Crockett and his Tennessee volunteers had arrived much sooner than Jamie had expected. He turned and walked to the cattle pen and saddled a fresh mount. With a packet of food and two canteens, Jamie rode south. It was bitterly cold on the afternoon of the 9th of February, 1836.

TWENTY-EIGHT

Jamie rode back into the Alamo days later.
His horse had been shot out from under
him by a war party of Kiowa and he had
been afoot for several days. Jamie finally
killed a scout from Santa Anna's forward
unit and took his horse. It was the 20th of
February. He dismounted stiffly, slapping
the cold dust from his buckskins. Travis,
Bowie, and Crockett rushed to meet him.

Their mouths dropped open when Jamie
said, "They'll be here in three days. They're
camped along the Rio Hondo." He told
them why he'd been gone so long.

"The Rio Hondo!" Travis exclaimed.
"That's only fifty miles away."

"How many?" Crockett asked, putting a
cooler tongue into the situation.

"Between five and seven thousand."

Travis and Crockett said nothing, letting
their expressions mutely state their inner
feelings. Jamie could sense that Travis did

not believe him. Bowie said, "May God have mercy on our souls." Then he took a drink of whiskey from a small flask and bent over double in a fit of coughing. He spat blood onto the ground.

Crockett and Travis appeared not to notice. "Get some food into you, Jamie" Bowie said. "And rest for a time. I'm sending you out again in a few hours with a message for Fannin. If this won't move him into action, then nothing else will — except perhaps a direct command from God."

Fannin, some ninety-five miles away, had renamed the Goliad mission Fort Defiance. He had received several earlier messages from Travis and Bowie, each of them urging him to mount his men and come at once. He had ignored them. He would later claim that he had sent messages back to the Alamo. No one knows for sure.

But Fannin felt he had more pressing matters to attend to than to concern himself with rumors and myths about a huge Mexican army about to attack the Alamo. On February 13th, acting governor Robinson had instructed Fannin to fortify and defend Goliad and do battle with enemy forces should they appear. Robinson had also taken over Sam Houston's title and now declared himself acting governor and commander-in-chief of the Army of Texas. He furthermore wrote Fannin and told him to ignore any orders he may have previously received from Houston.

In the days past, Fannin had received many communiqués from Travis and Bowie. Sometimes, when they were penned by Bowie's hand, they were quite blunt and to the point. These were not ignored, they just weren't acted on. But Fannin wasn't sure what to do. He would receive a message from the Alamo. He would write a letter to the advisory committee asking for orders. They would issue none.

As Santa Anna's troops neared the Alamo, the fate of the men and the few women and children now at the Alamo was sealed.

"God*damn* the man!" Bowie raged, when Jamie returned empty-handed, with no firm commitment from Fannin.

"I don't believe Fannin knows what to do," Jamie said to Travis, Bowie, and several more officers gathered around. "But I know from talking to the men that his supplies are very nearly gone. And he is really quite fearful of being attacked by General Urrea."

"General Urrea has about a thousand men and we're looking at six to seven thousand," the commander of the Alamo's cannon, Almeron Dickerson said. He shook his head and walked away. Dickerson and his men had worked like demons for days getting the cannon ready.

Travis looked at Jim. "Any suggestions, Bowie?"

"Yeah," Bowie said, winking at Jamie. "Get drunk!"

Travis glared daggers at Jim Bowie's back. He grew even angrier when he turned back to Jamie and he was smiling. "You find this amusing?" he demanded.

Jamie put a big hand on the commander's shoulder. "Loosen up, sir. I reckon we all have to deal with this in our own way."

Jamie turned and walked away. Travis watched him go, a slow smile spreading over his face. "Yes," he whispered. "I reckon we do, at that."

Several hundred miles to the north, in what was known as Indian Territory, snow had sprinkled the ground and it was very cold. A Shawnee scout entered the central lodge and faced Tall Bull.

"You have been gone a long time, Deer Runner. We were worried about you. You look exhausted," Tall Bull said. "Eat and rest here. Then we'll talk."

Deer Woman brought him a bowl of stew and Deer Runner ate hungrily. When he had filled his belly, he said, "Man Who Is Not Afraid is with the soldiers to the south. They have taken refuge in an old church in the town of San Antonio. They are doomed. Soon thousands of soldiers from the south will be upon them. They will all be killed."

Deer Woman said nothing. Her face did not change. Tall Bull grunted. "I despise Man Who Is Not Afraid, but I must respect his courage. However, I was looking toward the day when I would kill him."

"Little Wolf and Bad Leg will be disappointed," Deer Runner said.

Tall Bull waved that off. "Bad Leg is crazy in his head and Little Wolf's hatred of Man Who Is Not Afraid has clouded his mind, obscuring all else. What about Han-nah — Quiet Woman?"

"She is living with her husband in the dark swamps to the south and east. The wife of Man Who Is Not Afraid and their many children also live there. But I am told it is a terrible place, Tall Bull."

Tall Bull nodded his head. "There are runners in place to bring us news of this great battle?"

"Oh, yes. As you instructed. Many of

them. We will know the outcome within days."

But Tall Bull was not happy with his own plan. "I think we shall ride south, Deer Runner. Man Who Is Not Afraid leads a charmed life. He just might escape this death trap you say he is in. If he does, he will not escape me. Not this time. I have sought him too long."

"Tall Bull," Deer Woman said. "Don't go."

"What?" Tall Bull was clearly startled. His wife never questioned his decisions — well, not often.

"We have all heard of the strength and cunning and bravery of Man Who Is Not Afraid. I fear if you go, I will never see you again."

"Bah!" Tall Bull scoffed. "You talk nonsense, woman. Stop your babbling."

In the years since whites drove the Shawnee west, Tall Bull's band had shrunk. No more than a few dozen families now traveled with Tall Bull. But among those families were twenty-five of the bravest men, fierce warriors all.

"We'll leave ten men behind to protect our town," Tall Bull said. "You rest well, Deer Runner. We leave at first light."

That night, Deer Woman had a vision: she would never see her husband again.

On Sunday, February 21, Jamie rode back into the Alamo and stabled his horse. He went straight to Travis's quarters. "Santa Anna and his forward units are camped along the Rio Medina," he reported.

The Rio Medina was twenty-five miles from the Alamo.

Travis nodded his head in acceptance of Jamie's words. But incredibly, the man still refused to believe that an army of the size that Jamie reported was at hand.

Jamie left Travis's quarters and found Bowie. "He doesn't believe me. He still doesn't believe me."

Bowie coughed and shook his head. "He'll believe it when the first cannonball comes crashing against the walls."

"Any word from Fannin?"

"No," Bowie said softly. He stared at Jamie. "Get out of here, Jamie. Ride out and don't look back. You're far too young to die for people who don't appreciate what we're doing."

"They care, Jim. The majority of them don't even know we're here."

"Perhaps," Bowie said, taking a sip of whiskey. "Perhaps."

Jamie left the barricaded old mission and walked the streets of San Antonio. He could feel the panic that was now gripping the citizens. Many of them had already started packing up to leave. Few of them paid any attention to the tall, buckskin clad young man walking among them. Jamie stopped at a cantina. It was empty save for the bartender. He took a table and ordered food and drink.

"You are the scout from the Alamo?" the man asked, placing a plate of food before Jamie.

"Yes. One of them."

"You have seen Santa Anna's army?"

"Yes. They're camped along the banks of the Rio Medina."

The man crossed himself and whispered a quiet prayer. "When you are finished, señor, I will close the doors until this is over."

Jamie took a bite of food. "I don't blame you," he said.

At Fort Defiance, Fannin was sending couriers out daily, sometimes several times a day, pleading for orders from the advisory committee. None came. His men were becoming surly and restless. They wanted to help those at the Alamo, but would not do so without orders from their commander.

413

Fannin did not know what to do. So he did nothing. He waited for orders that did not come. He would, finally, act on his own, but it would be too late.

Jamie rode back to the mission on the afternoon of the 22nd of February. He quietly reported that Santa Anna's advance force was less than ten miles away. For reasons known only to Travis, Travis still refused to believe him.

Bowie finally let his terrible temper loose, in front of everybody. "You goddamn stiff-necked, little tin soldier son of a bitch!" he cussed a suddenly white-faced and trembling with anger Travis. "What the hell does it take to convince you — a handwritten message from God?"

"That will be quite enough, Colonel Bowie," Travis said, checking his own terrible temper, which he rarely unleashed.

"No it won't," Bowie responded. "I'll not see my men die here for naught. Abandon this place and we'll fight Santa Anna in a guerrilla fashion, like I've said all along we should do."

Actually, Bowie had never quite made up his mind just how the small force of Texans should fight the Mexican army.

"No," Travis said softly.

Shaking with fury, Bowie whirled about and stalked away, yelling for his men to form up. They were pulling out. Crockett walked over to the man and put a hand on his shoulder. He spoke softly to him for a few moments.

It was never recorded what Crockett said to Bowie. After a few moments, in a calmer voice, he told his men to relax. They were staying. He looked back once at Travis, then walked away to join his men. As he passed Jamie, the famous knife fighter smiled sadly and winked.

February 23rd, 1836.

"They're here, Travis," Bowie said, shoving open the door to Travis's quarters. Behind him, the sounds of the lookout in the San Antonio church ringing the bell reached him.

Travis slowly stood up from his desk, disbelief on his face.

"Still don't believe it?" Bowie taunted the man. "Well, since you won't believe Jamie MacCallister, send someone that you will believe. Or go yourself." Bowie turned and walked away.

Travis sent Dr. John Sutherland and a man named John W. Smith to investigate. They saw the long lines of cavalry, the cold

415

sunlight glinting off of polished lances. They watched as Mexican officers, with swords drawn, rode slowly up and down the assembled battle lines.

"My God, they're about to charge," Sutherland said.

He was wrong, but both men did say a very short but very fervent prayer to the Almighty, and then raced back to the Alamo. When the lookout spotted them galloping back, he began really ringing the bell.

In the bell tower, the private rang the bell and stared in horror at what looked like thousands of troops. He also breathed a short and very sincere prayer.

Sutherland and Smith leaped from their horses and reported to Travis and Bowie. "MacCallister's been right all the time, Bill," Sutherland said. "Santa Anna has arrived."

Jamie stood up and walked toward his saddled horse. Travis's voice stopped him.

"Where do you think you're going, MacCallister?"

"Wherever the hell he wants to go, Travis," Bowie said. "He's part of my bunch, not yours, remember?"

"I'm going to start driving those few cattle out yonder in here and put them in the pen," Jamie said. "We're running low on supplies."

Bowie laughed and Travis flushed. "Go on, Jamie," Bowie called. "Good thinking."

"Yes," Travis said. "Very good."

The rest of that day, those staying behind watched as the town nearly emptied of residents. Wagons creaked on the muddy, rutted road and wheels groaned. For many of the Mexicans in the town, it was not a matter of choice. They knew only too well the savage and ruthless mind of Santa Anna. Most of the residents of San Antonio had helped the Americans, and all knew there were informers who would be quick to point them out. They were running for their lives, taking as many of their personal possessions with them as was possible.

As the fleeing Mexicans looked toward the sound of the ringing bell in the tower, many wondered why the Americans were so willing to die for this? They could just not understand it.

After securing the cattle in the pen, Jamie rode out to see the sight, and quite a sight it was. He could truthfully say he had never seen anything like it. Crouched in a mesquite thicket, Jamie watched as hundreds of brilliantly garmented cavalrymen paraded up and down on their fine horses. An officer — Jamie did not know it but the officer

417

was General Ramirez y Sesma — was the most elegantly dressed of them all. He sat his horse and waved his sword, which caught the rays of the sun and reflected back in flashes of silver.

Jamie watched for the better part of an hour, as more and more troops came riding and marching up from the south. He estimated their numbers at close to three thousand. Taking a terrible chance he mounted up and, skirting wide, rode to the south to see what else he could report. He knew that Travis would not discount his reports now. He had never taken umbrage at Travis's disbelief in his earlier reports, for he knew that Travis felt that no man in his right mind would attempt to march a huge army across the arid plains in the windswept dead of a bitterly cold winter. But Santa Anna had done it, although at a terrible cost. He had crossed the Rio Grande with six thousand men, nearly two thousand pack mules, about fifty huge wagons, several hundred two-wheeled carts, and twenty-five cannon. The old Spanish road behind him was littered with dead animals and broken wagons and discarded equipment and more than a few dead men, who had dropped from exhaustion during the long forced march. But Santa Anna didn't care. He had revenge and retribution burning in his mind. He was going to stop this ridiculous independence movement once and for all and teach these goddamn upstart and arrogant Texans a lesson that would forever and ever live in history.

It did not take Jamie long to spot the huge clouds of dust coming from the south, the dust that seemed to spread for miles, whipped into the air by the cold wind, all coming toward him. That would be more mounted soldiers, the supply wagons, the artillery, and the infantry slogging along

"Thousands of them," he muttered. "Maybe more than I first reported back."

As Jamie rode back into town, the bell in the tower stopped ringing. The town was eerily silent. The normally busy plaza was deserted.

Jamie neared the Alamo and noticed that Travis had ordered all his men back behind the walls of the old mission. As he rode toward the still open gates, he whispered to the wind, "Goodbye, Kate. Just remember that I will carry your love in my heart even unto death."

The gates of the Alamo closed behind him.

Jamie dismounted and his horse was led away to the pen. He looked around him.

While the warning bell was still clanging, Captain Dickerson had galloped into the nearly deserted town to fetch his wife, Sue, and their baby daughter. There were other women inside the walls of the Alamo, but Sue Dickerson was the only American woman. There were several slaves behind the walls, including Bowie's personal man servant, Sam, and Travis's servant and cook, Joe.

Jamie could not find Travis, so he climbed up on a makeshift parapet and reported to Bowie, who was directing the realignment of cannon. Bowie listened to every word, his face growing grimmer. "We retreated once," Bowie said, his words low. "We shall never retreat again."

"Sir?" Jamie questioned.

"We came in here, from out there," Bowie explained, pointing. He looked out toward the empty cold landscape. "What you saw were the Dragoons, Jamie. And also Santa Anna's fighting engineers."

Jamie had seen much more than that, but he did not contradict Bowie.

Both men watched as couriers saddled up and rode out, Dr. Sutherland and Mr. Smith were heading to Gonzales, about seventy-five miles away, with a message from Travis, pleading for help. The second courier rode to Goliad, in yet another appeal to Fannin to send help.

Davy Crockett walked up, his rifle, Ol' Betsy, as he called it, in his hand. "I reckon Santy Anny's here, boys. He's been wantin' a fight, so let's make sure we give him a good one."

"Did you take that military commission Travis offered you, Davy?" Bowie asked.

"Nope," Crockett replied. "I come here to fight, not to order men about. You colonels just tell me where you want me and my sharpshooters, and there we'll be."

Bowie smiled.

Davy lifted a telescope to his eye and looked south for a moment, just able to see the long line of mounted soldiers. He lowered the glass. "Right purty, ain't they? If they can fight as well as they dress, we're in for a right good scrap." He handed the glass to Bowie and stepped down to the courtyard.

"You have any orders for me, Jim?" Jamie asked.

Bowie coughed and spat up blood. "No, lad. You've done more than your share. You just pick you a good spot from which to fight and get ready." Bowie stared at him for a moment. "You keep a horse saddled, Jamie. You hear me?"

"Yes, sir. Jim?"

Bowie nodded his head.

"How long can we hold out?"

"A good question. I would say ten or twelve days. No more than that."

Bowie very nearly pegged it on the money. They would hold out for thirteen days. Thirteen days of awful, bloody courage and greatness.

Standing on the windy parapet beside the legendary knife fighter, Jamie's thoughts drifted back for a moment to the Big Thicket country . . . and to Kate. He allowed himself a few moments of memories, and then shook them away when he became conscious of Bowie's eyes on him.

"Thinking of hearth and home, lad?"

"Yes, sir."

"You'll see your loved ones again, lad. I'm going to make certain of that. You're going to go on and do great things, Jamie. I sensed that in you the first moment I laid eyes on you."

"Why not young Fuqua yonder?" Jamie questioned, cutting his eyes to the boy called Galba. "He couldn't be more than sixteen or seventeen years old."

Bowie shook his head and evaded any reply. "I've been writing something, Jamie. But I've not yet finished composing. When

I'm done, I'll give it to you. See that it gets to the Telegraph and Texas Register. I'll admit, Jamie, that I'll be cutting it close. But if any man jack here can get out with the dying words from this garrison, that person is you. I'd be obliged if you'd do that thing for me."

"I'm in your company, Jim. I'll obey your orders."

Bowie smiled and clasped Jamie's arm. "Good lad. Now let's get ready for a fight."

Jamie noticed the smile on Bowie's lips.

"Tell me the joke, Jim?"

Bowie laughed and then coughed. "His Lord and Majesty General Santa Anna will ask for our surrender, Jamie. I've a bit of a surprise for him, that's all."

"Is this sure to irritate Colonel Travis?"

Bowie chuckled. "Probably." And he walked off without adding to that.

Jamie shook his head, wondering if Travis and Bowie would ever get along, even should they be admitted together through the gates of Heaven?

The answer was no.

Hell, either.

■ ■ ■ ■

Part Three:
The Siege

■ ■ ■ ■

Do not go gently into that good night,
Rage, rage against the dying of the light.
— Dylan Thomas

TWENTY-NINE:
THE FIRST DAY

Santa Anna's first real battle and his first encounter with Americans had been back in 1813, when he was a young man in the army of General Arredondo and sent to this very town to put down a civil insurrection by a bunch of Anglos trying to form a Republic of Texas. What nonsense, Santa Anna thought. His general had put everyone involved into a wild rout. Then came the punishments. Santa Anna enjoyed that immensely. Santa Anna felt nothing but scorn for Americans. Cowards, all of them.

He shifted in his saddle. He had been afflicted with *disentería* — in cruder terms, the shits — on the long march north, and he was not quite over it. That did nothing to improve his cruel temper.

It was time to enter the town. He had dressed in his finest uniform, with his chest filled with all the medals he'd won over the years of battles. His horse had been washed and groomed, his saddle, studded with silver, had been rubbed and polished.

Santa Anna had plans in mind for the residents of San Antonio, too. Dark savage plans. For he hated them. All of them. Years back he had been humiliated here, over a minor game of chance. And a not so minor incident of forgery — on his part. He had lied his way clear of any charges with his superiors, but he had never forgotten the laughter from the citizens of this wretched town. They would pay. Dearly.

And to further show how lightly Santa Anna treated the defenders at the Alamo . . . he planned to be *married* during the siege. To a lovely girl he had met only a few hours ago!

Santa Anna obviously did not believe in long courtships.

"Messenger comin' under a white flag, Jim," a lookout called from his post.

"They'll be wanting us to surrender," Bowie said, climbing up and standing beside a charged cannon.

The Mexican officer, all decked out in a fancy-colored uniform, called for the commanding officer. Bowie grinned and looked around for Travis. He was, as usual, in his office, writing reports.

"That's me, Amigo," Bowie replied cheerfully, in perfect Spanish. "Jim Bowie at your service. *Que haces?*"

"Your surrender, señor Bowie. General Santa Anna demands an unconditional surrender."

"I can but assume he's watching all this?" Bowie asked.

"*Sí,* señor."

"Run up the flag!" Bowie ordered.

Watching through a glass, Santa Anna's face reddened in rage as the red, white, and green Mexican flag, with some additions added, was hoisted up the flagpole inside the mission. Santa Anna cursed. The numbers 1824 were clearly visible, serving to remind him of the Texas constitution drafted in 1824.

Santa Anna told his aide, "The flag of no quarter. Now!"

The red flag was hoisted on the Mexican side, and every defender watching from the walls in the Alamo knew what it meant: a fight to the death.

Santa Anna issued another order and his cannon roared. They missed their target.

"Fire!" Bowie ordered, and the eighteen-pounder thundered out the Alamo's defiant reply.

Travis rushed from his quarters, furious.

Bowie had not told him of his plans to do this. From the parapets, Bowie smiled down at him.

"Jim's little surprise for Colonel Travis," Jamie muttered to Davy Crockett.

"I 'spect it did get ever'body's attention," Crockett drawled. "Damn shore got mine!"

"I wish a word with you, Bowie!" Travis yelled.

"Later," Bowie said, half turning his back to the man. "They've shown a man with a white flag. They want to parlay, and I got a man all ready to do that."

"I forbid it!" Travis yelled, his voice nearly a scream.

"Too late," Bowie said, then completely turned his back to the man.

Travis was outraged. He had suspected all along that Bowie had a plan to sell them all out. For to Travis, Bowie was a Mexican-lover.

He was right on one point: Bowie did love the Mexican people, he had married a beautiful Mexican girl. Then, too, Bowie knew the Mexican mind; how they thought. Travis was quite vocal in saying, often, that he doubted any Mexican even *had* a mind.

The Mexican artillery batteries continued to boom, but they were so far out of range, if they weren't careful, Bowie noted, the rounds just might fall on their own troops.

Jameson rode back. "Unconditional surrender," he shouted to Bowie.

Bowie gave his reply. He personally touched the flame to the hole of the cannon and let the freshly charged eighteen-pounder roar. Then he leaned over the wall and gave the clearly startled Mexican officer under a flag of truce a message for Santa Anna.

The Mexican officer's face paled and he shook his head. "No, señor Bowie. I cannot tell that to my general."

What Bowie had said was that, remembering that it loses something in the translation, Santa Anna's mother was a burro and his father was a vulture, and also that Santa Anna had sex with whores because he was so ugly no decent woman would have anything to do with him.

"Madre Dios!" the officer gasped. "I cannot say that, either!"

"Then tell him that Jim Bowie said *a besar cabo grosso!*"

The Mexican officer threw down the white flag and galloped away. He'd think of something to say to the general. He knew he'd better; he certainly could not repeat any of what Bowie had just said. Santa Anna would have him flogged. Or shot.

431

"What did you say to that officer?" Travis yelled, standing beside Bowie.

But Bowie only shook his head. "Just that we would, under no conditions, surrender unconditionally."

Travis didn't believe him, of course. But knowing that Bowie had his blood running hot for battle now, he had enough sense not to call him a liar. For had he done that, the Alamo would have lost one of its two commanders. And Travis knew it. Travis was no coward; far from it. He was a very brave man. He just had, on occasion, uncommon good sense.

"We are not going to surrender under any circumstances!" Travis informed Bowie.

Bowie shrugged his total indifference. But Jamie, watching from a reasonably safe distance, knew what the shrug meant: the idea of surrender had never entered Bowie's mind. He was ready to fight to the death. That was why he had so insulted the courier from Santa Anna.

Travis, still furious, climbed down from the parapet and lined up the men under his personal command. He gave them a rousing, if somewhat profane speech, and all agreed to never surrender. Then he stalked off to his quarters.

"I never thought the tin soldier had it in

him," Bowie said to no one in particular, after listening to Travis's speech. "Maybe I'll change my opinion of him."

Jamie thought that highly unlikely.

After listening to his courier's report, Santa Anna was so angry his dysentery returned and he had to rush to the outhouse for a time. When he returned, the courier had wisely disappeared, not wanting to repeat his lies for fear he could not remember all that he had said.

But he had told a junior officer what Bowie had really said. The young officer, seeking to appear favorable in his general's eyes, told Santa Anna all that Bowie had said.

Back to the outhouse.

The ineffectual cannon fire from the Mexican artillerymen continued throughout the afternoon. They hit nothing. San Antonio was now, for all intents and purposes, deserted. Only a few citizens remained in the town. The people in the town knew that when those in the Alamo really began to fight, their bigger and longer-range cannon could well destroy the town.

Travis's anger had slowly subsided and his logical mind began to see that Bowie had been right in his response to Santa Anna's demand for an unconditional surrender. But he sure as hell wasn't going to tell Bowie that.

Travis stepped out of his quarters and walked the compound. There was no sign of Jim Bowie. He had retired to his quarters to rest. The day had taken a lot out of him. He was much sicker and weaker than he would admit even to himself.

Crockett and several of his men had taken up positions along the walk with their long rifles, just waiting for one of Santa Anna's men to present a target.

So far, no one on either side had been killed, no one on either side had even gotten much upset — except for Travis's wild explosion of temper and Santa Anna's bowels — and no one had been seriously injured.

All that was about to change.

Davy Crockett had been watching as a lone Mexican soldier worked his way closer to the mission.

"You gonna let me have 'im, Davy?" one of his men asked hopefully.

"Nope," Crockett replied. "He's all mine. How far you reckon he is?"

"Long ways off, Davy," the Tennessee volunteer said. "You nail that one, it'll be something to write home about."

"I didn't know you could write," another one kidded the man.

"Hell, I cain't!"

Chuckling, Davy rested his rifle on a small bag of sand and sighted in. The long rifle cracked and the Mexican soldier went down bonelessly. Davy had drilled him through the heart from a nearly impossible distance and that was the first fatality of the battle. The Mexican soldiers knew then that the men along the walls of the Alamo were highly skilled riflemen.

Travis stood in the plaza and watched as the coonskin-capped and buckskin-wearing Tennessee men danced and whooped and hollered.

"You plugged 'im through the ticker, Davy!" one yelled.

Santa Anna shrugged off the report that one of his men had been killed. He had lots of *soldados*. They were all expendable. Santa Anna was thinking of his wedding day, and even more so, of his wedding night. He became sexually aroused and had to leave the room and wash his face in cold water. That didn't help a bit. He told one of his aides to bring a punta to his quarters. Two of them if possible. Three of them if the aide could find that many. And be sure they were young and pretty. And clean, for the general was a very fastidious man. Santa Anna fancied himself quite the lady's man, and very virile. He was also very vain and arrogant. And those were his good points.

Many of his officers held an intense dislike for General Santa Anna, but they kept that well hidden. Many of them did not like his streak of cruelty. Battles were one thing, but prisoners should be treated with at least some degree of compassion and dignity.

Santa Anna had little compassion, and on more than one occasion he had ordered helpless prisoners shot. But the officers were all professional soldiers, and they would obey their general. But they didn't have to like it.

Gradually, the gunfire subsided as evening fell and both sides settled down to supper. Travis watched from the open door of his darkened room as Jamie blackened his face and took up his bow and quiver of arrows. For a moment, he considered forbidding the young man to leave. But he stilled his tongue, not wanting another quarrel with Bowie.

My army, he thought. What an odd assortment of men, good men all, and brave men, but still a strange collection. Men from

New Orleans, from Tennessee, from half a dozen or more states over in America. There were even a couple of men from Scotland. Mexicans fighting alongside Anglos against their own people. What brought them here, to this place, at this time? Travis shook his head, unable to find the answer to his silent question.

He looked toward Bowie's quarters and sighed. Jim was a good man, a true man, and he wished they could get along. Travis admitted, to himself, that it was as much his own fault as it was Bowie's. They were as different as night was from day.

He watched as Jamie disappeared into the gloom near the west wall. The young man was going out to kill. Travis wished him luck. MacCallister was a mystery. Raised by Indians, Travis recalled someone telling him. Somewhat of a savage, he felt. But nonetheless, a very capable and likeable young man.

Even though William Travis was only a few years older than Jamie MacCallister, on this early evening, he felt the weight of command heavy on his shoulders.

"Colonel," a man called. "Come get some beef and beans and coffee, sir. It's gonna be a cold night."

It will heat up come the dawning, Travis

thought, as he walked toward the cook fire and took the offered plate of food in one hand and the cup of coffee in his other hand. "Thank you," he said politely.

"Please excuse me," Jamie muttered, lowering the body of the sentry to the nearly frozen ground. The man had died without a sound as the big blade of Jamie's Bowie knife nearly took his head off.

"Carlos?" a voice called out. "Where are you?"

"Por acá," Jamie softly called.

"Ah!" The man started walking toward Jamie and Jamie put an arrow directly into the soldier's chest. He dropped with a thud against the nearly frozen earth.

"Silencio!" a hard voice called, adding, *"Idiota!"*

Jamie did the silencing with an arrow in the middle of the man's back. The Mexican batteries began opening up, from about five hundreds yards away from the Alamo. Jamie's knife flashed in the night and he silently slipped away, his bloody souvenirs dangling from his belt. He slipped into the town, knowing he was taking a terrible chance, but feeling the Mexican soldiers ought to know a taste of fear. He was going to give them a taste of it, that night.

That Colonel Travis would not approve of this did not bother Jamie a twit. Bowie would be amused by it.

A drunken sergeant lurched out of a cantina that the soldiers had forced open, mouthing terrible things about *norteamericanos* in general and Texans in particular. Jamie left him sitting on the dirt in the alley, his back to the outside wall of the cantina, his chin on his chest, and his head glistening dark and wetly in the night.

Jamie flattened out against the wall of a building as a dozen or more cavalrymen walked their horses up the street, the hooves making a frightful echoing racket on the stones. Jamie used that noise to cover any slight sound he might make and slipped away. He made his way over to where a battery of artillerymen were swabbing out and reloading cannon. Then, Jamie supposed, they decided to take a break, for coffee or food or whatever, for they all walked away and vanished into the night. Jamie slipped over to the row of cannon and finding a bucket, began working quickly, scooping up mud and pouring it into the barrels of two of the eight-pounder cannon. Then he packed it in tight and rolled over into a ditch just as the men returned to their stations.

It was going to get real interesting when the order came for those men to fire their cannons.

Jamie collected three more scalps that night before he decided not to push his luck any further. He headed back for the Alamo, finding it almost ridiculously easy to wend his way unseen through the Mexican lines.

"Thanks, Tall Bull," he said under his breath, for the brutal training the Shawnee had given him on how to survive.

Reaching the rear of the Alamo, on the east side, near the cattle and horse pen, he called, "MacCallister. Coming over."

"Come on, Jamie," the sentry said. "How was it over yonder?"

"Busy," Jamie said with a smile, towering over the man.

"What that a-hangin' from your belt, son?"

"Scalps," Jamie told him, and walked on.

The man shuddered and muttered, "Travis ain't gonna like that a-tall."

Jamie told Crockett and Bowie what he'd done with the cannon and both men guffawed and slapped their knees in high humor. "Land sakes, boy," Crockett said. "You done fixed it so's we'uns can have quite a show this night."

Jamie wondered about Crockett's speech;

wondered just how much of it was affectation and how much was real? No matter, though. Davy was a fearless fighting man and a dead shot.

"My God, boy!" Bowie said, stepping back. "What have you got hanging from your belt?"

"Half a dozen scalps. I thought I'd give them to Travis as souvenirs." Actually, Jamie had no intention of doing that.

Bowie grinned. "No, lad. Let me have the honors." Before Jamie could stop him, he jerked the bloody scalps from Jamie's belt.

"What's going on up there?" Travis suddenly appeared in the night and called from the plaza. "Oh. It's you, MacCallister. What did you accomplish among the enemy this evening?"

"Killed half a dozen and fixed two of their cannon so when they fire, it'll surely backfire on them."

Travis climbed up onto the parapet and faced Jamie. "Report," he said.

Jamie told all that he'd seen and done — almost.

"Yeah, you want these, Bill?" Bowie asked innocently, then held out the bloody scalps.

Travis recoiled as if being handed a writhing poisonous snake. "What in God's name are those?" he demanded.

Crockett and his men — all skilled Indian fighters who had certainly taken more than their share of scalps over the years — could barely contain themselves. One swallowed his chewing tobacco trying to stifle his laughter.

"Scalps, Colonel," Bowie replied calmly. "Jamie took them. He thought you might want to keep them as souvenirs."

Travis drew himself up to his full height, which was eye to eye with Bowie, and smiled. "Why, yes," he said. "I certainly would. Thank you, Scout MacCallister. I am sure I shall treasure them always." He took the scalps and tucked them behind his own belt.

Crockett leaned close and whispered hoarsely, "He beat you on that one, Jimmy my boy." Then he burst out laughing.

Soon all the men along the parapet were howling at Travis having put one over on Bowie. But Jim was good humored and he soon joined in the merriment.

When the laughter had died down, Bowie stuck out his hand toward Travis. "Colonel, would you be so kind as to join me in my quarters and we'll have coffee and discuss, together and mutually, the defending of this bastion of liberty?"

Travis smiled and shook the hand of the

older man. "It would be my pleasure, Colonel Bowie. My great pleasure indeed." He chuckled, a rare thing for Travis. "Perhaps then, Jim, you can tell me what you really told that emissary from General Santa Anna this afternoon."

"Oh, that's easy, William. I just told him to tell Santa Anna to kiss my ass!"

Travis was startled silent for a moment. He blinked, then slowly started chuckling. Soon he was roaring with laughter and wiping his eyes with a handkerchief. Once again, the men along the parapet were howling with laughter.

From the Mexican battery of artillery, there suddenly came a mighty roar and a huge shower of flame and shredded metal and hardened mud. The flames touched off two more cannon and they blew apart. The blast from the first explosions knocked the two other cannons out of alignment and the cannonballs fell far short of their target and the scene was one of confusion and screaming and mortally wounded men.

Travis patted Jamie on the shoulder. "Good work, Scout MacCallister. Very good work. Colonel Bowie, shall we retire to your quarters to map out the battle plans?"

"After you . . . amigo."

So it was a truce. But would it have lasted

had Bowie not been terribly hurt in an accident the very next day?

No one knows.

THIRTY:
THE SECOND DAY

February 24, 1836

The Mexican artillery had kept up their bombardment all during the night, causing most of the defenders of the Alamo to sleep lightly at best, at their posts. This was to be the case for the next twelve days. A few of the men had managed to get a few hours good rest despite the bombardment: Bowie, Crockett, Jamie, and several others awakened rested. Most of the others had slept only fitfully.

Over coffee and beef and beans, which for the most part, was what the defenders would live on for the next twelve days, Jamie studied the one hundred and fifty or so men. The discussion that morning was not of the thousands of Mexican troops just outside the old church, but of the letter, drafted and signed by both William Travis and Jim Bowie, that a courier had taken to Governor Smith of Texas before dawn. That letter stated that Travis and Bowie would, from that date on, share command of the Alamo and orders to the men would be mutually agreed upon. That had come as a real shock to men loyal to each faction. But even though all considered it a good sign, most of the defenders' loyalty still went with Jim Bowie.

Most of the defenders still clung to the belief that reinforcements would come, and together they would whip the Mexican Army. It was a false hope, but it was all they had to keep them going. They had food enough for about three weeks, simple fare, but enough to keep them alive. They were low on powder and shot. But they had plenty of spirit, and that was something that Bowie and Travis had spoken of long into the shell-shot night.

"You know it's hopeless," Bowie had told Travis.

"I do not know of any such thing, Bowie."

"Bill, we're a hundred and fifty against six or seven thousand."

"Fannin will come."

"Only with his wife or a whore," Bowie said with a smile. "Fannin will do nothing without orders, and the advisory committee will never issue those orders. We're being sacrificed. But that's not without merit.

What we're doing here is buying time. Precious time. Time for Houston to get his army ready and in place."

Travis dropped his eyes to the grounds in his cup and was silent for a moment. "The men?"

"I think they know. The chaplain does."

Travis sighed heavily. "I have started writing a letter."

"So, too, have I."

"Mine is not yet finished."

Bowie poured them both fresh coffee. "Nor is mine."

"I expect to have mine finished by tomorrow . . ." He consulted his timepiece. ". . . This afternoon. I have asked Captain Martin to stand by to ride."

"I have not yet started committing mine to paper." He tapped the side of his head. "But I have it here. I shall start this evening. By then I should have time."

He wasn't aware of it, but he would have lots of time to write until the bloody, awful end, still some week and a half away.

"If I might make a suggestion . . . ?"

"By all means."

"Jamie MacCallister could take your message from these fortified walls."

Bowie smiled. "That's the lad I had in mind."

"Good! Good! The men tell me he's like a ghost in the night." Travis smiled at the knife fighter across the rough table. "I have some brandy . . ."

Bowie returned the smile. "I don't recall ever turning down a drink, Bill."

Brandy poured, the men sniffed and then sipped the explosive mixture.

Travis rose from the table and walked to a makeshift desk. He took out several pages of paper and handed them to Bowie. Bowie pulled the candle closer and read:

"To the People of Texas & all Americans in the world. Fellow citizens & compatriots — I am besieged, by a thousand or more of the Mexicans under Santa Anna — I have sustained a continual bombardment & cannonade for 24 hours & have not lost a man — The enemy has demanded a surrender at discretion, otherwise, the garrison are to be put to the sword, if the fort is taken — I have answered the demand with a cannon shot, & our flag still waves proudly from the walls — I shall never surrender or retreat. Then, I call on you in the name of Liberty, of patriotism, & everything dear to the American character, to come to our aid, with all dispatch — The enemy is receiving reinforcements daily & will no doubt increase to three or four thousand in four or five days. If this call is neglected, I am determined to sustain myself as long as possible & die like a soldier who never forgets what is due to his own honor & that of his country — Victory or Death."[*]

Bowie nodded his head in agreement with the words. "I can add nothing to this stirring tribute to the defenders of this mission, Bill. You've said it all."

"Then there is nothing left to do, is there, Jim?"

"Yes," Bowie said softly. "Fight and die for Texas."

The Mexican bombardment continued throughout the day, with very little damage to the makeshift fort, and no injuries or fatalities to the defenders. But Crockett and his sharpshooters played hell with any Mexican soldier who came too close to the walls. Because of the sharpshooters' deadly accuracy with their long rifles, the Mexicans were unable to move their light cannon any closer.

* *Actual wording of letter. Victory or Death was underlined three times.*

Inside the compound, the defenders were working frantically to get everything ready for the charge they knew was coming. They shored up the walls and reinforced any broken places in the walls. The hospital was made ready. The noncombatants, some twenty-five of them, were instructed to tend to the wounded, when that occurred, and all knew it would, and soon. For now, they saw to the keeping of fires, the preparation of food, the washing of the defenders' clothing, and to the rolling of bandages and the safekeeping of the meager supply of medicines.

It did not rain that day, and the sun was welcome, for it had been a cold and very wet month so far. The sun felt good and Bowie's cough was not nearly so pronounced as he worked to mount another cannon on the south end of the plaza, on a fifteen-foot platform.

Bowie's mind was not entirely on the placing of the cannon. The Mexican bombardment was continuous and distracting. During the night, the Mexican gunners had crept closer and now some of the cannonballs were actually striking the walls of the mission. Also, after he'd left Travis's company the night before, he'd gotten drunk and now he had a headache. And the ropes holding the cannon were badly frayed.

Whatever the reason for the accident, Bowie felt the heavy cannon shift on him. "Look out!" he called to the men below him. The men below scrambled out of harm's way. For a few seconds, all that held the heavy cannon was Bowie's tremendous upper-body strength. Men raced toward him with rope, but it was too late. The cannon shifted again and slammed into Bowie's side, crushing his ribs. Bowie fell from the platform and the cannon pivoted again, and stopped against a heavy support post sunk deep into the ground. Bowie lay nearly unconscious on the ground, a fearsome head wound gushing blood and each breath agony because of his broken ribs. Bowie passed out on the way to the hospital.

Still far to the north, Tall Bull and his small band of warriors made their way cautiously south, staying clear of any settlements. They were not a war party. Not yet, anyway. If by some miracle Jamie MacCallister escaped from the old mission, then and only then, would they become a war party. After only one white. Jamie Ian MacCallister.

Deep in the Big Thicket of East Texas, Kate sat out the cold winter with the children and waited for some word from Jamie. But none came. Finally, on the 24th of February, the day of Bowie's accident, a merchant from San Augustine brought her a letter that Jamie had written and posted several weeks back.

She carefully broke the wax seal and with trembling fingers unfolded the paper.

My darling Kate,

I do not know if this letter will even reach you, certainly not when. But as I take pen in hand, I first of all want to tell you how much I love you. I have loved you since the moment we met. I must be blunt, Kate, for I know of no other way to tell you this. I am going to the Alamo to fight for the independence of Texas. It is not in my plans to die, Kate. But if that is necessary to help free the people of this Republic from heel-grinding tyranny, then die I shall. If that should happen, you may take whatever solace there might be in the fact that I died standing shoulder to shoulder with brave and loyal comrades.

I do not know what fate has in store for me, Kate. I know only that I will carry your love in my heart to the end. Whether that will be soon or with you in my arms as the curtain of age falls around us and the light of life dims, is something that only God will decide.

Tell the children that I love them, and think often of them. You are among the best of friends, Kate. I have to smile when I think of our friends, Mexican, Indian, Nigra, and White. I think we have all proven something important in our little community, Kate. However, I am not sure I can express that in words.

But there is one thing I can express: I love you, Kate. Whatever happens, always remember that.

Your loving and faithful husband,

Jamie

Kate wept silently for a few moments, then dried her eyes and rose from the chair. She must be brave. For she knew she was not the only Texas woman who had a man at the Alamo. She wondered what it must be like at that place.

Jim Bowie was down and was not likely to ever rise again. That news spread like a raging fire throughout the compound. The regimental surgeon, Dr. Pollard, had left Bowie's quarters shaking his head in amazement that the man was still alive. He had allowed the men of the Alamo to file past Bowie's bed, to offer condolences and, many of the men knew, to say goodbye to the famous knife fighter. Bowie was dying.

When the last man had filed past, Bowie asked Jamie to sit for a time with him.

"Place those quills and the inkwell close by me, lad," Bowie requested in a weak voice. "It's come the time for me to write my farewell. Those scraps of paper, too, lad. Ah. Thank you. Have you written to your loved ones, Jamie?"

"Yes, sir. Before I arrived here. I posted it on the way in with Crockett."

"Good. I'm writing you out a bill of sale for my horse, Jamie. For when you leave here, you're going to have to fly. You know where my mount is hidden? Good. You think you can slip out of this bastion one more time, with your horse?"

"Easily, sir."

"A few miles outside of town there is a ranch that belongs to a friend of mine. His name is Ruiz. Take both our horses there and they will be stabled and grained properly. When the time comes, Jamie, you must leave with this message. You will not question my orders?"

"No, sir."

"Good lad. The doctor says I must not

have any whiskey. So would you please pour me a cup from that jug yonder?"

Jamie was not about to refuse his commander's request. He poured a cup and Bowie thanked him and sipped and smiled. "Now leave me, lad. Ah, one more thing before you go. Place that jug within arm's reach, would you? Thanks." He winked at Jamie. "I'll not die before the battle's conclusion, lad. When I close the door to this life, I shall do so in the company of my volunteers and all the men defending this bastion of independence. Pass that on to the men, would you?"

"Yes, sir." Jamie quietly left the man. He paused at the door. Bowie was writing, the only sound in the room the scratching of quill-point against the paper. Jamie stepped outside, gently closing the door.

Travis had been the first to call on Bowie. He now met Jamie just outside the door with a worried look on his face. "How did you find him, Scout MacCallister?"

"In good enough spirits." He told Travis what Bowie had said for him to tell the men.

"Good! Good! That will bolster their resolve." He patted Jamie's shoulder and walked away.

The cannonade had picked up, and the Mexican gunners were getting better, the balls and grapeshot crashing against the walls of the mission. Each time they paused to reload, Crockett and his sharpshooters would line the walls and take their shots, and the defenders were taking a toll on the cannoneers.

The defenders of the old mission were still in a good mood, many of them cracking jokes and laughing while the cannonballs drew ever nearer.

Perhaps, Jamie thought, they still believed that reinforcements were on the way. Jamie was operating under no such illusions. Although he could not say why he was so sure of his feelings, he felt the men of the Alamo were being abandoned. Bowie had said from the outset that they would fight and die alone; that they were being used as a way to rally Texas behind the independence movement.

"When we die, lad," Bowie had said, "all Texas will rise up and fight Mexico. As sure as the sun sets in the west, we are dead men. But we shall not die in vain. The blood spilled here will stain the conscience of all Texans and drive them to fight. Tough as hell on us," he added dryly, "but good for Texas."

As evening fell, Jamie slipped out of the mission, without telling anyone. Crockett and a few others watched him leave, but kept silent. They knew, to a man, that Jamie was not running from the fight, and that he would return. His reasons for leaving were his own, and none of their affair. But they also knew that Travis would soon miss him, and would probably demand answers. Travis did miss Jamie before an hour had passed, but he asked questions of no one except Bowie, and that was done in the privacy of Bowie's quarters.

"I sent him out," Bowie said, his voice a little stronger. "I wanted him to take my horse to a safe place." Bowie handed Travis the bill of sale he'd penned that afternoon.

Travis read it and nodded his head. "You think we're doomed, don't you, Jim?"

"I think everyone has written us off, Bill. I think we're being deliberately sent to our deaths. But I don't resent it. Houston is meeting with the convention at this time, I'm sure." He was, at Washington-on-the-Brazos. "Fannin is not going to move on his own, and the advisory council will not give him orders to come to our aid." Fannin never received any orders to aid those at the Alamo, but he would, finally, make an attempt to reach the Alamo. It would come too late. "Bill," Travis said, just before he closed his eyes to rest. "If I am to die, I could not ask to die in better company."

In an unusual gesture of comradeship, for he was not an emotional man, William Travis reached down and gently clasped Bowie's shoulder. "Nor I, Jim," he said.

Bowie's slave, Sam, sat in the darkness of a corner in the room and watched and listened. After Travis had left, he rose and came to Bowie's side. Bowie sensed his presence and opened his pain-filled eyes. He handed the young man a folded sheet of paper.

"I know you can't read, Sam. But this is your freedom. You're a free man, now. This paper states that. You get yourself a white rag and walk right out of those gates and keep going."

"I think I'll stay for a time, Mr. Jim," Sam replied.

"Don't be a fool!" Bowie said sharply. "Get out of this death trap, Sam."

Sam wet a cloth and bathed Jim's flushed face. "You rest now. "Time a-plenty for talkin' later."

Too weak and in too much pain to argue, Jim lay back and closed his eyes.

Sam retreated to a chair in the room and waited, ready to serve his master to the end.

Jamie made it easily through the enemy

lines, still very lightly manned, for the bulk of Santa Anna's army had not yet been placed, and rode to the Ruiz ranch outside of town. The Ruiz family was one of the oldest and most powerful of Mexican families in the area and even Santa Anna knew to leave the family alone. He was greeted warmly, as was and is the Mexican custom, and fed a huge meal.

"I don't understand this," Ruiz said, as Jamie ate. "You and your friends will gain nothing by dying at the old mission. You will accomplish nothing. I, too, want independence for Texas, but this way is . . . *folly!*"

"We'll prove a point," Jamie said.

"By *dying*? Santa Anna will not even bury your bodies. I know the man. He will order his soldiers to stack the bodies and put them to the torch and then scatter the ashes. What point will have been made?"

"That a free Texas is worth dying for," Jamie replied.

Ruiz looked at the tall and powerfully built young Anglo with the long yellow hair. He slowly nodded his head. "You will stay the night and rest?"

"No. I'll get back. Thanks for the meal, Señor Ruiz. You've been very gracious." Jamie stood up and moved toward the door.

Ruiz shook hands with him. "*Por nada.*

Vaya con Dios, Señor MacCallister."

Just after midnight, Jamie slipped across the irrigation ditch and over the east wall. The sentry there noticed fresh scalps dangling from Jamie's belt.

"Gonna give them to Travis, too?" he asked, a slight smile playing at his mouth.

Jamie smiled and shook his head. "Colonel Travis was forced into the humor of it the first time. I doubt he'd find a second time very amusing. How's Jim?"

"Bad. Reinforcements comin', Jamie?"

"No," Jamie said softly. "I don't think any help will arrive. Think we're all alone, Micajah."

Micajah cut his eyes to the hundreds of small fires burning all around them, in the enemy's camp. "We won't be for long," he said dryly.

Cannon fire from the Mexican lines once more began booming, and conversation was impossible. Jamie walked to his station along the wall, where he would fight and, whenever possible, sleep, and took up position.

"Was I you, I believe I'd a kept goin'," a man to his left said sourly.

"Nobody's holding you here," Jamie told the older man.

"For a fact," Louis Moses Rose said. "For

a fact." He spat on the ground and moved
off.

THIRTY-ONE:
THE THIRD DAY

February 25th, 1836

A cannonball crashing against the wall jarred Jamie out of sleep. He opened his eyes to the steel gray of early dawn. Inside the walls, men and women were moving about, tending fires, cooking food, and boiling coffee. Jamie stood up and stretched, getting the kinks out of his joints and muscles. The nights were bitterly cold and few men had ample blankets to keep warm. Jamie walked over to one fire pit and was handed a bowl of chile and beans, some tortillas, and a cup of coffee.

Jamie squatted down and ate his breakfast. On the Mexican side, brass bands were playing loudly. "Quite a concert," he remarked to a man who sat down on the ground beside him.

"Yeah. Travis says the cannons will start up soon as the bands quit playin'. Hope they wait 'til I've et. Lead's hard to digest."

Standing on a wooden parapet along the wall, Travis was not fooled by the concert. Santa Anna was not giving the defenders of the Alamo a band concert out of the goodness of his heart. He had a hunch that when the cannon began roaring, the smoke would be used to help hide a possible enemy advance across the San Antonio River. Travis also saw that if they succeeded, the wooden houses and huts that had been abandoned when Santa Anna's forces arrived, would provide excellent cover for the Mexican soldiers. If the soldiers reached those huts, they would be less than four hundred yards from the Alamo.

Travis jumped down from the wall and strode quickly to the center of the plaza. "I need two volunteers!" he yelled. "Men who can run fast and can laugh at danger."

A crowd surged forward instantly.

"You and you," Travis said, choosing two young men scarcely out of their teens, if indeed they were. One was a Louisiana boy from Rapides Parish, the other young man's name was Brown.

Travis set men working frantically making torches.

"You must fire the houses and huts," Travis told the two young men. "And then get back here."

"We'll damn sure do it, Colonel," the Louisiana boy said with a cocky grin.

"And we'll lay down coverin' fire for you," Crockett said. "Rifle and cannon when you're ready."

The two young men exchanged glances. "We're ready."

Their hands filled with torches, they moved toward the south gate. Crockett and his men had loaded up every rifle of their own and dozens more that were willingly handed to the sharpshooters. Many of the men had brought a half a dozen rifles with them to the mission. Captain Dickerson made ready his cannon, some of them loaded with deadly grapeshot.

"What's that Louisiana boy's name?" Jamie asked a man.

"Despallier. And he's a game one, he is."

Santa Anna and his personal contingent of bodyguards had ridden over a wooden bridge and had taken cover in houses near the Alamo.

"Go!" Travis told Despallier and Brown. The two youths raced out of the gate on foot as Dickerson's artillery roared and Crockett and his expert riflemen laid down a withering field of killing fire.

During the first fusillade a half dozen Mexican soldiers were killed by Crockett and his men, and Dickerson's artillery crashed into lines of Mexican infantry attempting to push closer to the Alamo. Their officers tried to beat them forward with the flat side of their swords, but the troops were having no part of that. The first wave fell back in retreat.

By now, Despallier and Brown had reached the houses and were beginning to put them to the torch. Wild cheering broke out from the defenders as the first spirals of smoke rose into the cold air. Soon the shacks and huts were blazing and Santa Anna was furious. He screamed at his men to capture the two Anglos.

But Travis had anticipated that when he'd been informed that the general had crossed the bridge.

"Look sharp now, Davy!" he called. "The Mex's will want those boys bad."

Jamie had taken his rifles and moved to a position on top of the barracks along the south wall, just west of the main gate. Bowie's room was at the other end of the barracks.

"Mr. Jamie?" a voice called from the ladder.

Jamie turned to look at Bowie's slave, Sam.

"Mr. Jim, he sent me up here to load for

you, sir."

"Come on, Sam. Keep your head down. Can you shoot, Sam?"

"Yes, sir."

"Then shoot. We'll both load."

Sam grinned and took a rifle, lying down beside Jamie.

"Sam?" Jamie said, in a voice only the newly freed slave could hear. "If you take arms against them yonder, you'll not stand a chance of leaving here alive."

"I ain't plannin' on leavin', Mr. Jamie. I plan on standin' by Mister Jim 'til the end."

"As you wish, Sam. There's a target; just to your left. Think you can hit him?"

Sam leveled the rifle and squeezed the trigger. Fire and sparks flared in pan and muzzle and the Mexican soldier fell in a lifeless heap on the cold and muddy ground.

Sam rolled to one side and began working with powder, ball, and patch as Jamie's eyes searched for a target. He found a flash of color and sighted in. He could not hear the man scream over the din of battle, but Jamie watched as the Mexican soldier crawled off to the safety of his lines, dragging a broken leg behind him.

The riflemen on the ramparts settled in to kill just as many of the enemy as they could that day, and kill them they did. Estimates ranged from three hundred and fifty dead to as many as eight hundred killed. No accurate count would ever be known. But one thing was for certain: the defenders of the Alamo took a terrible toll on the Mexican soldiers that day. The grounds all around the Alamo were littered with enemy dead.

Jamie and Sam lay on the roof of the barracks and killed or wounded their share that bloody day. On one occasion, the Mexican troops managed to get within a hundred yards of the Alamo's wall, but Crockett and his men drove them back with withering and deadly accurate rifle fire. By eleven o'clock on the third day, the Mexican force retreated in bloody confusion. Santa Anna had already raced from his dubious protection in the houses close to the Alamo back to the safety of the town.

The huts and houses around the Alamo were now blazing as Brown and Despallier had done their work and were now running full tilt back to the walls of the mission as rifle balls hummed and whined all around them from the Mexican lines. Miraculously, neither of them received a scratch. They hurled themselves through the open gates to the wild cheering of the defenders.

It was not yet noon of the third day, and the Mexican Army had been soundly trounced, the infantrymen running back in disorder, out of range of the riflemen along the walls.

Gasping for breath, the two young men gulped first water and then coffee and withstood with grins the congratulatory backpounding they received from the men around them.

"By God, we done it!" Davy Crockett yelled from the parapets, holding Ol' Betsy high over his head. "We put them greasers to the run, boys."

In his bed, Bowie heard the legendary woodsman's shout and smiled sadly. He had never liked the term "greaser," and he wondered how the Mexicans fighting alongside the Anglos in the Alamo would take it. But Bowie could understand how Crockett felt. The enemy was the enemy, and for doomed men, any term was certainly applicable.

His worry was needless. For Fuqua, Esparza, and the other Mexicans inside the Alamo, they grinned and cheered right along with the others.

Santa Anna was livid with rage. He stormed up and down inside the house he was using as his headquarters and cursed his officers and men for cowardly jackals. He kicked out at anything that he found

468

close to his polished boots. Finally, exhausted by his efforts, he sat down in a chair and glared at those around him.

Santa Anna pointed a trembling finger at his officers. "A repeat of today will not happen again," he warned them. Taking a moment to further compose himself, he said, "I want the bridge work completed by tomorrow evening. No excuses; just get it done."

The San Antonio river was over its banks due to an unusually wet winter. Santa Anna's fighting engineers were working furiously to build several bridges across the river.

"It will be done," Santa Anna was assured.

The weather had turned fickle and the wind had shifted and was now coming out of the north, dropping the temperature below freezing. Santa Anna's engineers were not only fighting time, but now they had to contend with the bitter cold. Inside the walls of the Alamo, the defenders, few of whom were adequately dressed for the winter, had to struggle to keep from freezing to death.

Travis ordered the men to exercise to get the blood flowing more freely. Some did; most ignored his orders.

After taking a head count and determining that everyone was safely inside, Travis decided not to push the issue and soon retired to the warmth of his quarters to do what he loved to do: write letters and reports to Houston.

The Mexican artillery barrage kept up all night. The men inside the Alamo huddled together to keep warm and the fire watch was kept busy maintaining the fires.

So far, no defender of the Alamo had been killed and what wounds they'd suffered were very slight. All that was about to change.

At the convention, Houston had talked until he realized his words were falling on deaf ears. The men at the Alamo were doomed; sacrificed on a blood altar. On this cold and bitter night, Houston stood outside his quarters and brooded. Governor Smith had earlier placed Houston on leave until March 1st, so Houston had no army to command. Houston had gone at once to meet with the Cherokee chiefs to get their word that they would not attack the Texans and would remain neutral during the war. They gave their word.

Houston looked toward the west, toward the Alamo, a hundred miles away, and lifted a hand in salute. "Farewell," he whispered to the cold wind and the darkness. "May

God be with you in your final hours." Bitterly, he added, "That's about all you have going for you."

Jamie huddled against the wall, listening to the crash of the Mexican artillery slamming against the walls. The ground trembled beneath the soles of his moccasins. Jamie was fortunate in one respect: he was dressed warmly enough and had the serape the Nunez family had given him. His hands were protected from the cold by the gloves Hannah had lovingly made for him. He dozed off, only to be brought back to consciousness by the never-ending artillery barrage.

Jamie wondered if he would ever see Kate and the children again.

Thirty-Two:
The Fourth Day

February 26th, 1836

Long before dawn broke, Jamie finally said to hell with trying to sleep, and left the protection of the thick wall and went in search of coffee. He got his coffee and a plate of beef and settled down to eat his breakfast while the Mexican gunners continued to bombard the old mission.

When dawn finally split the skies, all hint of rain was gone and the sky was a beautiful blue. The temperature remained quite cold.

When Jamie finished eating, he rinsed out his plate and took up his rifle and walked the nearly three-acre compound, speaking to others as he walked. He knew them all now, at least their first names or nicknames, and they knew him. But on this morning, Jamie could sense a mood of discouragement among the defenders. Even Crockett was no longer laughing and acting the fool and cracking jokes in an attempt to bolster the spirits of the men. The legendary frontiersman was somber, as he stood on the ramparts, staring out toward town.

Jamie climbed the ladder and joined him.

"That damn Mex general has done shifted men all about durin' the night, lad," Crockett said. "He's pretty well sealed us up tight."

Jamie could see through the smoke from the cannon that Santa Anna had blocked the roads leading east. "That isn't all he's done," Jamie said, after the crash of cannonballs had ceased for a moment. "He's blocked any possible help from getting to us . . . at least by the road."

"What help?" Crockett said, a bitter tone to his voice, as he and Jamie watched as yet another messenger was sent by Travis. The man galloped away. After several harrowing miles, he would circle wide and head for Fannin's location — if he wasn't killed by some Mexican patrol.

"How many do that make, Davy?" one of Crockett's men asked, moving close to be heard.

"Oh, eight or ten in the past few days," Davy replied. "He told 'em they could RIP if they wanted to."

"Rest in Peace?" the man questioned.

"Return if Possible," Davy corrected.

"Goddamnit!" the volunteer cursed, his breath steaming in the cold air. "They's got to be help on the way!"

"Don't count on it," Jamie said. "I think we're all alone in this fight."

"Surely the lad is wrong," Jamie heard another man say as he walked away, climbing down the ladder. "Ain't he, Davy?"

"I fear he's mighty right, boys. Mighty right."

Jamie walked to Bowie's quarters and looked in. Bowie was awake, but his face was pale and his eyes shiny with pain. He waved Jamie to a chair. "Get us some coffee, Sam. Would you please?"

"How does it look out there, Jamie?" Bowie asked.

Jamie brought the knife fighter up to date.

Bowie coughed and the pain nearly caused him to pass out. He spat blood into a rag and smiled wanly at Jamie. "I guess I'll die right here in this damn room, lad." He was one hundred percent accurate in his prediction. From that moment on, James Bowie, born in Logan County, Kentucky, around 1796, would leave that dark room only one more time until his death.

"Can I get you anything, Colonel?" Jamie asked.

"A new body would be nice. Jamie," he

said with a smile. "If by some chance you are trapped in here at the end, and I pray God that you are not, see to it that my knife is close to my hand, would you? I'll need it when I meet the Devil."

"Hush that kind of talk!" Sam said, bringing the men coffee.

Bowie laughed. "I gave him his freedom and now I got me an uppity darky on my hands, Jamie."

Sam wet a cloth and bathed Jim's face with gentle hands. "I got me a thought that the top man on the other side would let you pass free, Master Jim. Why won't you let me try?"

"I told you to git, Sam," Bowie whispered. "I'll write out a paper saying that you took no part in any combat."

"I'll stay," Sam said firmly.

"Not only has he turned uppity, he's stubborn as a damn mule to boot," Jim said. He cut his eyes to Jamie. "I'm still writing that letter, Jamie. I'll have it finished in time."

Jamie opened his mouth to lodge a protest and Bowie held up a hand. "I have officially assigned you to Travis's command, lad. It's all legal. Bill has said that you will be the last man over the walls with our messages. Them that can write have done so or are doing so. Or they're getting someone to do it for them. You'll carry the last words of farewell from this valiant garrison. That's firm."

"Yes, sir," Jamie said. "As you wish."

"Fine. That's settled. Now leave me. I've not been much for writing long missives and it's a chore."

"Jim?"

"Yes?"

"I don't want to be branded a coward."

Bowie smiled. "You won't be. How could you be faulted for obeying a direct order? Only a fool would RIP back to a certain death."

The sounds of the Mexican cannons intensified; the crash of ball and grapeshot slamming against the walls trembled the floor beneath Jamie's feet. Jamie left the room and Bowie took pen in hand and began slowly writing.

Events were now unfolding that would seal the fate of those trapped — albeit willingly — inside the Alamo. Fannin had finally decided to act on his own initiative. While Jamie was speaking with Jim Bowie, Fannin and a force of some three hundred men pulled out of Goliad, starting the march to aid those at the Alamo. At the same time, a small force of some thirty volunteers at

Gonzales, some seventy miles away to the east, under the command of George Kimbell, was making ready to ride to the Alamo.

Fannin's relief column got about a mile outside of Goliad — the fort was still in sight — when a wagon broke down. The column was halted while the wagon was repaired. For reasons that were, and are, known only to him, Fannin decided to camp there and wait until the next morning before resuming the march. During the night, the oxen used to pull the wagons got loose, or were freed, and the men spent the entire day of February 27th rounding them up.

Late that day, Fannin decided to return to Goliad. Again, no one knows why he chose to do that. If it was ever really known, the reasons have been lost over time. What is known is that Fannin, on that cold winter's late afternoon, called a meeting with his officers and shortly after the meeting, the column turned around and went back to the fort at Goliad.

While Fannin and his men were retreating back to Goliad, Kimbell and his tiny force of volunteers were making their way to the Alamo. They were moving cautiously, with as much speed as possible, for advance scouts had reported back that Mexican patrols were, "All over the goddamn place!"

At the Alamo, the siege had settled down to a nerve-grinding battle of artillery with only sporadic rifle fire from either side. The Mexican artillery had done little damage and killed no one. The defenders along the walls were dropping Mexican soldiers with nearly every round they fired.

Travis had not discussed it with anyone — he did not want to worry the seriously injured Bowie — and he had called no meetings with his officers. But he knew that Goliad was, at the very most, a four day march from the Alamo. If Fannin did not show up with reinforcements by the 27th, that meant, to Travis's mind, that Fannin was not coming at all.

Travis began to haunt the parapets and ramparts, taking chances at peering over the walls, straining his eyes to spot a relief column that was not coming. The men knew what he was doing; but they said nothing. However, they thought plenty.

Davy Crockett was a man of the forests and the open areas. He paced restlessly all about the walled-in compound. He did not like this type of fighting.

Jamie squatted on his heels, rifle in hand, his face impassive, waiting.

On his bed, his death bed, Jim Bowie wadded up and discarded page after page, not satisfied with his words. He alternately wrote his prose and cursed Fannin, Houston, Governor Smith, and everybody else he could think of who was in a position to send help, but who would not. The list was a lengthy one.

Every man in the Alamo knew they were running short of powder. Every man there realized, without doubt, they alone could not hold against the sustained charges they knew were coming. They all had been told that Santa Anna was not a patient man. If he had to sacrifice every man in his army to crush this rebellion, he would not hesitate to do so.

Reinforcements simply had to arrive. It was that basic. Without help, the men in the Alamo would die. All of them. And all of them knew this.

Some men cursed. Others prayed. Crockett paced the plaza like an angry panther. Travis stared out at thousands of Mexican troops. Still others, like Jamie Ian MacCallister, were impassive and stoic. The men thought of hearth and home. Those that had not yet written their farewells borrowed pen or quill and ink and paper and did so. The defenders of the Alamo all waited and watched for help that did not arrive. And would not arrive in any force large enough to be effective against Santa Anna's thousands.

The politicians talked and talked and debated and procrastinated and patted themselves on the back for their brilliance . . . while the men of the Alamo, as soldiers have done for centuries, waited to die.

Crockett ceased his pacing and squatted down beside Jamie. "Talk is, lad, that if help don't come by tomorrow, it ain't comin.' "

Jamie nodded his head in agreement with that. Like every man there, he needed a shave and he needed a hot bath. The women there were doing their best to stay up with the laundry, but they were running out of soap. The defenders were living on meager portions of beef and beans and corn — and that was running out as well. Coffee was now being rationed.

Crockett handed Jamie a slip of paper. "I ain't much for hand-writin', lad. But if you'd see this gets posted, I'd be obliged."

"I shall, sir. You know that Colonel Travis is sending me over the wall at the last moment?"

"I do. And a mighty important job it is, too."

Another man walked up and handed

Jamie a note. "I'd be obliged," was all he said.

Jamie nodded and put the short note into his pouch.

"You have a good memory?" Davy asked.

"Very good," Jamie replied, and he was not boasting; just stating a fact. "Why?"

"I spoke with Ol' Jim last night," Davy said, leaning close and lowering his voice. "He read me part of what he's puttin' to paper. It's grand, lad, mighty grand. Flowery and all, but words that'll run a chill up and down a man's spine. I 'spect you best commit it to memory when you get it. Just in case you lose that pouch."

Jamie thought about that. It was a good idea. He nodded his agreement. "But I'll ask him about it before I do."

Davy grinned. "I done done it. He said that he figured it was a good idea." Crockett sobered and said, "Son, you got some mighty powerful enemies that's put money on your head, you know that?"

"Yes, sir. I know."

"When this fracas here is over . . . not that none of us will be alive to tell of it," he added grimly and with more than a touch of fatalism, "you best hightail it out of Texas. I commenced to tell you whilst we was on the way here, so now I'll finish it. What I

481

know is this: the Saxon gang has swore to kill you, the Newby Brothers gang has swore to kill you, the Olmstead Brothers has taken a blood oath to do you in, and somebody name of Abel Jackson is worth considerable and has money on your head."

"I know," Jamie said.

"Powerful lot of folks got it in for you, boy."

"Not as many as this time last year," Jamie replied with a smile.

Crockett laughed and walked away. He knew all the stories about Jamie MacCallister, and knew them to be true. Jamie MacCallister was a man best left alone. Crockett also felt that Jamie was too good a man to be wasted in a foul-up like what was happening here. Jamie would never know it, but Crockett had also been instrumental in convincing Travis to send Jamie over the wall when all hope was gone. If he could make it, Crockett added silently.

All that day, Santa Anna had been beefing up his lines as additional troops arrived and were placed. If help should arrive, they best do it quick, the woodsman thought. For in a few more days, it would take a damn army to fight its way through.

One man might make it, Crockett felt. He knew that Jamie had left his horses some miles out of town, and when he left it would be on foot.

Crockett climbed back up on the rickety parapets, shored up on each end with dirt, and checked his rifle.

"Lookee yonder, Davy," one of his men said, pointing.

A Mexican soldier was brazenly standing some five hundred yards from the mission, taunting the defenders.

"You reckon Ol' Betsy can bang that fer?" the man asked, a gleam in his eyes.

Crockett spat on his fingers and rubbed a bit of spit on the sights. "That there Mex is gonna have a mighty sore butt," he said, considerable heat in his tone, for the Mexican soldier was braving the cold and had dropped his trousers, showing his ass to the men of the Alamo. Bad mistake. The soldier was dancing around, wriggling his bare buttocks in a very obscene way. Davy Crockett said some very ugly words.

Jamie had come on a run at the wave of a man and climbed up to stand beside Crockett. One glance told him that the frontiersman was very angry.

Davy leveled the muzzle-loader and sighted in, taking up slack on the trigger. The pan flashed and the muzzle spat fire. The screaming of the soldier could easily be heard. He was rolling and thrashing about on the ground, one cheek of his buttocks bloodied. Two men ran to his aid. The Tennessee sharpshooters brought them down with two rounds. No one else tried to reach the dead or badly wounded men.

The ass-shot soldier quickly crawled into a ditch and disappeared.

"I'm a man who can take insults with the best of them," Crockett said, reloading. "But I'll be damned if that's one of them."

As day four of the siege of the Alamo gave way to night, Santa Anna ordered his bands to play yet another concert. He ordered them to play gentle love songs. Santa Anna was a cruel man, and really, not a very intelligent person, but sometimes he felt he showed a streak of brilliance. The love songs, he reasoned, would make the men in the Alamo homesick and might cause some of them to desert.

He was wrong again.

Davy Crockett got his fiddle, and a Scotsman named MacGreagor, or MacGregor, got his bagpipes and together they managed to produce such an awful din that Santa Anna ordered his bands to play something, *anything,* just drown out the sounds of the fiddle and pipes.

So day four ended, with no Texas volunteer hurt or killed, more than fifty dead or wounded Mexican soldiers, and one shot in the ass.

THIRTY-THREE: THE FIFTH DAY

February 27th, 1836

Crockett had reversed his earlier thoughts of the Alamo being an exercise in foolishness and now confided in a few of his friends that he understood why it had to be.

"We got to hold up ol' Santy Anner for as long as we can, boys," he said to a small audience, of which Jamie and Bill Travis were a part. "We got to give them politicians time to palaver 'mongst theyselves and huff and puff and blow off steam." Which meant, in Davy's quaint way of speaking, give the Texans time to form a government and raise an army.

"So we die givin' them time to do all that?" one of his men finally brought the feelings of all out into the open.

Travis held his breath.

"Yep," Davy Crockett said. "That do just about sum it all up, boys."

"Wal, hell," one of the Tennessee volunteers said. "If we'uns is to die for freedom, let's do it up right. We got to have us a flag to wave."

"Yeah," a New Orleans volunteer said. "And not that damn Mex flag, neither."

All were adamant on that.

"You men think on it," Travis said. "Then we'll have the ladies here see what they can do."

"Mighty fine," Crockett said. "Back to the walls, boys. We got us a war to fight."

So now they had resigned themselves to their fate, or at least many of them had. One man hung back and viewed his surroundings with a sour expression. His name was Louis Rose; his nickname was Moses.

Travis continued to send out couriers, pleading for help and for supplies. He received neither. The bombardment from the Mexican cannon continued all day, and the old walls were beginning to suffer from the impacting balls. Travis pulled men from their posts to help shore up the crumbling walls with dirt and timbers. Santa Anna's army crept closer in a prelude to a charge. But the Mexican infantry was cautious, careful not to get closer than a couple of hundred yards. To crawl any closer meant certain death. Even now, days before the final charge, the area all around the Alamo was stained with Mexican blood and bodies littered the cold ground.

Santa Anna had ordered his men not to attempt to retrieve the bodies during the day, for Crockett and his riflemen just loved that. Not one successful daylight attempt had been accomplished. Even while the Mexican cannons roared, Crockett and his men exposed themselves to blast away at Santa Anna's soldiers.

Even though the defenders of the Alamo were low on supplies and pitifully, hopelessly outnumbered, on the fifth day of the assault, the men of the Alamo held on. They had no way of knowing, but the small band of volunteers from Gonzales (either twenty-five or thirty-two; it is unclear as to the exact number) were making ready to leave. They were bringing with them much needed powder and shot. But they would not arrive for two more desperate days.

At the convention, meeting at Washington-on-the-Brazos, which officially was not due to convene until the first of March, the still-confused and disorganized government of Texas had not declared independence from nor war against Mexico.

Had they known it, that would have come as a real surprise to the besieged men of the Alamo.

■ ■ ■ ■

"Know this well, men," Captain Albert Martin said to the band of volunteers preparing to ride from Gonzales to the Alamo. "We are marching to die. Any of you who are not prepared for that, step back now."

Not a man moved. In a few days, Colonel William Travis would draw a line in the dirt with his sword and throw down the same challenge to the men in the Alamo. Only one would refuse to take up the dare.

"We march in thirty-six hours. We know that we must carry as many provisions as we can. So get ready. We'll meet back here at dawn of the 29th."

Every man would return with as many provisions for the besieged mission as he and his horse could carry. Every man would return, knowing they were riding to their deaths. For freedom. For Texas.

Jamie and the other men of the Alamo worked frantically all the rest of that day, shoring up the crumbling old walls, which continued to take a terrible pounding from the cannon fire. Just as dusk began to lay her cloak of darkness over the land, a sentry yelled out, "Good God Amighty, boys! To your posts, to your posts. Here they come!"

Travis leaped to the parapet and stared out in horror at what appeared to be thousands of Mexican troops, all rushing toward the walls of the Alamo.

"Lower the cannons!" Dickerson yelled. "Quickly now, lads. They're almost on us."

The muzzles of the cannon were quickly lowered for minimum elevation and loaded with grapeshot. Davy Crockett and his sharpshooters, dozens of loaded rifles at hand, were sighting in, Jamie stood beside Crockett, half a dozen loaded rifles nearby.

At about two hundred yards, Dickerson let the four- and eight-pounders howl. When the smoke had cleared, the area was littered with the mangled bodies of dead and dying.

"Fire!" Crockett hollered, and a dozen rifles roared as Dickerson's crews worked quickly to reload.

The cannon screamed and the sharpshooters along the walls would fire. After one more unsuccessful charge, the Mexican officers ordered the buglers to sound recall. They had had quite enough of the guns of the Alamo for this day.

"My God!" Travis breathed, when all the smoke had drifted away and the grounds around the old mission were visible in the last rays of the setting sun. The sun glinted off of the bayonets of rifles lying beside the mangled bodies of at least several hundred Mexican soldiers.

"Hold your fire!" Travis yelled, as one defender started to shoot a crawling wounded man. He turned to Jamie. "Jamie, ride out under a white flag and tell the Mexican officer who meets you that we will hold our fire while they collect their wounded."

"Yes, sir."

Jamie rode straight up to the enemy lines, only a few hundred yards away from the walls. The lines were now heavily reinforced with earthworks, done at night to escape the bullets from the sharpshooters on the walls.

"My respects to you, sir," Jamie said to a man wearing a colonel's epaulets. "My colonel, William Travis, says to tell you that we will hold our fire so you may collect your wounded and see to their needs."

"Young man," the voice came from behind the officer.

Jamie noticed the colonel sprang to attention.

"Señor?" Jamie replied from the saddle.

"It took a tremendous amount of courage for you to ride right up to our lines. I thank you for your commanding officer's kind gesture."

He was still standing in the shadows and Jamie was not at all sure just whom he was speaking to.

"Would you please dismount and have supper and conversation with me? I give you my personal word that you will not be harmed in any way."

Jamie swung down from the saddle and a Mexican soldier took the reins. "I'll have some conversation and coffee with you, sir. And be honored. But I eat only what my comrades inside the walls eat."

The man chuckled. "I applaud your loyalty, young man. It is rare. Come. We'll sit in comfort and talk."

Jamie walked toward the man and was startled to find himself looking General Santa Anna straight in the eyes.

"They will all die," Tall Bull was told by the scout just returned from the south. He squatted down by the fire and warmed his hands, accepting the hunk of meat from the spit over the fire.

Tall Bull waited, a warm buffalo robe wrapped around him.

"The whites are barricaded in what appears to be an old place of worship. There are so many soldiers all around them it would be impossible to count them; it would be like trying to count the ants in a hill."

"Did you see Man Who Is Not Afraid?"

"It would be impossible to get that close."

"You were gone so long we were worried that you might have been killed."

"I had to hide my horse and walk most of the way. The soldier patrols are everywhere."

"You truly feel that the defenders of this worship place are doomed?"

"As surely as we are sitting close to this fire and the night is dark."

Tall Bull took a stick and drew in the dirt. "The defenders are here. Man Who Is Not Afraid left his home over here." He jabbed at the earth. We know there is but one trail that the whites travel, a road. It leads to this place called Gonzales. We shall leave in the morning to find a halfway point between the fort and the town. I think a nice place along this river . . ."

"The Guadalupe," the scout said.

"The what?"

"Guadalupe River."

"Stupid name. No matter. If Man Who Is Not Afraid does manage to escape death at the fort, or church, or whatever it is, he must travel this trail. We shall be waiting. I have spoken. Now I will rest."

"Why?" Santa Anna asked Jamie, after an aide brought them both steaming cups of strong coffee.

"Sir?"

"Why do you choose to die in that old mission?"

"I don't choose to die, sir. But if I must die, I can think of no better reason than for freedom."

"Freedom?" Santa Anna was startled. "From *what*?"

"From Mexico, General."

Santa Anna's aides stiffened, knowing what a volatile temper he had. But the general only chuckled. "You must know that you will not succeed."

"We might not, sir. But this is only the beginning. Where we fall, where each man falls, ten or twenty or a hundred will take their place. Killing us will only throw grease onto an already raging fire."

Santa Anna smiled. "Then what would you have me do, young man?"

Jamie paused, then chose his words carefully. "I think, sir, that the destinies of both you and your army, and those men in the mission . . . and to a larger degree, Texas, have been sealed. I think events are already locked in place and no matter what we say this night, they cannot be changed."

Santa Anna nodded his head slowly. "I think you are wise beyond your years, young man. What is your name?"

"Jamie MacCallister, sir."

"Señor MacCallister, you know I cannot offer you or your companions mercy."

"We understand that, sir. I would ask, speaking for myself, that you do not harm the women and the children in the mission. Or the slaves."

"I was not aware of any women or children in the fort!"

"Yes, sir. About twenty or so."

Santa Anna turned to an aide. "Note that. Advise the men that when the final assault comes, no harm is to come to women, children, or slaves."

"*Sí,* General."

"*Gracias,* sir," Jamie said.

"*Por nada.*" Santa Anna stood up from the camp chair and Jamie rose with him. The general smiled and saluted Jamie. Jamie returned the salute.

"*Buenas noches,* Jamie MacCallister."

"Good night, sir."

Santa Anna walked off into the darkness.

His horse was brought to him, and Jamie stepped into the saddle. He looked down at the faces of the Mexican soldiers who sur-rounded him. They were not unfriendly faces, just curious. "Good night, gentle-men."

He walked his horse away, back to the Alamo, amid a chorus of *buenas noches* and *vaya con Dios.* Travis and Crockett met him at the gate.

"We thought they'd taken you captive, lad," Crockett said.

"Are you all right?" Travis asked.

"Yes, sir. Fine. I had coffee and some conversation with General Santa Anna, that's all."

Crockett and Travis were speechless for a moment. And for both men, that sensation was quite a novel experience.

"You did *what?*" Travis finally found his voice.

Jamie told them of his encounter with the general.

"Incredible," Travis said.

"Well, I'll just be hornswoggled," Crockett said.

"Rider comin' with a white flag," a lookout hollered.

"Find out what he wants!" Travis called.

After a moment, the sentry said, "He wants to speak with you, Colonel Travis, and Davy and Jamie. Says Jamie speaks good Spanish and can translate if the courier loses his English."

The trio of men walked out the south gate and stood in front of the mounted courier.

"General Santa Anna says that he is calling for a cease-fire until noon tomorrow. He is giving you time to reconsider your position and to surrender. My general also wants you all to know that he is aware of the band of men coming from the town of Gonzales to help you. He has ordered cavalry to cut them off."

Travis, Crockett, and Jamie exchanged glances. That sure was news to them. Good news. They all wondered how many men were coming to their aid.

"You are alone here," the courier said. "And no help is coming. Your dying will accomplish nothing. My general is not a cruel man. He will accept your unconditional surrender. You have until noon tomorrow. After that time, surrender will not be possible and you will all be killed."

Travis replied, "Tell General Santa Anna we thank him for the respite, but he knows we cannot surrender."

"I am sorry, Colonel," the courier said, real emotion in his voice.

"So am I," Travis spoke softly.

The courier, a young officer, looked into

the eyes of the three men. "When you hear the *degüello,* pray to God. For it will soon be over for you all." He saluted, turned his horse, and rode back to his lines.

"What's the *degüello?*" Crockett asked.

"It's a song," Jamie said. "Means fire and death. It also means no prisoners will be taken."

"Total annihilation," Travis added.

"Well, we'll see about that," Crockett said. "I wonder how many men is comin' from Gonzales?"

"Certainly not enough," Travis said. "But any number will greatly improve the morale of the men. And they'll be bringing provisions, too."

"We hope," Crockett added.

"I'll go tell Jim the good news," Jamie said, and walked back into the mission.

"They're fools," Bowie said. "They're marching straight into hell. I admire their courage and love each and every one as I would my brother, but part of me hopes they don't make it and turn around and go back home."

Jamie told him about his conversation with Santa Anna.

"You hear that, Sam?" Bowie called weakly. "You don't fight no more now, you hear me? You just stand back and when the smoke clears, you can walk out with your head held high."

"Hush up," Sam told him. "And take your medicine like the doctor told you to."

"Not only has he turned uppity," Bowie said with a grin. "He's turned bossy, too."

"You hold his head, Mr. Jamie," Sam said. "And I'll pour this medicine down his throat."

"You won't have to do that if you'll just put a little whiskey in it," Bowie said with a laugh.

"You're a mean and ornery man, Mr. Jim," Sam said. "I'd leave, 'ceptin' I knows you can't get along without me. Now take this here medicine."

"Will you be quiet if I do?" Bowie asked.

"Yes."

Bowie held out his hand.

Thirty-Four: The Sixth Day

February 28th, 1836

Jamie stood on the parapet beside Travis and Crockett and watched the Mexican soldiers beef up their positions. Santa Anna had been true to his word: not one shot had come from the Mexican side that morning.

But his word was in no way etched in stone, for during the night, General Santa Anna had ordered his men to silently creep closer, trusting in the Alamo defenders to hold their fire. They did.

"The black-hearted son of a bitch!" Crockett cursed the trickery of Santa Anna.

"No honor," Travis said scornfully.

"I'd a-done the same thing he did," Jamie said with a smile. "I don't think there is any such thing as honor in a war."

Jamie jumped down from the platform and walked over to Bowie's quarters.

"Strange young man," Travis remarked.

Crockett said nothing.

Bowie was sleeping. When Jamie had pushed open the door, Sam stepped outside the darkened room to talk with him. "He's driftin' in and out, Mr. Jamie. Sometimes he don't even know who I is. He babbles some. He needs to be in a proper hospital. I tole him that and he tole me what difference does the place make when dyin' is a certainty?"

"Has he finished his letter?"

"Not quite, sir. But I heard him mumble that he was purt near done with it."

"Sam, you and Joe take up no more arms against Santa Anna," Jamie cautioned the slave. "Stay out of the fight."

"Yes, sir."

Jamie restlessly prowled the three-acre compound. He glanced up at the winter's sun. Noontime was near and when it came, Santa Anna would once more start his bombardment. The ultimatums of Santa Anna had been passed to all the men. The word surrender was met with cold, stony looks from the defenders.

Jamie ate his meager rations and once more moved to his position along the wall. Like all the others inside the mission, there were few things he could do other than wait, and think of family and home. And wonder if, when the time came, he would die well?

501

Jamie was inwardly torn with conflicting emotions. He certainly did not want to die — who does? — but he felt guilt at Bowie and Travis, and to some degree, Crockett's plans for him to slip out of the compound and flee. The men knew how he felt, and many had come to him, telling him his mission was an important one. Someone had to escape to tell the world the story. That made Jamie feel better. But not a lot.

The Mexican artillerymen began their bombardment, the first round landing inside the compound, smashing into the ground near the front of the old church. The truce was over. There was no turning back now. For those trapped inside the Alamo, only two ends existed: victory or death.

The cannonade that day had been the worst so far. A half a dozen defenders had been slightly wounded by shrapnel, although none seriously. But the psychological effects were beginning to show. The nerves of the men were ragged from lack of sleep, the bitter cold, the constant shelling, and lack of proper food. And the news that Bowie was drifting in and out of consciousness was very unsettling to the men.

Even Davy Crockett was affected by it,

the frontiersman becoming almost morose for a time.

Outside the walls, the Mexican infantry had become very cautious, taking great pains not to expose themselves unnecessarily. They had learned a painfully hard lesson about the deadly accuracy of Davy Crockett's sharpshooters along the walls of the Alamo.

Only the wounded Mexicans had been picked up during the surprise cease-fire called by Santa Anna, and the grounds all around the mission were littered with stiffening bodies of soldiers. Had it not been an unusually cold winter, the stench and following health problems would have been awful.

When darkness fell on the evening of the sixth day, Jamie went to Travis's quarters and found the man writing yet another report. Jamie, along with many of the other men, wondered just what in the hell the colonel found to write about.

"Yes, Scout MacCallister?" Travis said, looking up from the reports.

"I would like your permission to go over the walls and gather up powder and shot from the dead Mexican soldiers, sir."

"An admirable thought, MacCallister. But I believe the Mexican rifles are of a different caliber from ours."

"We have all kinds of calibers here, sir. Besides, the lead can be melted down and remolded to our caliber, sir. And we desperately need the powder."

Travis slowly nodded his head. He knew perfectly well that Jamie was going over the walls with or without his permission. This was the goddamnest bunch of independent-minded men he had ever commanded. The young man standing before him was just being respectful by asking his permission. "All right, Jamie. Go ahead."

Jamie stopped by to see Bowie. The man was in one of his more lucid hours and actually looking well. He grinned when Jamie told him what he planned to do.

"And just how do you plan on accomplishing that feat, Jamie?"

"By becoming a snake, sir. Just like the Shawnee taught me."

"Stop by and see me when you return. But change back into human form before you do," Bowie added dryly.

"Yes, sir," Jamie replied with a smile.

Jamie blackened his face with soot and tied a dark bandanna over his blond hair. He took only two pistols and a knife. Crockett stood leaning on his rifle, watching him.

"You larned well from them Shawnee, son," the man said. "Can you make like a mockingbird?"

Jamie's bird call was so much like the real thing Crockett was startled. "That way we'll know where you are and you won't get a ball in the brisket."

"Or in the butt," Jamie said, his eyes sparkling with good humor.

"That, too," Crockett said with a laugh.

Jamie left the mission by way of the cattle pen. He slithered on his belly like a huge reptile, slowly working from stiffened body to stinking body, removing the powder flask and shot pouch from each dead soldier. When he had retrieved a dozen, he worked his way back to the cattle pen, whistled softly, and handed the badly needed shot and powder to Galba Fuqua, who was manning the watch when Jamie returned.

They spoke softly in Spanish to one another.

"It must be terrible out there," Galba whispered.

"It isn't a picnic," Jamie admitted.

Galba handed the filled pouch to another man and gave Jamie an empty one. "Take care, amigo."

"I shall." And Jamie was gone again.

Jamie soon ran out of bodies closer in and

had to work his way further out from the Alamo. He worked so close to the Mexican lines that he could smell the fragrant odor of coffee and hear the lilting Spanish words of men far from home and loved ones. Soldiers are soldiers, he concluded. The world over.

He made five more trips back to the pen before Travis ordered him back inside.

"It's getting just too risky, Jamie," Travis told him. "Besides, you've brought back ample shot and powder. Take a much deserved rest."

For a fact, Jamie had brought back seventy powder flasks, all full, and sixty shot pouches, all full. Jamie did not argue with Colonel Travis. Bowie had assigned him to the regular army, and he would follow orders. In most cases.

Santa Anna was now under pressure to do something. He knew his men were becoming demoralized. Six days had passed and little, if any, damage had been done to the Alamo. As far as he could tell, the defenders had not suffered a single casualty. It was infuriating. He knew he had to do something to restore morale.

But what?

The arrival of an aide with news gave him

the thought.

"Sir! The troops from Aldama and Tolucca are within a few hours' ride of Bexar. Some two thousand strong!"

Santa Anna's dark face brightened. "We shall have a parade and much music. At first light, instruct the cooks to prepare a feast. Butcher some of the oxen."

With the arrival of those men, Santa Anna probably had close to seven thousand men at his disposal — the exact figure was never known — against some one hundred and fifty or so men holed up in the Alamo, who were low on powder, low on food, and cold — some did not even have shoes and were forced to wrap their feet in rags and strips of blankets to ward off frostbite.

But there was one thing the men of the Alamo did not lack, something they had plenty of, and because of that, the world would praise them for generations to come. The word *Alamo* would become a battle cry for freedom.

The one attribute the men of the Alamo had plenty of was Courage.

THIRTY-FIVE:
THE SEVENTH DAY

February 29th, 1836

"Joe," Jamie said to Travis's slave just after dawn. "Get him awake and to the walls. He'll want to see this."

Travis was at the door in jig-time. "What is it, Jamie?"

"Santa Anna's reinforcements have arrived. Or are arriving. Several thousand of them. With more cannon."

Travis paled just for an instant. Then he caught himself. Joe pressed a cup of coffee into his master's hand.

"And like the ones here," Jamie said, "they've brought their women with them."

Travis strode quickly to the walls and climbed up to the parapet. The sight before him was anything but heartening. The town of San Antonio de Bexar was filled with thousands of people. Several bands started playing, each one seeming to be competing against the other.

All Travis could say was, "My God!"

Crockett said, "Yep. I reckon it's time we all was callin' on Him. For a fact."

All that day the men of the Alamo crowded the walls, watching as more troops rode or marched in, with their colorful uniforms, flags and pennants waving, and the bands playing. The smell of cooking meat came to the men along the walls, the spices the Mexicans were using causing many a mouth to salivate. Since the Mexican army permitted their soldiers to bring their wives and kids and girlfriends and various female camp-followers along, the scene before the men of the Alamo was particularly unnerving . . . both above and below the belt.

Travis seemed to sense that the end was near. He retired to his quarters to write yet another plea for help. He wrote passionately but rationally to Governor Smith and to Sam Houston, telling about the hundreds of shells that had fallen in, around, and on the mission. He wrote that the morale of his men was still high, even though there now appeared to be no hope left for any of them. He implored Smith and Houston for help, particularly for shot and powder.

Travis closed with this: God and Texas — Victory or Death.

In Bexar, Santa Anna had forgotten all about the news of reinforcements coming in from Gonzales. He wanted all his men to enjoy the feast and the bands and the parades. He pulled in most of his patrols, giving the small band of men coming from the east a much better chance of making it, at least to the outskirts of town. Getting through the enemy lines to the Alamo was quite another matter.

Only a few cannons from the Mexican side roared that day, and the cannons of the Alamo were silent; Travis was pitifully low on powder, and what powder he had for his artillery was not much good. He knew he had to save his powder for the final assault.

"God help us all," he muttered.

By late afternoon of the seventh day, the volunteers from Gonzales had come to within a few miles of San Antonio. They took to whatever cover they could find and stayed out of sight, shivering on the cold ground until full nightfall. Then they abandoned their horses and struggled out on foot, each man carrying a heavy load of supplies.

Their plan was to reach the Alamo a short time after midnight; when the Mexican camp would be sleeping and most of the fires low. Of course they also had another worry: not to get shot by the men along the walls of the Alamo.

The men from Gonzales carried with them a homemade flag of silk. It was to be the battle flag of the Alamo. It had a hand-sewn picture of a cannon in the center and above and below the cannon, the words: COME AND TAKE IT. They had no way of knowing how prophetic those words would turn out to be.

The men from Gonzales crept along slowly, by some miracle making their way through the Mexican lines. Then they reached the ditch that surrounded the compound and stayed in it until they were at the walls.

A nervous sentry heard a noise and fired. The men from Gonzales went belly down in the muddy ditch.

"Goddamnit!" one said.

"Hold your fire," the captain of the guard yelled. "Them boys is *ours!*"

THIRTY-SIX:
THE EIGHTH DAY

March 1st, 1836

The men from Gonzales had reached the Alamo at about four o'clock in the morning. There would be no more sleep that night for anyone, not even for Bowie, who had managed to overcome his often coma-like malady and would remain lucid, if still very weak, for the next one hundred and twenty or so hours . . . and then the men of the Alamo would sleep forever.

Travis greeted Captains Kimbell and Martin and John Smith warmly. If the colonel had any disappointment about the small size of the group, and he certainly did, he did not show it. After the initial whooping and hollering from the defenders had died down, Travis took Captain Martin aside.

"You're the first of the relief columns, right, Albert?" he asked.

Captain Martin threw formality to the cold March winds. He shook his head.

"There will be no relief columns, Bill. We've been written off."

Colonel William Barret Travis sagged against the thick wall; its coldness felt to him like the icy hand of death touching his shoulder. "My God, Albert," he exclaimed softly. "You've come to die."

"Yes," was the reply.

"The men with you?"

"They know."

"Then so, too, will the others before dawn breaks."

"Probably. But I feel we shall not die for naught. We'll be the spark that ignites the fuse for independence."

"One hundred and eighty-nine men," Travis whispered, his words barely audible. "Against thousands."

Some accounts say one hundred and eighty-three men died at the Alamo, and estimates are that Santa Anna had under his command about five thousand crack, seasoned combat troops, with very few unwilling conscripts. That so few could hold out against so many for so long still, to this day, evokes wild stirrings of passion, and not just in Texas, for the men who fought and died at the Alamo came from all over the young nation and either nineteen or twenty-one were from foreign countries.

Martin gripped Travis's arm. "Bill, we shall not die in vain. I promise you."

"No," Travis said, rising to his height and straightening his uniform. "We most certainly shall not."

As the first rays of the sun touched the land, Travis assembled the men and raised the new battle flag of the Alamo. The wild cheering caused an aide to run to Santa Anna's quarters, where he'd been engaged in a bit of early morning dallying with his new bride.

Santa Anna was not happy at being interrupted. He was even less happy to learn that the volunteers from Gonzales had managed to slip through his lines and were now in place inside the walls of the old mission. He was unhappier still when he took his glass and viewed the new flag that now flew over the bastion of freedom and liberty in open defiance toward the Mexican government. The words on the flag made his stomach churn.

COME AND TAKE IT.

Santa Anna went into a wild fit of rage. He hurled the spy glass against the wall of the room and stomped around in his bare feet while his nervous aides tried to steer him away from the broken glass and sharp metal that now littered the floor from the

514

impact against the wall.

He finally calmed down enough to issue some rational orders. "Increase the cannonade. I want a steady bombardment and I want to see some damage done."

"Yes, General."

"I want to see some Anglo blood spilled."

"Yes, General."

"Then do it!" Santa Anna yelled. He took a step and his bare foot landed on a shard of broken glass. Santa Anna screamed like a panther.

When he stopped jumping around and hollering, Santa Anna found a chair and sat down. He was livid with rage. "I want all patrols increased in size and all roads and trails and paths leading to the Alamo found and guarded. No one leaves and no one enters that accursed place. Is that fully understood by all?"

His aides assured him it was.

"It better be," the general said menacingly.

The news had spread like a raging fire among the defenders inside the old walls. There would be no more help from the outside. Fannin was not coming. Houston was not coming. They were alone. They had been abandoned. Written off. Only death awaited them. Earlier that week, they had watched as a courier, Jim Bonham, had ridden out in the darkness with a final plea from Travis to Fannin to change his mind: For God's sake, man, help us!

All day long the Mexican bombardment slammed the Alamo, some of the batteries less than four hundred yards away; the heavier pieces set back nearly half a mile. If the powder Travis had at his disposal had been worth a damn, the defenders could have played havoc with the Mexican artillery. But as one artilleryman summed up the quality of gunpowder for the cannons, "We might as well be usin' dust from the road."

The powder the men from Gonzales brought with them was distributed equally and the defenders of the Alamo settled down to await the charge they knew was coming. What thoughts they must have had as they watched the thousands of Mexican troops that surrounded them. Surely all shared thoughts of home and family that they all knew they would never see again.

Men not on duty along the walls gathered in small groups and spoke, when the booming of cannons would allow it, of friends and family on the outside, of good dogs and fast horses. They spoke of last year's crops and of the plans they had for this year . . .

. . . Before they answered the call to arms.

History does not record any elaborate religious ceremonies being conducted by and for the men inside the walls of the Alamo. What praying there was — and surely there was a considerable amount of that — was done privately.

For several hours on that afternoon of the eighth day, the men of the Alamo were quiet; when they did speak, it was in hushed tones. Then, on the evening of the eighth day, just as afternoon was giving way to dusk, the men seemed to rouse; flagging spirits caught fire.

"I'll be damned if I'll sit around here lookin' like a lost calf," a man with rags wrapped around his feet said, rising from a squat. "Davy," he shouted to Crockett, standing on a parapet. "Get your fiddle and bow and do us up a tune. I feel like dancin'."

It must have been a sight. Davy struck up a slow reel and the man, whose parents had come over from Scotland, did a fling, his rag-covered feet kicking up dust in the plaza of the old mission. John McGregor got his bagpipes and joined in, and soon half a hundred men were dancing. Sam opened the door to Bowie's quarters so he could see the revelry and the famous knife fighter smiled at the antics of the men.

"They might overwhelm us, Sam," Bowie said. "But it won't be due to any lack of courage of the men out yonder."

The Mexican officers, upon hearing the music and the shouting, signaled for their cannons to stand down.

General Juan Amador galloped up and jumped from his horse. "What is happening?" he shouted.

"They are having a fiesta," a young lieutenant said.

"A . . . *fiesta*?" the general was astonished. "They are hours away from being dead men and they are having a dance?"

"*Sí.*"

What must the Mexicans have thought? Surely many must have thought: what manner of men are we facing? They are looking at total annihilation and still have the courage to sing and dance.

"Should General Santa Anna be informed of this development?" the young lieutenant asked.

"Good God, no!" General Amador was quick to say. He knew Santa Anna would fly into a screaming rage if he should learn of this. "No. Absolutely not. The general is . . . occupied at the moment."

"Should we resume the shelling, then?"

General Amador was silent for a moment, listening to the fiddle and the pipes. He shook his head. "No," he said softly. "Not yet."

"But General! There are quite a number in the plaza of the mission. They are exposed. We could kill many of them."

"We will kill them all very soon," the general said, weariness in his voice. "Are we such a barbaric gathering here that you would deny dying men a few moments of pleasure?"

"No, General."

"Then allow them what simple pleasures they can afford, Lieutenant. Resume the shelling when their festivities are concluded."

"Yes, sir."

General Amador turned, then stopped and looked back toward the faint sounds of music. He listened for a moment, sighed, shook his head, then swung into the saddle and rode back to the town.

A sergeant in command of a battery walked over to the lieutenant. "*Loco,*" he said, jerking a thumb toward the walls of the mission.

The lieutenant shook his head. "No, Sergeant. Just very brave men. Very brave men."

THIRTY-SEVEN:
THE NINTH DAY

March 2, 1836

Although the men of the Alamo never knew it, those delegates meeting at Washington-on-the-Brazos, on this date, officially rejected the Mexican constitution of 1824 and with a rousing cheer, adopted the Declaration of Independence, declaring Texas to be a Republic.

Had they somehow by magic learned of that decision, Davy Crockett would have more than likely spat on the ground and said, "Why, hellfire! We done that a week and a half ago! You boys is suckin' hind tit!"

Or words to that effect.

The bombardment from the Mexican cannon continued without letup. Miraculously, despite all the hundreds of shells that had dropped all around and inside the mission, none of the defenders had been killed and only a few had been wounded, none of them seriously.

Travis had given the order: "Save your powder, boys. Don't bother returning the fire. We'll need everything we've got when . . ." He stumbled over the last words. ". . . the time comes."

Bowie called Jamie to his quarters. Jamie was shocked at the man's appearance. Bowie had lost weight and his eyes were deep-set in his head. He looked much older than his years. He handed Jamie several sheets of paper.

"Commit it to memory, lad," Bowie requested. "Just in case something happens to your pouch. Sit down over there by the light and read it over and over. I'll rest while you're doing that. I am so damned tired!"

Bowie was dying.

Jamie committed the pages to memory over the rasping breathing of Jim Bowie. Sam walked over to his master and covered him with a thin blanket.

"He's asleep, now, Mr. Jamie. He might not wake up for hours. Them pages you read, was they most eloquent?"

"Yes, Sam. They were very eloquent."

"I knowed they would be. He mutters in his sleep a lot after he writes. Words like liberty and freedom and abouts how the men of this garrison gonna shed they blood for all Texas to be free. He can speak right good when he puts his mind to it."

"You like him, don't you, Sam?"

"He don't beat me none."

Jamie arched an eyebrow at that simple statement of loyalty and devotion. "Stay out of the fight, Sam. Stay clear out of it and when it's over, head for the high country and live out your life as a free man."

"We'll see," the freed slave said.

Jamie stepped out of the sick room and walked across the plaza. His patience was now wearing thin. While he no longer felt like a traitor because of his orders to leave the fort when the battle was nigh, he felt helpless locked inside the walls. And he was outraged that these brave men had been abandoned to die. He paused at Travis's hail from his quarters, changed direction, and walked over to the colonel.

"Yes, sir?"

"Bonham should be back tomorrow. I'm sending Smith out tomorrow night. You'd better go with him, Jamie." ·

"Is that an order, sir?"

Travis hesitated. "Ah . . . no, Jamie. It isn't. But I feel that Santa Anna will not wait much longer. For some reason, March sixth keeps creeping into my mind. I am not a man much given to premonition, Jamie, and have told no one else that."

"I won't repeat it, sir."

"I want you out of here no later than midnight on the fifth, Jamie. And that is an order. Those dispatches in your pouch will be our last farewells to the outside world."

"Yes, sir. I understand."

"You saw Bowie?"

"Yes, sir."

"His condition?"

"Worse. He's very weak."

Travis nodded, and then left when he was called by a work party along the log-reinforced south wall by the church.

"March the sixth," Jamie muttered. "Well, maybe the colonel is wrong."

He wasn't.

Thirty-Eight: The Tenth Day

March 3, 1836

The spirits of the men inside the walls of the Alamo were high, and for a time on this day, Travis still held out some hope that help was on the way. He had once more composed a letter and would be sending it out under cover of darkness that evening. John Smith would be the courier.

At midmorning, Bonham rode back into the mission and told Travis, "There will be no help, Bill. We are considered a lost cause. No help is coming."

"John is leaving this night," Travis said. "I have to keep trying."

"Don't ask him to return," Bonham pleaded. "We're doomed."

"Then why did you come back?" Travis snapped.

"To die shoulder to shoulder with my comrades," was Bonham's reply.

Travis's spirits sagged. He knew Bonham

was speaking the truth. The men of the Alamo had been abandoned. He walked dejectedly to his quarters.

"You're all fools," Louis Moses Rose told a gathering of stony-faced men. "Not cowards; just fools. Look, I've been a soldier all my life. Listen to me. This place has no strategic value. None. Let's get out of this death trap and fight Santa Anna Injun style. We can do Texas a lot more good that way."

"It ain't that this old mission has any value, man," Crockett said. "It's provin' a point to Mexico that we're doin'."

"What the hell is the point of *dying*?" Rose snapped back.

"How 'bout your friend, Jim Bowie?" Micajah Autry asked. "You just gonna leave him here?"

"Jim's dying," Rose said softly. "I went to see him just an hour ago. He didn't even know me."

"Go if you must," Daniel Cloud said. "I won't fault you. But as for me, I'm stayin'."

Cloud turned and walked away, the others quickly following him. Louis Moses Rose was left alone in the plaza.

Jamie had listened to the debate, squatting by the well. He harbored no ill will toward Rose. If the man wished to flee, then let him go. To go or to stay was a decision that each man had to make for himself. Jamie had heard others speak of Rose — the man had proven himself in combat more times than any of them. He was no coward. Perhaps, Jamie thought, the man was simply weary of it all.

But then, he silently added, who among us isn't?

The Mexican cannons began booming after a short respite. Jamie moved closer to the wall, next to the low barracks, and waited. Shot and shell dropped into the plaza, crashed against the walls, and the ground trembled beneath Jamie's moccasins. How many hundreds of rounds had been fired at the Alamo to date? With, so far, little effect.

His eyes found Louis Moses Rose, squatting with his back to a wall. He was alone, with not a man near him. The word had gone out quickly and the other men had chosen not to have anything to do with him.

Staying close to the walls, Jamie made his way over to the ostracized man. Rose looked up at Jamie's approach, surprise in his eyes.

"Ain't you afraid you'll catch something, moving so close to me?" Rose asked.

Jamie ignored that. "Look, Rose. Whether you stay or go is your choice and your choice alone."

"I ain't made it yet," Rose said. "You seen them ladders the Mexicans is building?"

"Yes."

"Won't be long now. They'll be crawling over the walls like ants to honey."

"Probably," Jamie replied, after the cannon barrage had momentarily ceased.

"They're all going to die here."

"They know that."

"It just don't make no sense to me."

Jamie knew then the man had made up his mind. He was going over the walls. The cannons began roaring again, and any further conversation was impossible.

Rose stood up and looked down at Jamie. "You had your decision handed you, Mac-Callister."

Anger filled Jamie and he stood up, towering over the man. "You think I asked for it?"

"No," Rose said, his voice just audible over the booming of cannon. "That ain't what I meant."

Jamie's anger faded and he put a hand on the much older man's shoulder. "I know it isn't. Sorry, Louis. Whatever decision you choose to make, Louis, I'm still your friend."

The man smiled. "I can use one about now," he admitted. And then further conversation was impossible as the cannons boomed. During an abatement, Louis said, "They have to be the worst goddamn gunners I have ever seen. They don't appear to know anything about elevation. If they did, there wouldn't be a platform or parapet left intact." He shook his head and walked off.

Jamie squatted back down against the trembling walls and waited. There just wasn't a whole hell of a lot else to do.

An hour later, just about an hour before sunset, the Mexican cannons fell silent. Jamie was eating a piece of bread and drinking coffee when Travis walked slowly out of his quarters and into the center of the plaza. He called for the men to assemble in front of him. All but Jamie.

"Scout MacCallister!" Travis called. "Stand lookout, please."

Jamie wondered what in the world was going on. Was Travis thinking of surrender? No. He immediately dismissed that. On his way to the parapet, Crockett stopped him and said, "You're out of this, lad. You just get them messages through. I done spoke to Travis. He's gonna give the men a choice. You stay up yonder on the platform."

Jim Bowie was carried out into the windy plaza, on his cot. He was lucid and feeling somewhat better. Sam put several pillows behind his head so he could see better.

Travis said, "I take full responsibility for our situation. And from the very depths of my heart, I apologize to you all. I did not even entertain the thought that we would be abandoned. That was, to me, unthinkable. But obviously, we have been forgotten. I was promised that help would come. It has not. It will not." He paused to let that sink in. "We alone stand in the way of Santa Anna's mighty army. We . . . *alone!*" No one there missed the emphasis on that last word. And no one there missed the true meaning of it. To a man, they knew that Travis was saying farewell to them all, in the only way he knew how.

"We have bought precious time for those delegates meeting at Washington-on-the-Brazos. Precious time for Austin and Houston to mount an army. Precious time for our allies on the outside to lay in powder and shot. Now I'm asking you to help me buy them more time. Two days; three days. Maybe longer. I will not surrender. If I must, alone, stand on those parapets and swab and load and fire the cannon, I by God will. Surrender is not a word I will ever let pass my tongue again."

The men cheered loudly at that.

"To give up would be far worse than dying," Travis continued. He shook his head.

"I could not live with that in my heart. I could not look another man in the eyes with that in my past. No. I am staying. Alone if I must. But I will never give up. I want the world to know that this old mission, soon to be stained with the blood of its defenders, was the young beating heart of what shall surely be the Republic of Texas. I intend to die right in it, within these walls. But I shall, with the help of God and this sword," he jerked his saber from its scabbard, "be surrounded by the bodies of my enemies."

The men went wild. Coonskin caps, sombreros, and battered old hats were slung into the air at Travis's words.

The Mexicans, now about two hundred and fifty yards away, must have wondered what in the world those beleaguered men inside the battered and crumbling walls had to cheer about. "Crazy gringos," must have been uttered a hundred times from the Mexican lines.

The men stood silent now, as Travis took his sword and started tracing a long line in the dirt, just in front of the row of men. That done, he walked back to the center of the line. Not a man there did not know what that line meant. But they waited for Travis to speak the words.

Travis, dressed in full uniform, held his

sword into the air, at arm's length. "I say I shall stand and die!" he thundered. He pointed the tip of his sword at the battle flag the men from Gonzales had brought, now fluttering in the cold winds. "For liberty, for freedom, for true justice, and for the Republic of Texas! Who will stand with me?"

There was no hesitation among the men. Several did standing jumps to be the first over the line. The others surged across. Only Moses Rose, Bowie, and Sam were left standing on the other side of the line.

"You stay here, Sam," Bowie said. "Don't you even think of crossing that line. Oh, boys!" Bowie raised his voice. "Some of you come over here and carry me across the line, will you?"

A half dozen men quickly ran to Bowie's side and lifted the cot, carrying Jim Bowie over the line Travis had drawn with the sword.

Louis Moses Rose now stood alone. He had made his choice and was not about to change his mind.

"It's your choice to make, Louis," Bowie called to his old friend. "Are you sure this is the way you want it?"

"I'm sure, Jim."

"God bless you, then," Bowie replied in a

surprisingly strong voice. "Tell all our friends we died for Texas."

"I'll do that, Jim."

"How are you goin' to get out, man?" another asked. "You know damn well some of them Mex bodies out yonder past the walls is playin' possum, just waitin' to use gun or knife."

"I'll get out," the old soldier said. "You just watch me." Rose looked squarely at each man standing behind Travis. The eyeballing took several minutes. To Rose's surprise, he found little animosity staring back at him. Most of the returning looks were friendly, curious, or a mixture of both. The defenders leaned on their rifles and watched him.

Dusk was rapidly settling all around the mission. The Mexican cannons remained silent. Rose hesitated, then left most of his powder and shot behind, laying the pouches and flask on the ground. "You boys will be needing these."

"Thank you, Louis," Travis said. "We do need them desperately. That's a fine gesture."

"I guess there is nothing left to say," Rose said. "Except farewell."

A woman stepped forward and handed the man a small packet of food. "Something to tide you over, Louis."

Rose was overcome with emotion as he took the food. He could not speak. He nodded his head in thanks and leaped for the rear wall and vanished into the gloom of dusk. Those in the Alamo waited for several minutes, no one moving or speaking. No shots were heard.

"By the Lord," a man said. "I believe he made it."

Louis Moses Rose vanished into history.

Thirty-Nine:
The Eleventh Day

March 4, 1836

Travis wrote no more reports to be sent outside the walls. He told Jamie, "I have no more dispatches for you, Jamie. There is nothing left to say. I cannot write of my own death before it happens. You may leave whenever you wish."

"I'll stay for a time yet," Jamie told him.

"Santa Anna's men are knocking at the gates now, Jamie. Don't wait too long."

Knocking at the gates was not far from the truth. During the night, the Mexican lines had moved to within two hundred yards of the walled compound. Under the now constant bombardment from Mexican cannon fire, the walls were crumbling at a much faster rate than the nearly exhausted defenders could shore them up. And they were out of timbers.

As Jamie moved around the plaza that day, men would call out to him.

"Take another scalp for me, MacCallister!"

"Godspeed, Jamie."

"Remember the Alamo!" another called. Jamie would, and that phrase would become the battle cry for freedom.

The men were tired, but their spirits were high. They had made their decision, and that had seemed to pull them closer together and lift the general mood. They were going to die, they had accepted that fact, but they were going to die for *By God Texas!*

The Alamo was no longer thought of as a church. It was a mighty fortress of defiance.

Outside the walls, Santa Anna had had quite enough of those inside the Alamo. He ordered his commanders to make ready for the attack. Thousands of troops drew additional powder and shot. Scaling ladders were made more secure. Knives, swords, and bayonets were sharpened. Men said goodbye to their wives and/or girlfriends and their children. The defenders of the Alamo had about forty-eight hours to live.

Jamie had worked out his escape. It was a simple plan, for he knew that the more elaborate a plan was, the more likely it was to fail. He gave his spare rifles to men along the parapets. He would leave with one rifle, two pistols, his knife, and his bow and quiver of arrows.

He was ready to go.

Santa Anna could not get the image of the tall, strongly built young man with the golden mane of hair out of his mind. If all the defenders of the Alamo are as that one, he thought but shared it with no one else, we will suffer terrible losses before we breach the ramparts.

He cut his eyes to his brother-in-law, General Cos, sitting across the room. Cos, Santa Anna knew, wished desperately to enhance his shattered reputation, for Cos still smarted over his earlier defeat by the Texans, many of whom, Santa Anna felt, were probably over there in the Alamo at this moment. Cos had given his word that he would never again return to Texas to fight, but had broken it without pause. So much for honor, Santa Anna thought with a cruel smile.

"You and your men will lead the charge," Santa Anna said abruptly, and watched as Cos's eyes widened. "You may redeem yourself in that manner."

That was all Cos was waiting to hear. He stood up and saluted. "Thank you. You will not regret your decision."

"I hope not," Santa Anna replied dryly.

"When do we attack?"

"Make your men ready. I will tell you when."

General Cos saluted and left the room.

Back at Washington-on-the-Brazos, the last courier from the Alamo had handed a delegate Travis's last communiqué. The man rushed into the meeting and bulled his way to the speakers' platform. He waved the tattered piece of paper and then read the plea for help aloud.

Pandemonium ensued. Men shouted and cheered and cursed and prayed. Some men shouted for all to mount up and get the hell to the Alamo to fight.

But calmer, cooler heads soon prevailed. Chiefly, Sam Houston. The room settled down as he began to speak. When Houston had concluded, it was agreed that no reinforcements were to be sent to Travis's aid. It was a decision that was to haunt Sam Houston for the rest of his life, but one that he knew he was right in making. Travis and the men under his command had to buy the fledgling government time. A day, maybe two, maybe three days. Precious time to establish a government for the Republic. Promised aid from the United States had not arrived. Without it, the shaky Republic could easily fall.

There were a dozen valid reasons why that fateful decision was reached that cold windy day back in March of '36.

"President Jackson was dragging his feet in sending help," one delegate said.

"We don't know even if he is sending help," another said.

"The Army is right over there in Louisiana," it was pointed out.

"Yes. And they marched right up to the border and stopped."

"That could mean they're not coming!"

"We don't even have a constitution."

"The world would condemn us," another delegate said. "For starting a civil war. Remember, technically, we're still a part of Mexico."

Someone made a very vulgar remark about Mexico and another very personal remark concerning the delegate who brought it up and what he could do with it.

A fistfight promptly ensued.

And so it went. It all amounted to the same thing: Travis and the men at the Alamo were to be sacrificed. There is no other word to use. Fannin refused to come to Travis's aid. President Jackson refused to send U.S. troops out of Louisiana into what was Mexican territory. Houston's hands were tied as surely as the destinies of those men at the Alamo.

No one liked the decision, most of all Houston. But it was done, and no one could undo it.

Only one thing could be done, and that was: Remember the Alamo.

FORTY:
THE TWELFTH DAY

March 5, 1836

General Cos stared at the walls of the place he had once commanded and cursed those inside it. "I will kill you all," he said. "I will not leave a single man alive."

Dawn began streaking the sky and Cos ordered his cannons to resume firing. The firing would continue all that day and into the night. He still didn't know when Santa Anna was going to launch his full-scale attack against the rabble in the Alamo, only that he, General Cos, was going to lead it.

He could hardly wait.

Inside the Alamo, shoring up the crumbling walls took most of the men from the parapets. Only Crockett and his sharpshooters and a small contingent of volunteers manned the parapets and platforms. Santa Anna had ordered all his cannon into play and the old walls were really taking a pounding.

Travis found Jamie standing beside Crockett and waved him from the parapet. "I feel in my heart that Santa Anna will attack this night, Jamie. I want you gone from here at full dark. Understood?"

"Yes, sir."

Since there is no record of William Travis being a clairvoyant, no one knows exactly how he reached his very accurate conclusion as to the time of the attack. But he was right almost to the hour.

"I'm ready to go, Colonel."

"Be sure and see Bowie before you leave. He thinks the world of you, Jamie. And Jamie . . . so do I."

"Thank you, sir."

"You better see him now, Jamie. Those moments in the plaza weren't good for him. It was far too cold. He's taken a turn for the worse."

"Yes, sir."

Bowie looked awful. But he was lucid. He took Jamie's hand in his own big hand and smiled up at him. "You're a fine young man, Jamie Ian MacCallister. It's been my pleasure knowing you. Travis just left me. You've seen him?"

"Yes, sir. He ordered me out at dark."

"Wise move. Travis seems to think Santa Anna will attack this night. I hate to have to agree with him . . ." Bowie tempered that with a chuckle. ". . . But I think he's right."

Bowie cut his eyes to Sam. "You think you could get him out, Jamie?"

"Yes. I believe so."

"I ain't goin', Mr. Jim," Sam said. "I done tole you an' tole you. It's time to hush up on it. Me and Joe done agreed on that."

The two men chatted for a couple of minutes and finally Bowie smiled sadly at Jamie. "What else can I say, my young friend, except goodbye."

Jamie again took Bowie's hand and gripped it gently for a moment. "Give them hell, Jim."

"I shall, Jamie. Godspeed, lad."

Those few moments of speaking had so tired the man, he was asleep when Jamie gently released his hand and placed arm and hand back under the blankets.

At the door, Jamie looked back once at the sleeping Jim Bowie. He would never see him again. "Goodbye, Sam."

"Goodbye, Mr. Jamie."

At noon, the wind shifted, the sky darkened, and the temperature plummeted to below freezing. Strange weather for this time of the year. Those recently killed Mexican soldiers began to rapidly stiffen in all sorts of grotesque shapes on the bloody ground around the Alamo.

The wind became so violent, it whipped the dust up and for a time, the Mexican cannons were silenced. And not just from the dust, for the weather was most foul.

Jamie found Travis and said, "This is a good time for me. The dust is so thick out there the sentries will be half blind."

Travis gripped his hand. "May God be with you this day, Jamie MacCallister."

"And with you, sir."

Travis drew himself up to full height and saluted Jamie. Jamie did his best to properly return the salute and then was gone, waving at the men as he headed for the irrigation ditch that ran under the walls.

The defenders of the Alamo watched him go and silently wished him Godspeed as the bitterly cold winds howled furiously and the swirling dust reduced visibility to nearly nothing.

Jamie had spent hours on the parapets studying the placement of troops, and knew where the Mexican army was the strongest, and where they were the weakest. It was really no big trick to slip through the lines. Outside of town, he alternately ran and walked to the Ruiz ranch. Some of Ruiz's vaqueros spotted him and escorted him to the sprawling home.

Señor Ruiz greeted him warmly and took him to the fireplace. Over coffee, Ruiz asked, "The Alamo?"

"It's still standing. Colonel Travis thinks the main attack will come this night."

"The men?"

"They're in good spirits. They know they're going to die and have resigned themselves to it. Bowie is very sick. When I left his side, only hours ago, he had a brace of loaded pistols and his knife at hand. He'll not go into death quietly."

Ruiz shook his head and sighed. "A waste. Such a waste."

"They don't think so, señor. The men at the mission are prepared to die for what they believe in."

"You will rest here for the night?"

"No. But thank you. I must be on my way." He tapped the pouch. "These messages must reach their proper destinations."

"I understand. Bowie's horse has been well taken care of and is ready for the trail. I will have him saddled while you eat and relax."

"*Gracias,* señor."

Ruiz did not ask where Jamie would ride first, and Jamie knew that was deliberate on his part. One cannot tell what one does not know.

But the food and the warm fire and the glass of wine took their toll on the weary young man. For days Jamie and the men from the Alamo had been battling intense cold and not enough food; they had been subjected to many hours of brutal cannon fire. Jamie's buckskins were filthy and he needed a bath in the worst way. He did not want to stretch out on Ruiz's couch, so he decided he'd nap for a few minutes on the rug; just for a few minutes only. Just for a few minutes. No more than . . .

Señor Ruiz returned and looked at the sleeping man with a knowing smile. He gently covered him with a blanket. So deep was Jamie's exhausted sleep that he did not stir at the blanket's warm touch. Ruiz ordered his servants not to disturb him. "Your messages can wait, young man," Ruiz whispered. "Nothing you have in that pouch can change what is certainly going to happen to those brave men at the Alamo."

He ordered the doors to the room closed and Bowie's horse to be unsaddled and returned to its warm stall. "Sleep, young man," he said. "Sleep."

FORTY-ONE:
THE LAST FAREWELL NINETY
MINUTES OF GLORY

March 6, 1836

Santa Anna ordered his cannons to cease firing just before midnight and the men of the Alamo wrapped up in their ragged blankets and tried to get some desperately needed sleep.

Travis had counted his defenders. One hundred and eighty-two men. Two slaves, Sam and Joe. Eight women, and a handful of children. Travis ordered the brewing of the last of their coffee; actually more than half of it was chicory. Crockett jokingly said if they could find some, a few rattlesnake heads would give it some flavor, and if they could spare it, some gunpowder might help, too.

The women, just as exhausted as the men, cooked up the last of the food and the men ate and drank and then tried to sleep.

Less than three hundred yards away, the Mexican army had received orders to attack the Alamo at five o'clock that morning.

March 6, 1836, turned out to be bitterly cold and, until dawn, an overcast morning. It was so dark that seeing one's hand in front of one's face was nearly impossible. Many of the older men behind the walls of the mission were ill, having come down with pneumonia. Others struggled to sleep in the intense cold as numbed hands gripped rifles.

Travis could not sleep. He carefully shaved and dressed in his best uniform. Then he knelt down and prayed. What he prayed for is unknown but to God.

Santa Anna slept well and awakened refreshed at three o'clock in the morning. After a quiet breakfast, he dressed in his finest uniform, complete with decorations, and ordered his horse saddled and brought around to the front of the house where he and his new bride were staying.

"The cavalry is ready to mount, sir," an aide told him.

"Good, good," the general replied. "The infantry?"

"In place and ready, sir. They are all within rifle shot of the Alamo."

"Excellent. The bands?"

"Ready to play, sir."

"At my orders, I want them to play the Degüello." The Fire and Death song.

"Yes, sir."

"General Cos?"

"Ready, sir."

Santa Anna shivered. "Get my coat. Damn this weather!"

With his warm coat around him, Santa Anna smiled, anxious for the Degüello to begin. He loved it. He'd loved the tune since he'd first heard its somber notes. The Degüello came from the Spanish word *degollar,* which means "to slash the throat" or "to behead." To Santa Anna, the tune brought out the ancient beast in him. It hottened the blood. It was stirring.

Travis had ordered several men to stand watch outside the walls, and several men to keep the fires going inside the walls. Those men outside the walls were never heard from or seen by their comrades again; or by anyone else for that matter. Handpicked men from the Mexican Army had crept forward in the darkness and sliced their throats.

Travis had grown increasingly restless. He had not taken his rifle, but a double-barreled shotgun, heavily loaded with rusty nails and whatever else the armorer could find, and mounted the parapet to stand by a cannon. He had consulted his timepiece before blowing out the candle in his room. It was four-thirty on the bitterly cold morning of March 6, 1836. Colonel William Barrett Travis had just about ninety minutes to live.

Miles away, Jamie Ian MacCallister slept the sleep of the utterly exhausted.

Jim Bowie stirred on his cot and suddenly became wide awake. "Sam?" he called.

"I'm right here by your side, sir."

"Make sure those pistols are ready, Sam. All four of them, and put them by my side. Two to my right, two to my left."

"Yes, sir, Mr. Jim. Is the Mexicans comin?' "

"They're here. Unsheathe my blade, Sam."

"Yes, sir. Now you be careful, Mr. Jim. That there blade is mighty sharp."

Bowie chuckled in the darkness. "Careful? An old pirate like me? Pour us both a drink, Sam. And make them good ones, now, you hear."

"You wants me to drink with you, sir?"

"That's what I said, Sam." He took the cup, brimming full of whiskey. "Thank you, Sam. Drink up. It'll be your last time to drink with me before I meet the devil."

Before Bowie's startled eyes, Sam, a man that Bowie felt almost never touched a drop, emptied the cup, smacked his lips, and said, "Ahhh! Mighty fine drinkin' whiskey, Mr.

Jim. Mighty fine."

Bowie had to laugh at Sam. "Is there any more in that jug, Sam?"

"Not narely a drop, sir."

Bowie downed his cup. "Well, Sam, like the lady told me one time, years ago: Get off me, boy. You done got all you paid for."

Sam and Jim Bowie shared a chuckle in the quiet darkness of predawn.

Jim said, "Now go over there in the far corner and sit down, Sam. When the soldiers bust through that door, you have your hands in the air just as high as you can stretch. Don't make any attempt to help me. I want your promise on that."

"I done served you for years, Jim Bowie. I can't make no promise like . . ."

"Sam!"

"All right, Mr. Jim. You gots my promise."

"I mean it, Sam."

"I knows you do. I'll do what you say."

The time was twenty minutes until five.

Davy Crockett tossed his blankets from him and rose, stretching the cold kinks out of his muscles. He picked up Ol' Betsy and climbed stiffly up to the parapet, to stand staring out into the darkness.

"She's a quiet one, Davy," one of his men said. "Too damn quiet."

"Ol' Santy Anny's a-comin' this mornin'.

That's why she's so quiet. As soon as his bands start tootin' on the bugles and beatin' the drums, they'll be hell to pay, all right. Get the boys up and ready."

Four forty-five.

Crockett left the platform and began rousing the men. "She's due to come any minute now, boys. I feel it in my bones."

"You feel it, too, Davy?" Travis called from his post.

"I damn shore do, Billy-Boy," Davy replied with a grin, knowing how Travis hated to be called that.

But Travis only laughed this time. "We'll make them pay in blood, Davy."

"Damn right, Colonel!" Crockett's strong voice boomed across the cold and windswept plaza.

Ten minutes to five.

Bowie lay on his cot, the blankets pulled up to his neck, but his hands were free. He thought fondly of his dead wife and children. "Just let me see them once more, Lord," he whispered. "And then you can send me to Hell. Just once more."

"You ain't goin' to hell, Jim Bowie," Sam whispered. "Ever'body knows God loves His warriors."

If Bowie heard him, he made no comment.

Almeron Dickerson kissed his wife on the lips, held her close for a moment, and then ran to his artillery battery.

"Return to me, Almeron!" she called.

"If it's God's will, Susanna!" he called over his shoulder.

It was not to be.

Five minutes to five.

Santa Anna rode his horse slowly through the silent streets to the house where he planned on observing the battle. He dismounted and entered the warmth of the building, accepting a cup of coffee from an aide. The coffee had not been sweetened. Santa Anna haughtily ordered the aide to sweeten his coffee and not to make that same mistake again.

Then, in an uncharacteristic burst of charity, he apologized to the young aide. Santa Anna stood by an open window, sipping coffee and humming his favorite tune: the Degüello.

FORTY-TWO:
REMEMBER THE ALAMO

Five o'clock. March 6, 1836
The heavy low notes of the Degüello sounded, and Travis yelled, "Here they come, boys! Here they come! To your posts, men. The enemy is about us."

They sure were. Some three thousand of Santa Anna's best combat troops surged up from the ground and charged the walls of the Alamo, all of them screaming loudly.

For just a very few seconds, the men of the Alamo were stunned by the enormity of it all. Then they rallied into action. Fifty Mexican soldiers were killed in the first volley of rifle fire from the walls.

"Give them what for, men!" Travis yelled, waving his sword with one hand and holding the double-barreled shotgun in the other.

And the volunteers at the Alamo did just that. Captain Dickerson ordered his cannon to be charged with grapeshot and fired nearly point-blank into the charging Mexican troops. It was carnage for the Mexican infantry.

Travis stood on the reinforced platform holding the battery of eight-pounders in the center of the north wall. He calmly brought his sword down on the cold metal of the cannon with a ringing slap and told the gunner, "Fire it, man. Do your duty. For God, Freedom, and Texas."

The cannon roared and an entire line of Mexican troops was blown into eternity, the grapeshot shredding their bodies.

Crockett and his men were guarding the front gate, and guard it they did. They stood calmly on the walls, fully exposed, and fired volley after volley into the charging troops until the Mexican commanders wisely decided to shift troops away from that part of the battle.

The Mexican troops had suffered so many wounded during the first rush, their pain-filled shrieking and screaming and pitiful calling for help was clearly audible over the crack and boom of combat. Some Mexican troops were beginning to retreat — never had these seasoned combat veterans faced anything like the cold fury of the men defending the Alamo. The officers screamed and cursed at the men, beating them with the flat side of their swords, commanding them to turn around and once more charge into battle. Some did; most did not.

The Mexican commanders ordered their buglers to sound recall; the first charge had failed miserably. Santa Anna went into a screaming rage as the first notes of the bugles reached him. His senior advisors tried to reason with him. It was no use. General Santa Anna was like a wild man in his fury. How was it possible, he screamed, that two hundred men could successfully beat back a charge by three thousand men?

His advisors had no reply to that.

Santa Anna jerked a very startled and very frightened young runner to him, holding the young man by the front of his jacket, and said, "You take this message to General Cos. He has one more chance to breach those walls. Just one. Now fly like the devil is nipping at your heels!"

The young soldier did just that. He found a colonel, gave him the message from Santa Anna, and then got the hell out of there. He found a riderless horse, swung into the saddle, and rode straight east, away from the battle. He was never seen again.

Incredibly, not one man defending the Alamo was killed or wounded during the first charge. When the ranks of the first charge broke, the cheering from the men inside the walls reached Santa Anna.

The first rays of the sun were blood red peeking over the horizon. Santa Anna whirled to face his senior officers. He pointed to the sun. "I want the ground inside those walls that color. By the time the sun is fully exposed, I want to be standing ankle deep in Anglo blood. Do it!"

"Reload and make ready!" Travis shouted his orders. "We held them, boys. By God, we held them. We can do it again."

"Not for long," Jim Bowie muttered from his cot, after hearing the faint call. He knew far better than Travis the temper of the Mexican people. He had lived among them, worked side by side with them, and married a Mexican lady. Bowie knew that when that Latin blood turned hot, Santa Anna's soldiers would be over those old walls, and then it would be man to man.

"Bring me a cigar, Sam," Bowie called. "I want one more smoke. And don't tell me the doctor said I shouldn't smoke. What the hell difference does it make now?"

Jamie's eyes flew open and he silently cursed himself for nine kinds of a fool and weakling and ran to the stable while the others in the house slept on. He quickly saddled up and was gone. A couple of miles from the grand home, he stopped and listened. He thought he could hear the very faint sounds of cannon; but he couldn't be sure. He touched his heels to the fine horse and headed for the road to Gonzales. The road itself was still some miles away.

Just off the road, in a stand of trees, Tall Bull and his band of warriors waited. Their faces were impassive as the cold winds whipped around them. Man Who Is Not Afraid would come. And when he did, they would kill him. Slowly.

The bands played the Degüello, the buglers sounded charge, and the Mexican army surged forward for the second time that morning as the sounds of cannonballs whistled over their heads. The balls crashed against the walls and this time portions of the battered old walls gave way under the onslaught. Great gaping holes were blown in the walls. Defenders rushed to plug the holes with their own flesh and floor, hastily throwing up human barricades with rifles and pistols in their hands.

On both sides, all knew that very soon it would come down to bayonets and knives at close quarter.

"Hold, boys, hold!" Travis's shout could

be heard above the din of battle.

And the volunteers held, beating back the second charge that morning.

General Cos retaliated swiftly, sending his troops back into the fray without a second's hesitation. The colonel had delivered the courier's message word for word, perhaps even adding some additional dialogue, since General Cos was not a well-liked commander.

It was six o'clock in the morning and the sun was blood red lifting into a cold and cloudless day when the first troops of the Mexican army breached the walls, pouring through a huge hole into the plaza of the Alamo.

William Barrett Travis turned to look with dismay at the Mexican soldiers running screaming with bayonets fixed into the plaza. "Hold, boys, hold!" he shouted, waving his sword, the blade catching the rays of the sun. "Hold for God and for Texas!"

Those were the last words the South Carolinian spoke. A single rifle ball caught the colonel in the center of the forehead, felling him instantly. He slumped to the platform, dead.

William Travis was certainly among the first, or even the first, Texan death. But outside the walls, it was terrible bloody carnage. Over a thousand Mexican soldiers lay dead or dying. And within the remaining fifty or so minutes, another thousand or more would be dead or wounded *inside* the walls. That so few men could inflict so many casualties against a force so huge would remain a lasting tribute to the fighting spirit of these defenders of the Alamo.

The Mexican army kept pouring men through the newly blasted-open holes in the wall. The fight became, for most of the Texans, hand to hand and eyeball to eyeball; the Mexicans used their long, needle-pointed bayonets, the defenders of the Alamo used their Arkansas Toothpicks and Bowie knifes. The walls and the grounds of the plaza became splattered with blood, most of it from the Mexican soldiers.

To the uniformed Mexican troops, the sight of the men of the Alamo came as a shock, for many of the defenders were literally in rags.

Ragged or not, the Texan force made it perfectly clear that surrender was not on their minds, and that they were prepared to fight to the last man.

The first seventy-five Mexican soldiers to come through the shattered wall died on the spot. Those who came behind them were forced to use the bodies of their fallen comrades as shields.

But within minutes, the Mexican troops had the upper hand. Once in the compound, the defenders had no place to go and death looked them square in the face.

But the Mexican troops still had a horrible, bitter, and bloody fight on their hands from the Texas force.

"Kill 'em all, boys!" Davy Crockett roared from his position along the walls. "Make 'em pay, by God. Make 'em pay in blood!"

With a mighty pantherlike scream that chilled those Mexican troops who heard him, Davy leaped from the platform, his men right behind him, screaming like wild banshees, and then proceeded to literally cut and club their way through the advancing troops of Santa Anna, making their way across the compound toward the old church itself. As they leaped from the walls, the Tennessee volunteers fired rifles and pistols and then used their empty rifles as clubs with one hand and their long-bladed and extremely sharp knives to open a way to the church. They left behind them frozen ground slick with fresh blood and littered with dead and dying, horribly mangled Mexican troops.

It was a scene that would haunt many of the surviving Mexican troops for the rest of their lives.

Crockett and his men and a few others took refuge behind the low wall that separated the main plaza of the Alamo from the much smaller plaza of the old church. They had the high walls of the building used as the hospital on one side, and a battery of artillery on the other side. The church lay to their backs.

Many of the Texans had retreated into the rooms in the buildings along the west, south, and east sides of the walls. Those left outside were quickly killed and then horribly butchered and the bodies mutilated, so great now was the rage of the Mexican soldiers.

"I could have told you," Bowie said aloud, as the sounds of knives and machetes striking cold dead flesh came to him in his room.

But at Travis's firm insistence, the rooms had been prepared for a last stand, and it was here that the defenders of the Alamo could, for the first time that bloody day, crouch behind cover and level their rifles and pistols at the enemy. Probably five hundred of Santa Anna's troops, at least, were killed in this action alone.

Davy Crockett, with an arm wound (left or right has never been firmly documented), was roaring like an enraged grizzly bear and killing Mexican troops as fast as he could load rifle and pistols. "You bastards will find Ol' Davy hard to kill!" he bellered.

His strong voice and unflagging courage gave the defenders new life. No hope, for they knew they were all minutes away from death, but new fighting spirit. Those who had run out of powder and shot started swinging their rifles like clubs, smashing open heads and smearing the ground and the walls with more blood. The Alamo defenders were all shouting and cursing and taunting the enemy. Many of the Mexican troops simply could not bring themselves to kill any more of these brave men. They threw down their weapons and refused to kill again. Not because they were afraid — for they certainly were not — but because courageous men like these should not be killed.

Their sergeants and officers shot those men dead.

Jim Bowie cocked his pistols and waited for the door to his room to smash open.

Sam sat on a stool in the corner.

Travis's slave, Joe, sat at Travis's desk, his hands by his side. Like Sam, Joe had been ordered to offer no resistance when the door was smashed open.

The plaza of the Alamo was now filled

with hundreds of Mexican soldiers.

Almeron Dickerson and half a dozen of his men were at the only cannons still in Texan hands. They loaded the two cannons with whatever they could find, lowered the elevation and touched a torch to the fire-hole. The cannon roared and the rocks and bits of rusty chain and broken pieces of muskets cleared a path fifty feet wide right down the center of the plaza, hurling bloody chunks of Santa Anna's soldiers in all directions, splattering other soldiers with the blood of their comrades.

The rifles of the Mexican troops cracked and the men manning the last battery of cannon fell dead.

Susanna Dickerson would see her husband one more time — to identify the body.

Troops kicked in the door to Bowie's quarters and the famous knife fighter lifted his first two pistols and shot two soldiers dead. He tossed the empty pistols aside and grabbed his last two pistols and fired. He had double-shotted these and the four balls struck three Mexican troops. Soldiers scrambled over the bodies of their comrades and pinned Bowie to the cot with bayonets, running him through. Jim Bowie roared in pain, blood spraying from his mouth and with the last of his strength, swung his big-bladed knife at a soldier who had the misfortune to get just a tad too close to Bowie. The knife took the man's head off clean just as another soldier drove his bayonet through Bowie's right eye, pinning his head to the wooden frame of the cot. The head bounced once on the floor, the eyes open in astonishment.

Sam sat with his face in his hands, unable to look at the bloody body of the man he'd been with for so long.

Davy Crockett could no longer take the time needed to reload as Mexican soldiers swarmed him. He was swinging Ol' Betsy like a club, smashing heads left and right. He was bleeding from half a dozen wounds and forced to lean up against the side of the hospital to stay on his feet as his massive strength was ebbing away. Around him lay the bodies of twenty Mexican soldiers. A squad of soldiers rushed him and pinned Crockett to the wall with bayonets, running him through. Davy's last act was to close one big hand around the throat of a Mexican sergeant and squeeze with all his might. Davy Crockett, with blood leaking from his mouth, grinned in a ghastly manner and said, "Come along, son. We'll continue this fracas on the other side."

He died still holding on to the terrified

sergeant. Davy slumped over the bayonets that had pinned him to the wall. The sergeant died seconds later, his throat crushed.

No one knows who the last Texan was to die in the Alamo. It might have been Crockett. It might have been a major named Robert Evans, or it could have been a volunteer named Walker. It does not matter. They were all dead.

Santa Anna's troops had taken the Alamo, but the price they paid was unbelievably high. When the last shot was fired — some fifteen minutes after the last defender was dead — some eight hundred Mexican bodies were sprawled in death in the plaza alone. It was six-thirty in the morning on March 6th, 1836.

Approximately one hundred and eighty-two men had killed over two *thousand* Mexican troops, over five hundred of those killed in brutal hand-to-hand combat. Many of the dead Alamo defenders still had their hands on their knives, the knives buried to the hilt in soldiers' bodies. Some still held on to the throats of Mexican soldiers, locked in a death grip.

Many of the Mexican soldiers, much to the disgust of some of their officers and sergeants, threw down their rifles, sank to their knees, and wept openly and unashamedly. They were not weeping for their fallen comrades alone, but for all the brave dead.

Still other Mexican soldiers, their blood hot with rage, went from body to body and fired countless rounds into the dead Texans, then took their knives and mutilated the bodies. It took the officers more than fifteen minutes to regain control of the enraged Mexican soldiers.

Santa Anna still had not made his appearance inside the walls of the Alamo.

Susanna Dickerson, the six or seven other women, the children, and Sam and Joe, remained where they were, under guard of more compassionate and older soldiers. They wished no harm to come to noncombatants.

High overhead, the buzzards, who millenniums past had made a pact with death, were tiny black specks in the cloudless blue sky. They had patience; they could wait. The buzzards were born with the knowledge that sooner or later, death came to everything living.

It was about eight-thirty that morning before Santa Anna rode his horse up to the battered walls of the Alamo, carefully picking his way through the hundreds of bodies of his soldiers. He dismounted and stood for a moment, his nose wrinkled at the smell of death.

"Very distasteful business," he said to a colonel.

"Quite," the colonel replied. "But this will surely teach the Anglo revolutionaries a lesson."

"I'm certain it will," Santa Anna agreed, then stepped into the plaza through a hole in the wall.

FORTY-THREE

Santa Anna turned to his left upon entering the Alamo. He walked across the wooden bridge over the irrigation ditch and then followed the wall to the officers' quarters. He looked in, sniffed at the sight of the sprawled and mutilated bodies, and walked on. At the north wall, he stopped and stared up at Travis's body.

"Colonel Travis, sir," he was informed. Travis's body had not been hacked on. Neither had the body of Bowie or Crockett. Most of the other dead were unrecognizable.

"One shot through the head," Santa Anna said. "I wonder if he killed himself in despair?"

Some historians have toyed with that theory, but reports from Mexican soldiers who were there, both officers and enlisted men, state unequivocally that William Travis fought bravely and was felled by a shot from a Mexican rifle. He did not commit suicide.

Santa Anna shrugged his shoulders and walked on, after giving this command, "Separate the bodies of my brave fallen from this Texas rabble. I wish my men to be buried with dignity."

They were not. Reports state that many of them were tossed into the beds of wagons, taken some distance from town, and left to rot and be eaten by animals while others were simply rolled into ditches and others thrown into the river.

Santa Anna looked up at the flag that still fluttered proudly over the dead defenders of the Alamo. "Take down that goddamn flag!" he ordered.

What happened to the flag the men from Gonzales brought with them to fly over the mission is unknown. The only flag to survive was the flag the volunteers from New Orleans brought with them. It read: THE FIRST COMPANY OF TEXAN VOLUNTEERS FROM NEW ORLEANS. It was sent to Mexico City.

Santa Anna and escort left the site of Travis's death and walked over to the east wall, to the artillerymen's quarters. He looked in. Many of the bodies had been hacked with machetes so fiercely they resembled nothing more than heaps of bloody rags. From there he walked to the edge of the hospital building and his eyes narrowed and his lips turned to cruel slits when he saw Davy Crockett's big hand still locked in place around the sergeant's throat.

"Get that hand away from the throat of that brave soldier," he ordered.

"We tried, sir," a lieutenant said. "The fingers are in a death grip."

Santa Anna turned cruel eyes on the officer. "Then either break the fingers free or cut them free."

"Yes, sir."

Santa Anna turned to go and stopped, looking back at the buckskin-clad frontiersman. "Who is that man?"

"Davy Crockett, sir."

Santa Anna grunted. "He wasn't as tough as he thought he was, was he?"

All present wisely decided not to comment on that rather ridiculous question. Any fool could plainly see that Davy Crockett had personally killed twenty-five or thirty soldiers in this spot alone before he was bayoneted to death.

Several senior sergeants cut their eyes to one another, then looked Heavenward. Remarks like that only made them believe more firmly that most officers were so stupid they needed help to piss.

Santa Anna looked toward the church,

toward a group of men guarding the entrance. "Prisoners? I said no prisoners."

"Women and children and two black slaves, sir."

"Ahh! Well, we'll see about them in a bit." He pointed to another building. "What's over there that is so interesting men must gather around and gawk?"

"The body of Jim Bowie, sir."

Santa Anna gave one more look at Crockett's badly mutilated body and then walked over and looked in. Sam had been removed to the church. Bowie's body still lay on the blood-soaked blankets.

"Start the men gathering wood to burn the bodies," Santa Anna ordered.

"The commanders, sir?" he was asked.

"The what?"

"Travis, Crockett, and Bowie?"

"What about them?"

"Do we, ah . . . bury them or, ah . . . ?"

"Burn them with the rest of this Texas rabble!"

It was slow going for Jamie. Several times he'd had to very quickly find hiding places from the roaming Mexican patrols. Finally he decided to ride parallel from the road, staying some five or six miles south of it and ride cross-country. By doing that, he

571

cut down the chances of being spotted by any Mexican patrol. It slowed him considerably, for the country was rough, but Bowie's horse was a stayer, and he loved the trail.

Jamie had more than ample provisions, for Ruiz had insisted on outfitting him as if he were going on some far-flung expedition. It was almost seventy miles to Gonzales, and Jamie was not going to kill a good horse in some wild ride. Jamie had no news to tell the citizens of Gonzales; he did not know if any final battle had taken place or not. So he took his time, the pouch containing the precious last words from the defenders of the Alamo under his buckskin shirt, next to his flesh.

When the sun was directly overhead, the heavy thought came to Jamie that it was probably all over back at the mission. There was no way that one hundred and eighty-odd men could withstand for long a sustained charge from thousands of the enemy. He sagged in the saddle, saddened by that thought. Jamie had made many good friends with the men of the Alamo during the short time he'd been there. If indeed they were gone, their memory was not, and would never be as long as he was alive.

Travis, Bowie, Crockett, Dickerson, Esparza, Walker, Evans, Bonham, Jameson,

Fuqua, Pollard, Holland, Cloud, Autry, Martin, Kimball, McGregor, Baugh . . . and all the others.

Jamie began angling more closely to the main east/west road, for he knew that the farther he rode away from San Antonio, the less likely the chances of running into any Mexican patrols. The Mexican army had learned the hard way that small patrols did not last long roaming about alone in the Texas countryside. Those that were sent out had a habit of not returning. And never being seen again.

He decided he would make his camp for that evening at about the midpoint between San Antonio and Gonzales. Along the banks of the Guadalupe River.

FORTY-FOUR

Susanna Dickerson, wife of Captain Dickerson, the other women and children, and the two slaves, Sam and Joe, were escorted out of the church and separated. Susanna Dickerson and her daughter, Angelina, were taken to a house in town, but not before the last shot to be fired in the Alamo boomed, an accidental discharge from a rifle. The stray bullet hit Susanna in the leg, felling her. Mexican soldiers rushed to her aid, picking her and the child up and carrying the mother and daughter into town. It is rumored, but never proven, that Santa Anna had the man who fired the shot, either flogged or hanged or shot. There is no proof that anything was done to the soldier who fired the last shot, or even that anybody knew who he was.

It is also rumored that General Santa Anna was so taken with the lovely Mrs. Susanna Dickerson that he offered to marry her on the spot, and take her and the child to Mexico, where they would be well cared for.

If that is true, once Mrs. Susanna Dickerson got over her fury and shock, her reply to this bizarre proposition was, more than likely, unprintable.

Suffice it to say, Mrs. Dickerson declined the magnanimous offer.

Jamie awakened with a start and lay very still for a moment, trying to determine what had awakened him. He cut his eyes to his picketed horse. The animal was standing with ears pricked, eyes fixed on the blackness to Jamie's immediate right. The fire had burned itself out. Not a live coal remained to glow in the cold night.

Jamie tensed his muscles, then threw himself from his blankets, rolling with rifle in hand as dark shapes moved out of the night, rushing where he had been seconds before.

Shawnee! Jamie recognized the distinctive hair even in the dark. He lifted a pistol and fired, the big ball stopping a Shawnee in his tracks. Jamie fired his second pistol at a shape and drilled the Shawnee through the brisket, doubling him over and dropping him to the near frozen ground.

"Take him alive!" Jamie heard the voice of Tall Bull shout. "I want to see how well he dies."

After silently rolling a few yards from where he had fired his last pistol, Jamie lay still on the hard ground. He knew he was invisible in the cloudy, moonless night. He had slept hard, for he had still not recovered from those last days of going without sleep, and had no idea what time it might be. He guessed it was after midnight.

He heard a rustling off to his right, and knew that had been a deliberate act, trying to draw his fire. The Shawnee were masters at this type of warfare and would make no noise in their stalking.

Tall Bull! His hate must be strong to have carried him this far in his search for revenge. The wind shifted and Jamie could smell the familiar odor of grease and woodsmoke coming from the bodies and the buckskins of the Shawnee.

A Shawnee threw himself out of the brush, a club in his hand, raised to strike at Jamie's head, and Jamie rolled over on his back, pulling his knees to his chest and kicked hard with both feet. His feet caught the Shawnee in midair and the wind whooshed from the man as Jamie propelled the Indian through the air to land on his belly. The

Shawnee must have landed on one arm, for Jamie heard the sharp crack of a major bone breaking.

Jamie recovered and rolled away, his rifle still clutched in his left hand.

"Good, Man Who Is Not Afraid," Tall Bull's voice reached him. "You are a mighty warrior, as I always predicted you would be."

"He is a great hulking ox," the contemptuous voice of Little Wolf said. "He will scream like a woman when I cut the flesh from him."

Jamie smiled in the darkness and remained silent.

Bad Leg put his mouth into action. "I have the ultimate disgrace for you, White Hair. I will use you like a woman."

Jamie couldn't resist it. "Unless you've grown somewhat below the belt, Bad Leg, you couldn't make a hummingbird flinch."

Jamie used the noise of Bad Leg's angry screaming and snorting and threatening to back up a few yards, closer to a tiny offshoot of the river, and then move a few yards to his left.

Tall Bull chuckled. "Very, very good, Man Who Is Not Afraid. You have sharpened your tongue in manhood. This will be a great game we play this night."

"How is Deer Woman?" Jamie called, then again shifted position, putting himself very close to the tiny offshoot. He had loaded one pistol, and was now quickly loading the second.

"She is well. Older, as we all are," Tall Bull replied. "I forbid her to ever speak your name, but I can tell that she misses you."

"I did no harm to you or to anyone in your town," Jamie called. "I just wanted to return to my own people, as did Hannah. You cannot fault me for that."

"Oh, I don't fault you, White Hair. But you disgraced me in the eyes of my followers. I will be redeemed when I show them your scalp."

"That'll never happen, Tall Bull. You've already lost two this evening, with a third one hurt. Doesn't that tell you anything?"

There was a long silence. That was followed by a sigh. "It tells me that you are a mighty warrior, Man Who Is Not Afraid. But we are many."

"I've fought three and four times your number, Tall Bull. I'm here and they're dead." He slipped down the bank and silently crept along in the sand, angling to get behind Tall Bull and however many men he had with him.

"I do not doubt your words," Tall Bull replied.

Jamie paused, seeing a Shawnee standing beside a tree. That was a favorite Shawnee trick: making oneself part of the earth, and it worked, most of the time. The man was standing with his right side to Jamie. Jamie squatted down and felt around carefully in the shallow water until he found a rock about the size of a small apple. He dried his hands on his buckskins and then carefully gripped the rock. He took aim, judging the distance, and let the rock fly.

Jamie missed the man's head, the rock striking the Shawnee on the side of the neck, just below the jaw. But it had been thrown with considerable force and the Indian went down, choking and gasping, both hands to his surely badly injured throat. The Shawnee kicked and moaned for a half a minute or so, and then lay still.

Four down, Jamie thought, as he silently worked his way around the twisting little offshoot.

He almost walked right into two of Tall Bull's band. They were wading in the stream, working toward the river. Jamie heard the rustle of water and stopped, pressing himself against the cold bank, both hands filled with pistols. He hated to give away his position, but felt he had no choice in the matter.

From a distance of about five feet, Jamie fired both pistols. At almost point-blank range, the balls tore great holes in the chests of the men and flung them into the water. Jamie immediately changed positions, coming out on the other side of the offshoot and taking cover in some low brush.

Jamie remembered well how Tall Bull operated and knew that he seldom took more than ten or twelve warriors with him on a raid, unless it was to be an all-out battle with another tribe. Jamie felt he had cut Tall Bull's band down by at least half this night. Tall Bull would not only be angry, but would be twice as dangerous and cunning.

"Running Bear is dead," Jamie heard Little Wolf's call. "White Hair clubbed him on the neck."

The thrown rock, Jamie thought. Must have crushed his throat so he couldn't breathe.

"Circle," Tall Bull ordered.

Circle where? Jamie thought. That was a ruse on the part of Tall Bull. Tall Bull really had no idea where Jamie was. So that order was merely an attempt to get Jamie to move, thereby possibly exposing his position, something Jamie had no intention of doing.

The wind died down to nothing and the night was very still. Jamie could not take a chance on reloading his pistols, for the slightest noise would bring death. He waited.

After a moment, he heard a gasp from the banks of the offshoot and knew that someone had found the two warriors Jamie had shot. There was a rustle of moccasins against sand and earth, and then silence. Whoever had found the bodies was reporting back to Tall Bull.

Jamie had killed five and put another one out of action. That left three, possibly five warriors to face. But they would be the most dangerous, the most experienced, and in the case of Little Wolf and Bad Leg, the ones filled with the most hatred for him. Tall Bull was by far the most skilled manhunter.

Jamie was not overconfident. He knew this night was fraught with danger. His life was much more threatened here than at any time in the past few weeks. The odds of a cannonball dropping on his head had been slight. As long as he stayed out of sight, behind the walls of the Alamo, no Mexican sharpshooter could hit him. But here, on this cold night, danger could be and probably was, all around him. The Shawnee would be moving in for the silent kill, coming slowly.

The wind picked up and Jamie used its soft sound to quickly reload his pistols. A dry twig snapped to his left. Moving only his eyes, Jamie could just make out the shape of a man, standing rock still after his foot had snapped the twig. He was about twenty-five feet away from the brush Jamie was hiding in. The Shawnee would be silently cursing himself for that bad move. The warrior moved and when he did it was sudden. One second he was there, the next instant he was gone.

Returning his eyes to the front, Jamie watched as a dark shape came over the bank of the offshoot and was gone. Tall Bull, and Jamie was certain it had been Tall Bull, had found his moccasins tracks in the soft earth and sand and knew approximately where he was.

When the second dark shape materialized for only a moment, his head and upper torso exposed, Jamie fired one pistol and instantly came out of the brush, running hard for the bank. But he had missed his target. The shot had caused the Shawnee to belly down, however, and Jamie leaped over him and into the water. He jumped for the far bank, ran a few yards, and then was out of the watercourse and onto dry land. He ran for a clump of trees and bellied down, catching his breath while his eyes searched the darkness and his ears were attuned for any sound.

Escape was out of the question. The dispatch pouch was under his saddle and Tall Bull would have left one warrior at the camp site. This was a fight to the finish, and Jamie felt that Tall Bull realized it, too.

He shoved his pistols behind his belt and quickly checked his rifle. A shadow movement across the offshoot caught his attention and Jamie lifted the rifle to his shoulder. The shot would give away his position, but Jamie knew he had to cut down the odds. When the shadow became a man, Jamie fired. A choking scream told him his ball had flown true. He reloaded and waited.

If his attackers had been any other but Tall Bull, they would have more than likely given up this fight, for the Indian saw no percentage in taking this many losses. There was always another day. But this was Tall Bull; this was personal. This was a fight to the finish.

Jamie was in a good position; probably the best defensive position he could have chosen. The river twisted here, the water to his left and right and back. Tall Bull and however many he had left, must now attack from the front. Jamie made himself as comfortable as possible and waited.

Jamie was alert, whatever sleep he had gotten refreshing him. He had his rifle and two pistols, and ample shot and powder. But his bow and quiver of arrows was back in camp. Jamie now felt there had been twelve in the attacking band. Tall Bull, Little Wolf, Bad Leg, and nine others. Six were dead, one wounded. He faced five.

"We can wait," came the strong voice of Tall Bull. "Forever if it comes to that."

Jamie made no reply and knew the Indian expected none. Tall Bull and the one other older warrior would be the hardest to kill. They would have the patience that Little Wolf and Bad Leg did not possess. Bad Leg was basically a coward. But that was not necessarily a good thing for Jamie, for cowards, when cornered, can be formidable and dangerous foes.

"The road is miles north from here," Tall Bull went on. "There are no farms or villages within a day's ride. There is no one to help you, Man Who Is Not Afraid. So now is the time to be afraid."

Jamie heard the giggling of Bad Leg. "Now I know why you brought him along,

Tall Bull," he called. "Does Deer Women know you share your blankets with the likes of Bad Leg?"

Bad Leg immediately began cursing Jamie and Jamie pulled his rifle to his shoulder. From the sound of his voice, there was only one place Bad Leg could be, and that was behind a small clump of bushes that stood out even in the darkness. Jamie squeezed the trigger, then quickly began reloading.

Horrible screaming erupted from those bushes and Jamie could just make out the shape of Bad Leg as he stumbled to his moccasins. He lurched forward in a peculiar hunching movement. His screaming became more of a wild shrieking. He staggered along, crying out for help. But Jamie knew that no one would expose themselves. Bad Leg was on his own. Bad Leg fell down to his knees in the dirt. He seemed to be holding his lower belly.

Bad Leg hurled foul curses at Jamie for a moment, and then toppled over to one side. He lay there, moaning.

"And then there were three," Jamie called, during a respite in Bad Leg's moaning.

"His medicine is very good this night," Deer Runner whispered to Tall Bull. They were behind a jumble of old logs piled there by floodwaters years back.

"Perhaps too good," Tall Bull said. "But if I must die in order to kill Man Who Is Not Afraid . . . so be it."

"I am ready," Deer Runner said.

"We are nearing old men," Tall Bull whispered. "There is much more behind us than what lies in front of us. I think this night will be a good night to die."

"If any night is a good night," Deer Runner replied, rolling his eyes at the darkness. "Perhaps if we are killed together, our spirits will wander together?"

"I would like that, old friend. I cannot think of another warrior I would rather have with me through the eternal years."

Bad Leg began shrieking more loudly than before, thrashing about in the dirt.

"He is shot in the lower belly," Tall Bull said. "His death will be long and painful, and he is not dying well at all."

"Did you really expect him to die well?"

"No. He was always a fool and is dying like one. Little Wolf will die no better," he added, disgust in his voice.

"Why should he? He does not have your blood in his veins."

"True." Tall Bull sighed. "I adopted two sons. Both of them failed me."

"You love him, don't you?"

"Who?"

"Man Who Is Not Afraid."

Tall Bull was silent for moment. "Yes," he spoke the word very softly. "And it is because of that love that I must kill him."

"Or be killed," Deer Runner said.

Tall Bull was thinking of his wife's vision when he replied, "Only the mountains never die."

FORTY-FIVE

By midafternoon on the day the Alamo fell, the bodies had been separated and the defenders of the Alamo were placed on huge funeral pyres. There was a layer of wood, then a layer of bodies, the bodies and wood soaked with grease and oil. There were half a dozen or more of the pyres, all of them much higher than a man's head.

Just before the torches were thrown onto the pyres, Santa Anna said, "This will teach those damn Texans a thing a two. This is the only kind of independence they'll ever get!"

The torches were hurled onto the pyres and the smell of burning flesh was so overpowering the men were forced to move back some distance in an effort to escape the odor.

"These damn Texans are offensive to me even in death," Santa Anna said, holding a white handkerchief to his nose.

Another bunch of Texas volunteers would prove to be a whole hell of a lot more offensive to him in about six weeks time. At a place called San Jacinto, where the Texas Army, under the command of Sam Houston, would wipe out Santa Anna's entire command and, a few days later, force the arrogant Santa Anna to accept unconditional surrender.

But on this late afternoon, Santa Anna gave Susanna Dickerson a horse, some provisions, and a black man who had been serving as his cook to go along as escort. He told her to ride to Gonzales with this message: "Tell the citizens there what happened here at the Alamo. Tell those people to never again rise up in rebellion against me. Now, go!"

Susanna would be found, some six or seven days later, by a group of Texas scouts who were on their way to the Alamo to see what had happened there.

Just about forty-five minutes before dawn, during the darkest hour, Jamie heard the three remaining Shawnees coming for him. Bad Leg had died a few hours before, whimpering and sobbing and still begging for someone to come to his aid. Just before he died, he cursed his friends for deserting him.

Jamie had to make the loads in his pistols and rifle true ones, for when the rush came, there would be no time for reloading. He made certain his Bowie knife was at hand, for he felt — no, he *knew* — the final minutes, and maybe seconds, would be knife to knife, and probably with Tall Bull, one of the most skilled knife handlers Jamie had ever known, outside of Jim Bowie.

Something flitted to Jamie's left, casting a quick shadow. But the move brought no gunfire from Jamie, for he knew it was a ruse. Many whites felt the Indian to be stupid, or dumb. Jamie knew better. They were some of the finest fighting men on the face of the earth. If he had fallen for that maneuver, that quick shadow, and fired, he would more than likely be dead, for he knew that at least two rifles were pointing at him.

He waited.

Jamie had changed positions earlier, and had replied to none of the probing questions from Tall Bull, Deer Runner, and Little Wolf since then. He had darkened his face and hands with dirt and had put himself in the least likely spot; the one that offered only the barest of protection, right at the northern edge of the clump of trees.

And whoever it was coming in from the north was very nearly on him.

Deer Runner. And he was moving as silently as a ghost, making only inches of headway at each forward move. Jamie could make out only part of the man's features, but enough to see the long scar that ran from Deer Runner's eyebrow down to the point of his jaw.

Jamie's hand was on his knife, on the ground, and he brought it up swiftly and powerfully, the cutting edge up, and nearly took Deer Runner's head off. Just as the knife impacted against flesh, a rifle roared and Jamie felt a white hot burst of pain in his left shoulder. Using his feet, he pushed himself back, deeper into the heavier growth. It was a good move, for a second rifle roared and the ball slammed into the tree where, only seconds before, Jamie had been.

Jamie pulled out a bandanna and stuffed it under his buckskins, plugging the bullet hole and slowing the bleeding as best he could. He sheathed his knife and waited, gritting his teeth against the waves of pain. He felt the slow flow of blood wetting his flesh. His fingers felt about the base of the tree and found some moss. He pulled some loose and placed it, he hoped, under his buckskin shirt at his back, where the ball had torn through. He knew the pain he was feeling now was nothing compared to what it would be when the shock wore off.

Silver was showing in the eastern sky when Little Wolf seemed to come out of nowhere and made his leap for Jamie. Jamie lifted a pistol and shot him. Little Wolf landed on top of him, his knife slicing Jamie's left leg from just below the hip down to almost his knee. Jamie kicked the Shawnee off him and tore Little Wolf's shirt to use to bandage his leg. He could not tell how deep the knife had penetrated, but it felt like a serious wound. He bound it tight and quickly reloaded his discharged pistol.

"Just the two of us now, Man Who Is Not Afraid," Tall Bull's voice reached him. "I felt sure Little Wolf would fail, but I was confident that Deer Runner would take you."

"You were right about one and wrong about the other," Jamie said.

"Something has changed in your voice. I think you are badly hurt."

"That's a hell of a lot better than you're going to be, Tall Bull."

"What do you mean?"

"You're going to be dead."

Tall Bull chuckled. "I taught you well, my son."

"That you did, father. And I thank you for it."

Tall Bull's laugh held no humor. "Perhaps I taught you too well."

"We'll soon know, won't we?"

"That is true."

Jamie could tell with each reply that Tall Bull was slowly working his way closer. He was in the cluster of trees now. Jamie did not know if he could stand up; did not know if his wounded leg would support him. But he did know he was now no match for Tall Bull if it came to hand to hand with knives. He had to shoot him; had to get lead into the man. Tall Bull was an enormously powerful man, perhaps not as powerful as he'd been when Jamie was a child in the Shawnee town, but Jamie knew if Tall Bull ever got his hands on him, the fight was over — and Jamie would be the loser.

Tall Bull made only one mistake in his deadly advance: he waited too long to make his move. The skies were growing lighter by the minute and Jamie's eyes were sharp. He saw a lower branch move and a brown hand reach up to still it. Jamie put a heavy caliber ball right through that hand. Tall Bull made no sound, even though Jamie knew the pain must have been awful, for he'd seen the sudden splash of bright red color the dead leaves.

Jamie laid that pistol aside and picked up his second pistol, muffling the cocking with his left hand. Waves of agony lanced through him when he moved his left arm and bright lights of pain erupted behind his eyes.

Tall Bull burst out of the brush running hard. There was a knife in his left hand, his ruined right hand dangling and dripping blood, and a wild cry on his lips. His face was pure savage and his eyes were alive with victory.

Jamie lifted his pistol and shot Tall Bull in the chest, watching as if events had suddenly slowed down to only a fraction of life's speed. Tall Bull stopped and looked down at the hole in his chest, just below the V of his rib cage. Blood was pouring out.

"Iiiyyee!" he cried. "I died at the hands of a true warrior!" He stumbled forward and fell, the knife driving deep into Jamie's side.

For just a few seconds, the eyes of Jamie and Tall Bull met. Tall Bull gasped, "My son! My son! Only Man Above knows how much I loved you."

"You sure picked a funny way to show it," Jamie said, just as darkness began to take him.

"Deer Woman was right," Tall Bull whispered, lowering his head to Jamie's chest. "She said I would not return."

"So we both lost the war," Jamie's voice was very weak.

"Both sides always do," the Shawnee chief said, as his eyes and the eyes of Jamie Ian MacCallister closed and they were spun whirling into a world of shadows.

FORTY-SIX

Little Wolf crawled to his knees and staggered toward the river to splash water on his wounds and try to bandage them. Then he would return and take the scalp of Jamie MacCallister. He made the river only to pass out again. He lay with his legs in the cold water and his upper torso on the bank.

Jamie opened his eyes to a world of pain. It was full daylight and the sun was bright. About eight o'clock, he guessed. He did not try to pry the dead fingers of Tall Bull from the hilt of the knife. He doubted he had the strength left in him to do that and then pull the blade from his side. He gritted his teeth, summoned all his strength and willpower, put one hand around Tall Bull's wrist and the other around the dead Indian's closed hand, and jerked.

He screamed and passed out from the pain.

By the river, Little Wolf stirred at the

sound, but could not drag himself to consciousness.

Jamie pulled himself back to white-hot awareness and pushed Tall Bull from him. He did not yet have the strength to stand, so after gathering his pistols and rifle, he began the painful crawl back to his camp. Twice he had to stop and rest. At his camp, he built up the fire and dressed his wounds as best he could with what he had and could find, the latter provided by nature.

He forced himself to eat and drink some coffee and then, working in stages, for he was very weak, he packed up and saddled up. His horse did not like the smell of blood, but Jamie quieted the animal and got the saddle on him. Next came the task of getting himself into the saddle. After three tries, all of them hideously painful, he made it.

He pointed the nose of the horse north, toward the road. He was very tired, and wanted very much to just lie down and rest. But he knew if he allowed that, he would not get up. He would just die.

How he stayed in the saddle for as long as he did was something short of a miracle. He was only half conscious much of the time. When he reached the road, he turned east and ran right into a Mexican patrol.

Through the painful haze behind his eyes, he saw them and lifted his rifle. It seemed to weigh a thousand pounds. The Mexican patrol literally blew him out of the saddle. Jamie was unconscious before he hit the ground. He was not aware of the gentle rain that started falling from the clouds. It was a warm rain, and it signaled the beginning of spring.

Jamie lay sprawled on his face and belly in a ditch by the side of the road. His horse had raced off as soon as Jamie was shot out of the saddle. Two of the Mexican cavalrymen tried to catch the animal, but the horse was too fast for them and they gave up.

Jamie was covered with blood from his newly received head wound to his knees, and the officer took one careless glance at him and said, "Dead."

Jamie had been carrying the pouch on the outside of his coat to prevent any blood from leaking through and the Mexican officer ripped it from him and pawed through the letters. He could read and speak English and he saw quickly that there were no military dispatches among the bits of torn paper. He shook his head and cursed and threw the papers on the dampening ground and swung back into the saddle.

He looked over at Jamie's horse, about a

half mile away, grazing. "Too bad," he said. "That was a fine animal. I would have liked to have caught him."

The patrol galloped off, toward San Antonio, as the rain began turning the ink on the papers once more into liquid.

Kate straightened up from her work and looked westward. An almost physical stab of fear had suddenly filled her. She clutched at her breast and gasped. What was wrong with her? She'd never before experienced anything like this.

Jamie Ian and Ellen Kathleen, now in their ninth year, and both very bright and quick, looked at their mother and then at each other. Ellen shook her head at her brother.

Andy blurted, "Are you all right, Mommy?"

Kate turned from the stove and forced a smile. "Yes. I'm fine. Get me some potatoes, will you, Andy?" She looked out the kitchen window. Sarah and Hannah were walking up the path, coming over for afternoon coffee and conversation. The men were in the fields.

Kate took a deep breath and calmed herself. She just couldn't understand that sudden moment of anxiety. It was gone now. She sighed and took the potatoes Andy handed her and thanked him. She had to smile as she looked at the children. Everyone of them blond and blue-eyed. The boys all looked like Jamie and the girls all looked like Kate.

Kate stepped to the door to greet her friends. What's happening, Jamie? she thought. What is going on where you are? Are you safe? Well? This waiting is becoming harder and harder to bear. Come back to me, Jamie. Come back to me.

San Antonio was very quiet. Over at the Alamo, ashes from the funeral pyres were cold. All that remained of over one hundred and eighty men were a few teeth and some bones that had managed to survive the intense fires.

When asked what he wanted done with the ashes of the defenders, Santa Anna said, "I really don't care. Let someone else worry about it."

No one really knows what happened to the ashes of the men who fought so gallantly and died at the Alamo.

A Mexican family found Jamie. The man was getting a shovel from the wagon when his wife screamed. He ran to her side.

"He moved!" she said. "His hand. His

hand moved."

"Impossible, woman! The man is *dead. Madre Dios,* look at him!"

"I tell you his hand moved."

The man knelt down in the rain beside the sprawled body. He recoiled in shock when he saw Jamie's eyelids flutter. He looked up at his wife. "This is truly a miracle. He's *alive!*"

Jamie's horse had wandered over. The woman tied the reins to the back of the wagon and then she and her husband struggled to drag Jamie over to the wagon. It took them three tries to get him into the bed of the wagon, for Jamie was a big man.

"I wonder what happened to him?" she asked, when they were on their way.

"Bandits, surely," the husband replied. "This is a dangerous road."

Neither of them knew anything of the fight at the Alamo.

"What are we going to do with him?" she asked.

"Give him the dignity of dying on a pallet with a roof over his head. We can't leave him for the coyotes and the buzzards. That would be a sin."

At their farm, the man and woman and their children carried Jamie into the house and undressed him. They all gasped when they saw his fearsome wounds, then set about tending to him. When they had done all they could do, they covered Jamie and sat at the table, looking at him.

"It's in the hands of God now," the woman said.

"I wish the priest would come by. He would know what to do."

The man wasn't nearly as devout as his wife, but he wisely made no comment. He rose from the table to see to Jamie's horse. When the horse was stabled and rubbed down and fed, the man gathered up Jamie's weapons, unloaded them, and cleaned them of mud and blood.

He and his wife had carefully cleaned the wounds, then stopped the new bleeding with cayenne pepper. They applied poultices to the wounds and then sat back and waited for Jamie to die. The man and his wife had done all they knew to do.

It would be days, in some cases, even weeks, before all the Anglos in Texas knew what had taken place at the Alamo. While Jamie lay hovering between life and death, sometimes conscious enough to drink herbal tea brewed by the Mexican woman, Houston was putting together and pulling together his Texas army.

When Mrs. Susanna Dickerson was found by Houston's scouts, she told them what had happened at the Alamo and also that General Santa Anna had ordered a detachment of his troops to march to Gonzales and either drive out or kill all Americans.

A pall settled over the tiny town of Gonzales. The entire force of Texans at the Alamo had been killed and their bodies burned. But soon despair turned to outrage and cold fury. Who in the hell did Santa Anna think he was to treat human beings in such a manner? To mutilate and butcher and then burn the bodies like so much garbage. Goddamn the man!

"We retreat," Houston said, and then waited for the howls of protest to die down. "We have no choice in the matter. Send a rider to Goliad and order Colonel Fannin to pull out and link up with us . . . here." He pointed to a crude map. "Tell him to destroy the fort and get the hell out of there. And tell him that by God I want this order obeyed!"

A rider was immediately dispatched to Goliad, to Fannin at Fort Defiance.

Houston immediately had Gonzales evacuated. His plan was to fall back across the Colorado River. The rain that had started a few days earlier fell in abundance now, turning the poor roads into roads of mud. The soldiers and the frightened refugees had a very tough time of it, but they made the Colorado with Santa Anna's troops right behind them. Houston's men crossed the river just before it poured over its banks and flooded everything. A full Mexican division was looking at him from the west side of the river. Houston was counting on Fannin for help, and wondered where in the hell the man was.

But Fannin once more had difficulty in making up his mind. He decided to delay leaving Fort Defiance. That decision would cost him his life and the lives of his men. When he finally decided to abandon the fort, he got some four or five miles outside of Goliad and found himself looking at about two thousand Mexican soldiers, under the command of General Urrea. Fannin had slightly over four hundred men under his command. He ordered his wagons circled and made his stand. They fought for several days, killing over three hundred Mexican troops, but finally had to surrender. There was no hope left. Urrea assured Fannin he and his men would be treated fairly and humanely.

A week after Fannin surrendered, on a Sunday morning, Fannin and his men were taken outside of Goliad and shot . . . on orders from Santa Anna. The thirty or so badly injured men, unable to march out of town, were carried outside the makeshift hospital and also executed.

When the news of the slaughter at Goliad began leaking out over the countryside, many of the civilians went into a panic, quickly packing a few possessions, and taking off for safer ground.

Nearly three weeks had passed since the fall of the Alamo, and the news had finally reached Kate and the others living in the Big Thicket country just east of San Augustine. She was devastated; but she could not bring herself to believe that Jamie's ashes were among those scattered to the wind around the Alamo. She knew her Jamie, and knew that among his virtues was the ability to survive.

"Kate," Sam Montgomery told her, as the month of March drew to a close. "You've got to accept it. Jamie is gone."

"No!"

"Kate, Kate, I don't like it, either. I'm heartsick at just the thought. But there were no survivors."

Kate looked up at the sounds of a lone horseman making his way up the lane. It was the man who ran the livery in San Augustine. He dismounted and took off his hat. "Ma'am," he said. "Sam. I got news. Some of the women that was in the Alamo is talking. They say that just hours before the fall, Colonel Travis sent out a man with a pouch full of messages from the defenders. They said it was Jamie MacCallister."

Kate's heart swelled and she nearly swooned. Sam steadied her arm and she leaned against him.

"How straight is this news?" Sam asked.

"Pretty straight, Sam. And the patrol that found Susanna Dickerson said they come up on a place where there had been one hell of fight 'tween somebody and some Shawnees."

"Shawnees?" Kate asked. "There are no Shawnees near San Antonio."

"Well, not many, leastways," the liveryman replied. "Anyhow, whoever is was that fought these Shawnees killed more than his share, according to the patrol. They counted eleven bodies. All Injun."

"And the white man?" Sam asked. "Assuming it was a white man; what about him?"

"Not a trace, Sam. Looks like he got away clean."

"Did not," the heavy voice spoke from

606

behind them, startling them all.

They whirled around. It was the huge Cherokee, Egg. He had slipped up on them as silently as a snake.

"Get wagon," the Cherokee enforcer said. "Pack provisions for a long trip. I will take you to your man."

"He's *alive*?" Kate cried.

"Yes. Badly hurt. Long way off."

"I'll go with you, Kate," Sam said.

"You stay here," Egg told him firmly, in a tone that Sam had learned meant the subject was closed. "No one will bother us. I have man with me to drive wagon. We leave in one hour." He looked at Kate. "No more faint. You must be strong. Move!"

Houston now had about a thousand men. He could never be sure because of the desertions and new additions that were arriving every day. Houston formed a cavalry unit, and assigned men to man the cannon, of which he had six, all mounted.

Meanwhile, Santa Anna had left San Antonio and joined up with General Sesma. It made for an awesome force of trained, combat-experienced soldiers. Santa Anna felt confident that this time, he would drive every American out of Texas . . . or kill them where they stood.

Then he made a fatal mistake.

He split up his huge army into several groups. He sent over twelve hundred troops to the south, about nine hundred to the north, and he took personal command of a select group of infantry and cavalry and crossed the Colorado river — his objective was San Felipe.

That move was to be Santa Anna's Waterloo.

On April 21st, 1836, Kate arrived at the home of the Mexican couple who had cared for Jamie. On that same date, far to the east, Houston and his army were preparing to meet Santa Anna's troops in the battle that would turn the tide for Texas independence.

Kate knelt down beside the wasted body of her husband and let her tears bathe his face. Jamie was alive and conscious, but his hideous wounds had ravaged him. He had lost about seventy-five pounds and was only a shell of what he had once been.

But he was alive.

Kate pressed a hundred dollars in gold coin into the hands of the Mexican couple. They gasped at the money. That was a small fortune. They had never seen so much money. They tried to return it, but Kate would have none of that.

"I wish I had more to give you," she told them in Spanish. "You have done so much. I could never repay you all that I owe you."

Jamie was so weak he could scarcely speak. For the fevers, more than his wounds, had nearly killed him. Egg picked him up in his arms and carried him to the wagon — the bed had been filled with straw — and gently placed the man on the softness. "Now we go home," the huge Cherokee said.

FORTY-SEVEN

Far to the east, between a bayou and the San Jacinto River, Houston was preparing to launch the battle that would finish Santa Anna's reign of terror in Texas.

The battle cry of the Texans was, "Remember the Alamo, Remember Goliad."

Houston's men had blood in their eyes and slaughter on their minds. And that is exactly what it would turn out to be for the Mexican troops.

On the 20th of April, Houston's men and the Mexican troops exchanged a few rifle shots and that was about all. The Mexican army was well-dressed in their colorful uniforms. Houston's men were dressed mostly in rags, for their clothing had taken a beating during the long days and nights of marching. Their clothing was tattered, but their spirits were high.

Santa Anna viewed the newly formed army of Texans with contempt. His scouts had told him they were filthy, all dressed in rags, had no food, and the mounts of their small cavalry unit were scrawny and looked as though they had not been fed in days.

"We shall send them fleeing for their lives with the first charge," Santa Anna was told.

"Very well," Santa Anna said. "In the morning we shall finish with this distasteful business and then make ready to go home."

They were going to go home, all right. To their maker.

On the afternoon of the 20th of April, Houston knew he could contain his men no longer. To do so would light the spark of insurrection, for his men were ready for a fight and his commanders had told him their men were, by God, going to fight, whether Houston liked it or not.

The thinly timbered field of San Jacinto was all that separated Houston's army from Santa Anna's army. At about three o'clock that afternoon, Houston gave the orders: Move out. But do it silently. The Army of Texas moved out, silently as ghosts, flitting through the timber, advancing to the open field where the Mexicans were camped. The cannon were being pulled along by men to cut down on the noise horses might make.

Santa Anna was asleep in his tent.

About two hundred and fifty yards from

the huge encampment of Mexican soldiers, many of them resting, Houston shouted, "Remember the Alamo. Remember Goliad!"

Houston's small battery of cannon roared, shattering the tranquility of the balmy afternoon.

Many of the men had lost friends at the Alamo and at Goliad. They screamed out the names of the dead and opened fire with their rifles.

The Mexican Army was caught flatfooted. Why Santa Anna's guards had not detected the advancing Texas army remains a mystery. But they did not. Many of the Texans had moved into a position only a few yards from the sprawling Mexican army and the afternoon turned into a slaughter. Houston's fifers were tootling and the drummers were pounding as the startled and frightened Mexican army sprang to their feet and grabbed rifles. Santa Anna's cavalry, the dragoons, ran for their horses, which were not saddled. Houston's cavalry galloped into the Mexican camp, their sabers flashing in the afternoon sun. Within seconds, the sharpened steel was dripping with blood, and blood splattered the clothing of Houston's cavalrymen and their mounts. The Texan cavalry rode down many of the panicked Mexican soldiers, the hooves of their mounts smashing the life from the soldiers.

Santa Anna was in the saddle, waving his sombrero, attempting to rally his men. "Fight them, goddamn you!" he shouted, his voice just audible over the howling din of battle and the cries of badly wounded men.

But his men were in panic. They looked for their leaders and could not find them. The advancing line of Texans was about three quarters of a mile long and coming at a run. It must have seemed to the Mexican soldiers to be an endless line of soldiers. It was not; it was a very thin line but Santa Anna's troops did not know this. It was not the Mexican policy for the officers to share much intelligence with line troops.

The Mexican soldiers went into total panic and confusion. They began running in all directions and Houston's men chopped them down. The battle turned into a slaughter.

Houston had his horse shot out from under him. He swung into the saddle of a riderless Mexican horse and had that animal shot out from under him. On foot, he was felled by a musket ball to his left leg, knocking him to the ground, the bullet breaking his leg. He crawled into the saddle of yet another horse and rallying some men, led a charge, waving his sword. Houston leaped his horse into the fray. Swinging his sword, he beheaded a Mexican colonel and turned in the saddle just in time to see a Mexican general riddled with bullets from the rifles of the Texans.

"Let them surrender!" Houston shouted. "They're trying to surrender, boys!"

But the Texans were having none of that. The blood-splattered walls of the Alamo and the terrible slaughter at Goliad were too fresh in their minds. The Texans went after Santa Anna's men with a vengeance. They gave no quarter as they ripped and shot and slashed their way through the Mexican lines.

Santa Anna and many of his senior staff officers managed to escape in all the confusion. As one sergeant in the Texas Army put it, "They took off like their asses was on fire!"

The actual battle lasted just over fifteen minutes. But the blood lust was hot in the veins of the Texans, and they more than got their revenge for the slaughter at the Alamo and at Goliad. To say the men under Houston's command went berserk would be putting it mildly. They were bent on killing and nobody was going to stop them.

About eight hundred Mexican troops were killed that late afternoon, and over six hundred finally taken prisoner when the blood lust had cooled and the men began to take stock of what they had done.

Houston, in great pain, lay on blankets and took reports from his commanders. He had lost eight men and had nineteen wounded.

"Santa Anna?" Houston questioned.

"Gone."

"Not far," Houston said. "Order patrols out and tell them to look for a man dressed like a peasant or a common soldier. He's an arrogant bastard, but he isn't a fool."

Santa Anna was no fool, but he had a lousy sense of direction. He got lost and wandered around in the night like a goose. Not only that, but he lost his horse and was on foot. Instead of heading for his own army, located about forty miles away, on the Brazos, he turned and walked straight back toward the killing fields of San Jacinto. That night, a patrol picked him up and by daylight, he was standing in front of Sam Houston. Santa Anna was one scared man, but still full of bluster.

"I demand to be treated as befitting a man of my rank," he said.

Houston told him, quite bluntly, where he could put his demands.

Nobody had ever suggested *that* to Santa Anna, but it sure got Santa Anna's attention real quick. He stood trembling with fear and indignation.

Houston added, "You're damn lucky I don't have you shot on the spot."

Santa Anna was sure now that he was a dead man.

But Houston spared General Santa Anna, feeling that the man was much more valuable to him alive than dead. He made Santa Anna write out a letter, acknowledging Texas's independence from Mexico, and also had him put in writing that from that moment on an armistice between Texas and Mexico was declared.

Houston's men didn't like it; they wanted to hang Santa Anna right then and there, but Houston was firm on the matter: Santa Anna would be spared.

Santa Anna also wrote out a message to be delivered to his troops at Fort Bend and Houston sent two men to deliver the message. The same day the message was received, nearly five thousand Mexican troops began packing up and pulling out of Texas.

"I may go now?" Santa Anna asked, considerably humbled by the experience.

"Not yet," Houston told him.

Santa Anna would be held prisoner, albeit treated well, for almost seven months, to make sure that Mexico kept its promise, then he was released. For all intents and purposes, the war was over. Texas was free of Mexico's domination.

FORTY-EIGHT

Jamie's recovery was long. But under the care of family and friends, he soon began to show signs of improvement. Slowly his strength began to return and by midsummer, he was taking walks around the cultivated fields in the Big Thicket country. He sent one of the Nunez boys down to Galveztown, or Galveston, as some were now calling it, with a note to the newspaper editor there, telling him of the dispatch pouch he had left the Alamo with, and of the messages carried therein. The editor did not come himself, but did send a friend to talk with Jamie. The man did not believe Jamie's story, dismissing his claims. Had Jamie been fully recovered from his wounds, the man would have returned to Galveston with a busted jaw, along with other contusions and abrasions.

But the owner of the paper, while interviewing Santa Anna at a later date that summer, was startled to learn that Santa Anna himself remembered the tall young man with the courage of lions, as Santa Anna put it. The editor made a note of it and mentally vowed to visit the Big Thicket country to personally speak with Jamie Ian MacCallister.

As for Jamie, Kate watched him recover and noticed that his gaze often turned longingly to the west.

"We'll be leaving soon," she told her circle of friends.

"What?" Sarah blurted. "Leave? And go where? And why?"

"I don't know exactly where," Kate admitted. "West, I'm sure. I know Jamie."

"But, this is your home!"

Kate smiled and cut her eyes to Hannah, who had said nothing. She, too, knew Jamie, and Kate's announcement had come as no surprise to her.

"We'll all go," Hannah said, causing Swede to swallow his chewing tobacco.

Sam remained silent. Like Kate, he had seen the signs of restlessness growing in Jamie. Jamie had not confided in him, but Sam knew the Alamo had changed Jamie. He could not know to what degree, only that it had.

By August, Jamie had fully recovered and

announced that he was riding south to meet with the editor of the paper at Galveston.

"I have to try," he told Kate. "I have to try to get Bowie's message to the public. It's important."

He had never told anyone what Bowie had written. But he knew every word by heart.

The owner and editor believed him, but without at least some modicum of proof, he felt he could not publish what Jamie had memorized.

"Those are Bowie's words, sir," Jamie told him. "And Crockett's words and Travis's words. It's important for the sake of history that they be recorded and preserved."

"I agree, young man. Wholeheartedly. And as you see, I've written them down, word for word, just as you told them to me. Maybe someday. But not this day."

Jamie returned to the Big Thicket, a bitterly disappointed man. Moses Rose knew Bowie and Travis and Crockett had given him messages, but Jamie could find no trace of the man. Louis Moses Rose had dropped out of sight.

Little Wolf, like Jamie, had recovered from his wounds. The Shawnee had dragged himself into the brush and lay like a wounded animal for several days. He was in the brush when the patrol came along and found the bodies of the dead. But Jamie was not among them. Little Wolf was now consumed with hatred. It was what kept him alive. The patrol had not buried the dead, and that infuriated Little Wolf. That the whites would allow Indian dead to be left for the scavengers was unthinkable to Little Wolf. It showed how unfeeling they were. The fact that he had left a dozen or more of white bodies to rot under the sun or be eaten by animals did not enter his mind.

Little Wolf did not have the strength to bury his father and his friends. He tried, but could not. He prayed that his father would forgive him. Little Wolf did not try to return to his mother's village, far to the north.

As he slowly healed, Little Wolf had only one thought in his mind: to kill Jamie MacCallister.

Jamie rode into San Augustine and bought a wagon from an American who had just emigrated from the States. Along with the wagon, he bought six big Missouri mules. It was October 1836.

"We'll leave in the spring," he told Kate.

"Everyone is going," she replied.

Jamie was not surprised.

Jamie rode to the Nunez family's cabin and told a very startled Juan he was giving his land to him. "You're a good farmer, Juan. You'll treat the land well. Be happy."

Egg came to see Jamie one last time. The huge Cherokee, now out of a job since Texas had declared its independence from Mexico, shook hands with Jamie.

"What will happen to you now?" Jamie asked.

Egg smiled. "I will survive. I shall live quietly in this land of swamps and forests. Soon no one will remember Egg."

But Egg would not survive to live out his remaining years in peace. He and the remaining band of Chief Diwali's Cherokees, including Diwali's son, were massacred on the banks of the Upper Brazos River in 1839, while trying to flee to Mexico.

Jamie watched Egg walk toward the swamps. He felt he would never see the man again. Jamie owed Egg a great deal; probably his life.

"Egg!" Jamie called.

The Indian stopped and turned around.

Jamie made the sign for brother. Egg smiled and returned the gesture, then stepped into the gloom of the swamp.

Jamie never saw him again.

Kate came to his side and Jamie put his

arm around her waist. "All you have to do is say no, Kate. And this will be our home forever."

She smiled up at him. "I only have one objection, Jamie Ian MacCallister."

"Oh?"

"Yes. With all the kids we have, you should have bought *two* wagons!"

In West Texas, Little Wolf had made friends with a small band of renegade Kiowa and Comanche and they spent the winter making life miserable for the few settlers who lived in that area. Little Wolf's reputation as a fearless warrior grew, and soon more renegades joined his ranks. These were Indians who had been kicked out of their tribe for one reason or the other, usually for stealing or coveting someone else's wife . . . or murder. They were the worst of the worst and they liked the idea of killing Jamie and of taking the blond Kate for their own use. But riding into East Texas was not such a great idea, for the people there had no patience for warlike Indians.

However, two half-breed Kiowa renegades did step forward, agreeing to travel into East Texas and scout out the area. Since Spanish was their first language, they felt they would have no trouble with whites. The saddles on their horses would be Mexican — stolen, of course. They would dress as Mexicans, act as Mexicans, and speak Spanish. They would see what they had to see and return as quickly as possible.

The fever of moving west into uncharted lands soon caught on with everybody in that one little pocket of the Big Thicket. It took some convincing, but Moses and Liza soon agreed to move west, as did Sally and Wells. It would be a big enough wagon train to discourage all but a very large war party of hostiles.

That winter everyone worked on wagons, repairing or replacing harness, making spare wheels, and getting ready for spring. The women, of course, hated to leave their snug cabins, but the growing excitement of the children soon became infectious and all looked forward to spring's budding.

Little Wolf's scouts had ventured into the area, actually never entering the Big Thicket country but instead gathering their information by hanging around San Augustine and listening to talk and gossip. It did not take them long to learn all about Jamie's plans to move west. As soon as they learned all there was to know, they were back in the saddle and heading west to report to Little Wolf.

They had learned that Jamie planned to visit the Alamo, then cut north and west from there, heading for the big mountains, hundreds of miles away. Little Wolf smiled his insane curving of lips.

"Perfect," he said.

And it was perfect for Little Wolf and his band. Texas was not going to tolerate much more from the Indians. The philosophy among the settlers was quickly becoming that the only good Indian was a dead one. The climate was rapidly beginning to get very unhealthy for the red man.

"There is only one way they can go," it was pointed out to Little Wolf. "When they reach this vast emptiness, we can strike."

"No," Little Wolf said. "Once they leave the settlement of San Antonio, they will be on guard. And if they are with Man Who Is Not Afraid, they are fierce fighters all. Even the women. I despise Man Who Is Not Afraid, but he is a warrior without equal. I know," he added bitterly. "So we must strike before they reach the settlement. We have time to plan carefully. They will not leave until spring warms the land. I think it would make my father rest easier if we took them along the same river where my father's bones are now scattered. Yes. I think that is where Jamie MacCallister will lie rotting. And I will take his wife like a dog beside his body. Or perhaps allow him to live long enough to watch while I humble her; to hear her shrieking in pain and disgrace while we take our turns with her. Yes. That is a good plan. A very good plan." Little Wolf laughed insanely. His followers knew that Little Wolf was a tad off-center, but they did not know to what extent.

Little Wolf was as crazy as a lizard. But like many insane people, he was also cunning. Little Wolf did not fear death, as long as he saw Jamie die with him. He did not care if every man who followed him died. He cared only in seeing Jamie MacCallister dead.

Dead. Like his father. Little Wolf's eyes began shining with a mad glow. Those renegades close to him slowly backed away, for Little Wolf's temper was a terrible thing to behold. And he was cruel and quite inventive when it came to torturing prisoners — man, woman, or child.

His followers smiled. The taking of this wagon train should prove to be fun. There would be hours, perhaps days, of the screaming of prisoners under torture. There

would be women and girls to rape and sod-
omize.

Fun for everyone.

FORTY-NINE

When spring began greening the land and flowers were blooming in the meadows, Jamie and his band of westward-bound pioneers closed the door to their cabins and hitched up the teams. Juan Nunez and his family had decided to go with Jamie and the others: twelve adults, five teenagers, and a whole passel of kids. The Nunez boys would be in charge of taking care of the fine horses Jamie raised, the women would drive the wagons, and the men would act as outriders and scouts and hunters. The older kids would take turns spelling the women at the reins.

"How far you reckon them mountains are, Jamie?" Swede asked.

"About a thousand miles, I'd guess."

"It'll be a grand adventure, for sure," Sarah Montgomery said, looking around her at the fields that should have been plowed and planted by now.

Kate was at the tiny cemetery, placing wild flowers on the graves of Baby Karen and Ophelia. Jamie walked over to stand beside her.

"She's not here, Kate," he told her. "She's with God in Heaven."

When she did not reply, Jamie said, "I guess it's harder for the mother than it is for the father."

Kate smiled up at him, her eyes wet from crying. "You might say that, Jamie."

He felt totally helpless and awkward at moments like these. His Shawnee warrior training nearly always prevented him from showing much emotion. Severe beatings will etch that training forever in one's mind.

"All you had to do, Kate, was to say you didn't want to go," Jamie said gently.

"Don't be silly." She wiped her eyes and laughed. "When that minister said 'til death do us part, I took it *seriously*!"

They walked over to the wagons and Jamie helped Kate onto the seat. She picked up the reins and winked at him. "Let's go to the mountains, Jamie Ian MacCallister. I've read about them, heard about them, and now I want to see them."

Jamie swung into the saddle. "Maybe we'll run into Grandpa there."

"We won't if you don't get moving, love."

Jamie laughed and rode to the head of the wagons. He twisted in the saddle and looked back for the last time. He did not know why he felt they must leave and go traipsing off into the wilderness, only that they must.

His eyes touched the eyes of Moses, white-headed now, before his time. A more dear and faithful friend no man could ever hope to find. His youngest son, Jed, was driving a wagon filled with tools and spare parts and wheels and anything else they felt they might need.

Sally was driving a wagon, with Wells sitting his horse alongside her.

Jamie locked eyes with Sarah, and she smiled at him from the wagon seat. He looked at Hannah, and she laughed openly. Jamie knew the Swede would never understand the special bond between him and Hannah; a bond so tight that only death would ever break it.

Maria Nunez was handling the reins of her wagon, Juan sitting his horse beside the wagon. Two very fine people who raised well-mannered kids and who knew only hard work and grinding poverty while working the land.

The kids were spread out among the wagons, and Jamie rode slowly down one side and up the other side, counting heads;

blond heads, nappy heads, shiny-black-haired kids with flashing button eyes.

What a mixture, Jamie thought. But we made it all work with no friction. So it can be done, if people will only try. And now we're going to do it again.

Jamie rode to the head of the column and lifted his arm. "Let's go see the mountains, people!" he called.

The wagons rolled through San Augustine and the people there came out to see them off, standing and waving and calling their hail and farewells for the last time. The owner of the general store handed Jamie a package and from the smell, he knew what it was: hard candy for the kids.

It would be the last store candy the kids would see for months, perhaps years. Quicker than any of them would have liked, the tiny village was behind them and silence stretched out before them. Just outside of San Augustine, Jamie turned the wagons slightly south. They were going far out of their way to visit San Antonio, but all wanted to see the Alamo.

They would not see another town or village or any type of settlement until they crossed the Trinity and a few miles southwest of there was a trading post. But that was miles ahead and days away.

The area was not void of people, for thousands of Americans had moved into Texas just prior to the war for Texas independence, most of them settling in the eastern part of the state. Lots of people, but few towns.

Jamie was once more in the peak of health, and roamed away from the wagons, always choosing the best crossing of sloughs and creeks. The "road" they followed was actually an old Indian trail, not much more than two wagon wheel ruts in the ground.

There were no incidents with Indians, for the settlers in East Texas had resolved that problem. In only a few short years, there would be no Indians left in East Texas except for a few peaceful Alabama and Coushatta. Jamie felt certain they would have trouble with the Kiowa and Comanche once they left San Antonio, but he was not expecting any trouble until then.

At the trading post, they bought a few supplies, exchanged pleasantries with the people there, and moved on. Jamie set a leisurely pace, for all knew they were seeing this country for the last time. Except for Jamie, they were also seeing it for the first time.

At a trading post on the Colorado, later to be known as La Grange, Jamie halted the wagons and they spent a couple of nights. Again they resupplied, talked with the people there, and rested. Most of the citizens had heard of Jamie MacCallister and many questioned him about the Alamo. He answered their questions patiently and truthfully. But it was painful for him, for the memories of Jim Bowie, Bill Travis, Davy Crockett, and the others were fresh in his mind, and it still rankled him that the editor of the paper would not print Bowie's last statement.

Several weeks after leaving the Big Thicket country, Jamie led the wagons onto the road that would take them to San Antonio and Jamie instantly felt suspicions seize him. He halted the wagons and sat his saddle for several moments, looking at the trail stretching out before him.

While the others chatted and rested by the road, Hannah came to him and he swung down from the saddle to stand beside her.

"What's wrong, Jamie?"

"I don't know," he spoke the words softly. "But I sense trouble ahead."

"You're certain that Tall Bull was dead?" she questioned in a whisper.

"Yes. But I don't know about Little Wolf. I know that I shot him. But whether it was

633

a killing shot . . . I don't know."

"Is there anything between here and San Antonio?"

"Walnut Springs. Just a trading post and a few cabins."

"It would be like Little Wolf to ambush us at the very spot where his father died."

"That's my thinking, Hannah."

Together, they walked back to the wagons, Jamie leading his horse. "I hope I'm wrong," Jamie told them. "But I think we're going to have some trouble when we near the Guadalupe River. Two days from now."

"Little Wolf?" Kate asked.

"Yes. It sounds silly, I know, but I have this . . . feeling. So from now on, keep the kids in the wagons and no walking alongside. Load up the extra weapons and keep them handy." He looked at Sam and Swede. "When, or if, the attack comes, it will come silently and swiftly. There will be no warning. If Little Wolf survived that fight, he's banded with other Indians. Maybe renegades. If that's the case, they'll be more vicious and cruel than anything any of you have ever seen. They'll be looking not just to kill me, but to take prisoners alive for torture. I don't have to tell you women what lies in store for you if you're taken. Hannah has made that perfectly clear to all of you.

Little Wolf, if he's alive, is quite mad. That makes him doubly dangerous. Let's go. Close the wagons up and keep them tight. Lookouts keep a sharp eye out for anything unusual. Call out if you see anything that looks suspicious."

But Jamie knew that the odds of any of them spotting anything were slight. He knew that when the attack came, if it did, it would come silently and deadly and with no warning. And he felt the attack would come at or near the river. Hannah knew Little Wolf's mind as well as Jamie did.

Jamie had spoken with the men who had found the battle site, months back. The bodies had not been buried, but one scout said the body of what appeared to be an older man had been partially covered. Jamie would bet that was Tall Bull; Little Wolf had been wounded so badly he could not properly bury his father. That his father's bones were scattered, left for the animals, and not wrapped and presented in the traditional manner to the Gods, would only serve to heighten Little Wolf's madness and craving for revenge.

The closer they came to the river, the more convinced Jamie became that Little Wolf was alive and waiting for him.

He stopped often to scan the terrain ahead

of him. To sit his saddle and sniff the air. For just as the white man smells differently to an Indian, an Indian smells different to a white man. If one knows what to sniff out. And Jamie certainly knew.

A few travelers had passed them, heading east. Sam was curious as to why Jamie had not questioned them.

"Because they wouldn't know anything, Sam. Little Wolf will let a hundred people pass his hiding place. He wants me. He wouldn't expose himself for anyone else. Not until I am dead."

"His hate must be wild," Swede commented, one second before a rifle cracked and he was knocked from the saddle.

FIFTY

Jamie left the saddle and was in the trees along the river in two blinks of an eye. He did not have to look back to see what those in the wagons were doing. They had rehearsed it so many times it would be second nature. When he did look around him from a concealed spot, the wagons were circled tightly, the stock inside the circle, and the defenders forted up. Out of the corner of his eye, Jamie had seen Swede jump to his feet and run for the wagons, his left arm bleeding. So the wound was not a serious one.

Jamie took stock of their situation and found it pretty good. Little Wolf, if this was Little Wolf and Jamie felt certain it was, had chosen his ambush point well, and the time of day. It was about an hour before dusk, a time when any travelers would be holed up for the evening.

The odds of anyone coming along to aid

them were slim to none.

Jamie had been riding with his bow and quiver of arrows on his back. He had his rifle and two pistols and his knife. He strung the bow and notched an arrow. Then he waited motionlessly.

"You die this day, Man Who Is Not Afraid!" Little Wolf called out.

Jamie did not reply. It seemed to him he had played this scene before. With a rueful smile, he hoped he fared better than the last time.

One of Little Wolf's band foolishly exposed his upper torso and a half dozen rifles roared from the wagons. The Indian was dead before he hit the ground. Another tried to dart across the road and Moses's shotgun belched fire and smoke, the heavy load catching the renegade in the belly and flinging him back into the ditch.

Two down. How many left? Jamie thought. A dozen? Twenty? More than that? Jamie doubted it. Twelve or fifteen at the most. If it had been a larger band, they would have tried another method of attack, he felt. But with Indians, one just never knew. Trying to second guess a seasoned warrior had cost many a white his or her life. To fight Indians, one had to think like an Indian. Most whites could not — Jamie could. And Hannah would be quietly coaching those in the circled wagons. The sides of one of the wagons had been reinforced, and would stop a bullet. The kids were in that wagon, belly down on the floor of the bed.

For anybody west of the Mississippi River, these were dangerous times, and the kids had been well schooled on what to do and what not to do in case of attack.

Jamie had located two of Little Wolf's band. During the first seconds of the ambush, they had shifted locations to work closer to the wagons and their cover was not good. Jamie slowly lifted his bow and let an arrow fly. He heard a grunt of pain as the arrow struck true. The Indian rose to his feet, the arrow embedded in his side, and a rifle cracked from the wagons, the ball taking the warrior in the head.

Three down.

Jamie laid aside the bow and picked up his rifle. He sighted the second warrior he had spotted and squeezed the trigger. The rifle roared and the Indian's face blossomed in crimson. He died in a sitting position, his back to a tree.

Four down.

"They'll talk now," Hannah whispered to the others within earshot. "They'll decide if their medicine is good or bad." She had doctored and bandaged Swede's arm. He squatted behind a wagon wheel, a pistol in his good hand.

One renegade decided on his own that his medicine was very good; that he was invincible. He charged the wagons, screaming. A very stupid thing to do.

Rifles and pistols roared and the renegade was stopped cold in his tracks and slammed to the ground.

Five down.

Jamie heard the rustling of brush as the remaining Indians pulled back. This was not going according to plan. They were taking too many losses and gaining nothing. They would have to think about this.

Jamie moved from his position and worked his way through the trees and brush along the bank of the river. But he need not have done so. The sounds of galloping horses reached him. Little Wolf and his band had decided to wait for another time. Their medicine was not good on this day.

When he was certain the renegades were indeed gone, and would not be back this late afternoon, Jamie looked at the dead. Two Comanche, two Kiowa, and one Ute, he thought; but he wasn't sure about the last. He walked over to the wagons.

"How's Swede?"

"I'm all right," Swede answered. "I jumped from my horse when the ball hit me. It's just a flesh wound. Will they be back, Jamie?"

"Not this day. Their medicine is no good. They'll probably wait until we leave civilization behind before they hit us again. But they will hit us. Count on that."

"Is this where you fought Tall Bull?" Hannah asked.

"Four or five miles south of here," Jamie said. "I think. But here is as close as the road comes. Were any of the children hurt?"

"Not a scratch," Kate told him. "The Indians really didn't get off that many shots."

"They'll be back," Jamie said grimly. "And maybe sooner than we think."

Little Wolf returned that night, just as the guard was changing. And when he struck the attack came hard, without a lot of skulking about. They came on horseback, and several managed to leap their horses into the inner circle. Swede took one's head off with a mighty swing of a double-bit axe and the horse, panicked with a spray of hot blood across its flanks, galloped across the small circle and leaped out into the night, dead hands still gripping the mane.

Jamie jerked a renegade off his horse and

snapped his back across his knee like breaking a stick of kindling wood. He looked up at the sound of a shot and for a second, his eyes were on Kate, standing with a rifle in her hands, a dead Comanche at her feet.

That broke the mounted attack.

"They'll be coming on foot now," Jamie called. "Everybody load up every gun and stand to your posts." Then he had an idea. "Little Wolf!" he shouted. "Can you hear me?"

"I hear you, Man Who Is Not Afraid. Are you trembling? Have you pissed your pants in fear?"

"Not hardly, Brother."

"I am not your brother!" Little Wolf screamed. "I was never your brother!"

"Do you know what our father said to me just before he died?"

"Nothing! He would say nothing to dog shit like you!"

"You are wrong, Brother. After I shot him, he called out and said, 'I died at the hands of a true warrior.' "

"Liar!"

"That's not all he said, Brother."

"I am not your brother!"

"Tall Bull said, 'My son. My son. Only Man Above knows how much I loved you.' "

"He did not say that. He never loved you.

642

Only me. He loved only me. Lies roll off your tongue like water over a falls. You are a liar!"

"You're not Shawnee, Little Wolf. You're white. Like me. You were taken as a baby. Little Wolf and Deer Woman adopted you. Just like they did me."

"I am not white!" Little Wolf screamed. "I am Shawnee. You are a liar!"

"A Shawnee with eyes the color of a bright new leaf in spring?" Jamie called out. "I doubt it. Your skin is as white as mine, White Boy."

Little Wolf cursed him until he was out of breath.

"That's your new name, Little Wolf. White Boy."

Little Wolf went wild with rage. He cursed and stomped around in the trees. He was so angry he could not speak any words that made sense.

"Besides being white, you're a coward, too," Jamie continued to taunt him.

"I will cut out your heart and eat it!" Little Wolf shouted.

"No, you won't," Jamie's words were calmly spoken. "Tall Bull couldn't do it, and he was ten times the warrior you are. You are nothing. You are puke on the ground."

Little Wolf was so angry he could not speak. He screamed in frustration.

"Why are you doing this, Jamie?" Kate asked.

"Hush," Hannah shushed her. "If Jamie can make Little Wolf fight him one on one, when Little Wolf is dead, the others will be leaderless and leave."

"But Jamie might be killed!"

"No, he won't. I've heard Tall Bull and Deer Runner and Stalking Bear and the others say a hundred times that Jamie was the better of the two . . . there was no comparison. Little Wolf never bested Jamie and he won't this time."

"Show me you have the courage of Tall Bull," Jamie shouted into the night. "Meet me one on one, White Boy. If you have the courage to face me alone. Which I doubt, since I'm sure you still squat to pee."

It was only with the greatest of efforts that Little Wolf managed to finally get his terrible temper under some sort of control. He was very nearly hyperventilating and one of his men went to the river to wet a cloth for him to use to bathe his face.

"Don't do it, Little Wolf," a Comanche said. "He's only trying to bait you."

"What did I tell you all?" Jamie raised his voice, as if speaking to those behind the wagons. "I told you Little Wolf-White Boy was nothing but a damn coward."

Something snapped in the already crazed mind of Little Wolf. He threw down his rifle and shouted, "Then step out, White Hair!" he shouted. "Face me with knife in hand, if you have the courage."

Jamie smiled and leaned his rifle against a wagon wheel. "Let me hear you give the orders for your followers not to interfere no matter how it goes," he called.

Little Wolf gave the orders in a harsh tone, then called out of the darkness, "Now you do the same with your people, Man Who Is Not Afraid."

"No interference," Jamie said, loud enough for Little Wolf to hear. "They go free if by some miracle I should fall, Little Wolf. Let me hear your word of honor on that."

"They will go free. They will not be harmed. I give you my word. But I will not need help from Man Above to kill you."

"Confident bastard, isn't he?" Swede muttered the question.

"He's a fool," Jamie said, then drew his big Bowie knife from its sheath and stepped out of the circled wagons.

From out of the cool night, Little Wolf walked toward him, knife in hand. "I have been dreaming of this moment for years," Little Wolf said.

"In a couple of minutes, White Boy, you'll be able to dream forever," Jamie told him, sarcasm thick off his tongue. "You'll have the sleep of the dead."

Little Wolf screamed and leaped at him. Jamie sidestepped and Little Wolf's knife cut nothing but night air.

"Clumsy," Jamie said. "You move like a fat cow."

Little Wolf cursed him.

"Our father would be disgraced at your behavior, White Boy."

Little Wolf's knife whistled close to Jamie's belly. Jamie laughed at him and clubbed him on the side of the head with a big fist.

Little Wolf backed up, shaking his head to clear it of a sudden painful buzzing from the blow.

Jamie pressed him, moving his left hand from side to side to distract his foe. He lunged and the tip of his razor-sharp knife drew first blood as the point slashed across Little Wolf's belly. The wound was not serious, but it was painful, and sudden fear leaped into Little Wolf's eyes at the ease with which Jamie had cut him.

Little Wolf backed up, conscious of the warm flow of blood leaking down across his lower belly. He feinted but Jamie would not play that game. All his false move got him was a cut across his left arm, between shoulder and elbow. Little Wolf felt more fear clutch at him as he stared into the eyes of Jamie, who was confidently smiling at him in the light of the moon.

"Shoot him!" Little Wolf suddenly yelled to his warriors.

It was not unexpected and Jamie tensed, ready to leap at the sound of a rifle or pistol being cocked.

"No," a Kiowa said. "This is a test of honor. We gave our word and we will not break it, Little Wolf."

"I gave you all an order!" Little Wolf screamed. "Obey me."

"You are a coward," a renegade Comanche called. "We are through with you. Die alone, Little Wolf."

A few seconds later, Jamie heard the rush and pound of hooves as Little Wolf's band left him.

"Leave," Jamie told the man who was once his brother. "Go and take care of Deer Woman. Ride out."

"I cannot," Little Wolf said softly. "And you know I speak the truth."

"Then step forward and taste my blade."

Little Wolf cried out and jumped. Jamie

stepped to one side and cut the Indian across the back, rendering his left arm useless as his big blade severed muscles. Blood gushed and Little Wolf almost went to his knees. Slowly, he turned to face Jamie.

There was pain mixed with resignation on Little Wolf's face as he said, "Did my father really say all that you said?"

"Yes."

"I am adopted?"

"Yes."

Little Wolf tried to jump at Jamie. He lost his balance and fell heavily to the ground. He cursed and pulled himself to his knees. "Kill me!" he cried.

"No," Jamie said. "I will not."

"You must!"

"I will not."

With a wild scream of hate and fury, Little Wolf drove his knife into his own stomach, burying the blade to the hilt. When the first waves of intense pain had passed, and with blood leaking from his mouth, he said, "I have no right to ask this of you, Man Who Is Not Afraid. But will you bury me near the place where my father's bones are scattered?"

"Yes, Little Wolf, I will do that."

"Take my horse. I will not need him where I go. For my father is afoot in the darkness as well. He's a good horse. I stole him from a stupid Pawnee."

"I will make sure you have weapons to take with you to the beyond."

"Thank you, Man Who Is Not Afraid." Little Wolf's voice was growing weaker but other than that, he made no sounds of complaint, even though the pain must have been terrible. He remained on his knees, both hands clutching the handle of the bloody knife buried in his stomach.

Hannah came out from the wagons, carrying food wrapped in a cloth. "You will not go hungry as you journey into the darkness, Little Wolf."

She placed the food beside him, away from the growing puddle of blood around his knees, and returned to the wagons.

"I must say this as my time slips away," Little Wolf said. "You are the greatest warrior I have ever met, Man Who Is Not Afraid."

Little Wolf fell over on his side, closed his eyes, and died.

At daylight, Jamie took the wrapped body of Little Wolf to the spot where he had killed Tall Bull and the others. Only Hannah accompanied him. He recognized the area by the human bones scattered about, including a rib cage. Jamie stood for a few minutes, looking at the old battleground, then he sighed and made ready for the simple service. He presented Little Wolf's body to the gods, with weapons and food. Hannah gave a Shawnee prayer for the dead and sang to the Gods. Then Jamie and Hannah returned to the wagons, walking through the brush and the sparse timber, holding hands.

"You're awfully quiet, Jamie," Kate remarked.

"Seems like to me you'd be happy that all this is over," Sam said.

"I do not wish to ever return to this place," Jamie said. "For the ghosts of Tall Bull and Deer Runner and Bad Leg and Little Wolf will forever wander here, unable to leave."

"Do you really believe that, Jamie?" Swede asked.

"Yes," Jamie said, and swung into the saddle.

FIFTY-ONE

After all these months, no traces of blood remained on the stones in the plaza or on the long and shot-gutted walls of the Alamo. Jamie entered the place alone. Kate had started to follow him through the gate, but Hannah held her back.

"Not yet," she said. "He'll call us."

Jamie walked the grounds and looked into each room. In his mind he could hear the voices of the dead. Davy Crockett, Jim Bowie, William Travis, Kimball, Martin, Bonham, Dickerson, Pollard, McGregor, Holland, Cloud, Autry, Esparza, Fuqua, Jameson, Walker, Evans, Baugh, Malone, Moore, Sewell, Bailey . . . and the one hundred and sixty-one others, including some sixteen or so whose names are forever lost from the roll call of the gallant.

Jamie could not bring himself to look into Bowie's room. He had seen the bloodstains still on the walls of the other rooms, and could not bring himself to see Bowie's blood splattered. Juan Nunez had personally spoken with several Mexican soldiers who had fought at the Alamo, and deserted soon after, sick to their hearts at the savagery they had both witnessed and taken part in. They had told him that all the bodies of the defenders had been horribly mutilated, then burned. Both of them had sworn to Juan that they would never again take up arms against a fellow human being . . . unless of course, it was an Indian. They didn't count.

No one ever really found out what happened to the ashes of the defenders of the Alamo.

Jamie motioned for the others to join him and the group walked the grounds and stared in awe at the bullet-and shell-ravaged walls and buildings. Jamie would not let the children look inside the blood-splattered rooms.

All were glad to leave the compound, Jamie especially, for to him it seemed that the ghosts of the fallen heroes were everywhere. The feeling of their presence was so strong, he had to fight the temptation to look over his shoulder. Years later, when friends came to visit him in the mountains, they would all tell him that the ghosts were still there, roaming the grounds of the old mission. Some would say they could faintly hear McGregor's bagpipes, the sawing sounds of Crockett's fiddle, in Travis's quarters, the sounds of his restless pacing, and in Bowie's room, the scratching of his pen as he laboriously wrote the stirring last farewell that the editor had refused to print.

Jamie sent the others on to where they were going to camp for a couple of days, while the ladies provisioned up for the long trip that lay ahead of them. He stood and sat and squatted for over an hour, staring at the outside of the walls of the Alamo, letting memories flood him. He knew, without any doubt at all, that if he lived to be a hundred and fought in that many more battles, he would never stand shoulder to shoulder with any braver men than those who died at the Alamo. For Freedom. For Texas.

Finally, he mounted up and rode away, leaving it all behind him. Except for the memories. Those, he would take to the grave.

Visiting the cantinas of San Antonio, Jamie found four men, two Mexican and two Anglo — all of whom Señor Ruiz vouched for — who agreed to drive additional wagons west and north into the mountains for Jamie and the others. Where they were going, there would be no stores, no neighbors, no nothing — not for hundreds of miles. Jamie did not yet know about Bent's Fort, but where he had in mind to take his people was still a couple of hundred miles from the junction of the Arkansas and Purgatory Rivers, where the Bent Brothers build their huge fort.

It was here, at San Antonio, that Jamie called his little group together for one last chance for anyone to change their minds, if any chose to do that.

No one did.

Jamie shrugged his heavy shoulders. Of them all, only he had any idea what the high mountains were like, and that came from talking with mountain men who had been there; lived there for years. It was going to be brutally cold in the winters, with a short growing season. He had reminded them of that.

"If there is dirt, things will grow," Swede said. He grinned at Hannah, who was pregnant again, she felt sure. "Including kids."

"We pull out in the morning," Jamie said.

Of the newly hired men, Carbone and Martine (whose sons would grow up to be feared gunfighters) and Jones and Williams, only Martine had been up to the Rocky Mountains, and he warned Jamie that it was going to be a tough pull for wagons.

"I'd rather see you with oxen, señor," he told him. "But these mules will make it, providing you take enough grain along to add to their grazing."

"That's what you and Jones will be hauling in those big wagons."

"Then we shall be ready to go in the morning."

That night, Jamie stood with his arm across Kate's shoulder, and together they looked at the candle and lamplights of San Antonio.

"Hold the sight in your mind, Kate. For odds are good that you will never see its like again."

"I won't miss it," she said with a smile. "I've come to enjoy the solitude of the wilderness. I want our children to grow up knowing and loving the wild country. And with Sam and Sarah along, they'll also be educated. We're going to have the best of all worlds, love."

"Regrets, Kate?"

"Not a one, Jamie. Not a one."

The weather turned against them. Rain

developed that night, and by morning it was coming down in torrents.

"No point in setting out in this," Jamie said to the others. "We'll stay right here until it clears. We have time."

Rain soaked the land for two days and nights, turning roads into quagmires and making trails impassable. Finally the sun shone in welcome rays and three days after the torrential rains had ended, Jamie felt they could start the next day. At noon, Martine came to him.

"Men in town looking for you, señor. Talk is, they plan to kill you."

"Why?" Jamie asked.

"Something about their brothers and a big fight they had with you some years back."

"Lord knows I've had some fights," Jamie acknowledged. "But I thought all that was over and done with." Jamie was thoughtful for a few seconds. "Don't mention this to anyone else, all right?"

"As you wish. There are at least five of them, and I suspect more are lounging about town. Do you wish me to accompany you?"

Jamie shook his head. "I'll kill my own snakes, Martine. But thanks."

Martine watched him ride toward town,

then turned and walked over to Carbone. "Saddle up your horse and come with me. Señor MacCallister might need our help."

Carbone, never one to avoid a good fight, smiled and quickly saddled his horse. Both men checked their guns, inspected the sharpness of their knives, and rode into town.

"Eight men, Señor Jamie," the liveryman told him. "They ride in yesterday. I do not like their looks at all. I believe they are here looking for you."

"Gracias," Jamie thanked him, and handed him the reins to his horse.

Jamie ducked out the back of the huge building. Keeping to the alleys, he made his way to a cantina at the edge of the village, one mostly frequented by the area's less than desirable citizens.

The fight that was only moments away from erupting would be talked about in San Antonio for years. Jamie Ian MacCallister, twenty-seven years old and already a legend for many of those years, was about to enhance that saga.

As Jamie peeked into the bar from the storage room, he didn't need a guide to spot those hunting him. Three of them were standing at the plank bar, swilling whiskey.

The bartender spotted Jamie standing in

the gloom of the back room and with a slight nod of his head, the others standing at the bar quietly took up their glasses and moved away. They were all rough men, some of them outlaws and gunrunners to the Comanche and Kiowa, but they all knew Jamie and liked him for his fairness and respected him for his courage. And deep down, none of them wanted any trouble with Jamie MacCallister.

Jamie pulled both pistols from his belt and cocked them, then stepped into the big room, filled with cigar smoke and the sour smell of whiskey and unwashed bodies.

"I'm Jamie MacCallister," he said. "Are you the gentlemen looking for me?"

The bartender hit the floor with a thud as the three men turned and drew their pistols.

"You mighty right about that, you son of a bitch!" the biggest and ugliest of the trio said.

Jamie shot him in the belly, the heavy ball doubling the man over and knocking him into the second man, sending both of them to the floor. Jamie lifted his other pistol and drilled the standing man in the center of his chest. He covered the short distance from the doorway to the storage to the bar in a heartbeat and jerked the third man to his boots and hit him with a crashing right fist that pulped the man's lips and sent yellowing teeth flying and blood splattering. Jamie bodily picked the man up and threw him across the room. The man landed against the wall and the sounds of bones breaking was loud.

Jamie took two pistols from the dead man, checked them, and stuck them behind his belt. He took two pistols from the gut-shot and moaning man, checked them, and stuck them behind his belt, at his back. He quickly reloaded his own pistols, and carrying them in his hands, he walked outside.

"MacCallister!" the shout came from a man standing in the middle of the wide street.

"That's me," Jamie said.

"You kilt my kin a few years back. He were ridin' with Olmstead and Jackson."

"He should have picked better company," Jamie replied, cocking the heavy pistol.

"You're a dead man, MacCallister!"

"No, I'm not," Jamie said. "But you damn sure are." Then he shot the man right between the eyes at a distance of about a hundred feet.

Standing a half block away, Carbone and Martine exchanged glances. *"Asombroso!"* Martine breathed. "What a man!"

Jamie filled his right hand with a loaded

pistol and turned at the sounds of running feet. Two unshaven and dirty men, both with pistols in their hands, came to a sliding stop about fifty feet from Jamie.

"Tonight that whore you married will be a widder woman, MacCallister!" one yelled.

Jamie plugged him and the man standing beside him and left them flopping in the mud of the street. He went in search of the last two. A ball knocked adobe from a building and bloodied Jamie's cheek. Another ball tore up ground at Jamie's feet just as he lifted a pistol and drilled his assailant in the belly. The man sat down in the mud on his butt and began screaming. The eighth man jumped out into the street with a loud oath and leveled a rifle. Jamie turned sideways to present a smaller target, lifted the pistol, and fired, the ball taking about half of the man's head off.

Jamie quickly reloaded and called out in a calm voice to Martine and Carbone, who were standing awe-struck by a building, "Collect all their weapons and shot and powder. Take them back to our wagons."

"*Sí,* señor!" both men said.

Jamie walked back into the cantina just as the man he'd hurled against the wall was getting up. Jamie returned him to the dirty floor with a ham-size fist. The sounds of the man's jaw breaking were loud in the quiet room. Jamie found a bucket of water and threw the contents onto the man's face. He stood over the utterly terrified man and glared down at him.

Jamie must have looked like a mountain to the man.

"I'm going to leave you with a horse pointing east, and these words of warning," Jamie told him. "If I ever see you again, no matter what the circumstances, I will kill you where you lie, sit, squat, or stand. Is that understood?"

The man was unable to speak because of his shattered jaw, but he nodded his head vigorously.

Jamie turned his back to the man and walked out, and yet another chapter was added to the mushrooming legend of Jamie Ian MacCallister.

FIFTY-TWO

"Any trouble in town?" Kate asked, noticing the tiny cuts on Jamie's cheek from the flying adobe.

"Not much," Jamie said. "I just met with some ol' boys who came out west to see me."

"Were they glad to see you?" Kate asked, her tone dry enough to empty a well.

"I don't think so," Jamie replied, washing his face and hands in a bucket of water and drying off with a rag. "But I'm the last thing they saw before they met the devil."

"Uh-huh. You missed the nooning; we've already eaten. But I saved some stew and bread for you. You think you can stay out of trouble long enough to eat?"

Jamie grinned, bent down, and kissed her. "I will sure try, darlin'."

Kate blushed as the kids giggled. She shoved at him, perhaps moving him an inch, at best. "Oh, go on, you!"

Jamie sat down and began eating, as Martine and Carbone returned and began whispering to the others. Hannah smiled, and the others shook their heads in astonishment.

A few minutes later, a delegation from town rode out and approached Jamie warily, after making certain Jamie could see they were not armed. "Sir," a well-dressed man said. "Those men back there . . . ah, the recently deceased, they were carrying ample funds."

"I don't want it," Jamie said, sopping a hunk of bread into the seasoned stew.

"They had no papers on them, so we don't know where to send the money."

"How about the man with the busted jaw?"

"He left town quickly. Heading east. He was in considerable pain but would not let the doctor examine him."

"Smart man. Do whatever you want to with the money. Give it to the poor."

"Will you be leaving soon, sir?" another man asked nervously.

"Come the morning."

All the men seemed to sigh.

"How many men did my husband kill?" Kate asked.

"Ah . . . seven, ma'am."

"Is that all?" Kate said with a straight face. "A few years ago, he killed forty."

"Forty!" a rather plump gentleman blurted. "Good God!"

Jamie sighed and finished his bowl of stew. He hoped Kate would hush up, for he knew only too well what a wicked sense of humor she had.

Kate smiled at him and walked over to the wagon to finish packing away supplies. Jamie breathed a bit easier. "We'll be leaving in the morning," he told the delegation. "And I apologize for the trouble in town."

"It wasn't your fault, Mr. MacCallister," another man said. "What bothered some people was your . . . coolness about the entire affair. There was quite a crowd gathered to witness the, ah, demise of the last, two, ah, gentlemen."

Jamie grunted. Then he stood up, swiftly and silently as was his fashion. The group of businessmen all quickly backed up and that move infuriated Jamie. But he very carefully held his temper in check and smiled and was cordial as he shook hands with the men, bidding them good day.

When they had departed, he heard the sounds of muffled giggling coming from the wagons. He turned to see all the women gathered up in a knot, aprons covering their mouths to stifle the laughter.

"Very dangerous fellow there, Kate," Hannah said, then bent over double with laughter.

"Yes," Sarah said. "How can you sleep at night knowing such a brigand is lying next to you?"

"Isn't it a disgrace?" Kate said, trying her best to keep a straight face. "I've never been run out of town before."

The women all started laughing and Jamie shook his head and walked off, leaving the women howling at the disgusted expression on his face.

Swede caught up with him. "What in the world is all that about, Jamie?"

"I just got run out of town."

"And they think it's *funny*?"

"Hysterical."

Sam and Juan walked up. "What set the women off? They're laughing like a bunch of idiots."

"Jamie just got run out of town," Swede said.

"Run out of town? And they think that's *funny*?"

"I guess."

"What's so funny about that?" Juan asked.

"I don't know," Swede said. "You'll have to ask Jamie. He told me."

"Jamie . . ." Sam started.

"This is where I came in," Jamie said. "Excuse me." He walked off just as Moses and Wells walked up.

"What's wrong with the women?" Wells asked.

"Jamie got run out of town," Sam said.

"And they think that's *funny*?" Moses asked.

Jamie covered his ears with his hands and went down to talk to the horses.

Just as dawn was splitting the sky with color, Jamie swung into the saddle and took the lead. "Let's go see the mountains," he said, and the wagons moved out.

Outside of town, Jamie swung off to one side and looked back at the Alamo as the wagons and livestock lumbered past him. The sun was touching the old mission, bathing it in a pure light from the Heavens.

Jamie smiled, recalling Bowie's words as he read them by the dim candlelight in Bowie's room. He imagined Bowie when he was full of life and how he might have spoken those words. He could almost hear Bowie's strong voice.

"My fellow Texans, and to freedom-loving people all over America. These are my final words from this post. I pray God they will

666

be read over and over, for years to come. For these words, these thoughts, these emotions, they are not just from me, but from all the brave men gathered here who have chosen to die for liberty and freedom.

"Oh, but shed no tears, for we shall not die in vain. For in the pools of our spilled blood in this old mission, shall be written the song of freedom for Texas. Nay, not just for Texas, but for the whole of the United States. Sing it loudly, men and women of America. Sing it to your children and to your children's children and to every generation until the whole world knows the tune. Sing it so we shall never be forgotten. Sing it before armies go into battle. Remember the Alamo. Let it be a battle cry that rolls off of every tongue in every conflict from this moment on. Don't forget us, Americans. Don't. I beg you. Don't let our memories die. Don't have these brave boys die for naught.

"Santa Anna thinks this will be an easy victory. But we are going to teach Santa Anna a hard lesson about men's dreams of freedom. I think after the smoke has cleared, and the last ball is fired, Santa Anna will know he's been in a fight. I have my brace of pistols and my good knife. So let them come. I shall soon be in the arms of my darling Ursula.

"It will be over for us in a few hours. And I want everyone to know that William Barret Travis has my respect. He is a brave and resourceful leader and I would follow him through the gates of Hell and probably will.

"So — life ebbs and comes down to this. I wonder what the thoughts are of those men huddled against those walls, seeking relief from the bitter cold and the loneliness of separation from family and home. Much like mine, I would think. Sad, perhaps mingled with a touch of fear. Oh, not fear of the act of dying itself, but fear of the unknown. For who among us knows what lies beyond the veil? Ah, well, we'll all soon know.

"So — I will close with these thoughts: Remember the men of the Alamo. For we will never surrender. We shall fight to the last man, until the last breath is gone from the last defender. And these final words I dedicate to the men who wait to die outside this warm room. They are gallant men. Brave men. Free men. And they are dying for you.

"These words come from a garrison valiant and steeped in courage. And our last word must be — farewell.

"Farewell."

"Goodbye, Jim," Jamie whispered. "You won't be forgotten. The men of the Alamo will never be forgotten. For I shall tell my children, and they will tell their children. And the world will know that on that awful bloody day, men of more courage than most possess fought to the last man. They died for God and for Texas."

ABOUT THE AUTHOR

William W. Johnstone is the *USA Today* bestselling author of over 130 books, including the popular *Ashes, Mountain Man,* and *Last Gunfighter* series. Visit his website at www.williamjohnstone.net or by email at dogcia@aol.com.

The employees of Thorndike Press hope you have enjoyed this Large Print book. All our Thorndike, Wheeler, and Kennebec Large Print titles are designed for easy reading, and all our books are made to last. Other Thorndike Press Large Print books are available at your library, through selected bookstores, or directly from us.

For information about titles, please call:
(800) 223-1244

or visit our Web site at:
http://gale.cengage.com/thorndike

To share your comments, please write:
Publisher
Thorndike Press
10 Water St., Suite 310
Waterville, ME 04901